WHAT MAKES A MAN TURN INTO A MURDERER OVERNIGHT?

FAMINE

The Greek-looking man said: 'This food in here—you think that you're going to keep it all to yourself? All of it? Just because you're a storekeeper you think you've got some God-given right to survive while everybody else starves?'

Nicolas didn't even want to think about it. He said: 'I'm giving you three. You understand me? Three, and then I shoot.'

The first shot missed. The revolver bucked in his hands, and he heard the bang of broken glass at the back of the store, followed by a sudden rush of green olives from three broken jars. He fired again before he could allow himself to think, and the Greek's shoulder burst apart in a spray of gory catsup. And then there was a deep, deafening *bavvooom*! and Nicolas realized with strange slow horror that the Greek had fired back at him with his shotgun, and that he'd been hit, badly hit, in the belly and the thighs . . .

GRAHAM MASTERTON

Famine

timewarner
paperbacks

A *Time Warner* Paperback

First published in Great Britain by Sphere Books 1981
Reprinted 1984, 1986, 1987, 1988, 1991
Reprinted by Warner Books 1992
Reprinted 1994
Reprinted by Time Warner Paperbacks in 2004

Copyright © 1981 by Graham Masterton

*All characters in this publication are fictitious
and any resemblance to real persons, living or dead,
is purely coincidental.*

The right of Graham Masterton to be identified as author of this work
has been asserted by him in accordance with the Copyright, Designs and
Patents Act 1988.

All rights reserved.
No part of this publication may be reproduced,
stored in a retrieval system, or transmitted, in any
form or by any means, without the prior
permission in writing of the publisher, nor be
otherwise circulated in any form of binding or
cover other than that in which it is published and
without a similar condition including this
condition being imposed on the subsequent purchaser.

Printed and bound in Great Britain by
Clays Ltd, St Ives plc

ISBN 0 7515 0388 6

Time Warner Paperbacks
An imprint of
Time Warner Book Group UK
Brettenham House
Lancaster Place
London WC2E 7EN

www.twbg.co.uk

'They are as sick that surfeit with too much,
As they that starve with nothing.'
                    – Shakespeare, *Merchant of Venice*

Book One

One

He was crossing the red-asphalt yard in front of the farmhouse when he heard a car-horn blaring from the direction of the north-west gate. He shifted the saddle he was carrying to his right arm and raised his hand to shield his eyes from the dazzling scarlet glare of the setting sun. A Jeep Wagoneer was bouncing along the track towards him, stirring up a high trail of shining dust, and whoever was driving it was in enough of a panic to ignore South Burlington Farm's strict 5 mph speed limit.

He laid the saddle down on the ground as the Jeep squealed and bucked to a stop in front of him. The door swung open and out scrambled his cereal-crop manager, Willard Noakes, as quickly as if the Jeep were about to explode. He was one of those skinny, awkward, jerky kind of people, Willard Noakes, and Season had once compared him to a Swiss army knife. 'He seems to have so many arms and legs. He can open a door, and light a cigarette, and knock over a mug of coffee, and scratch his head, all at one time,' she had laughed.

But there was nothing funny or awkward about the way Willard hurried across to him now. Willard's bony, sun-leathered face was smudged with dirt and there was dust in his walrus moustache. He said: 'Ed, you'd best come quick. And I mean quick. It's something real serious.'

'What's wrong, Willard?' Ed asked him. 'You came down that track like Evel Knievel.'

'I'm sorry, Ed. But it's something you got to see.'

'An accident? Someone hurt?'

'Well, you could call it some kind of accident, although I'm darned if I know what sort. And if anybody's going to get themselves hurt, it's going to be you.'

'Okay.' Ed raised his arm and beckoned to one of his engineering hands, who was hunkered outside of the garage, cleaning out a fuel-oil pump. The man laid down

3

his tools and came across the yard, wiping his hands on a rag.

'You wanted something, Mr Hardesty?'

'Yes, please, Ben. Take this saddle into the house for me, would you, and make sure it's hung up right. And tell Mrs Hardesty I might be a half-hour late.'

'Sure thing, Mr Hardesty.'

Ed climbed up into the Jeep's passenger seat while Willard started the engine. They swung around the yard and then headed back towards the north-west gate, past the stables and the garages, and out through the white-painted fence.

The Jeep's FM radio was playing *Coward of the County*, almost inaudibly. Ed reached across and switched it off.

'You want to tell me what's wrong?' he asked Willard.

Willard glanced at him. They were driving along the wide dusty track that ran beside one of their finest stands of shellbark hickories, and then out across the twenty-three thousand acre expanse of South Burlington's northern wheatfields. The sun was almost melted away now, except for one smouldering crimson crescent and the miles of ripening wheat appeared to be an odd bright pink.

'I don't know,' said Willard, unhappily. 'I think maybe you'd better see it for yourself. I don't think I'm competent to judge.'

'*You're* not competent? How competent do you think *I* am?' demanded Ed. 'You've been growing wheat for nearly forty years, and all I've been doing is sitting on my butt in a stuffy New York office, telling little old ladies how to salt away their surplus dollars for a rainy day.'

Willard thought about that and then shrugged. 'All I can say is, I've never seen anything like it before. I've never even *heard* about anything like it before. But I'm not asking you to take a look at it because I think you might know what it is. I'm sure you won't. I'm asking you to take a look at it because it's your farm.'

'Is it the crops?'

Willard nodded. 'I can't even describe it, Ed. I've never seen anything like it before. I mean that. Forty years or not.'

The Jeep sped them across the flat, early-evening landscape. The sky faded gradually from a florid rose-colour to a dusky ceramic blue and a cold and creamy moon hung above the horizon. Ed sat sideways in his seat, his arm slung over the back, watching his fields revolve slowly around him.

His fields. He still couldn't quite believe it. The idea that he actually owned all eighty-five thousand acres of South Burlington Farm – the idea that each handful of dirt he could dig his fingers into for more than ten miles was his own personal property – it all seemed like a strange waking fantasy.

South Burlington had always been his father's, by ownership and by deed and by that special kind of title that only a lifetime of sweat and pain and sheer arrogance can earn. His father, Dan Hardesty, had been short, stocky, and pugnacious, a tough little bustling pig in Levis. He had built his farm by aggressive mechanisation, shrewd marketing, ruthless buying of agricultural real-estate, and by never sleeping for more than four hours a night.

To Ed, and to Ed's mother, and to Ed's older brother Michael, the old man had seemed to be immortal and indestructible and it was only when he had collapsed from a stroke in the middle of last year's harvesting, felled in one of his own fields under a sky like boiling blue ink, that the family had come to understand at last that he wasn't going to live for ever. Dan Hardesty, the creator of South Burlington Farm, the wealthiest, toughest man in King-man County, Kansas, was only days away from death, and someone was going to have to take over.

Michael, as stubby and proud as his father, had been the legal and natural successor. During his teenage years, Michael had stayed on the farm, learning the modern and computerised business of growing wheat, while Ed, who was tall and wiry and thoughtful, like his maternal grandfather, gravitated away from the farm, and then the county, and eventually, the state. In the years of Kennedy and Johnson, flower-power and Vietnam, Ed had gone to Kansas University in Manhattan, Kansas, on a financial study course and then to Columbia Business College, and eventually made his way to New York, where he had been taken on by a smart new investment corporation called Blyth, Thalberg & Wong.

As a boy, Ed had always disliked the farm – maybe for no other reason than he knew it was never going to be his. The farm was all dust and heat and just like his father had been demanding of his mother, he had been equally demanding of Ed, as if he was trying to test him, and maybe break him. Whenever Ed had tried to slip out on a date with one of the girls from the neighbouring farms, or from town, his father had invariably caught him at the gate and given him some last-minute chore like folding sacks or sweeping up dust, so that if he ever made it to the girl's house, he was always at least an hour late and perspiring, and prickly as a scarecrow with wheat chaff. One pretty and unkind young girl had nicknamed him Li'l Abner.

On the day before Dan Hardesty's funeral, however, as the family were solemnly gathered on the farm to pay their last respects to the man who had built their lives for them, Ed's whole existence had been turned upside down. Michael had been obliged to drive over to Wichita late in the afternoon for an urgent meeting with the bank. On the way back, just after midnight, he had tried to overtake a truck on route 54 where it crossed the South Ninnescah River, and he had failed to see another car coming towards him in the mist. The Kansas Highway Patrol had estimated the collision speed to be 125 mph, head-on.

Henry Pollock, the bald and breathy family accountant, had taken Ed aside after his father's burial and said: 'If you want South Burlington, son, it's all yours. You only have to say the word.'

He remembered glancing across towards Season, who had been standing a little way away from the family crowd in her black veil and her black suit like a beautiful and elegant raven; and he remembered thinking – *she knows that Pollock's offering me the farm, and she knows that I'm going to have to say yes. Why doesn't she come across and support me? Why doesn't she take my arm and say it's all right?*

Well, he knew now why she hadn't, he thought to

6

himself, as Willard drove the Jeep across the pale reaches of ripening wheat. He sure knew now.

Willard switched on the Jeep's headlights. 'The worst of it's just about a half-mile up ahead, right over there, to the left. Do you mind if I take her staight across the wheat?'

'If you have to,' Ed told him. His father had always gone apoplectic with fury if he found tyre-tracks across the fields, and Ed had tried to keep the same rule about respecting the crops. There was only one way to run a farm like South Burlington, and that was efficient and hard, and with no favours to anyone. He sat uncomfortably in his seat, while Willard veered off the road and drove through the tall, rustling crops.

'I don't make a habit of this, Ed, I can tell you,' said Willard, as if he sensed his employer's discomfort.

Ed didn't answer, and for a short while there was nothing but the whining sound of the Jeep's transmission, the pattering of wheat ears on the bodywork and the occasional tap of a moth on the windshield. Ed thought: if you could drive a car into the ocean, this is what it would be like.

Willard was leaning forward in his seat now and straining his eyes to see where he was. Eventually, a white marker stick appeared through the twilight and a flashlight was waved at them. Willard turned the Jeep in a semi-circle and stopped it. They climbed out into the warm, breezy night.

'Hi, Mr Hardesty,' said the man with the flashlight. 'Glad you could make it so quick.'

'Hi, Jack,' said Ed. 'Willard just caught me going into supper. What goes on here?'

Jack Marowitz was one of Ed's senior farm managers. He was young – only twenty-eight – but he had a silo-full of honours from the Iowa State University of Science and Technology in the agricultural uses of advanced chemistry, automation and computer techniques. It was Jack's job to make sure that what grew in the fields came out of those fields in optimum condition and was delivered to the right place at exactly the right moment. Jack could plan the

7

harvesting of ten thousand acres down to the last half-hour.

He was quiet, almost diffident, with a thick brown head of hair and Coke-bottle glasses, but Ed liked him because he didn't rant and rave and he did his job well.

Jack held up an ear of wheat in the palm of his hand and directed his flashlight on it.

'What do you make of this?' he asked Ed. Ed peered at it closely, and then poked it with his finger.

'It's rotten,' he said. 'The whole damned thing's rotten.'

The ear of wheat was blackened and every grain inside it was dark and slimy with decay. Ed took it out of Jack's hand and sniffed it, and he could smell a distinctly sour odour, like whisky mash.

'It appears to me like some kind of blight,' said Jack. 'The only trouble is, *what* kind? It certainly isn't rust, and it sure as hell isn't smut.'

Ed stood straight and looked around. 'How much of the crop's been affected?' he asked. 'Maybe it's just some localised soil complaint. Maybe these seeds weren't dressed.'

'Well, that's the problem,' put in Willard. 'And that's why I wanted you to come take a look for yourself. It covers something like five acres at the moment, but it's spreading.'

Ed took the flashlight from Jack and walked a little way out into the wheat. He shone the beam this way and that, quickly, and every way he shone it, he saw the same thing. The ears of wheat were drooping on their stalks and they were all dark brown with decay. The smell of sourness was carried on the breeze, and under the light of that pale and emotionless moon, silently suspended on the horizon, Ed felt as if the world had subtly changed position on its axis, as if things would never be quite the same again.

'You never saw anything like this at Ames?' he asked Jack, switching off the flashlight and walking back.

'Nothing at all. And, believe me, I saw some pretty grotesque stuff.'

'When did you spot it?'

'Round about two this afternoon,' Willard explained. 'We were making out the harvesting rota, just along the track there-a-ways. I was standing on the roof of the Jeep, looking around to see how the crops were lying, what with all those winds we've been having and all – and I could see a dark patch from the road. At first I thought it was the shadow from a cloud. But when it didn't move, like the other shadows did – well, then I knew there was something wrong.'

'Two this afternoon?' asked Ed. 'It's only eight now. How can you tell if it's spreading?'

Jack cleared his throat. 'At two this afternoon, it was only covering two to three acres.'

'What do you mean? You mean it's spread two acres in six hours? That's crazy.'

Willard's expression was indistinguishable in the dusk, but Ed could tell from the tone of his voice that he was embarrassed. 'I'm afraid it's true, Ed. We didn't measure exactly, or nothing like that. But it seems like it's going through the wheat like some kind of a slow fire.'

Ed stood silent for a while, his hand over his mouth, staring at the dark patch of decaying wheat in the middle of his field. If the blight could spread at the rate of two acres in six hours, that meant it could eat up eight acres a day at the very least. The danger was that as the circumference of the blighted area increased, so the speed at which the disease burned up his crops would increase. Willard was right. It was just like a slow fire.

'Let's get in the Jeep,' Ed suggested at last. 'Then let's circle the affected wheat and see how much of a problem we've got on our hands. I want to watch this blight in action. I want to see it actually spreading.'

They climbed into the Wagoneer, and Willard started up the engine.

'Make sure you only drive over unblighted wheat,' Ed told him. 'If it's any kind of a fungus, I don't want it spread around the farm on the tyres of your Jeep.'

Willard nodded and backed up a few feet before turning the wheel and taking the Jeep in a slow, bumpy circle around the darkened edge of the crops. Ed reached into the pocket of his red plaid shirt and took out a pack of small cigars. He stuck one between his lips without offering them around. He knew that neither Willard nor Jack smoked, although Willard had been known to make short work of a half-bottle of Old Grandad.

Jack said, 'It must be some kind of airborne fungus. Otherwise, it couldn't spread so damned fast. But the question is – what made it start here? And where did it come from?'

'You haven't had any reports of it elsewhere on the farm, have you?' asked Ed.

'Not so far. But I've been kind of incommunicado today. My walkie-talkie's been on the fritz for for a week, and I put it in for repair.'

'I think we'd better take the chopper out at first light, and see if there's any more of it,' said Ed. 'If it's spreading as fast as you say it is, we could finish up with only half a crop, or maybe no crop at all.'

He turned around to Jack, who was sitting in the back seat. Jack gave him an uneasy grin, almost as if the blight was his fault.

'You've taken samples, I suppose?' said Ed.

Jack nodded. 'I took about twenty or thirty while Willard was going down to the farm to get you. I'll try to analyse some of them myself, but the rest of them can go to Dr Benson, down at the State Agricultural Laboratory.'

'You think Benson's capable of finding out what it is?'

'He's as capable as anyone. I mean, sure, he's a little eccentric, but there's nothing wrong with his technique. He isolated that seed fungus way before the Federal people came up with anything.'

'All right,' said Ed. 'But I don't want to have to wait for a week while he fiddles around with crackpot theories, the way we had to with that boosted fertiliser.'

'I'll tell him to play it straight.'

'And sober, I hope.'

'Sure.'

They had reached the crest of a gentle rise in the ground, and now, by the light of the moon, they were looking down on the five-mile slope that took the northern wheatfields of South Burlington as far as the Mystic River, a tributary of the South River, itself a tributary of the South Ninnescah.

Ed felt the skin on the back of his neck tingle at what he saw. Across the silvery wheat, a dark corroded stain had already spread for a mile in each direction, and westwards it reached as far as he could see.

He touched Willard's arm and whispered, 'Stop.' Then, when the Jeep was halted, he climbed down into the wheat and stood there silent, unmoving, like the witness to an accident which he was helpless to prevent.

Willard and Jack watched him as he knelt down and studied the ears of wheat all around him. Some were blighted, some were still clear. But even as he watched them, the clear wheat gradually began to darken, and within minutes it was as rotten as the rest. He stayed where he was for a while, and then he stood up and came back to the Jeep.

'What do you think if we burn a circle around it?' he asked Willard. 'Isolate it, like a fire with a firebreak?'

'We could try,' said Willard. 'Do you want to go back to the farm and round up the men?'

Jack said: 'If the blight is airborne, which I think it is, then clearing a firebreak really isn't going to do much good. The wind's erratic tonight, west to north-west. It's going to spread the fungus all over the farm before you can do anything worthwhile about it.'

Ed looked at him. 'Have you got a better idea?' he asked. He tried to control the sharpness in his voice, but it was difficult. His father had always taught him that it was better to do something than nothing, and he knew just what Jack would have suggested. Sitting on their backsides waiting for the laboratory report, while the whole eighty-five thousand acres turned black all around them.

'We could try spraying,' said Jack. 'Maybe a dose of Twenty-four D would do it.'

'Oh yes, and who's going to fly a crop-duster at night? And what are we going to say to the health authorities, when they find that the fungicide levels in our grain are ten per cent higher than anybody else's? We might just as well set fire to the whole damned farm, or let it go rot.'

'Ed – there's no need to lose your cool,' said Willard, gently. 'I'll try anything you say. But even if we wait until

11

morning, we're only going to lose a fraction of the total crop. I think the best answer is to leave it alone until we have some reasonable idea of what it is.'

'And supposing nobody can find out? Even you, Jack, or your eccentric Dr Benson?'

Willard tugged at his moustache. 'They're just darn well going to *have* to find out. That's all. I've put too much of my life into South Burlington Farm to see a whole year's wheat harvest go bad, and Jack knows that. Don't you, Jack?'

'We'll isolate this blight, don't you worry,' said Jack. 'I know it's serious, but I'm going to take it back to the farm right now and spend some time on it and Kerry can run some samples over to Wichita first thing in the morning.'

Ed stared out at the acres and acres of drooping black wheat. 'You really don't believe that a firebreak would hold it back?' he asked, almost as if he was speaking to himself.

'I don't think so,' said Jack. 'I just think you'd be using up energy and manpower and money for no good reason.'

Ed rubbed his eyes. 'Okay, then,' he said, 'Let's get back. I'd like to put a call in to Charlie Warburg and see if we can claim some compensation for any profits we lose. Henry Pollock ought to be told, too.'

They climbed back into the Jeep and made their way back across the fields to the track. The moon was higher now, and the light that fell across South Burlington Farm was alien and cold. Ed smoked his cigar half-way down, then stubbed it out in the ashtray. Nobody who worked on a wheat farm ever tossed a glowing butt out of the window.

As they approached the farm buildings, they could see the pattern of lighted windows in the farmhouse and the outbuildings which meant that all twenty of South Burlington's John Deere tractors were in for refuelling and maintenance, that all the Jeeps and all the trailers were parked away for the night, and that Season Hardesty was waiting at home for her husband to come back and eat.

Willard halted the Wagoneer on the red-asphalt yard. 'I'll call you later,' he told Ed. 'Maybe ten or eleven o'clock. I'd like to know what Charlie has to say.'

'Okay,' said Ed, and then he turned around to Jack. 'I

want you to call, too, just as soon as you've made up your mind what that blight could be. Or even if you can't decide what it is at all.'

'I sure will,' said Jack.

'Whatever happens,' said Jack, 'I want us all here by six o'clock sharp tomorrow morning, with Dyson Kane if he can make it, and I want us to make a complete chopper tour of the whole spread.'

'Yes, sir,' said Willard.

Ed climbed down from the Jeep and closed the door. He looked at Jack for a moment and then he said, 'Good luck.' Willard released the Jeep's handbrake and drove out of the yard and Ed stood with his hands on his hips watching its red tail-lights disappear along the eastbound track. Then he walked slowly across to the house and climbed the verandah steps to the front door.

Two

Season was sitting with her feet up in the living-room, reading a copy of *Vogue*. The television was tuned to a special programme about Mid-Eastern oil, but the volume was turned down to a mutter. She didn't even look up as Ed came into the room, unzipped his tan leather jacket, and sat down in the big library chair that had once been his father's. Season always called this chair 'the witness stand', and she had wanted to throw it out when they first moved in; but to Ed, sitting in his father's once-sacrosanct seat was one of those small but important parts of taking over South Burlington. It was no fun being an emperor if you didn't have the throne that went with the job.

The living-room was decorated in soft blues – stylish, tasteful, with antique French furniture upholstered in ultramarine velvet. There were tall vases of flowers all around and a marble bust of Ralph Waldo Emerson on a slender mahogany torchère. The room was a perfect reflection of Season's personality – cool, ordered, stylish, and discreetly expensive.

13

'You're late,' said Season, turning over a page.

Ed unlaced his boots. 'Didn't Ben tell you I was going to be held up?'

'Yes,' she said. 'But the fact that I was told doesn't alter the fact that you're late. It was a fish soufflé, and I've had to throw it away.'

'You threw away my supper?'

She turned another page. 'You don't really care for *flat* fish soufflé, do you? I wish you'd told me. I would have kept it for you.'

'Season – ' he said.

She looked up at last. She was a tall girl of thirty, with a thin oval face and alarmingly wide blue eyes. Her blonde hair was scraped back on her head and held with a tortoiseshell comb. In her silk Japanese pants suit, all pastel colours and loose pleats, she looked as if she was all wrists and ankles. She was pretty, and sharp, and Ed had loved her from only about three minutes after meeting her.

Some men found Season intimidating, both physically and conversationally. But Ed was a good four inches taller, and he had a slow dark masculine assurance about him – thick black hair, dense black eyebrows, deepset eyes of refreshing green – and the warm seriousness of whatever he said had always seemed to be able to enfold itself around her prickliest comments and render them harmless.

'I've asked Dilys to make you an omelette,' she said.

'What about you?'

'I don't feel hungry any more. The act of cooking was enough to satisfy me.'

'What about the act of throwing it all away?'

'That satisfied me too.'

'So I've come home to a satisfied wife?'

'If you like.'

'We've got a serious problem out there in the fields.'

'Oh, yes?' she asked. 'Don't tell me the computers are striking for more off-time. Or is it a human problem?'

'It's a crop problem. There's a kind of blight. The wheat's rotting right in front of our eyes. So far it's spread over fifteen or twenty acres, and it's still spreading.'

'What are you going to do about it?'

14

'I'm not sure yet. I don't even know what kind of a blight it is.'

'It's probably a curse from your father.'

'Season – we've got twenty acres of rotten wheat out there and that isn't funny.'

Season uncurled herself from the sofa, stood up and walked across to the inlaid French drinks cabinet. 'I'm sorry,' she said. 'I don't think I've drunk enough yet to be funny. Do you want one?'

'Scotch,' said Ed. He pulled off his boots and laid them down beside his chair. Season glanced at them as if she was expecting them to start tap-dancing on their own. She mixed herself a strong daiquiri and pineapple juice and poured out a Chivas Regal on the rocks for Ed.

'There you are, my lord and master,' she said, handing him his glass.

'Sally in bed?' asked Ed, drinking, and then wiping his mouth with the back of his hand.

'She went up about a half-hour ago. She despaired of her father, just like I did.'

Ed let out a short, testy breath. 'Listen,' he said, 'I'm sorry about the soufflé. Willard came down like a bat out of hell and wanted me to go take a look at this blight. It's very serious. Jack's doing some tests on it tonight and tomorrow we're going to send some samples across to Wichita. I had to go. I didn't have any choice.'

Season sat down again. 'All right,' she said, more softly. 'Abject apology accepted. I just don't think I'm ever going to get used to the way I went through a wedding ceremony with an actuary in New York City and wound up married to a wheat farmer in Kansas. What do they call it? Not culture shock. Maybe horticulture shock.'

'I'm just hoping this blight doesn't spread in a compound ratio,' said Ed.

'What do you mean by that?' asked Season, trying to look interested.

'Compound growth means that the wider it spreads, the wider it spreads. It starts off by blighting two acres, then six, then ten, and so on. If it goes on like that, we won't have a farm by the middle of next week.'

'I hope you really don't believe what you're saying,' said Season, wearily. She stirred her cocktail with her finger, and then licked it.

'I don't know,' said Ed. 'I've seen samples of rust, and the rot you get when you don't dress your seeds with fungicide, but America has fewer wheat-disease problems than almost any other country in the world. What America spends on crop fungicides in any one year wouldn't keep the town of Emporia in hotdogs. The only real problem we get is drought.'

'Well, Farmer Hardesty, you should know,' said Season, sipping her drink and looking at the television.

Ed stood up. 'I guess I'll go say good night to Sally. Do you want to tell Dilys to start my omelette?'

'What did you say?' asked Season, her attention momentarily distracted by a television picture of running camels.

'I said I'm going up to say good night to Sally.'

'Well, don't. She'll be asleep by now.'

He ignored her and went all the same. When he was half-way up the curving staircase, he heard her call, 'Your seven-league boots are squeaking because you left them behind.'

He paused, and said, 'Tell them I'll send my magic socks down to pick them up later.'

Season appeared in the doorway, holding his boots in her hand. 'Take the goddamned things now!' she snapped, and hurled them after him, one at a time. 'Every time you come home you make the living-rooom look like a goddamned thrift store!'

The boots clumped on the stairs and then rolled back down again. Season kicked them across the hallway and then stalked back into the living-room. Ed slowly descended the staircase, collected them up, and went up to see Sally with an expression that Season had once described as his 'Grant Wood face'.

Sally was lying curled up in her old-fashioned carved oak bed, under the early-American patchwork comforter that Season had bought for her at a fashionable store on Lexington Avenue in the eighties. She was almost asleep, but not quite, and when Ed looked in at the door, she stirred and raised her head from the pillow and smiled at him.

'Hi, Daddy,' she said, sleepily.

'Hi yourself.'

'I waited for you but you didn't come home. Mommy threw your supper down the sink-disposal.'

'I know,' said Ed, sitting on the edge of the bed and running his hand through his daughter's long blonde curls. 'Dilys is going to fix me an omelette.'

'You'll have indigestion if you don't eat regular. My teacher told me.'

'Your teacher's quite right. I was busy on the farm, that's all. Some of the wheat went bad.'

Sally looked up at him. Although she was only six years old, she looked exactly like her mother. Fair-haired and leggy, with those wide blue eyes like some startled character out of a Disney cartoon. Ed leaned over her and kissed her, and she had that childish smell of soap and cookies and clean clothes.

'I love you,' he said, with a grin.

'I love you, too,' she told him.

They were silent for a moment. Then Sally said, 'Is this a darned farm?'

'What makes you say that?'

'I don't know. Mommy was talking on the telephone to Auntie Vee today and she kept saying "this darned farm".'

Ed touched the tip of her nose with his finger. 'Darned is one of those words that grown-ups use when they mean pesky.'

'What does pesky mean?'

'It means something that irritates you. Something that gets on your nerves.'

'Does the farm get on Mommy's nerves?'

'Sure it does. It gets on *my* nerves sometimes. But it's important. It's what people call a heritage. It's something that's been handed down from father to son, something that belongs to one family, and stands for everything that family is. You're a Hardesty, see, and this is the Hardesty farm. When people meet you, they think – aha, that's the

17

little girl who lives on the big wheat farm in Kingman County, Kansas.'

Sally thought about that and then she said, 'Will you come with us?'

Ed frowned. 'Will I come with you where?'

'To Los Angeles. To visit Auntie Vee.'

'I didn't know you were going to Los Angeles to visit Auntie Vee.'

'Well, Mommy said so on the telephone. She said we'd try to get away some time this week.'

Ed sat up straight. 'Did she? Well . . . I guess if she said so, then you must be. I don't know if I'll be able to come with you, though. August is a pretty busy time on the farm.'

'Try to come, won't you? I want you to come.'

Ed kissed her again and then stood up. 'Sure, I'll try to come. Now why don't you get yourself some sleep?'

He tucked her in tight, and then closed her door and crossed the landing to the master bedroom. Once more, Season's taste and stylishness was all around. The rugs were rich pink and there was white-and-gold rococo furniture everywhere, chairs and commodes and side-tables all genuine eighteenth-century French. The bed was a half-tester, draped with pink velour and covered with a gold-embroidered bedspread. Ed watched himself thought-fully in the gilt cheval mirror as he stripped off his plaid riding-shirt, his faded blue jeans, and his undershorts. Naked, he was lean and muscular, with a crucifix of black hair across his chest. Since he'd taken over South Burlington, he'd lost twenty pounds.

He was tying up his bathrobe when Season walked in. 'Dilys is just beating your eggs now,' she said.

He turned around. 'That's good. Sally's teacher thinks I'm going to suffer from indigestion if I don't eat regular.'

'Is Sally still awake?'

'Only just.'

Season went to her dressing-table and began to take off her diamond earrings. 'You haven't asked me how my day went yet,' she said.

He stood behind her, so that she could see his face in the mirror. 'I don't have to ask. I know you were bored stiff.'

18

She put her earrings away, and then she started unbuttoning her silk suit. Underneath it, she was nude, except for a small pair of white backless panties. She had a skinny, fashion-model's figure, with small wide-nippled breasts and long, lean thighs. She took the comb out of her hair and began to brush it. She left her pants suit on the floor for Dilys to pick up later.

'Actually,' she said, 'I wasn't totally bored. The day did have its moments.'

'Like when?'

'A man came to steam-clean the rug in the hall. He was quite good-looking in an artisan kind of way. He told me he had eight children.'

'Anything else?' he asked her. His face was expressionless.

'Mrs Lydia Hope Caldwell phoned. She wants me to join the Daughters of Kansas. She spent twenty minutes telling me what a great privilege it was and how it was hardly ever accorded to newcomers.'

'What did you tell her?'

'I told her I was overwhelmed, of course.'

He watched her naked body in the mirror. He wondered if it was just her nudity he found so desirable, or whether it was her nudity combined with her sharp and critical personality. He stepped closer to her and laid his hand on her shoulder and kissed the side of her forehead. She kept on brushing her hair as if he wasn't there.

'Then, of course, you called your sister in LA,' he told her.

'That's right.'

He ran his hand down the soft curves of her back, and slipped it under the elastic of her pants, so that he was cupping the cheek of her bottom. The tips of his fingers were almost touching her vulva, but not quite.

'You called your sister in LA and told her how sick you were of this darned farm. All these tedious acres of wheat, all these simple, honest farming folk. All these tractors and all these crop-dusters.'

'All these down-home actuaries,' she put in.

'That's right,' he nodded. 'And then you invited yourself

19

to spend a few weeks in Beverly Hills, along with Sally, totally ignoring the fact that Sally has to go back to school, and that I'm going to need you this month more than I've ever needed you before.'

Season stood utterly still, as if she was pretending to be a statue. Their two faces were reflected side by side in the mirror, and neither face betrayed anything at all. They were playing their usual game of testing, questioning, and teasing, to see whose façade cracked first. In New York, they had played it in fun, and only occasionally. Here in Kansas, it had started to become much more than an amusement, and much more to do with the survival of their relationship.

Ed's fingers stayed where they were.

Season said, 'I haven't rushed into this, you know. I've had plenty of time to think about it.'

'You didn't mention it to me.'

'Of course I mentioned it. What do you think we've been doing, every single night since we came here? Butting our heads together just to see how much it hurts? Ed, my darling, I'm bored with South Burlington, I'm bored with Wichita, I'm bored with the entire state of Kansas, God bless it, and I have to escape for a while.'

'Is that it? You're bored?'

She gently reached behind her back and took his hand away. Then she went over to the bed and sat down. There was a silver cigarette box on her bedside table and she took out a Kool and perched it at the side of her pale-lipsticked mouth as if she was Humphrey Bogart.

'Isn't it enough?' she asked him. 'I used to be a magazine editor. Now I'm like something out of an A. B. Frost drawing.'

'Who the hell's A. B. Frost?' he demanded. 'For Christ's sake, isn't that typical of you? You complain that you're discontented, and when I ask you why, you say that it's because I've condemned you to live like some person in some picture by some goddamned obscure artist I've never even heard of. A. B. Frost, for Christ's sake.'

'A. B. Frost was very well known,' said Season, lighting her cigarette. 'He travelled through Kansas and Iowa in the

20

eighteen-nineties, sketching farmers. Good, devout, God-fearing, crop-loving farmers.'

'You make that sound like a disease.'

She blew out smoke. 'I don't mean to. But this bucolic existence is just about driving me crazy. I have to get away.'

'You knew what it was going to be like. We talked about it for long enough.'

'Of course I knew what it was going to be like. Well, I had a fair idea. But it was what you wanted, wasn't it? Even if I'd told you that wild mules wouldn't have dragged me to South Burlington, you still would have found a way to get me here.'

He looked at her for a long time. The way the bedside lamp shone on her long blonde hair, and cast those curving shadows from her breasts. 'Do you really hate it that much?' he asked her.

She tapped ash from her cigarette and shrugged. 'I don't know. Maybe I'll get used to it.'

'Do you want me to give it up?'

'How can you give it up? You've signed all the papers, you've taken out all the loans, you've made yourself responsible for the lives and jobs of hundreds of people.'

'I could sell it,' he said.

'Oh, sure, you could sell it. And then you'd spend the rest of your life complaining because I made you give up the only thing you ever really wanted to do. Face it, Ed, that's been your destiny since you were born. To reap and to sow, to plough and to mow, and to be a farmer's boy.'

He sat down next to her. She didn't look at him, but smoked her cigarette as if she was racing to finish it.

'It's me, too, isn't it?' he said. 'It's not just South Burlington.'

She still didn't look at him. 'I don't know,' she said. 'These days, I find it hard to separate one from the other. It's just like you're always telling Sally. The Hardestys are South Burlington, and South Burlington is the Hardestys. It's one of those homespun equations that don't make any logical sense, or even any genetic sense, but which people believe in like E equals mc squared.'

'I love you, you know,' he said simply.

21

'You love the idea of me. I don't know whether you actually love me. Not me, as a person. Not me, as an educated and independent person who suddenly finds herself isolated by her husband's chosen way of life – cut off from friends and style and civilisation. I'm getting neurotic, do you know that? I have fantasies of shopping at Gimbel's. I wake up in the night with unnatural cravings for one of Stars' pastrami sandwiches.'

He took her hand. Her Tiffany engagement ring winked a tiny rainbow at him. 'Listen,' he said, hoarsely, 'you can go to New York whenever you want. Fly tomorrow, if you feel like it.'

'Ed,' she said, slowly shaking her head, 'that just isn't the point. I want New York but I want you, too. New York on its own isn't enough. I'm your wife, I happen to love you, but I also happen to have mental energies and psychological requirements which aren't being fulfilled. At the moment, the two most important needs in my life are totally incompatible, and that's the problem.'

He stared down at the shaggy pink rug. 'I don't know what to suggest,' he said. 'You don't want to stay here and yet you don't think it's a good idea if I sell the place.'

'I think if you sold the place it would gradually destroy our marriage,' she said. 'Not staight away, but gradually and very effectively.'

'So going to Los Angeles for a while is going to hold it together?'

'I don't know. But it's going to give me some time to think. You too.'

He said, unhappily, 'I don't think I feel like thinking. Not about us.'

Season leaned over and kissed him, twice, very gently and lovingly. 'We have to,' she said. 'And if I were you, I'd go down to the kitchen and see if that omelette's ready, otherwise you're going to feel like you're eating a window-cleaner's leather.'

He stayed where he was for a while. He felt tired, and trapped, and he wasn't sure which way to move. Somehow, in New York, he had found it much easier to be positive, much easier to make clear-cut decisions. But on a farm like

22

South Burlington, clear-cut decisions weren't called for. You needed to sniff the wind, and make guesses, and alter your guesses to suit the changing weather. Farming was a life of constant compromise, and somehow the compromises were beginning to creep into his marriage.

Maybe Season was right. Maybe if she took a short vacation in Los Angeles it would help them both. But on the other hand, maybe it wouldn't. Maybe it would take them even further apart. After all, once Season began to mix with those Hollywood types, all those BPs and would-be movie stars, life at South Burlington would probably seem even duller than ever.

Maybe she would begin to think of Ed as nothing more than a stolid farmer. Something out of A. B. Frost.

'Are you going to bed now?' he asked Season.

'I was considering it,' she said. 'But I won't if you can think of something else to do around here.'

He shook his head.

'That's what I told Vee,' she remarked. 'Farming in Kansas is nothing but fertilising, furrowing, fooling-around and fornication.'

He got up. 'I won't be too long,' he said. 'I have to call Charlie Warburg.'

'Charlie Warburg? From the finance company?'

'That's right.'

She frowned as she watched him walk across the room to the door. 'He's in charge of losses, isn't he?'

'Kind of.'

'So what you were saying about that wheat blight – you were serious about that? Is it really so bad?'

'I don't know yet. It could be.'

'Ed – ' she began.

He paused by the bedroom door. She looked as if she was about to say something, but it was plain that she couldn't find the words. She sat there, with her arms crossed over her bare breasts, and looked at him with an expression that could have meant I'm sorry, or I wish we'd never met, or anything at all. Ed waited a moment longer, and when she didn't say anything, he closed the door and went downstairs.

23

Three

It was a quarter after six the next morning when the Hughes helicopter rose from the small pasture at the back of the South Burlington farmhouse and tilted its way northwestwards into the bright, snappy sky. The rotor blades flashed in the sunlight as it headed out past the hickory stand, and the *flack-flack-flack* of its engine was echoed by the outbuildings and the fences.

Dyson Kane was at the controls. He was South Burlington's most experienced flyer – a small, lightweight, white-haired man as sprightly as a jockey, with a pinched face and eyes that could have punched holes in leather. Dyson had smoked a huge briar pipe, with a bowl as big as a coffee-cup, but three years ago his doctor had warned him of lung-cancer, and now he sucked butterscotch Life Savers as if his life depended on them, and it probably did.

Ed sat next to Dyson in the front seat, and behind them sat Willard and Jack. From the dark smudges under his eyes, it didn't look as if Jack had slept too well.

'Keep following the track,' Ed told Dyson. 'I'll tell you when to turn off.'

'Sure thing, Ed,' said Dyson. 'You're the boss.'

Ed turned around to Jack and said, 'I don't suppose you've had any more ideas since you called me last night?'

Jack shook his head. 'I tested for everything. It sure isn't rust, and it isn't smut, and it's no kind of mildew that I've heard of. But I'm keeping an open mind. We've had some pretty humid weather lately and mildew thrives in humid conditions.'

'Is it worth spraying for mildew?' asked Ed.

'I suppose we could try dusting with sulphur, although I've never known sulphur do much for really serious cases.'

'Any other options?'

'Well, there's a compound called Bayleton, but that's not registered for use in the United States and we'd have to seek

24

emergency exemption to dust with that. The same goes for that British stuff from ICI, Vigil.'

'Would either of those do any good, even if we were allowed to use them?'

'I don't know. Until we get an exact analysis of what we're up against, we're only guessing. Kerry's taken the samples over to Wichita, but there's no telling how long they're going to take to decide what it is.'

Willard said, 'I can't believe it's mildew. Mildew looks kind of greyish-green, you know and it usually breaks out before the grain forms. It affects the leaves so that photosynthesis can't occur properly. But I can't believe it's that. We haven't had an outbreak of mildew on South Burlington for fifteen, maybe sixteen years.'

Dyson Kane suddenly said, 'Jee-sus! Take a look at that!'

He angled the helicopter away from the track without waiting for Ed's instructions, and took it out across the same stretch of field that Ed and Willard had visited the previous evening. Below them, Ed could make out the tracks of their Jeep through the wheat – but instead of the tracks running around the edge of the dark and blighted crops, they had now been overtaken by the darkness and swallowed up. Everywhere around, like a company of sad, arthritic widows, the rotting stalks hung their heads in the morning wind.

'It's spread,' whispered Jack. 'Fifty or sixty acres at least. Maybe more.'

Dyson took them low over the field, so that their down draught left a flurrying trail in the wheat. They were flying at sixty or seventy knots, but as Ed peered through the purple-tinted plexiglass ahead of them, it seemed as if the ocean of crops had been stained by the blight as far as he could see, and as far as they could fly. He opened the airvent, and the cockpit of the helicopter was filled with the warm, sour stench of decaying wheat.

Willard said, 'This disease sure knows how to eat up a crop, and that's no mistake.'

Ed told Dyson, 'Higher. Take her up higher. I want to see how far this stretches.'

The helicopter climbed into the shining sky. Ed slipped

on his aviator sunglasses, and looked around in all directions. The dark stain on the wheat now spread all the way southwards from the north-western trail to the banks of the Mystic, in an irregular shape that roughly resembled the state of Idaho. Jack's estimate of fifty or sixty acres was conservative. From up here, Ed would have guessed a hundred.

'We've got ourselves a real bad one here, Ed,' said Willard. 'I think we're going to have to dust, and dust quick.'

'Even before we know what it is?' asked Ed. 'We could end up doing more damage with crop-protection compounds than the blight's doing on its own.'

'We could end up with eighty-five thousand acres of rot,' retorted Willard.

'Take it south,' Ed told Dyson. 'Let's make a circuit round the whole farm, and see if there's any more of this stuff.'

'You bet,' said Dyson, and the helicopter turned away from the blight-stained areas of wheat and beat its way noisily over the Mystic River and out across the silvery-golden stretches of South Burlington's south-western acres.

'What did Charlie Warburg have to say for himself?' asked Jack, taking out a stick of gum.

'He was pretty inconclusive,' Ed replied. 'He admits that all the loans we took out for equipment and farm facilities are covered by insurance, but he isn't certain if an unknown blight is going to go down very well with the underwriters.'

'It isn't going down very well with me, either,' said Willard, caustically.

Ed said, 'The whole crop's protected, of course, under the Federal Crop Insurance Programme. That's as long as we can convince them that this blight is officially a peril of nature, like a drought, or a hailstorm. But all they can do under the law is compensate us for the cost of putting in the crop. They can't pay us for any profits we might have made.'

Dyson looked out across the farm. 'Looks like your first year at South Burlington won't be too happy, then. All work and no profit.'

Ed nodded. 'It could be worse than that. If we can't isolate this blight, and find out how to lick it, then I daren't plant again next year.'

Willard leaned forward in his seat. 'With respect, Ed, have you tried to think what your Daddy might have done, under the same circumstances?'

'I'm not my daddy, Willard.'

'No, I know you're not. I don't expect you to be. But your daddy was never averse to calling on his friends, whenever he needed a helping hand, just like his friends were never averse to calling on him.'

'You're trying to tell me something, aren't you?' said Ed, raising his voice above the roaring of the helicopter's motor.

'I'm trying to *suggest* something,' said Willard. 'I'm trying to suggest that when we get down, you might put in a call to Senator Shearson Jones.'

'Shearson Jones? That old twister?'

Willard shrugged. 'He may be a twister, but he's got himself some pretty powerful friends in the Department of Agriculture. What's more, when your daddy died, he still owed your daddy for two notable favours, one of which was covering up for him over that wheat-dumping scandal in seventy-eight.'

'Why should Shearson Jones still think he owes this family anything now that Dad's dead?'

Willard grinned. 'Because this family still remembers, that's why. And as long as there's just one Hardesty around who knows what the upright and honest Senator Jones tried to do with a hundred and forty-two thousand tons of best Kansas grain, then the upright and honest Senator Jones is going to continue to smile whenever a Hardesty asks him to.'

'That sounds like blackmail to me,' said Ed.

Willard grinned. 'You might call it blackmail in New York City. Here in Kansas we call it mutual assistance.'

'Hm,' said Ed.

'You don't believe me?' asked Willard. 'You call him when you get back, and see if I'm not speaking the truth. You ask Senator Jones if the Department of Agriculture maybe can't find some extra compensation for the victims of new and unusual crop diseases.'

'Willard,' said Ed, 'you should have been a politician, not a farmer.'

'Being a farmer and being a politician are one and the same kind of talent,' said Willard. 'Everything you do, you do by careful planting, and careful fertilisation, and watching and waiting – so that when the right moment arrives, you can go *shhhklukk!* and the ripe ears of wheat fall straight in your hand.'

Jack suddenly frowned. 'What's that?' he said. 'Look – up ahead there. Just over to the right.'

Ed turned in his seat. Far in the distance, maybe three miles away, he thought he could make out a shadow on the wheat. A brown, irregular stain that covered five or six acres at least.

'Well, I'm damned,' said Willard. 'There's more of it.'

The helicopter banked in a wide circle around the field, and approached the stain from the south-west. There was no question about it. The blight had spread here, too – almost five miles to the south of the first outbreak. Ed told Dyson to hover by the edge of the dark area while he took a long look at it. Dust and wheat flew up all around them, but Ed could see for himself that the blight was creeping from one stalk to another, from one acre to the next, and that only quick and decisive action was going to save South Burlington from the most disastrous crop in its entire history. That was if any action could save it at all.

'Okay,' Ed told Dyson at last. 'Let's go check the eastern acres.'

It took them until two o'clock in the afternoon to make a thorough airborne check of the whole farm. By the time Dyson brought the helicopter back into the pasture behind the farmhouse, they had counted seven major areas of blight, and three smaller outbreaks.

The helicopter settled on the grass and the rotor blades whistled slower and slower. Ed opened the door and climbed out, followed by Jack and Willard.

'Well,' said Jack, cleaning his glasses on his shirt-tail. 'What are we going to do now?'

Ed said, 'I don't know. Nothing, right now. First of all I want to hear what Dr Benson's got to say.'

'And then you'll call the senator?' asked Willard.

Ed glanced at him. Willard was brushing his moustache with his fingers and looking exaggeratedly innocent.

'I may,' Ed told him. 'Just to make his acquaintance.'

'Okay,' said Willard. 'I'll make the call to Dr Benson, if you like, and see if he has any ideas yet. I can reach you at the house?'

'Yes. I should be there for most of the afternoon.'

Ed walked across the pasture, vaulted the split-rail fence, and made his way around to the front of the house. It was a neat, well-proportioned house, with white carved balconies and shuttered dormer windows and a shingle roof that sloped all the way down to the roof of the front verandah. It didn't look like the kind of house that Dan Hardesty would have chosen for himself, but only recently Ed had discovered that it wasn't. An early partner of his father's called Ted Zacharias had constructed it, and sold it to his father along with twenty thousand acres of arable land. Ed hadn't been surprised by the discovery: his father had always been a man of business, not of taste.

As Ed crossed the yard, he saw the grey Cadillac Seville parked in front of the steps, and the buff-uniformed chauffeur leaning against it smoking a cigarette. His mother was here. He rubbed the muscles at the back of his neck as he walked through the verandah and opened the gentian-blue front door. His mother always gave him a feeling of suppressed tension, and it sometimes took Season an hour of gentle talk and a massage to calm him down after the old lady had gone.

Mrs Ursula Hardesty was another reason he had left home.

She was standing in the hallway as he came in, primping her hair. She was tall, bony as a clothes-horse and wearing a light green Yves St Laurent dress that was at least twenty years too young for her. Her eyes were as pale and watery as Little Neck clams, and her neck was withered and white, although it was sparklingly decorated with three strands of diamonds and pearls. She gave him a lopsided smile, and raised her arms like someone signalling to a passing ship.

'Edward. My dear. I thought I'd surprise you.'

'Hello, Mother.'

He embraced her as circumspectly as he knew how. Curling his arm around her waist and yet not quite touching her; kissing her cheek from a fraction of an inch away.

'You're looking peaky, dear,' she said. 'Are you still taking that tonic wine I brought you?'

'When I remember. I've just had a bad night, that's all.'

Mrs Hardesty glanced towards the living-room, where Ed could see Season's arm on the back of the settee, holding a smoking cigarette.

'I hope you're not having any *trouble*,' she said, her voice as brittle as fractured porcelain.

'You mean you hope I'm not having too many arguments with Season? Is that it?'

Mrs Hardesty looked pained. 'I've never had anything *against* her, Edward, but I can't say that she's really cut out to be the mistress of a wheat-farming empire, can you? I mean – fashion and style are all very well, but has she bought herself any galoshes yet?'

'Mother,' Ed told her, 'I'm not having you start all that again. Season's settling in pretty well, all things considered. It's a big change to come to Kansas from New York City. A big shock to the system. Season's going to have to be given time to get used to it.'

'Well . . .' said Mrs Hardesty, disapprovingly, turning her mouth down at the corners.

'Well nothing, Mother,' Ed retorted. 'And as to when she's going to buy herself any galoshes . . . she'll do it when Gucci bring out some galoshes with red-and-green bands round the top.'

'It's your loss,' Mrs Hardesty said. 'If you want to carry the whole burden of South Burlington yourself . . . it's really up to you. I can't influence you.'

'No, you can't,' said Ed. 'Now come and have a cocktail before I start getting mad at you. I've got enough problems on the farm without getting mad at my mother.'

'No *serious* problems, I hope?' said Mrs Hardesty, as they walked through into the living-room.

'Moderately serious. Some sort of crop disease. We're not sure what it is yet.'

Mrs Hardesty frowned. 'Is it bad? You're almost ready for harvesting.'

Ed walked around the back of the sofa, clasped Season's hand, and bent over to kiss her. She was dressed in tight dark blue velvet pants and a cream-coloured silk blouse. Her hair was freshly washed and shining, and she had let it hang loose to her shoulders.

'How is it?' she asked.

Ed shrugged. 'Hard to tell yet. But it's still spreading. We saw patches of it all over.'

'Did Dr Benson call yet?'

'Willard's trying to get in touch with him now.'

Mrs Hardesty sat down in the velvet-covered armchair by the fireplace, facing the library chair which had once been her husband's. She sat stiff and erect, raising her head like an inquiring eagle. 'You've sent samples across to Dr Benson?' she asked. 'Your father always thought that Dr Benson was a quack.'

'Perhaps he is,' said Ed. 'But he's our first line of assistance. Jack's been trying to isolate the blight all night, and he can't make out what it is.'

'I could give you Professor Kornbluth's number,' said Mrs Hardesty. 'He did some wonderful work for us on seed dressings.'

'That's very kind of you, Mother, but Professor Kornbluth is an expert on the protection of germinating crops, and that's it. This is a blight of the whole ripened ear.'

'Has it spread very far?' asked his mother.

'Two, maybe two hundred and fifty acres.'

'Two hundred and fifty acres? And you're leaving it to Dr Benson? My dear, you can't do that!'

'What else do you suggest I do?'

'Go over his head. Your father would have done. Go straight to the Department of Agriculture.'

Ed sat down in his father's chair, and crossed his legs in a

31

deliberate effort to show that he was relaxed. 'Mother,' he said, 'Dr Benson is the Kansas state expert on crop protection. Whatever father thought about him, and however erratic he might seem to be – '

'Alcoholic, more like,' sniffed Mrs Hardesty.

'All right, alcoholic. Erratic. Whatever. But he's still the man I have to do business with, week in and week out, and if I go over his head now there's never going to be any chance of my getting a favour out of him in the future. I know what he's like. I'm not dumb. But I told Willard to kick his keister if he dragged his feet, and I think he'll be able to help us.'

Mrs Hardesty suddenly and unexpectedly turned to Season. 'What do *you* think, my dear?' she demanded.

Season shrugged. 'I don't think anything. I don't think I've ever met Dr Benson. Whatever Ed decides to do is fine by me.'

Mrs Hardesty rose to her feet. 'Isn't that *marvellous*?' she said, in a frivolously sarcastic tone. '"Whatever Ed decides to do is fine by me." Have you ever heard any wheat-farmer's wife come out with such a positive and helpful contribution? Do you know something, my dear, when I was mistress of this farm, I used to spend all my waking hours finding out about crops and how to grow them. I was as much an expert on wheat as Ed's father was. I could talk about planting and harvesting with the best of them, and I could take a tractor to pieces with my own bare hands. This region is *lousy* with sidewalk farmers, who commute to their farms from Wichita and Kansas City, and *lousy* with suitcase farmers, who spend most of their time in Chicago and Los Angeles, and only fly in for the sowing and the harvesting. Well, Dan Hardesty wasn't one of them, and neither was I. We lived on our land and we took care of our crops and we produced more grain on these eighty-five thousand acres than most farms that were twice our size. We did it together, Dan and I, and that's why I can hardly believe my ears when I hear you saying that you don't care about it.'

'I didn't say that I don't care about it,' put in Season. 'I simply said that I respect Ed's judgement.'

32

'Come on, Mother,' said Ed. 'We all know what you and Daddy did to build up South Burlington. It's part of the family's history. But can't you just leave it alone?'

'I see,' said Mrs Hardesty. 'You're prepared to talk about your father and I as ancient history – a bedtime story for Sally, maybe – but you're not prepared to take my advice?'

'Mother, this is my farm now.'

Mrs Hardesty looked out of the window across the sunlit yard. Her hands were clasped together in controlled anguish. 'Yes,' she said. 'I know it is. And I also remember what it cost this family for you to have it.'

Season turned around. 'That, Ursula, is a grossly unfair remark,' she said, coldly. 'Ed was just as hurt as you were by what happened to his father and what happened to Michael. Good God, you're talking as if he killed them with his own bare hands.'

Mrs Hardesty stared at her. 'My only regret,' she said, 'is not that Edward took over the farm when his father and his older brother both died. My only regret is that he should have brought to South Burlington a wife who treats the farm and everything that it means to this family with such obvious contempt.'

Season was about to say something caustic in return, but she held herself back. Instead, she reached over to the low gilded coffee-table and opened the cigarette-box.

'I'd really appreciate it if you sat down and made yourself comfortable,' she told Mrs Hardesty. 'I hate to see anyone feeling ill-at-ease in my home, no matter who it is.'

Mrs Hardesty looked to her son, but Ed simply said, 'Sit down, Mother. I'll fix you a cocktail.'

'You will stay for some supper, won't you?' asked Season. 'Perhaps you'd like to stay the night?'

The telephone over on the French bureau started to ring. Ed said, 'Excuse me,' and went across to pick it up. It was Willard, calling from the office on the far side of the yard.

'I hope I'm not interrupting anything,' he said. 'I saw the old lady's car outside.'

'Just the usual,' said Ed. 'Did you get hold of Benson?'

'I sure did. And I hope you're sitting down.'

33

'Has he found out what it is?'

'He has some ideas. But it turns out that we're not the only farm that's been hit. He's had samples in this morning from as far away as Great Bend and Concordia. Seems like the whole state's been affected.'

'The whole state? You're kidding.'

'I wish I was,' said Willard. 'But I called Arthur Kalken over at the Hutchinson place just to check, and he told me their whole south valley is nothing but two thousand acres of blight. He's had it for two, three days now.'

'There hasn't been anything about it on the news.'

'Well, the state agricultural people have been trying to keep it quiet until they know what it is. They don't want buyers boycotting Kansas wheat just because they're afraid it might be contaminated or something. And also, the thing's only just hit. Most of the farmers were like us – they thought they were the only ones who'd got it.'

Ed ran his hand through his hair. 'What's going to happen? Did Benson have any ideas?'

'He's still trying to isolate it. He's sent some samples to the federal laboratories, too. But meanwhile, George Pulaski's arranging an emergency meeting for all the state's wheat farmers – probably in Kansas City and probably on Thursday morning.'

'Okay,' said Ed. 'Did Benson give you any ideas about interim control? Sulphur spraying, anything of that kind?'

'He said to leave it alone. It's not rust, and it's not powdery mildew, and it could react adversely if you dust it.'

Ed put the phone down. Season was watching him intently, and she said, 'You've got your *Aristotle Contemplating The Bust Of Homer* face on again. What's wrong?'

'Willard talked to Dr Benson. It seems like South Burlington isn't the only farm with the blight. The whole state's affected.'

'And I suppose Benson still doesn't know what it is?' asked Mrs Hardesty.

'No, Mother, he doesn't,' said Ed. 'But it seems like he's taken your advice, and sent the problem over his own head.

He's asked the federal laboratories to look at it, too.'

'Well,' said Mrs Hardesty, 'it won't be the first time the wheat crop's failed in Kansas. For some of those part-timers, it's a regular occurrence.'

'The whole wheat crop, throughout the whole state?' asked Ed. 'South Burlington's wheat crop, too?'

'The crop's insured, isn't it?' Mrs Hardesty asked. 'And at least your father isn't around to see it fail. He would have tanned your hide.'

'Mrs Hardesty, the blight isn't Ed's fault,' said Season.

Mrs Hardesty lifted her head, more like an eagle than ever. 'Poor farmers always blame everything except their own lack of talent. Drought, floods, hail, mildew – they're all an excuse.'

'Mother,'said Ed, 'you're going to make me mad in a minute.'

The telephone rang again. It was Willard. 'Dr Benson called me,' he said. 'Told me to watch the two-thirty news on television. Seems like the state agricultural department has just put out a statement.'

Ed pointed to the television, and twisted his hand to indicate to Season that she should switch it on. Then he asked Willard, 'Any more news about the analysis?'

'Not a thing. Looks like it's one of those diseases that's going to baffle modern science for years to come.'

'I'll keep in touch,' said Ed, and put the phone down again.

The news was just beginning. After a lead report about fighting in Iran, the anchorman said, 'Trouble of a different kind here at home. Reports from the wheat-growing states of Kansas and North Dakota tell of a rapidly-spreading and so-far unidentified crop blight. Apparently the blight is attacking ripe ears of wheat and causing them to rot right on their stalks, and hundreds of acres of crops have already been destroyed. Local and federal agricultural experts are working around the clock to isolate the cause of the blight – so far without success. George Pulaski, chief of the agricultural department for the state of Kansas, the country's number one wheat producer, says that he's confident the blight will be brought under control before the damage ruins more than a nominal percentage of the year's crop. But, he warned, many farmers may face substantial losses, if not bankruptcy.'

That was all. Ed walked over and switched the television off. 'I think I could use a drink,' he said, quietly.

'Thank God your father isn't here,' said Mrs Hardesty.

'Thank you, God,' said Season, and Mrs Hardesty gave her a frosty stare.

Four

That evening, after supper, he went upstairs to his small library and placed a call to Senator Shearson Jones in Washington. The telephone rang for a long time before anyone answered, and then an irritated voice said, 'Senator Jones's residence.'

'I'd like to speak to the senator, please.'

'The senator isn't here. He's in Tobago, on vacation.'

'He spoke in the Senate yesterday afternoon, on soybean subsidies.'

'So?'

'Well, either he has an incredible talent for throwing his voice, or else he's still in Washington. You tell him it's Ed Hardesty, son of Dan Hardesty, and you can also tell him one hundred and forty-two thousand tons.'

'That's the message? One hundred forty-two thousand tons?'

'That's the message.'

There was a lengthy pause, during which Ed could faintly hear someone laughing. Then there was a series of clicks, and the phone was put through to Senator Jones.

'Jones here.' The voice was thick, and slurred with tiredness or drink.

'Senator Jones, you don't know me, but you knew my father.'

'That's right. What's this cockamamie message about one hundred and forty-two thousand tons?'

36

'I'm not a blackmailer, Senator Jones. That was just a way of getting you on to the phone.'

'All right, you got me. What do you want?'

'You've heard about this wheat blight in Kansas?'

'Sure. Something about it. But it doesn't look too disastrous from where I'm sitting.'

'You're sitting in Washington, DC, Senator Jones. I'm sitting right in the middle of eighty-five thousand acres that are very rapidly turning black.'

'Well? You're insured under the Federal Crop Programme, aren't you? Why don't you go talk to that nice Mr Deal?'

'I shall,' said Ed. 'But you know as well as I do that the Federal Insurance Programme only covers the cost of re-planting.'

'Name me an insurance policy that covers anything else,' demanded Senator Jones. 'You could be Cartier-Bresson, and every photograph you ever took could make you ten thousand dollars, but if the laboratory fogs one of your films, what can you claim? The price of the film, that's all. And it's the same with crops.'

'I'm aware of that,' said Ed. 'But since this blight is so damaging, and so completely unknown, I was wondering if there might be a possibility of further aid from the Department of Agriculture.'

'No,' said Senator Jones.

'Is that a refusal to help, or an admission that you don't have the clout to help?'

'That's a refusal to help. What's the matter with you farmers? You get deficiency payments, you get guaranteed floor prices, you get nationwide federal insurance. What more do you want? You want me to come out there and harvest your crop for you? You want me to ride a tractor?'

'Senator Jones, the way this blight is spreading, there isn't going *be* any crop.'

'Well, you'll just have to grin and bear it. I'm sorry, Mr Hardesty, but farming's tough, and there's nothing that you or I can do about it.'

Ed drew a breath. 'Listen, Senator Jones, my daddy may have been a tough and wily old turkey, and he may have

37

built up one of the most successful wheat farms in south Kansas, but he was heavily overstretched on his spending. When I took over this farm, it was right on the verge of financial collapse. Sure – we were harvesting a regular, high-quality crop, and we had all the latest techniques. But we were overmanned, and we'd relied too much on credit, and too much on favours, and the simple fact was that we had a super-efficient farm that wasn't quite super-efficient enough to meet its interest payments.'

'I hope you realise you're breaking my heart,' said Senator Jones.

'I hope you realise I was lying when I said I wasn't a blackmailer.'

Senator Jones sniffed. 'This doesn't sound like a Hardesty talking. Your daddy was one of those men who always stood on his own two feet. He'd expect a favour from his friends, sure. But he never crawled for anything.'

'I'm not crawling, Senator Jones. I'm asking. My daddy did you a favour, and now I want you to do him a favour in return. Because if this farm goes bankrupt, which it surely will if we don't get more than a federal insurance payment, then my daddy's name is going to be dragged all over the Kansas papers like dirt.'

'Hunh,' said Senator Jones.

'You can "hunh" all you like,' said Ed. 'I know you're thinking that I don't sound like my daddy, but the reason for that is that I'm *not* my daddy. He was a farmer, but I'm a businessman, and the way this farm was falling to pieces when I took over, that's probably just as well. My daddy was very good at what he did, but when it came to the financial jiggery-pokery, he relied too much on people like you. He didn't know a floor price from a floor mop.'

'Mr Hardesty,' said Senator Jones, with exaggerated patience, 'I have to tell you that I'm very sorry for you, and that I'd really like to help. But the truth of the matter is, I'm very busy right now on this soybean problem in Iowa, and I really can't see that I'm going to be able to spend the time on one single disgruntled wheat farmer from Kansas.'

'All right,' said Ed. 'If that's the way you feel, I'm going straight to the papers with the facts on the wheat-dumping scandal.'

'Who the hell do you think you are?' snarled Senator Jones. 'Nancy Drew? Don't come at me with that going-to-the-papers shit.'

'You think it's shit?' asked Ed, although he was trembling with the tension of what he was doing. 'You read it in print in the *Washington Post*, and then tell me it's shit.'

There was silence. Fifteen seconds, thirty seconds of utter silence. Then Senator Jones said, 'This is a state-wide problem, right? As I understand it.'

'Kansas and North Dakota. That's what I heard on the news.'

'Well – if it's a state-wide problem – I may be able to pressure for federal emergency aid. I may be able to arrange a special financial allocation to help farmers wiped out by the blight.'

'That sounds more like it.'

'I can't promise anything, and I think we ought to meet. I'll have to get my assistant to do some digging on the background, too. You have to understand that I'm coming into this cold.'

'So am I,' said Ed. 'I only found the first traces of blight yesterday evening.'

'All right,' said Senator Jones. 'Is there any chance you can get down to Fall River at the week-end? I have a cabin there, by the lake.'

'It's possible.'

'Then let me call you tomorrow, or maybe Thursday, and I'll be more in the picture by then.'

'Good,' said Ed.'

'I'll tell you something,' said Senator Jones, 'you certainly inherited one of your father's most important qualities.'

'Oh, yes?'

'Oh, yes. You can bluster like hell. Now, give me your number so that I can call you back.'

At last, Ed put the phone down. On the scribble pad beside him, he saw that he'd written the word 'Compensation' in elaborate, illuminated letters, and sketched a picture of an ear of wheat.

He sat back in his creaking sheriff's chair, and rubbed his eyes with his fingertips. Then he looked around him at the leather-bound books on the bookshelves – *The Farmer's Frontier*, by Gilbert White, *The Great Plains*, by Walter Prescott Webb – and at the pipe-rack his father had left and at the bronze statue of plough horses from the early days of dry farming. Stacked on the corner of his desk were the accounts books for the past five years at South Burlington, and as Ed had come to learn since he moved into the farmhouse last fall, these books told the whole story of his father's greatest successes and his greatest failures.

He heard a slight noise at the door, and he swivelled around in his chair. His mother was standing there, in her white bathrobe, her hair done up in curlers.

'Mother,' he said. 'I thought you'd gone to bed.'

'I heard you talking,' she said. 'I came along to say good night.'

'All right,' he said, nodding. 'Good night, then.'

She remained where she was, her face shadowed by the half-open door. 'Was that true, what you said to Senator Jones?' she asked him.

'Was what true?'

'You know what I mean, Edward. Was the farm really on the edge of ruin?'

He stood up, and ripped the doodles off his notepad. 'Sometimes you have to say things just to put pressure on people,' he said. 'Whatever happened, it's all past, and Daddy's dead, and that's all you have to worry about.'

'But I want to know.'

He turned around and looked at her. 'You didn't know when Daddy was alive. He kept it all hidden from you. Why should you want to know now?'

'Because he was my husband. Because I want to understand some of the problems he had to face.'

Ed picked up one of the accounts books, and flicked through it. 'You can look if you want to. You may not understand what it all means, if you don't have any training in reading accounts. Henry Pollock will tell you what went on, because Henry was Daddy's right-hand man. But what it all amounts to is over-spending, under-capitalisation, arbitrary investment and near-sighted financial planning.'

Ursula Hardesty slowly shook her head. 'I don't understand it. He was such a good farmer.'

'Oh, yes. No doubt about it. His irrigation system is still one of the finest in the country. You know what people said about him – he could grow wheat on a parking lot. But he relied too much on his personality, and on scratching people's backs, and having his own back scratched in return. The day he died, the financial future of this farm was hanging by a thread. That's why the bank needed to talk to Michael the night before his funeral.'

'Are you trying to say that your father killed his own son?'

'Mother, don't talk nonsense. Michael died because of a terrible and tragic accident.'

'But that's what you're saying isn't it?' his mother insisted. 'If the farm had been financially stable, Michael wouldn't have had to drive into Wichita. If your father hadn't over-spent and mis-managed the farm, Michael could still be alive.'

'Mother, for God's sake, you can't talk like that.'

The old woman stood up straight. 'This is my house. I can talk how I like.'

There was a pause, and then a quiet, firm voice said, 'No, Ursula. This isn't your house. Not any more. And if you want to be welcome in it, you're going to have to keep a check on those irrational outbursts of yours.'

Season was standing at the far end of the corridor, by the door of the master bedroom, in a long lacey negligée. Mrs Hardesty touched her forehead with her fingertips as if she felt a sudden twinge of headache, and then abruptly turned and walked back to her bedroom, without a word. Season stayed where she was, waiting for Ed to say something.

'I'm going into Wichita tomorrow to see Dr Benson,' Ed said. 'If I'm going to press for extra compensation, I think I'm going to have to get myself all the technical information I can lay my hands on.'

'Of course,' said Season. There was an odd, slightly

41

challenging note in the way she said it.

'Do you want to come with me?' he asked her. 'You could do some shopping at the civic centre.'

'It depends what time you go,' she said. 'I'm catching an eleven o'clock flight to Los Angeles from Wichita Mid-Continent Airport.'

'Season?' he said, quite urgently; but she had already gone back into the bedroom, and closed the door.

'Season?' he repeated, knowing that she couldn't hear him.

Five

Senator Jones walked back into his lavish Moroccan-style living-room, with its multi-coloured mosaic tiles and its North African draperies and its elaborate brass-topped tables and stood silent for a moment, lighting up a cigar.

'Well?' asked the red-headed girl in the silky emerald-green wrap, stretching herself out on the ottoman sofa.

'Well what?' said Senator Jones, as he *pup-pup-pupped* his Havana into life.

'Well, who is it who's so burningly fascinating that you're prepared to break off right in the middle of courting your favourite newspaper lady? Usually, my darling, you're not even prepared to answer the phone for the President.'

'The President's a Democrat,' growled Senator Jones. 'Apart from being an uninteresting asshole.'

'And was this a Republican? An *interesting* asshole?'

'If I told you who it was, and why he'd called me, you'd rush back to the office and print it,' said Senator Jones.

'It's as scandalous as all that?'

'It's no more scandalous than anything else that happens in American politics. Tell me one worthwhile political achievement since seventeen seventy-six that hasn't been scandalous. It was scandal that made this nation great.'

Senator Jones lowered his bulky body into a large

carved-oak armchair, upholstered in a zig-zag fabric that resembled camel blankets. He crossed his legs by tugging at his left ankle with his right hand and he puffed at his cigar for a while reflectively. He had always been a big man. There were photographs upstairs in his study which showed him as a linebacker for the Washburn University football team. A serious, solid young man with thick lips and eyebrows that looked as if they had been drawn across his face with a black felt-tip pen. He had remained reasonably athletic while he worked in his father's law firm in Topeka; but when he entered politics, in the Eisenhower landslide of 1956, as one of the state's youngest-ever representatives, he quickly learned to enjoy the fruits of political success, as well as the steaks and the lobsters and the truffles and the fine vintage wines. By the time Ike's term was over, Shearson Jones weighed over 250 pounds, and Washington wags were calling him 'Shearson Jones, Incorporated.' *Time* magazine printed a famous picture of him sitting in a committee meeting with his belly protruding so much that they captioned it 'Kansas Representative and Friend.'

He may have been overweight, but he stayed light on his feet, both physically and politically. The hours he spent over dinner weren't wasted, because he chose his dinner-partners carefully, and by the time Kennedy was elected he was known as one of the toughest and most knowledgeable negotiators in Congress. His main power base was the Department of Agriculture, where he formed intricate and lasting alliances with the most influential members of the bureaucracy, the faceless officials who really decided what went on. He ran for senator in 1964, and during the Johnson years he built up several enduring friendships with the heavyweight Southern Democrats who controlled the Agriculture Committee. In 1971, he was the prime mover behind a small but forceful group of senators who blocked attempts to abolish or adjust the parity ratio – the ratio between income and expenditure which was supposed to show how well America's farmers were faring. The parity ratio usually showed the farmers were doing badly, and that they urgently needed federal support, so that by 1973 the government was handing them more than 2·5 billion dollars a year.

What the parity ratio *didn't* show was that most larger farmers were actually doing very well, and that many of those larger farmers were paying Shearson Jones hundreds of thousands of dollars to maintain their subsidies. By 1973 – when the federal farm programme was eventually changed under the Agriculture and Consumer Protection Act – the senator from Kansas was worth well over seven million dollars.

He was said to have made another million out of illegal sales of rice to the North Vietnamese, but an exhaustive investigation in the *Washington Post* failed to come up with any concrete evidence. Shearson Jones had raised his fist in the Senate and asked God to strike him dead *instantly* if he had ever been guilty of illegal trafficking in grain or rice.

Today, Shearson Jones was big, balding and buoyant – a huge and ebullient man at the peak of his career. He had occasionally been mentioned as vice-presidential material, although *The New York Times* had ruled out the possibility of his ever making the White House. 'Too fat in an age of austerity,' they had remarked, dismissively.

The red-haired girl said, 'What are you going to do now? Kiss me? Kick me out? Or are you going to sit there and seek oral gratification from that cigar for the rest of the night?'

'I'm thinking,' said Shearson.

'Oh, you're *thinking*. In the middle of our romantic courtship, you have to think?'

He ignored her. 'Make me another drink,' he said. 'I want to make one more phone call.'

She got up from the ottoman, walked over, and kissed him on his bald forehead. There were pinpricks of sweat on his brow, and he still smelled of garlic from lunchtime. He glanced up at her and gave an appreciative 'hmmph,' but then he was used to the attentions of pretty young women. He was very rich, and very powerful, and apart from that the sheer bodily size of him exerted some sort of grotesque attraction over the unlikeliest girls. One of his mistresses had ecstatically described his love-making as 'something between riding on Moby Dick in a rough sea, and bouncing on a huge feather bed.'

He had known Della McIntosh for just four days. He had seen her before, of course, because she was the Washington bureau chief for the *Kansas City Herald-Examiner*, and whenever he held a press conference or handed out prizes or opened his mouth in the Senate, Della McIntosh would have to be there. She had even interviewed his wife Margaret once, for a piece that had run under the headline 'Living With The Stomach Of The Senate.'

But four days ago, Margaret had been fortuitously out of town, visiting her diabetic sister in San Diego. And when Shearson and Della had found themselves together on the balcony of Senator Karl Leiderman's elegant Georgetown house, both taking an oxygen break during a seven o'clock cocktail crush, it had been animal attraction at first sight, with nothing to hold it back.

Della was petite – snub-nosed, green-eyed, with vivid red hair in a shaggy Farrah bob. Although she was small, her breasts were enormous – *Playboy* playmate size – and Shearson had taken one look at her and felt an almost irresistible urge to dig his podgy fingers into them. Della had been wearing a low-cut cocktail dress in electric blue, with a small sapphire cross dangling in her cleavage, and Shearson had walked across the balcony in his huge black tuxedo and loomed over her like Mount Baldy on a dark night.

'That cross,' he had rumbled, 'is resting in the most desirable spot in the whole of the District of Columbia.'

They had left the cocktail party separately. There was no way in which Shearson could ever slip out from anywhere unnoticed. They had met up an hour later at Le Faisan Restaurant, where he had treated her to dinner, and to the unparalleled spectacle of an average Shearson Jones repast. He had steadily eaten his way through turtle soup, fresh trout, roasted quails, rack of lamb, *boeuf en croûte*, salad, cheese, and a heaped plateful of *profiteroles*, smothered with hot chocolate and cream.

They had toasted each other wordlessly in Hospices de Beaune.

Now, over by the African-style cocktail cabinet – stained oak topped by minarets and pierced with mirrors – Della mixed them two vodka tonics. Shearson opened a brass-inlaid box and took out a telephone.

'Are you sure you can trust me?' asked Della, squeezing the limes.

Shearson punched out a number. 'No,' he said, 'I'm not sure at all. But if I see one single word of this in the *Kansas City Herald-Examiner*, I'll have the whole damned paper closed down.'

'You and whose army?'

'Me and Mr Wendell Oliver, the chairman of Western States Communications, who happens to control a majority shareholding in your newspaper, and who comes around here for dinner twice a month.'

She glanced at him. He plainly wasn't joking at all. She said, 'Oh,' and brought him his drink. Then she sat on the edge of the ottoman, her wrap slightly parted to reveal her breasts, while he puffed and popped away at his cigar and waited for his number to ring.

'Alan?' he said, at last.

A wary voice said, 'Who is this?'

'Alan, this is Shearson. That's right. Well, I know it's kind of a strange time to be calling you, Alan, but as it happens something pretty interesting has come up.'

'What do you mean by "interesting"?' asked the voice. It was a rich voice, fruity, with a strong Georgia accent.

Shearson pulled a face. 'All kinds of interesting, Alan. Politically interesting – the kind of thing that would show a fellow up in a favourable light when it came to election time – and financially interesting, too. In fact, the very best kind of interesting.'

'Go on.'

'You've heard about this crop blight they've been experiencing in Kansas and North Dakota? The wheat disease?'

'Sure. It was on the news tonight. I've already asked Wilkins to get together a dossier on it.'

Shearson nodded. 'That's good. You've told the media what you're doing, have you? Good. Because from what I hear, this blight's pretty serious. Hundreds of acres gone to rot, and nothing the farmers can do about it.'

'Spreading all the time, too,' put in Alan. 'So far they're projecting the worst wheat harvest for ten years, even if they can bring it under control by mid-week.'

'Well, that's what I hear, too,' said Shearson. 'Not that it's really going to hit our grain reserves too badly. We've got more damned grain stored up than we know what to do with – especially after we stopped selling it to the Soviets. And if you ask me, it won't do the farmers much harm, either. It's about time Mother Nature slapped them down a bit, and gave them a genuine reason to be grateful for all those subsidies we give them.'

Alan said cautiously, 'I still don't quite get your drift, Shearson.'

'The drift is this,' Shearson explained, with a smug smile. 'This blight is spectacular, and damaging, and right now it's newsworthy. That means that the situation's just getting ripe for some strong emotional rhetoric. You know what I mean. How the honest farmers risk their whole livelihood just to fill the nation's bread-basket; how this strange and terrifying blight is going to drive countless small farmers to the wall; how they're going to need more than their usual guaranteed floor prices to stay in business.'

'I'm not sure you're making sense,' said Alan.

'Oh, I'm making sense all right,' said Shearson. 'Because out of all this stirring talk, we're going to propose a special emergency rescue fund – maybe call it the Blight Crisis Appeal. We'll swing a vote in the House for some modest starting donation from the federal government – say ten million dollars – and then we'll ask private industry to donate as well. As an acknowledgement, we'll take out whole page advertisements in *Fortune*, with headings like 'The grateful farmers of Kansas thank the following for their donations . . .' All good heartwarming commercial stuff. The public will like it, the government will like it, industry will like it, and even farmers will like it.'

'I'll buy that,' Alan said. 'But where's your angle?'

Shearson grunted in amusement. 'You're being slow tonight, Alan. The angle is that you and I will administer

47

the fund, and that we'll have total and legal control over the distribution of the money. Naturally, we'll have to be paid a modest salary by the fund for the work we put in, and then we'll have expenses to cover, and it might even be necessary for the fund to purchase extensive tracts of farmland for research purposes. You've always fancied a nice stud farm for your retirement, haven't you, Alan? Well, you could have that, and serve the American people, too.'

There was a long silence on the other end of the telephone. Then Alan said, 'Legal? You sure?'

'I'll have Joe Dasgupta set up the framework. He may cost a little more, but he'll make it watertight.'

'What if the laboratories find out what's causing the blight, and what if they manage to arrest it before it does too much damage? What happens then?'

'Alan, my friend, you're being naïve. The federal agricultural research laboratories are under *our* jurisdiction.'

'You mean – even if they *do* find out what it is – we don't have to accept their findings?'

'That's right. We can keep this blight going just as long as we need to. Apart from our own laboratories, the only other people working on any kind of analysis are the local yokels in Wichita, and you know how limited their facilities are. They couldn't analyse a cow flop.'

'Well,' said Alan, thoughtfully, 'it seems like you've thought of all the possible wrinkles. What are you going to do now?'

'I have a farmer,' said Shearson. 'One representative farmer, whose crop is turning as black as Sammy Davis Junior all around him. I used to know his father, before his father passed on, and so there's a good old-time friendship story for the newspapers in that. This farmer's going to be my mouthpiece for all the struggling crop growers of Kansas and North Dakota. He's articulate, and he's out for extra compensation on top of his crop insurance, and with the right handling he could be very appealing. I haven't met him yet, but provided he doesn't look like Quasimodo, I don't think we're going to have any problems at all.'

There was a longer silence. Eventually, Alan said, 'All right, Shearson. I'll leave the ball with you. But don't forget to keep me in touch. I don't want you using my authority for deals you conveniently forgot to tell me about.'

'Alan,' said Shearson, warmly, 'would I ever do a thing like that?'

'Yes,' replied Alan, and put the phone down.

Della sat watching Shearson with a mixture of amusement and respect. 'You amaze me,' she said, as Shearson picked up his cocktail and took a long swallow.

'I amaze you? Why? I'm only doing my job.

'Your job is to set up personal slush funds disguised as emergency appeals for stricken farmers?'

Shearson shook his head. 'My job is to make the people who elected me happy. That's why they voted for me. With this Blight Crisis fund, the agricultural aid supporters in Congress will get to feel happy, the private industries who donate money and have their names published in the papers will get to feel happy, the farmers will get to feel happy, and the public will get to feel happy.'

Della stood up and walked across the Arabian rug. The loosely-tied belt around her silky wrap came undone, and Shearson glimpsed her small see-through nylon panties. He raised his eyes to her and saw that she was smiling.

'We mustn't forget *you*,' she said. 'You will get to feel happiest of all.'

'You don't begrudge me a little satisfaction out of life? A little financial compensation for all the selfless effort I put into this nation's affairs?'

'You still amaze me,' she said. 'To take a situation like this wheat blight, and twist it around into a profit-making venture with only a couple of phone calls and a few minutes' thought – well, that's what I call genius. Black genius, perhaps. But genius all the same.'

He watched her closely, and then he held out his fat-fingered hand for her. She stepped a few inches closer, and he grasped her wrap.

'I still don't know if I can trust you or not,' he told her, in a thick voice that had all the warning rumbles of an earth tremor. 'I still don't know if I should have let you overhear what I was saying.'

'I don't even know who you were talking to.'

He grunted. 'Don't give me that. It was Alan Hedges, the chairman of the Agriculture Committee, and you realised that as soon as I started talking.'

'All right,' she smiled, 'I did.'

'The question is,' he said, 'are you going to rush into print with this tasty little morsel of scandal, or are you going to accept my offer?'

'Offer?' she asked, tilting her head to one side. Shearson was tugging harder at her wrap now, and her right shoulder was bare. She didn't make any attempt to resist him. Her skin was pale and freckled in the subdued light from the pierced-brass Moroccan lamp.

'Come on, Della, you're an intelligent woman,' said Shearson. 'I'm going to need someone to oversee this little fund-raising operation for me. A manager.'

'Don't you have anyone in the Department of Agriculture to do your managing for you?'

He shook his head. 'They're all too busy digging knives into each other's backs and trying to outsmart me. I need an outsider. Someone new, and bright, and fresh, and personable. Someone like you.'

'You don't know anything about me.'

'I know that you're twenty-seven years old, born in Pauls Valley, Oklahoma, daughter of a horse-breeder and his wife. I know that you studied at Oklahoma College of Liberal Arts at Chickasha, and then found yourself a job in Oklahoma City as a copy girl for the *Oklahoma News-Messenger*. I know that you married a printer called George McIntosh when you were just twenty-one, and that you bore him a daughter. I know that your daughter died of meningitis when she was two, and that not long after, you and George split up. You went to Kansas City, and found a job on the *Kansas City Herald-Examiner* – and George – do you know what happened to George?'

'No,' said Della, white-faced. 'I haven't heard from George in two or three years.'

'Well, that's not surprising,' said Shearson. 'George died

in a very nasty multiple road accident on the Indian Nation Turnpike, a couple of miles outside of McAlester, just about a year ago.'

'How do you know all this?' asked Della. 'You've only been dating me for four days. And, my God, nobody told me that George was dead. I didn't even get a letter from his mother.'

Shearson shrugged, but didn't release his tight grip on her wrap. 'I know because I have to know. I'm an influential man, Della, and influential men are at permanent risk from chisellers and con artists and sweet-talking whores with big tits. You – you're different. You talk sharp and you don't let me get away with treating you like dirt. I like you a lot. And that's why my friends at the Federal Bureau of Investigation were only too glad to fill in a little background for me.'

Della looked down at his fist, gripping her wrap possessively.

'You want me to give up the newspaper?' she asked him. He nodded.

'How much would it pay? I mean – running an emergency fund isn't a career, is it? What would I do when it was all over?'

'You wouldn't have to do anything. A fund of this kind can raise up to three hundred million dollars. Maybe more. You and me and Alan Hedges – we'd all be working for a percentage. In rough figures, you may come out with a million and a bit.'

'A million and a bit? A million *dollars?*'

'You heard me. That's the offer. But if you don't take it, I don't want a single word about this Blight Crisis Appeal turning up in the *Kansas City Herald-Examiner*, or any other newspaper for that matter. This is offered to you in confidence, because I like you, and because I think I can trust you.'

Della stood silent. Shearson watched her for a while, the sweat shining on his forehead, and then he heaved himself out of his chair, and stood over her.

'You know why I like you?' he growled. 'You're a smart bitch. A real smart bitch. Even now, you're playing smart.

Even though I know damned well what you're going to say.'

He seized her emerald-green wrap in both hands, and pulled it right down over her shoulders, baring her breasts. They were big and white and heavy, with soft pale nipples, and Shearson looked down at them with the theatrical pleasure of a stage pirate who has just prised open a casket of gold.

'You're smart,' he said, 'and you're damned sexy.'

He gripped her breasts in both hands, digging his fingers in deep. She raised her head, and closed her eyes, and he leaned forward and kissed her neck, and then bit it, until he was leaving bruises all over her skin. His fingertips worked at her nipples, tugging them and rolling them around the ball of his thumb, until the pink areolas crinkled, and the nipples tightened and stood up.

He was breathing hard now, from exertion; but he peeled off his dark businessman's vest, loosened his cufflinks, and took off his shirt. Underneath, his body was huge, with sloping breasts that were almost as big as Della's, and a belly that swung with its own ponderous weight. He leaned forward, panting, and took down his pants, and then his undershorts.

Della said, 'Now? You want to do it *now*?'

He kicked aside his discarded clothes with his feet. He was naked now – a vast bulky Buddha – pale and hairy and imposing. He stood with his thighs apart, his fists on his hips, and the erection that rose from between his legs was dark crimson and challengingly thick. Unlike many fat men, whose sexual functions declined as their weight increased, Shearson Jones had kept up a greedy interest in women, and the size of his penis was renowned amongst more than a few Washington hostesses whose husbands occasionally found themselves posted abroad on State Department business.

Mrs Gene Bolsover had called it 'the only pole I'd salute whether they ran a flag up it or not.'

Shearson took hold of Della's arm, and pulled her towards him. Her wrap was hanging around her waist now, and he tugged it right off, so that she, too, was naked, except for her panties. He kissed her mouth, and pressed her close to his big pillowy belly, and squeezed her breasts until they hurt.

'You're a bitch, you see,' he panted. His face was laced with shining sweat. 'You're a bitch who has to be *taught* to be appreciative.'

She had seen him in this mood before, but never so fiercely. He had never actually hurt her before, despite his bulk, but now it seemed as if he was going to try to force her to do whatever he wanted, both in bed and at work. She arched her back to get away from his thick-lipped kisses, but he wrapped his arms around her in a massive, spine-cracking bear-hug from which she just couldn't break herself free. Apart from being huge, Shearson was also overwhelmingly strong.

'I'm offering you everything a woman could want,' he whispered, close to her ear. It was a harsh, uncompromising whisper that frightened her. 'Everything you ever desired. Money, fur coats, pleasure, popularity. You can't tell me that you're going to say no.'

'Shearson – ' she said, but he gripped her even tighter. Her lumbar vertebrae felt as if they were being compressed in a vice.

'Come on, Della, you can't say no! A million dollars, maybe more than a million dollars, and me, too!'

'Shearson – I can't – ' she gasped. 'Shearson – I can't – breathe properly – '

Shearson suddenly released her, and raised his arms, like a boxer showing the referee that he's broken completely free from a clinch. His eyes were giving nothing away at all. They were bland and bulbous and they didn't even blink. He backed away, his thighs wobbling, his hands still raised.

'Well, then, Della,' he said, softly, 'you can do whatever you choose. But if you decide you want to stay with that newspaper of yours, you'd better get yourself dressed and leave this house right now, and there's something else you'd better consider, too. You'd better consider my friendly association with Mr Wendell Oliver, and how that might adversely affect your career. What's more, you'd better think about all those confidences to which you've accidentally become a party, and how dangerous those kind of confidences can be. Why, I've known people with information like that get themselves into all kinds of trouble.'

In the dim Moroccan room there was no sound at all, save for Shearson's laboured breathing. Then, the senator reached out behind him for the ottoman, and sat down on it, still breathing heavily, and still watching Della with those intense, vacant eyes of his.

'If you decide you want to take up a new career in my employment, of course, your whole life's going to be different,' he said. There was no expression on his face at all. 'You're going to discover a whole new world of diamonds, and mink, and Cadillacs. That part of life which my good friend Alan Hedges calls "The Gravy".'

He lay back, his belly spreading wide, his thighs crowding underneath its fleshy overlap like the carcasses of two white whales being towed along by a factory ship. But between them, his erection rose as strong as ever, and his balls were as tight as a fist.

'Are you coming?' he asked her.

She stayed where she was while an unseen clock ticked away another minute in her life. A brass-and-ebony clock which had ticked away the lives of unknown Moroccans in Tangier, and which Shearson had brought back with him from North Africa on one of his regular antique-plundering trips.

During this minute, she didn't look pretty, even though her hair was shining bright red, and the shadows which fell across her nearly-naked body were soft and flattering. But then she approached the ottoman, and looked down at Shearson's massive body, and smiled. The smile of a sensual woman, possibly – even the smile of a hooker. But she knew what she had to do and the smile went with it.

While Shearson lay on his back, she climbed on to him, straddling his thighs first, and then leaning forward, so that his erection was touching her stomach. She held it in her small fist, her small fist with the thin gold rings on every finger, and she slowly rubbed it up and down, until the head swelled purple and glossy, and the slit in it began to gape the same way that Shearson's mouth was gaping.

'Good girl,' breathed Shearson. 'Good girl.'

She lifted herself up a little, and from where he was lying Shearson could see the gingery pattern of pubic hair through the transparent nylon of her panties. But then she reached down between her legs, and pulled the nylon aside, exposing the glistening pink flesh of her vulva. And with an easy, rhythmic motion like a rider settling herself in a saddle, she couched the head of Shearson's erection between her open lips, and sat down on him, quickly and easily, and right up to the hilt. He let out an odd chuffing sound, like the air brakes on a large truck.

'You big pig,' Della told him, with that same hooker's smile. 'You great gross hog of a man.'

Shearson didn't make love like other men: he was too fat for that. Instead, he expected his lovers to gallop on top of him, while he responded with a kind of wallowing undulation. But he was big enough to go very deep, and to stretch his women to their utmost, and while his body may not have been agile, he had hands that could twist and squeeze, or could just as arousingly touch and tickle and tease. While Della moved up and down on him, sliding up and down with ever-increasing excitement and tension, he gripped the round soft cheeks of her bottom and parted them like a diner breaking a soft bread-roll, and then sent his middle finger on a dark and erotic exploration of the doughy interior. Della, in spite of herself, in spite of everything she felt, found herself pushing her hips harder and deeper on to Shearson's cushioned thighs, and it was only on the very brink of orgasm that she had a vivid and uncompromising insight into what she was actually doing, and that she saw Shearson's fatness for what it was.

Then – it was too late. Her body was already quaking; her breasts were already shuddering; and Shearson was ejaculating inside her in measured, laconic spurts of sperm.

She climbed off him too quickly. He sensed her distaste. But he stayed where he was on the ottoman and watched her with dispassion as she stepped across the room and picked up her wrap. She found it easier to face him once she had covered herself up, although he had left her with a slimy reminder of his appetites which was sliding down her thigh.

'Well,' he said, easing himself up into a sitting position. 'I suppose that means yes. What you did, I mean. I suppose that amounts to acceptance.'

She nodded, her head jerking like a marionette. 'Yes,' she said, in her briskest liberated-female-reporter manner. 'Yes, it does. I'll send in my resignation to the *Kansas City Herald-Examiner* as soon as your fund raising committee is ready to roll.'

'You're a sensible girl,' he said. 'Will you pass me my undershorts? And my cigar?'

She carried over his drooping white undershorts with as much grace as she could manage; and his cigar, pinched between finger and thumb like some kind of unpleasant dropping. He lit it again, and puffed up some figured clouds of pungent blue smoke.

'This isn't an easy world, Della,' he said, as if he was trying to excuse himself for what he had just forced her to do. 'We all have to go out and get what we want, as rough and as tough as we have to. It's the only way.'

'Yes,' she said. 'You'll excuse me if I go to the bathroom.'

Shearson sat on the ottoman for a minute or two after she'd gone, and then heaved himself up and laboriously stepped into his undershorts. He was mopping the sweat from his forehead with his handkerchief when, in complete silence, his Puerto Rican manservant Billy appeared at the door. Billy was a small man, slender and nervous and narrow-chested, with a face as oval and white as a blanched almond.

'Peter Kaiser on the telephone for you, sir.'

Peter Kaiser was his personal assistant. Shearson waved his hand dismissively. 'Tell him to call back in the morning. What time is it, Billy?'

'Eleven, sir. He says it's very urgent, sir.'

Shearson took his cigar out of his mouth and frowned at the smouldering tip. For some reason, this one wasn't burning right. 'Very well,' he said. 'But this is the last call tonight. You understand that? Mrs McIntosh and I have a great deal of important business to discuss.'

'Yes, sir,' said Billy, without a single hint of insolence.

Shearson waddled over to his armchair, sat down, and picked up the telephone.

'Peter?' he said. 'What the hell's so damned urgent you have to call me at this hour? I have guests.'

'I know, Senator. Billy told me.'

'All right,' said Shearson, in a patronising tone. 'You can cut out the little-league superiority. All I want to know is why you're calling.'

'It's to do with this blight, Senator. You know the wheat problems they've been having in Kansas?'

'I do have a passing acquaintance with the problem,' said Shearson. 'As a matter of fact, I've just been discussing a Blight Crisis Appeal with Alan Hedges. I was going to fill you in tomorrow.'

'Well, the fact is, Senator, it's worse,' said Peter.

Shearson sniffed. 'Worse? What do you mean by worse? Worse than what?'

'Worse than it was before. Much worse. I've had two urgent and confidentials from Dick Turnbull in the past three hours. The wheat blight is spreading like crazy. Dick estimates five hundred thousand acres already. And now we've got nine major farmers in Iowa reporting a similar kind of blight on their corn and soybean crops.'

'Are you serious?' asked Shearson. 'Corn and soybean too?'

'All the reports have been authenticated,' said Peter. 'There are six or seven more which haven't been checked back yet, including two reports of fruit and vegetable blight in California.'

Shearson rubbed his jowls thoughtfully. 'What about the media?' he asked. 'Any trouble from them yet?'

'Not too much, although the *Wall Street Journal*'s been pestering me for most of the evening. That may give us a little time – maybe until the morning – but we won't be able to hold it back for very much longer. It seems like every darned crop in the whole darned country's going rotten.'

Shearson said, 'Listen, Peter – I want you to keep a tight rein on what the media get to hear about. Right at the moment, I don't want a panic. I'm trying to set up this appeal fund to help farmers whose crops have been destroyed by the blight, and if everybody starts running about like blue-assed baboons, then it's going to spoil the whole presentation. The minute the public themselves start to feel threatened by what's happening, they'll lose all interest in giving aid to the farmers.'

'Well, all right,' said Peter, dubiously. 'But what am I going to tell the press if they put it to me point-blank?'

'*Tell* them there's a crop blight crisis. *Tell* them it's serious. But tell them we have whole teams of experts working on a solution, and we expect to be dusting with proven antidotes within the week. If they want figures, tell them we don't anticipate anything worse than an eight per cent cereal crop shortfall.'

'I don't know,' said Peter. 'Supposing they go take a look for themselves?'

'Use your head,' retorted Shearson. 'All press and television people are up against deadlines. You think they're going to be able to take a look at the whole of Kansas before tomorrow morning's editions? They'll take one or two stock shots and leave it at that.'

'All right, Senator, if you say so,' said Peter. 'Do you want me to keep you in touch throughout the night?'

'Tonight, I'm busy,' Shearson growled. 'Call me at seven tomorrow morning. Oh – and there's one thing you can do. Get in touch with the agricultural research laboratories and see how they're progressing with their analysis.'

'Okay, Senator. I'll call you tomorrow.'

Della appeared at the living-room door, with her hair brushed and her make-up restored. There was a faint stiffness about her smile, but Shearson was too pleased to notice it. 'You wait till you hear what's happened,' he grinned. 'It seems like every damned farmer in the whole middle West is getting hit by this blight. So if we play our cards right, if we can keep the public's personal anxiety way down low and their sympathy way up high, we might be in for more than we originally bargained for.'

Della said, 'Good,' in an abstracted voice, and then walked over to the cocktail cabinet, where she poured herself three fingers of scotch, straight-up, and drank it back without blinking.

Six

It was a dry, hot, windy morning. The sky over southern Kansas was already the odd mauvish colour of burned notepaper. Ed drove Season and Sally along Highway 54 into Wichita with the air-conditioning in his Caprice stationwagon right down to freeze. Every time he glanced in his rear-view mirror he could see the three Gucci suitcases packed in the back, with the tags that read LAX.

Season was wearing a smart camel-coloured suit, and her hair was tied back with a scarf. Sally had brought along her favourite dolly, a floppy and unsavoury rag creature with bright pink hair. Its name was Merry, for reasons that Ed and Season had never quite managed to understand.

They didn't talk much. There wasn't very much to say. He had tried this morning to ask her not to go, as they lay side by side in their soft curtained bed; but she had kissed him, and said that it was necessary for her own survival. He had made love to her, more doggedly than passionately, and afterwards she had lain there amongst the rose-patterned sheets and smiled at him gently, but still without changing her mind. He knew she had to go, too. She needed to remind herself that Kingman County wasn't the whole world, and that South Burlington wasn't the sum of her life and her intelligence.

All he had said to her over breakfast was, 'You'll come back, won't you, when you've made up your mind?'

Sally had looked up from her bowl of Grape Nuts, puzzled. Season had touched her lips with her fingertip to tell Ed that he shouldn't say any more. But a few minutes later, she had said, gently, 'You know I will.'

The early sun had shone through the window across the

59

breakfast table, and with Dilys bustling at the stove in her gingham apron, the kitchen had taken on all the appearance of one of those happy 1950s television series, the ones where hearty neighbours kept popping in through a swing door, and everybody ate heaps of bacon and sausage-links and wheatcakes, and never suffered anything worse than an occasional misunderstanding.

'I'll call you when we get there,' said Season, as they approached Wichita Airport. A DC10 was making its approach over on their right and it flashed silver in the morning light before it sank towards the runway. The going-away smell of airplane fuel penetrated the car's air-conditioning, and Ed suddenly felt very lonesome and even frightened, as if he would never see Season again. Not to hold anyway, and not to love.

He turned right into the airport, and drove them up to the terminal building. 'I didn't buy you anything to take with you,' he said. 'Do you want a book, a magazine, something like that?'

Season shook her head. 'I believe I'll have quite enough thinking to do. And Sally's never flown over the Grand Canyon before. We'll keep busy.'

He turned to her, and placed his hand over hers. 'Well,' he said hoarsely, 'there's one thing I'd like you to take with you.'

She looked at him, but didn't say anything. He lowered his head, because somehow that made it easier to hold back his emotion. 'I'd like you to take my love with you,' he said, wishing the words didn't sound so much like a Valentine card. 'And I'd like you to take my best wishes for everything that you do. I love you, Season, and there ain't two ways about it.'

She kissed him, and her lips were very warm, and she smelled of Joy. 'I love you, too, Ed. Really dearly I do. And I'm going to miss you badly. But I know that when I get back, I'm going to have my head straightened out and everything's going to be fine.'

'Why don't you come, Daddy?' asked Sally. 'You could take me swimming and everything, and Auntie Vee says we'll go to the ocean.'

Ed turned in his seat and took her hand. 'I've got to harvest all of our wheat, honey, or we won't have any food to eat for the next year. But maybe I'll be able to come next time.'

'I love you, Daddy,' said Sally. 'And Merry loves you, too.'

Ed kissed her. 'I love you, honey.'

He got out of the car. The day was roastingly hot, even though it was only ten o'clock, and the sun rippled off the sidewalk in corrugated waves. He opened the back of the stationwagon, and hefted out their cases. A sky-cap with a bright red face and prickly hair was waiting to collect them.

'Los Angeles?' the skycap asked.

Ed nodded. Then he went around to open the car doors for Season and Sally.

'Listen,' he said, 'I won't wait. I have an appointment with Dr Benson at the agricultural laboratory.'

Season held him close. 'Goodbye, Ed,' she said, and she was crying. She took hold of Sally's hand and the two of them walked quickly across the sidewalk and into the reflecting doors of the terminal. Ed stood watching them go, and then he slowly took out his handkerchief and rubbed the sweat from the back of his neck, and maybe some of the tension, too. He climbed back into his car and started the motor.

For a moment, he closed his eyes.

He hadn't said much to Season this morning about the wheat blight. It was a little worse, he'd admitted, but he was sure they could get it under control. What he hadn't told her was that Willard had come knocking at the kitchen door at six-thirty in the morning, while Ed had been sitting at the table drinking his first cup of coffee of the day and reading the papers, and that Willard had already been out with Dyson Kane on a circular helicopter tour of the whole spread.

Willard had calculated that almost an eighth of their total wheat acreage had been blighted during the night, and that the disease was spreading even faster than before. If they didn't find some way of curbing it by Monday or Tuesday, they were going to lose everything.

Ed had shown Willard the news story in the *Kansas City Herald-Examiner*. Considering how widespread the blight had been, and how many major Kansas farms had been hit, the coverage had seemed almost offhand. It had rated only a second lead on page three, and 'Our Agricultural Desk' had simply reported that 'several Kansas wheat farmers have noticed an unidentified blight on their late crops', while 'Our Washington Bureau' had remarked with distinct unconcern that 'federal researchers are busy analysing the blight and working on new methods for bringing it under prompt control.'

In fact, Ed had been so disturbed by the paucity of the news story that he had already called Walter Klugman, who owned the neighbouring Penalosa Farm, and checked if his crops were just as seriously affected.

'Oh, you bet,' Walter had said. 'If anything, mine's worse than yours. I've got thirty per cent of my wheat crop turned rotten, and if the state don't come up with something soon, I'm going to burn the whole damned spread.'

Even when Ed and Willard had turned on the television for the early-morning news, the stories about the wheat blight had been dismissive and superficial. 'Not a good year for the wheat farmers of Kansas and North Dakota,' ABC had reported. 'They're bothered by a mystery disease which is turning hundreds of acres of harvest-ready crops into black, stinking decay. But federal scientists are said to have the problem in hand, and there's also news that Kansas Senator Shearson Jones, known for years as the "Farmers' Friend", is planning on setting up an appeal fund to help those farmers who might face financial hardship because of the blight.'

Willard, helping himself to a cup of coffee, had shaken his head and whistled. 'Financial hardship? The way things are going, we're all going to be wiped out.'

As he drove over the Wichita Valley Flood Control gully, and along Douglas Avenue to the civic centre, Ed tuned into the news on his car radio. But there was nothing at all about the blight – just some long-winded story about a teacher from Wellington who was trying to bring back compulsory prayers. 'We've been without God for nigh on thirty years,' she was saying. 'It's time we turned our faces back in his direction.'

Ed parked the stationwagon in the civic centre parking lot, and took his brown-tinted sunglasses out of the glove-box. Then he walked across the wide, glaring pedestrian precinct, until he reached the shiny office building which announced itself as the Kansas State Agricultural Laboratory – not only with a plaque of brushed stainless-steel, but with a bronze statue of a smiling family growing out of a giant ear of wheat.

Inside, it was cold, echoing, and smelled of polish. A girl receptionist with bright red lipstick and a Titian-tinted beehive hairstyle directed Ed to the ninth floor. He stood in the elevator next to a man in a white lab-coat who was carrying a cardboard box marked 'Infected Rodents' and humming *Peace In The Valley*. There were times when he agreed with Season about Kansas. If you came from New York, or any city larger than Cleveland, you could quite readily believe that the Kansas state mentality was solid cereal from ear to ear.

He walked along the ninth-floor corridor until he reached a half-open office door marked Dr Nils Benson, Head of Disease Control. He knocked.

Dr Benson was standing by the window, peering at a 35mm colour slide. He shouted, 'Come in!' very loudly, and then swung around on his heels to see who his visitor was. 'Ah!' he said. 'It's Mr Hardesty, isn't it? Mr Hardesty of South Burlington Farm.'

'You came around at Christmas when I was having that seedling problem,' said Ed. 'How are you doing?'

Dr Benson shook his hand. He was a tall, sixtyish man with a marked stoop of the shoulders – mainly brought on by his chronic shortsightedness and his habit of attacking anything that interested him like a Greater Prairie Chicken. He wore large round eyeglasses, and his hair was fraying and white, but whenever he took his glasses off, he looked strangely boyish and young. It was common knowledge in Wichita that Dr Benson had lost his homely but vigorous wife to an interstate truck driver, and that for years he had suffered an alcoholic problem. Some of his unkinder colleagues called him 'Booze Benson'.

'Sit down,' said Dr Benson, lifting a heap of *Scientific Americans* off his desk, hesitating a moment, and then dropping them on to the floor. The floor was already littered with stacks of alphabetical files, graph paper, magazines, books, and empty Kentucky Chicken boxes. On the walls there were federal information posters on the comparative effects of various fertilising agents.

'You mind if I smoke?' asked Ed, taking out one of his small cigars.

'Why should I? Everybody's entitled to kill themselves whichever way they want. I've got some early results for you, incidentally. We did some chemical and ultra-violet tests on those samples your fellow brought in, and it looks like we might be having some success.'

'You know what it is?'

'Well, not exactly. But we know what it *isn't*.'

'I see,' said Ed. 'And what isn't it?'

'Sit down,' repeated Dr Benson. 'Make yourself comfortable, at least.'

Ed, awkwardly, sat on the edge of a small bentwood chair that was already piled with newspaper cuttings and torn-open letters. Dr Benson picked up pieces of paper and flung them systematically into the air as if he were performing some arcane manufacturing process.

'It isn't powdery mildew,' he said. 'Nor any from of powdery mildew of any kind whatsoever. *Erysithe graminis*, that's the technical name for it. And it's not *that*. Which is quite a pity.'

'Why is it a pity?' asked Ed. 'I thought you would have been relieved.'

'Oh, no, I'm not relieved at all. If it had been powdery mildew, even in its worst form, we might have been able to spray for it. I'm not saying we could have done very much good, but it would have been better than nothing at all. As you know, federal regulations only give us the option of using sulphur, but I'm sure a little bit of political finagling could have given us an emergency exemption to use Vigil or something like that.'

Ed nodded. 'My crops manager mentioned Vigil. Do you

think it's still worth trying to get a clearance to use it?'

Dr Benson stopped flinging paper, stared at Ed for a moment, and then shook his head. 'Not worth it. Wouldn't do any good at all. The tests we've done so far indicate some runaway kind of virus infection – not at all simple and not at all ordinary. In fact, if I didn't think that it was completely impossible, I would hazard the opinion that it was a cultured virus, specially developed for the purpose of destroying cereal crops.'

Ed frowned as he lit his cigar. 'What do you mean – "specially developed"?'

'Genetically engineered,' said Dr Benson. 'Created by human intention in a virus laboratory, for the specific task of destroying our crops.'

'That can't make sense,' said Ed. 'How the hell would anybody be able to spread a virus all over Kansas and North Dakota without being noticed?'

Dr Benson took off his eyeglasses, and attempted to wipe them on a crumpled piece of notepaper. 'My thoughts exactly. Kansas covers something like ninety-two thousand square miles. Nobody could go around to every wheat farm in the state with enough virus-carrying compound to cause this kind of damage within the space of a week or so, not by car. And if they tried to overfly all those farms in an airplane – well, they'd have to fly very low, and somebody would have noticed them.'

Ed moved the letters off his seat, laid them on the floor, and then sat back. 'You're presupposing that anybody would have a motive for destroying our crops.'

Dr Benson pulled a face. 'Of course. But don't you think the Soviet Union would be likely? "You held your wheat back from us, now we're going to make sure that you can't have it either." Maybe I'm talking baloney. I don't know. I'm not what people call a political animal.'

There was a difficult silence. Ed respected Dr Benson's scientific talents, but he wasn't at all sure about some of his wilder theories of political conspiracy. Last year, when Ed had asked him to evaluate a new boosted wheat fertiliser for him, Dr Benson had suggested that the compound was deliberately designed to weaken the growing crops in such a way that yet another of the same company's strengthening agents would be needed. He saw a dark and elaborate plot behind everything.

Ed said, 'All right – let's leave aside any idea that this virus might have been spread deliberately – and let's think about how serious it is.'

Dr Benson opened one of his desk drawers, and then slammed it shut again. Perhaps, a long time ago, that drawer had contained a bottle of Jack Daniel's. 'Well,' he said, 'it's very serious indeed. It's a highly sophisticated, highly selective, highly virulent aerobic virus. It could have developed naturally, the same way that Chinese influenza develops naturally, or it could have been sprayed on your crops in some technically calculated way which released it when the weather conditions developed into what they are at the moment.'

'Dr Benson – ' said Ed. 'I'm not really interested in how the virus arrived on my farm. What I'm really interested in is how to get rid of it.'

'That's the whole point,' said Dr Benson. 'Although I may be proved wrong – and I hope to God that I am – there is no way of combating this virus until we find out whether it's natural or manufactured – and *who* manufactured it. I find this terribly difficult to explain to anyone without a basic understanding of DNA and genetic structure – but these days it's quite possible to develop viruses that are so complex and malignant that almost nothing can be done to destroy them.'

Ed ran his hand through his hair in exasperation. 'And you think it's the Russians?' he asked, incredulously. 'What did they do – drop it by satellite?'

Dr Benson shook his head violently. 'No, no, they couldn't have done that. If they released a virus from a satellite in orbit, the whole global atmosphere would wind up polluted, and every crop on Earth would die. And if they tried to send the virus to Earth in directional capsules, they would be spotted at once. I do read my news magazines, you know.'

'So what did they do? Hang around at Lubeck's Seed-Dressing Factory, and squirt a bit in every bag?'

Dr Benson held up his hands. 'They might have done. Who knows? I'm only trying to make an educated guess.'

'Well – let's put it this way,' said Ed, 'if anybody ever tried to overfly South Burlington Farm and dump anything on my crops, I'd sure as hell get to know about it. I know there are miles of wheatland in Kansas where somebody could do it unnoticed. But right now we're talking about farms that are well-kept and supervised. They're just as badly hit as any place else.'

Dr Benson nodded. 'You're right, of course, and if this virus has been spread on purpose, then I just don't know how. But I think you ought to know that in my opinion, based on the broad tests that I've been able to make so far, the virus is unstoppable. At least for this year's harvest.'

Ed looked at him carefully. 'You're trying to tell me that I can't do anything about it? That it's going to wipe out my whole crop?'

'I'm afraid it is.'

'But you've sent samples to the federal agricultural research laboratory – surely they've got people there who can isolate it?'

Dr Benson smiled. 'I wish they did. I only sent the samples there out of scientific protocol. They don't have anyone there who knows as much about wheat as I do. If you want expertise, you should never go to the federal people. You should come here, or to the State Experimental Farm at Garden City. *They're* doing some more tests for me, I might add – longer term stuff. Give them ten years, and they might discover what it is.'

Ed said, 'I hope you know what you're saying, Dr Benson. If I lose this crop, then the chances are that I'm going to lose the farm altogether. I had to borrow thousands of dollars this year. I had to work my butt off, until my marriage went to pieces. I had to get up at five in the morning and stay on my feet all day until ten at night.'

'Farming's a risky business,' said Dr Benson. 'It always has been, and it always will be.'

'That's my family farm!' Ed told him, and his voice was quivering. 'My daddy created that spread out of nothing! My daddy died for that farm, and I gave up everything

67

outside of Kingman County! My career, my wife, my daughter – everything!'

Dr Benson said, 'I'm sorry. I really am. But it doesn't look as if you're going to be the only one. I've had samples in from all over, and they all tell the same story. What's more, I've been talking on the telephone to some of my friends in Des Moines, Iowa, and Corvallis, Oregon, and worst of all in Modesto, California.'

'What do you mean?' asked Ed. 'What are you talking about?'

Dr Benson opened and closed his desk drawer again. 'The blight is appearing on all kinds of crops in all kinds of regions. Not just on wheat in the plains states. But on apples and pears and broccoli and peas and tomatoes and you name it. Every region is concerned about it, but so far it doesn't appear to have spread widely enough for anyone in the Federal Department of Agriculture to have twigged on to what's happening. So the grape growers lose a few table grapes. So the tomato growers lose a few bushels of tomatoes. Every farmer has his problems, and farming's an industry with plenty of natural wastage.

'But,' said Dr Benson, walking across to the window and staring out at the shadowed courtyard below him, 'all my conversations yesterday afternoon and early this morning with research staff in six states – just to ask for ideas to begin with, just to seek opinions – all my conversations seem to have led me to one very uncomfortable conclusion. Which is why I started wondering about a Soviet conspiracy. The one very uncomfortable conclusion is that all these crop disorders are caused by manifestations of the same basic virus. Maybe a slightly different version for celery. Maybe a specially high-powered one for potatoes. But all the same fundamental malignancy – all causing the same kind of effect. Blackness and decay and a rot that spreads like a forest fire.'

Ed could hardly believe what he was hearing. 'You mean, all of these states are suffering the same sort of problem – and nobody's taken an overview? Nobody's realised that it's the same thing?'

'Why should they? It's all happened in the space of a few

days. Maybe a week or two at the most. And you have to remember that most state agricultural departments work in a very bureaucratic way. They have no reason to operate otherwise. It takes a long time for one farmer's complaint about a few blighted nectarines to filter its way through the office structure and then the research structure and finally arrive on some responsible officer's desk, so that he can connect it with another farmer's complaint about blighted celery. That's if he ever connects it at all.'

Dr Benson turned around, and the light from the window made a crescent of reflected whiteness in his glasses. 'You also have to remember that many of our agricultural research people aren't exctly – well, to put it quite charitably – they aren't exactly *hotshots*. The fellow I talked to in Modesto had examined twenty-eight samples of blighted fruit and vegetables, and he wasn't even considering the possibility of a virus.'

'Supposing he was right and you're wrong?' asked Ed.

Dr Benson smiled. 'I don't think there's any chance of that, Mr Hardesty. I may have my problems and I may have my reputation, but I'm the best damned agricultural scientist in the Middle West.'

Ed rubbed his eyes. There was nicotine on his fingers, and it stung. 'What are we going to do now?' he asked. 'What am *I* going to do?'

'I don't know yet,' said Dr Benson, 'but the first priority is to hand over all this information to the Department of Agriculture in Washington. Then – if we're lucky, and they don't shilly-shally too long – we might see some concerted action to find a preventive.'

'More bureaucracy?' asked Ed.

'There's nothing else that we can do, is there? I don't have the facilities here to deal with a nationwide virus. And if you project the effect of this blight to its ultimate conclusion – well, it's terrifying. We could survive the loss of one year's wheat. We could survive the loss of one year's corn. But *everything*? Fruit and vegetables and grain? We'd end up with a nation-wide famine.'

Ed reached into the pocket of his shirt. 'Wait a minute,' he said. 'It so happens that my father was a close buddy of

Senator Shearson Jones. In fact, I was talking to Jones on the telephone last night, trying to work out if I could get some extra compensation for the damage at South Burlington. I have some clout there – not much, but maybe enough to have him pull out some of the bureaucratic stops.'

'Shearson Jones, huh?' asked Dr Benson, with a grimace. 'Not exactly my favourite representative of the people.'

'Nor mine. But I think we're going to have to pull whatever strings we have to hand, don't you?'

'I had a hell of an argument with Shearson Jones once,' said Dr Benson, reflectively. 'Have you ever been to his house out at Fall River? It's an incredible place. Overlooks the lake. A friend of mine in the agricultural department told me it cost him one and a half million dollars.'

Dr Benson slowly shook his head at the memory. 'There was a party out there for everybody in the state agricultural department who had helped him push through his special wheat prices programme. I was invited, too, because I did some background research. Well, I was drinking pretty heavily in those days, and when I saw Shearson Jones I just had to tell him what I thought of people who ran the farming economy from behind a desk, and got fat on the proceeds. I nearly lost my job. I certainly lost any chance of promotion. You don't breathe whisky fumes over Senator Shearson Jones and tell him he's an office-bound profiteer and get away with it. No, sir.'

Ed stood up. 'I think I'll call him all the same. If you're right about this virus –'

'Oh, I'm right about it. I wish I wasn't. And you go ahead and call him. I don't suppose he remembers one boozed-up Kansas has-been from five years ago.'

'Can I reach you here?' asked Ed.

Dr Benson checked his watch. 'Sure. I have to drive out to Garden City late this afternoon, but you can catch me here until four.'

'I'll call you,' said Ed.

He left the laboratory and stepped out into the hot mid-morning sunshine again. He paused by the statue to put on his sunglasses, and for a moment he stood looking at the smiling family who were sprouting out of the giant ear of wheat. Then he walked across the plaza to the parking-lot, and his shadow followed him like a nagging doubt that wouldn't be shaken off.

Seven

In the cold air-conditioned offices on Independence Avenue which Senator Jones's fifteen-strong staff probably knew better than their own houses and apartments, Peter Kaiser was completing the complicated groundwork for the Blight Crisis Appeal, and completing it fast. Throughout the windowless, fluorescent-lit warren of partitions, telephones were ringing and typewriters were nattering and girls were hurrying backwards and forwards with messages and memos and files.

Peter Kaiser was tall, black-haired, and good-looking if you liked men who wore permanent-press suits and striped ties and grinned a lot. His friends said he resembled George Hamilton. He had been a promising junior in the early days of the first Nixon administration, and it showed. He still believed that Nixon could make a comeback. Pierre Trudeau had, Mrs Indira Gandhi had – why not the most competent and misunderstood president of all time?

On Independence Avenue, Peter was known as 'The Machine'. He was never inspired, and rarely original, but once Shearson Jones had set him a task, he went through it like something inhuman. Nobody ever saw him eat in the office, although he grudgingly permitted the rest of the staff to send out for Big Macs and shakes when they had to work through their lunch-hour; and Karen Fortunoff, one of the prettier and wittier secretaries, said she had once seen him take a covert swig from her can of typewriter oil.

The only sign of real life which Peter ever exhibited was when he touched the girls' bottoms – always slyly, and always quasi-accidentally, so they were never absolutely

71

sure if he meant it or not. He dated one or two of the girls occasionally, but his affairs rarely lasted. One girl had complained that he was 'all boxed roses, Frank Sinatra mood music, and fumbles under the table.'

These days, Peter lived with his sixty-two-year-old mother in a stuffy, high-ceilinged apartment in the old Wellington Hotel. Or rather he slept there: like most of his staff, he spent most of his waking hours in the office, particularly when there was a panic project on, like the Blight Crisis Appeal.

During the morning, Peter had called Joe Dasgupta, the brilliant and expensive Indian constitutional lawyer, and Joe Dasgupta was already working on a legal structure for the fund and considering how it should be registered. Peter had also called Fred Newman, the chairman of the Kansas Wheat Growers' Association, at his home in Palm Springs. So far, Fred Newman's own farm had suffered little damage, and he agreed with Peter Kaiser that the financial interests of Kansas farmers would best be served by 'soft-pedalling the blight, media-wise'. He also accepted Peter Kaiser's invitation to act as expert adviser to the Blight Crisis Appeal, in return for 'necessary expenses'. Shearson Jones had recognised the importance of having Fred Newman attached to the fund from the beginning, since most of the suitcase farmers who owned land in Kansas were strong Newman supporters.

Fred Newman had always argued that 'Just because a man doesn't actually dig the soil with his own bare hands, that doesn't mean his heart isn't in farming,' and that sentiment had won him the votes of almost every wheat grower who preferred to spend fifty weeks of every year in New York or Los Angeles – in fact, anywhere except out in tedious Kansas, amongst all that tiresome wheat.

While Peter Kaiser had been making those calls, his staff of eleven girls had been canvassing major industries all over the country – particularly those industries connected with farming, farm machinery, fertilisers, and food transportation. By lunchtime, they had rustled up pledges of more than five million dollars in contributions, and by mid-afternoon, after CBS and ABC news had both run stories on the Kansas wheat blight, with serial footage of the blackened crops, they had jumped to eight million dollars, all tax deductible.

In the Senate itself, Shearson Jones spent the morning smoking a large domestic cigar and gathering support for his emergency aid bill among Republicans and Democrats alike. He ate a heavy lunch with Wallace Terry of the *Washington Post*, and told him that he was leaning heavily on anyone who owed him a favour, and a few people who didn't, 'simply to rescue those poor beleagured farmers in Kansas.'

Shearson drew so much attention to his own state during the course of the afternoon that hardly any comment was passed by the media on those scattered reports coming in from Iowa and Oregon and Washington and California that outbreaks of blight were appearing everywhere. At the Department of Agriculture, the press officer was still talking about the crisis as 'the Kansas wheat problem' and sidetracking any press questions about similar blights in other states as 'alarmist' and 'quite usual for the time of year.'

Two of Shearson Jones's best speech-writers were working on a draft TV statement which the senator hoped to make to the press during the evening. Peter Kaiser had seen the first outlines, and he was particularly taken by a phrase which talked about 'those earnest, honest, caring farmers who are still living the kind of American life that *Saturday Evening Post* used to celebrate on its covers.'

At three-thirty, Joe Dasgupta called back. Peter Kaiser was sitting in his chilly, beige-carpeted office, dictating a memo on how contributions should be followed up, accounted for, and banked. He waved his hand to Karen Fortunoff to leave him for five minutes while he talked.

'Okay, Joe,' he said, once Karen had left. 'How's it shaping up?'

'So far, it's fine,' said Joe Dasgupta, in his distinctive Delhi accent. 'I've advised Shearson to set up the Blight Crisis Appeal as a private foundation, with someone entirely nondescript as manager, and himself as president.'

73

'You didn't think we should try to form it as a federal corporation under an Act of Congress? It would've seemed like it was a whole lot more respectable.'

'Well – that was the choice,' explained Joe Dasgupta. 'Respectability or practicality. As a private foundation, you can still persuade Congress to vote you money, yet you won't have them breathing down your neck so hard. Also, you'll have more room to manoeuvre with the IRS.'

'Sounds reasonable,' nodded Peter Kaiser. 'How soon can we start collecting money? We have close on nine million dollars pledged so far.'

'I'll have the papers sent around to your office. All I need now is a couple of notarised signatures from Shearson and Alan Hedges, and you're in the Blight Crisis business.'

'You've done an incredible job, Joe,' said Peter Kaiser. 'Remind me to take you out to dinner real soon.'

'That won't be necessary,' Joe Dasgupta told him, with polite disdain. 'I'll just send my invoice around with the papers.'

Peter Kaiser put down the phone, and pressed his desk buzzer for Karen to come back in. Karen Fortunoff was a petite, dark-eyed brunette, whose smart cream suit didn't conceal a trim figure. She had come to Washington two years ago from Duluth, intoxicated with ambition and heady ideas about working in Congress. She had left behind her two bewildered suburban parents who still kept her room made up for her, with all her dolls and her Raggedy Andy books, and who still called her 'Baby' on the phone. She had worked as a secretary for a magazine printing company for a while, but then she had met a girl at a party who had helped with the catering at some of Shearson Jones's fund-raising picnics. 'Now, Shearson Jones is *power*,' the girl had said. 'Pure, naked, disgusting, unadulterated *power*.' Karen had liked the sound of that. After all, power was the very magnet which had first drawn her to Washington. She had called Peter Kaiser the next morning.

'Where were we?' asked Peter, as Karen sat down with her steno pad and crossed her legs.

'We'd gotten as far as Banking Procedures (ii),' she said.

74

'Oh, yes,' said Peter. 'Banking Procedures (ii). How to pay in corporate cheques, and the clearance of charitable funds.'

Karen said, 'Don't you ever take a break?'

Peter's hands were clasped in front of his mouth, his elbows propped on his desk. He looked up at her, his eyes refocusing slowly, as if he were tired, or drugged.

'A *break*?' he asked, as if he didn't know what the word meant.

'Yes. Don't you ever relax?'

'Karen,' he said, 'we're on Banking Procedures (ii). If you want to talk about relaxation, you'll have to do it in your own time.'

'You're not that much of a machine, surely.'

'I'm busy. I have fifty-five other things to do before we close down for the night. That's all. It's nothing to do with being a machine.'

'Don't you even drink coffee?'

Peter sat back in his revolving leather armchair, but his fingers still tensely gripped the edge of his desk.

'Karen,' he said, 'are we going to finish this dictation or not?'

'I only asked you a question out of human consideration,' she told him. 'You work with people, you want to know what they're like, what makes them tick. Well, I do, anyway.'

'What makes me tick is irrelevant to Banking Procedures (ii). It is also none of your business.'

'All right. I didn't mean to be offensive. I simply said that –'

Peter pressed the buzzer on his desk. Almost immediately, the door opened, and Fran Kelly, Karen's own assistant, stepped in.

'Mr Kaiser?'

'Bring a steno pad and a sharp pencil. We have two hours of dictation to do.'

Karen sat up straight. 'What goes on here? Just because I asked you a simple personal question –'

Peter stared at her, hard. 'I'll tell you what goes on here,' he said, in a level voice. 'What goes on here is work. Not talk. Not personal consideration. Not fraternisation. But work.'

Karen, pale-faced, stood up. 'Work, huh? I suppose feeling my fanny by the water-cooler is work?'

'Just leave my office,' said Peter. 'Type up whatever notes you've made so far, and make sure I get them before five.'

'You're not going to fire me?'

'Why should I? When you're not interrupting me with ridiculous questions, you're good at your job. And besides, I don't particularly want all the time-wasting hassle of sorting out your compensation.'

Karen slowly shook her head. 'You know something,' she said. 'I don't believe you're real. I just can't believe that you're an actual human being.'

'I assure you I am. Now, are you going to go type those notes before I change my mind about firing you?'

Karen was going to say something else, something spiteful and absurd and angry. But she managed to check herself and take a deep breath instead. She didn't want to lose this job, not really; and a small, sane voice inside her said that Peter Kaiser was too thick-skinned to care about insults. He'd only enjoy the spectacle of her making her a fool of herself.

She closed her steno pad, smiled shakily at Fran, and said, 'It's all yours.'

'And man the telephone,' put in Peter, as she left the office. 'I don't want to be disturbed for the next two hours.'

Karen nodded, with mock-graciousness, and closed the door.

Back in her own office, a small windowless cubicle along the hall, decorated with nothing more than two postcards from Mount Shasta, Karen put down her pad, and leaned against the wall. She shouldn't have let Peter shake her up like that. He was only a political office-boy, after all, and a cold-blooded s.o.b. to boot. But she could never get used to his abruptness, and his total lack of feeling. As one of her friends had remarked, you didn't really object to Peter Kaiser fondling your backside in the corridor, because it was no more interesting than accidentally walking into the handle of an electric floor-polisher.

76

I could quit, she thought. I could tear up his goddamned banking procedures and stalk out. But that was why women failed in business. They took it too personally. Karen wanted to make it up the tree to those creaking branches where the heavyweights like Shearson Jones were perched, and walking out on Peter Kaiser wasn't going to help her do it.

Just say after me: One day, Peter Kaiser, I'm going to fix your wagon. Then take seven deep breaths. Then sit down, take the cover off your self-correcting IBM and start typing up his fucking notes.

She had inserted the paper and aligned it and was all ready to start, when the phone rang. She picked it up and said smoothly: 'Peter Kaiser's office. Who's calling?'

There was a ringing noise on the line, as if the call was coming from a long way off, then a voice said, 'Is Senator Jones there? I'm calling long-distance.'

'Senator Jones is at his office in the Senate right now. Peter Kaiser is his personal assistant. He's here.'

'My name's Ed Hardesty, from Wichita, Kansas,' said the voice. 'I spoke with Senator Jones last night about the wheat blight.'

'Yes?'

'Well – I have some more information on the blight. Some really important scientific stuff. Do you think you could give me the Senator's number?'

'I could have him call you back. What did you say your name was?'

'Hardesty. Ed Hardesty. Senator Jones used to be a friend of my father. Tell him it's Dan Hardesty's son.'

Karen could hardly hear him. 'Do you have a message for him?' she said, loudly.

'The message is that the wheat blight is probably a virus of some kind . . . and that it's attacking crops all over the country . . . the same kind of virus . . .'

'Wait a moment,' said Karen, 'I just broke the point on my pencil. Now, what did you say about a virus?'

'It's the blight,' repeated Ed. 'The blight is spreading all over the country. Not just on wheat, but on corn, and soybeans, and everything. The agricultural laboratory here in Wichita has already made tests . . . Dr Benson says the whole nation's food supply could be at risk . . .'

'Dr Benson? How do you spell that? Like Benson in *Soap*?'

'That's right. Like Benson in *Soap*. Now, do you think you could please pass that message on to Senator Jones, and have him call me? It's very urgent.'

'Okay,' said Karen. 'I'll try.'

There was a fizzing sound, and then the call was cut off. Karen said 'hello?' a couple of times, but there was no answer, and she put the phone down. She glanced at the scribbled notes she'd made, and then she typed a message for Peter Kaiser.

'Mr Ed Hardesty called from Wichita, Kansas, at three forty-five p.m. . . . he said that the wheat blight was probably a virus . . . and that it's spreading all over the country on corn, soybeans, everything. Dr Benson in Wichita has made tests, and says whole nation at risk.'

It was only when she had finished typing it that she realised the implications of what she had just written. She tugged the notepaper out of the IBM and re-read it. That was what the man had said, wasn't it? 'The blight is spreading all over the country. Dr Benson says the whole nation's food supply could be at risk . . .'

The way Karen had heard the blight story on the news, it was nothing more than a minor seasonal problem affecting a few farms in the depths of Kansas. And who on earth ever worried about what went on in Kansas? But now, this Ed Hardesty had called to say that *everything* was blighted. Not just wheat, but everything. Karen suddenly felt unreal, and cold, and she read the memo over again, and couldn't stop herself from shivering.

She was still looking at it when she heard a slight movement at her doorway. She looked around, and there was Peter Kaiser, leaning against the door-jamb, watching her. His face was expressionless, but the way he was standing, with one hand on his hip, somehow told her that he was more relaxed than usual.

'I'm, er – I'm just starting your typing now,' she said, looking away.

'That's all right,' he told her. 'I've come to tell you that I'm sorry.'

'You're sorry? Why should you be?'

'Why shouldn't I be?'

'Well,' she said, 'you're Peter Kaiser, nicknamed "The Machine", and you're the most efficient administrative executive in the whole of the Republican party organisation, bar none, and any stupid chit of a secretary who wastes your precious time by asking fatuous questions about coffee and time off – well, she hardly deserves an apology, does she?'

Peter smiled. 'I like you,' he said. 'You're spunky.'

She turned and looked at him. 'The last time anybody said that to me, I was seven years old, and I'd just come last in the egg-and-spoon race at school, and managed not to cry.'

'You've changed since then,' Peter said.

'In some ways. I still don't cry.'

'All right,' he grinned, 'I'll allow you that. Will you come out to dinner this evening?'

'Where are we going? The nearest Exxon station?'

'I don't understand.'

She shrugged. 'The way you've been acting, I thought you only fed on gasoline.'

'Karen,' said Peter, 'I am a human person. I do have feelings. If you cut me, do I not bleed?'

'I don't know. You might ooze a little grease.'

He laughed. It was an odd laugh, strangely high-pitched. 'Okay,' he said. 'I've come to say I'm sorry, and I'm sorry. So will you still let me take you out to dinner?'

Karen thought for a moment. One voice said: *no, tell him to go screw himself, or even his mother*. But the other voice said: *if Peter Kaiser likes you, he'll introduce you to Senator Jones, and if Senator Jones likes you . . . the sky's the limit. Or at least the dome of the Capitol's the limit. It's what you came to Washington for. You political groupie, you.*

'All right,' she said. 'Invitation accepted. What time do we eat?'

'Nine, nine-thirty. That's not too late for you, is it?'

'I should have just about digested my Big Mac by then.

79

By the way, here's a message for the senator, when you talk to him next.'

Peter took the memo and quickly looked it over. Then he read it again, more slowly, and frowned.

'Three forty-five?' he asked. 'Just a couple of minutes ago?'

'That's right.'

'And is this all he said? Nothing else?'

'That's all,' shrugged Karen. 'The blight is some kind of a virus, and it's spreading. Kind of creepy, isn't it?'

Peter forced another grin. 'Just one of those crackpot messages you always get when this kind of thing happens. I won't be surprised if we get more in the next few days. Viruses . . . death-rays from Mars . . . punishments from Heaven . . . you'll get used to it.'

'It frightened me, as a matter of fact,' said Karen. 'The man sounded so sane.'

'They always do,' Peter assured her. 'Now – do you think you can put me through to Senator Jones?'

'Whatever you want. Particularly since you're buying dinner. And particularly since I seem to have escaped two hours of solid dictation.'

'Okay,' said Peter. 'I'll take it in my office. And – well, I'll see you later.'

Karen picked up the phone and dialled through to Senator Jones's office. It was almost a minute before anybody answered, and then she heard Della McIntosh's voice, slightly out of breath. 'Yes? Senator Jones's office?'

'Mrs McIntosh? I have Peter Kaiser for the senator. I think it's pretty urgent.'

'Hold on,' said Della, and Karen heard her put the phone down on the table. In the background, she picked up the distinctive rumble of Senator Jones saying, 'What does that frosty-faced asshole want now? Right in the middle of – '

Then Senator Jones, louder and closer, said, 'Yes? Is this Peter?'

'I'll put you through, Senator,' said Karen, and she connected him to Peter; but at the same time she held her hand tightly over the mouthpiece of her own phone, and listened in.

'Peter?' growled Senator Jones. 'I hope you realise you've called me at a goddamned awkward time.'

'I'm sorry, Senator, but I've had an urgent message from Ed Hardesty, in Kansas. I thought you'd want to hear it straight away.'

'Hardesty? That blackmailing son-of-a-bitch? His daddy's whelp, that's all he is. What the hell has he got to say that justifies your interrupting my personal rest-period?'

Peter Kaiser took a long, steadying breath. 'He says he's had some results from the research people in Wichita. They seem to believe that this blight is caused by some kind of virus, although they don't seem to have put a name to it yet. The worst thing is, though, that they've definitely connected the virus with those corn and soybean blights in Iowa. In fact, all those reports on fruit and vegetable diseases that Dick Turnbull's sent us over the past couple of days . . . it seems like they've tied up the virus with *those* blights, too.'

Senator Jones said, 'Virus? What are they talking about?'

'I don't know specifically, Senator,' Peter told him. 'But Hardesty did say that someone called Dr Benson had made tests and reckoned that the whole of the nation's food supply was at risk.'

'Benson? I remember Benson. A goddamned drunk. He came to Fall River once and spewed all over my Cherokee rug. I thought they'd kicked his ass right out of Kansas after that.'

'It seems like they didn't,' said Peter, patiently. 'And if he's right, we could be in big trouble with the Blight Crisis Appeal. Benson only has to tell the press that the entire country's crops are going down the sink and nobody's going to feel like allocating anything to two dozen Kansas farmers.'

'How are the federal analysts doing?' asked Senator Jones.

'I haven't called them yet. But I checked with Professor Protter this morning, and he said their progress was strictly limited.'

'In other words. they haven't gotten anywhere at all.

That's typical, isn't it? One alcoholic quack in the middle of Kansas can analyse a disease, but a whole team of agricultural supermen in Washington can't work out the difference between wheat and birdseed. Get on to Protter again, and tell him to work faster, or I'll kick his ass from here to next week.'

'Yes, Senator.'

Senator Jones cleared his throat, and sniffed. Then he said, 'There are two things you have to do, Peter. You're right about the Blight Crisis Appeal. We have to get as much of that money into our bank account as we can, before people start to panic. How are you doing so far?'

'Nine million dollars promised, as of three o'clock. If I really hustle, I guess I can get hold of most of it by the weekend. Say seventy per cent. We'd have to arrange for special clearance on the cheques, of course.'

'Just lay your hands on as much as you can,' grunted Shearson. 'It may only be a fraction of what we originally planned to raise, but it'll do. The second thing you have to do is put maximum pressure on Professor Protter. Maximum, do you hear? It's Protter's job to come up with an antidote, and real fast.'

'But if we find an antidote, and announce it publicly, won't that slacken off contributions?'

Shearson sniffed. 'It's a question of picking the right moment. The right political moment, the right scientific moment, the right psychological moment. We may find an antidote tomorrow, but that doesn't mean we have to announce we've found it tomorrow. What we do is, we hold it back while the contributions are still rolling in, and we only announce it when the blight has become so critical that contributions are falling off in any case. The media are going to bust the blight situation wide open sooner or later. They're bound to. But it's *then* that we say we've discovered the answer to everybody's problems, and pick up all the political credit for saving the day. Some people call it brinkmanship. I call it the Lone Ranger syndrome. Don't shoot that silver bullet until you really have to.'

'Supposing Protter draws a blank?' asked Peter. 'I mean

– supposing we can't stop it, and the crops really *do* get wiped out?'

'Well, there's another little job for you. Call Frank Edison, and check the nation's food storage situation. Government stocks, private silos, military supplies – anything and everything. Then talk to some of the top supermarket people, and work out an estimate of how long their shelf supplies would be likely to last under crisis conditions.'

Peter jotted down a few notes. 'You want a picture of the worst that could possibly happen?'

'That's right,' said Senator Jones. 'But don't go scaring anybody. If they want to know why you're asking, just tell them it's for a federal contingency plan, in case of freakishly bad weather.'

Peter said, 'Isn't anyone else getting reports of this blight? I would have thought the president would have wanted a brief by now.'

'Oh, that's already been done,' said the senator. 'I sent him a personal memorandum this morning, telling him that, yes, we had problems with a new and unexpected blight in Kansas and North Dakota, but that all of our top agricultural scientists were working on it, and they were only hours away from cracking the problem wide open. I admitted there were outbreaks of blight in Iowa and Oregon and parts of Washington, but I told him that considering the humidity, they weren't unexpected, and we didn't anticipate a serious shortfall in output.'

'So you're not getting any flak from the White House?'

'Not yet. It'll come, but not yet.'

'Don't you think you ought to do something about Dr Benson? I mean – he could be talking to the newspapers now.'

'I've been considering that,' said Senator Jones. 'I think I might send Della over to Wichita to have a quiet word with him. Tell him how important it is for scientists not to scuttle around panicking everybody. I was going over to Fall River at the week-end in any case – I can send her on ahead.'

'And Hardesty? What about him? If he doesn't get any

response from you, he's likely to blow the whistle.'

'Hardesty is a professional pain in the ass,' breathed the senator. 'But I still want to have him as my Kansas Farmer figurehead. He'll be good copy. The young, dedicated, second-generation wheat farmer. And if he's been as hard hit by this blight as he says he has, he's going to be glad of a few extra dollars. Maybe I'll get Della to talk to him, too. She's good at sizing people up.'

Peter was tempted to answer, 'You can say that again, Senator,' but he held his tongue. 'Do you want me to call him back?' he asked Shearson.

'Yes, do that. Do that right away. I made a mistake once, years ago, in some political scandal you won't even remember. I took care of all the big people but I forgot about the little people. And if you're not careful, it's the little people who can put you under.'

Peter wrote down two more lines of notes, and then he said, 'Okay, Senator. I'm sorry I disturbed you. Maybe we can meet up later and I'll put you in the picture on the food supplies.'

'Good,' said Shearson. 'And for Christ's sake keep this as quiet as you can. Until those donations have cleared the bank, we're still running on the skyline. You understand me?'

Peter glanced at the anti-bug light beside his telephone. 'Yes, Senator,' he said, crisply.

Peter put down the phone, and as he did so, Karen Fortunoff put her phone down, too. Within a few seconds, there was a buzz from Peter's office, and a light flashed on her handset.

'Yes, Mr Kaiser?'

'Ah, Karen. Get me my mother on the phone, will you?'

'Now, Mr Kaiser?'

'*Now*, Karen. That's if you don't mind.'

Karen dialled the Wellington Hotel, and waited while the dialling-tone warbled. Then she heard Peter's mother say, 'Mrs Kaiser's suite. Who's calling?'

'It's your son for you, Mrs Kaiser. Hold on, please.'

She put the call through to Peter's desk, but again she clamped her hand over the mouthpiece and listened in.

'Mother?' she heard Peter asking.

'What's the matter, dear? I have Mrs Kroger here for tea.'

'Mother, this is very important. I want you to listen, and I want you to do exactly as I tell you.'

'Peter, dear, what on earth's the matter? You sound quite peculiar.'

'Listen, Mother, I sound quite peculiar because it could be that something quite peculiar is just about to happen. I've got wind that we could be suffering some very severe food shortages over the coming winter.'

Mrs Kaiser sounded perplexed. 'Food shortages? What do you mean? I haven't heard anything about food shortages. I don't eat much anyway. I'm on a diet.'

'Mother, I know all about your diet. But you still have to eat something. And the way these shortages are shaping up, it looks like there may be hardly anything to eat at all, except canned stuff, and frozen stuff, and maybe meat.'

'Peter – are you sure?'

'I wouldn't be calling you if I wasn't sure. Now, listen, will you, and stop asking questions. I want you to call Mr Parker at the general store in Connecticut – yes, *that* Mr Parker – and I want you to ask him how much he wants for all of the foodstuffs in his store. Yes, Mother, *all* of them. Canned foods, dried foods, flour, TV dinners, everything. The whole damned stock, except for the toys and the corn dollies and the cigarettes. Right. Then I want him to drive the whole lot up to the house at Litchfield and get the key from Mrs Lodge and store everything in the cellar. Tell him to buy a couple of new deep-freezers if he needs to. Just make sure the whole contents of that general store are tucked away in our house, that's all.'

There was a long silence. Then Peter's mother said, 'Are you feeling all right, dear? You're sure you're not running a temperature?'

'Mother!' snapped Peter. 'Will you just do what I tell you to do? It could be a matter of life or death! *Your* life or death!'

'Peter, I hardly think –'

'What you hardly think and what's actually happening

are two different thngs, Mother. Sixty per cent of the wheat crop in Kansas has been wiped out by disease in two days. A third of the corn and soybean crops in Iowa are going down with the same blight. We've got tomatoes rotting in Florida, grapes rotting in California, broccoli dying in Oregon, potatoes going mouldy in Idaho . . . this whole damned country's been hit by the biggest crop failure ever.'

'Well, dear, I've heard about the wheat. That was on the news today. But nobody's said anything about tomatoes, or broccoli. I'm not particularly fond of broccoli, in any case.'

'Mother –' said Peter, in a bottled-up voice.

'Oh, very well dear. I'll call Mr Parker. I'm sure he's going to think that I'm quite mad. Shall I tell him to make sure to stock up again, because of the shortages?'

'Don't tell anybody anything. The whole reason I want you to call Mr Parker is because he doesn't know I work for Senator Jones. It's important we don't start a panic, otherwise everybody's going to start stock-piling food and the shortage is going to be even worse.'

'I see, dear. All right. Can I tell Mrs Kroger?'

'Don't tell anybody. I'll call you later.'

Peter banged the phone down. Karen, biting her lip, replaced her own receiver. She could scarcely believe that any of what she had heard was real. Surely, in a country like the United States, with all those newspapers and television stations, somebody would have realised what was happening and warned the public? Surely one man like Senator Jones couldn't suppress the news so easily? Yet it seemed as if nobody really cared – as if reporters and politicians and government experts were all quite happy to take whatever they were told as the gospel truth, provided it was couched in reasonable-sounding language. Even the president had accepted Shearson Jones's waffle about 'cracking the problem wide open', and 'not anticipating a serious shortfall.'

Karen's telephone light flashed again. She picked up the receiver and said, 'Yes?'

'Karen – can you try to get me Mr Ed Hardesty, at South Burlington Farm, near Wichita?'

'Yes, Mr Kaiser. I won't be a moment. I have one other call to make first.'

'Okay, Karen. But don't make it too long.'

'No, Mr Kaiser.'

Karen pushed a button to get herself an outside line, and listened to the dialling tone for a moment. Then she punched out a number with a 218 code. The phone was answered almost immediately.

'Mom?' she said. 'It's Karen. Yes, it really is. I know. But, please, Mom, I've got something terribly important to tell you.'

Eight

As the sun set over South Burlington Farm, Ed and Willard and Dyson Kane stood waist-high amongst the blackened wheat, smoking in silence and watching the smoke drift diagonally across the decaying reaches of the south-eastern fields. Usually, smoking was totally forbidden in the crops, but now it didn't matter any more, and they had lit up in the same way that Hitler's staff had all lit up, once the Führer was dead and the Third Reich was over for ever.

The Hughes helicopter rested a few yards away on a slight slope, white and clean and shining amidst all the oily and stinking devastation in the fields around it. A flock of birds wheeled and turned overhead.

Ed was tired and unshaven, dressed in jeans and a red plaid cowboy shirt. Beside him, Willard stood with his arms folded, his eyes hidden behind dark sunglasses, but his whole posture betraying how defeated he felt.

'I just never saw anything like it,' he said, after a while. 'We didn't even get the chance to try to fight back.'

Ed turned towards Dyson. 'How much of the crop do you think we've lost up to now?' he asked him. 'Sixty, seventy per cent?'

'Hard to tell exactly,' said Dyson. 'But I'd say near on

eighty. There won't be anything worth saving by the week-end.'

'Did you have any luck with Senator Jones?' asked Willard.

'I had a bad connection. He's supposed to be calling me back. To tell you the truth, I feel pretty embarrassed about using that wheat-dumping scandal against him.'

'I shouldn't,' said Willard. 'He'd use it against you, if you were in his place, and he were in yours. The way I see it, this farm is pretty damned important to you, and if you want to keep it going, then you're going to have to play the same dirty tricks as everybody else.'

Dyson Kane hunkered down, and picked one of the rotten ears of wheat. The smell in the wind was sour and unpleasant, but by now they'd grown almost used to it.

'You know something?' Dyson said. 'These crops don't *rustle* any more. It doesn't even sound like summer. In summer, that's all you ever hear, usually, out in the fields. That rustling sound, of ripe wheat.'

'Dr Benson thinks it's a Soviet conspiracy,' said Ed. 'He reckons the Communists found a way to poison our wheat when we weren't looking.'

Willard shook his head. 'I don't think poor old Dr Benson has ever been quite the same since he dried out. He used to see giant ladybugs, when he had the DTs. Now, he thinks everybody's plotting to overthrow Kansas.'

'There's no way that anybody could have spoiled this kind of acreage without spraying,' said Dyson. 'And if you're going to spray poison, or something of that kind, you have to do it real low. Nobody could have flown over this farm without my knowing about it. Not that low.'

'That's what I thought,' said Ed. 'I think Dr Benson's probably right when he says it's some kind of a virus, but it looks natural to me. I just hope he finds some way of curing it.'

'You're going to burn these fields?' asked Willard.

'What do you think?'

'I think you're going to have to. It looks like a pretty smoky finish to the summer. I'm sorry.'

Ed nodded. 'I'll talk to the senator one more time, just to make sure that nobody wants to look the crop over before they start paying out compensation. Then I guess we'll set it all alight.'

The radio-telephone in the helicopter bleeped. Dyson walked over to it and picked it up.

'Yes. Yes, he's here. Ed, it's for you. Somebody from Senator Jones's office.'

Ed took the receiver, covered one ear with his hand to cut out the sound of the breeze, and said, 'Ed Hardesty speaking.'

'Mr Hardesty? Hi, my name's Peter Kaiser. May I call you Ed? It seems from what the senator's been telling me that we could all be working together quite soon.'

'Did you get my message about the virus?' asked Ed.

'Sure. We told Senator Jones straight away. The only trouble is, Ed, that we've been doing some pretty thorough tests on the wheat right here in Washington, at the Department of Agriculture's own laboratories, and we're not at all sure the cause is a virus at all.'

'Are you close to finding out what it is?'

'Oh, yes. Right on the brink. But we don't want to give out any public releases on the blight until we have a more definitive idea. If we said it was a virus, you see, it could cause unnecessary panic; and we might find that farmers were destroying their crops without any real justification. It's one of those situations we have to handle with kid gloves, if you know what I mean.'

'Dr Benson is convinced it's a virus,' said Ed. 'What's more, he thinks all these other blights are caused by different versions of the same basic infection.'

'We-e-ell,' said Peter Kaiser, 'without being unfair, Dr Benson has pretty limited facilities over at Wichita, compared with what we have here, and he isn't exactly renowned for his personal stability. Don't get me wrong. He's a talented man. But the last thing we need in a serious situation like this is for anybody to jump to conclusions.'

Ed said, 'Okay. I get your point. Did Senator Jones get

very far with his ideas for federal compensation?'

'Haven't you been watching the television news today?'

'Only once. I've been tied up here at the farm for most of the afternoon.'

'In that case,' said Peter, 'I'm happy to be the first to tell you that we've already set up a Kansas Wheat Farmers' Blight Crisis Appeal, legal and official and ready to roll in the money. We have full backing from some really heavyweight people in the Senate, including the chairman of the Agriculture Committee, and the whole structure's been arranged by one of Washington's top lawyers.'

Ed looked towards Willard and pulled an impressed face. 'I didn't know Shearson Jones could work so fast,' he told Peter.

Peter gave a synthetic chuckle. 'Well,' he said, 'outward appearances can be deceptive. He's overweight, sure. But I can tell you one thing. When any single person in Kansas of any political persuasion is threatened by fire, or drought, or crime, or you name it, Shearson Jones can be pretty damned nimble on his feet. He's a caring man, Mr Hardesty, whatever people say about him. Why, here at the office, behind his back, they call him the Fat Samaritan.'

Ed frowned. 'Is he going to be able to persuade Congress to vote the fund any money?'

'Oh, I'm sure,' said Peter. 'But meanwhile we've been taking pledges from industry. So far today we've chalked up nearly three million dollars, and we're sure we'll get more.'

'Well, I'm amazed,' said Ed. 'And pleased, too. I thought politicians were all foot-dragging and red tape.'

'Not Shearson Jones,' Peter told him. 'And I want to assure you of something else, too. As soon as the first donations to the Blight Crisis Appeal have cleared the bank, they'll be paid straight out. No waiting, and no arguments. All you'll have to do is satisfy the appeal board that your farm meets the legal requirements for compensation – which I'm quite sure that yours does – and you'll be eligible for your share of the three million.'

'I'm gratified to hear it,' said Ed.

'I'm gratified you're gratified,' Peter told him. 'You see,

Senator Jones believes that we'll be able to collect a lot more money for the appeal if we have a figurehead – one person who represents the whole plight of every unfortunate farmer. Somebody who can talk on television about what's happened in Kansas, and how difficult life can be on a wheat farm. Somebody who represents the best in American farming. A young man, struggling against the weather, and fluctuating prices, just to keep up the traditions that made this country what it is today.'

'Are you reading that from a script or making that up as you go along?' asked Ed.

'Come on, Ed, don't be cynical,' said Peter. 'You know what I'm talking about.'

'Well, I guess so. And I also guess that you want *me* to be your figurehead.'

'Why not? This extra compensation was your idea to start with. Why not take it the whole way, and identify yourself publicly with what you believe?'

Ed ran his hand through his hair. 'Let me think about it, will you? I've got your number.'

'I'll let you do more than think about it,' said Peter. 'Shearson Jones has arranged for his personal representative to fly to Wichita tomorrow to meet you. She's going to talk to Dr Benson first, to find out what he's discovered, in case he might have turned up anything helpful. Then she can come out to South Burlington and talk to you.'

'*She?*' asked Ed.

'Mrs Della McIntosh,' Peter explained. 'Right up until Monday, she was Washington correspondent for the *Kansas City Herald-Examiner*. But when she saw how strongly Shearson felt about the blight, and what he was going to do for the wheat farmers, she quit her job on the spot and offered to help. Shearson Jones has that kind of effect on people.'

'I see,' said Ed, uncertainly. 'All right – I'll expect her.'

'Shearson himself will be down at Fall River by Sunday. I guess he'll want to meet you. Meanwhile – good luck with the crop.'

'The crop?' asked Ed. 'There isn't any crop left.'

'Well, I know,' said Peter, slightly flustered. 'What I

meant was, good luck with the insurance, and the compensation, and whatever you need good luck with. I'll talk to you later.'

Ed put the radio-telephone down, and stood thoughtfully beside the helicopter for a few moments. Willard said, 'Who was that? Is anything wrong?'

'I don't know,' said Ed. 'I've had experience of loan sharks, and phoney accountants, and speculators. But I'm out of my depth when it comes to politicians. They talk a whole lot of bullshit – or at least you *think* it's bullshit. It's only when you think about it for a long time afterwards that you realise the calculated importance of every single damned rubbishy word they spoke.'

'Shearson Jones?'

'His sycophantic sidekick. But at least he had some reasonable news. Shearson's set up a special compensation fund, and it looks like we may be able to save South Burlington.'

Willard couldn't help grinning. 'Well, that's something to celebrate. You want to come back to my place and sink a couple of beers?'

Ed looked around the black, rot-flattened crops. The sun had almost gone now, and the silence over the wide plains of Kansas was enormous. Ed remembered walking out into the fields when he was a boy, on a dark and windless night, and believing that he was the only person left in the whole world. People from Kansas know what you mean when you describe that feeling; only a city-dweller will go 'huh?'

Ed said, 'Yes. I think we ought to celebrate.'

'Is your mother still staying with you?' asked Willard, as they climbed back into the helicopter.

'Just for a couple of days. She thought she ought to take over the house now that Season's gone.'

'She's a strong woman, your mother.'

Ed clipped up his lap-belt. 'We're all strong, here on South Burlington. But it didn't protect us from this, did it?'

'We'll get through it. You wait and see.'

Dyson Kane started up the motor. The helicopter warmed up for a while, and then tipped up into the air. They flew at low level across the ocean of stained wheat, until they circled at last around the small tree-bordered house where Willard lived. Dyson put the helicopter down beside Willard's Ford pick-up and switched off. They climbed out into the darkness, and ducked under the whistling rotors.

Willard was a widower. His wife Nanette had worked in the kitchens at South Burlington Farm when Ed was a boy; but at the age of forty-five she had contracted cancer of the face, and died. Willard had kept his house pretty much the same through the years that followed, and if anyone had walked into it without realising Nanette had been gone since 1961, they would have thought that she was about to come singing down the stairs at any minute. Willard wasn't morbid about her, just very gentle with her memory. Beside the oak sofa, on a small table, her knitting still lay where she had left it the day she died. It wasn't sacrosanct. Willard didn't mind if anybody picked it up and looked at it. But it was something she had been doing on the day he left her, and that's why he kept it there.

Ed and Dyson sat down in the living-room while Willard went into the kitchen to find the beer. Dyson called out to Willard, 'Mind if I switch on the television? Maybe we'll catch the news.'

'Sure,' said Willard, from the kitchen, popping the tops on cans of Coors. Dyson leaned forward in his armchair and pressed the switch on the big old walnut-veneer set. The picture flickered sideways for a while, and then they saw Magilla Gorilla grinning out of his pet-store window.

'News is after this,' said Willard, coming back in with the beer. 'Does anybody like pretzels?'

'I'm only the world's greatest pretzel-addict,' said Dyson. 'I took three cures at St Joseph's Hospital before they finally gave up and let me eat as many as I wanted.'

Ed glanced around the room. It was four or five months since he'd been in here, but it hadn't changed. The cheap ornaments still stood on the mantelpiece over the fire, and on the walls hung the framed portrait of Nanette, and the painting of Mount Sunflower, the highest peak in Kansas, at sunrise. There was also an aerial photograph of South Burlington Farm, in colour, with the ballpen inscription,

'To Willard. With thanks for everything you've ever done here. Ursula Hardesty.'

Ed sipped his beer. He agreed with his mother, in a way. It was better that his father hadn't seen South Burlington reduced to this rotten waste of collapsing crops. He wished only that his father had left him with enough capital not to have to go begging to people like Shearson Jones. He didn't doubt for a moment that Shearson Jones would one day expect an equal favour in return.

'I thought we were supposed to be celebrating,' said Willard. 'Here's to the blight compensation fund, and everybody who donates to it.'

Ed smiled, and raised his tankard. 'Here's to South Burlington,' he said. They drank, and then Willard opened a box and passed round his King Edward cigars.

'Quiet now,' said Dyson. 'Here's the news.'

The lead story was about renewed tension in the Middle East. Then there was a lengthy report about severe flooding in Colorado. After that, a film report of the president's visit to a new sanitarium in upstate New York. Ed and Willard and Dyson glanced at each other and waited for what they thought was the most devastating news of the hour.

Eventually, it came. A wheat-ear symbol was superimposed on the screen behind news reporter John Magonick, with the headline 'Kansas Wheat Crisis.'

'This looks like being a disastrous year for wheat farmers in the Middle West. A mysterious blight has stricken crops in most parts of Kansas and North Dakota, in some cases ruining fifty to sixty per cent of a farm's entire harvest. Fortunately, grain stocks are very high after last year's excellent weather, and President Carter's embargo on selling US wheat to the Russians has also helped to keep the silos topped up. So – Department of Agriculture experts are saying today that there is no immediate cause for public concern.

'In Washington, Kansas Senator Shearson Jones has acted promptly in setting up an appeal fund for farmers who lose their wheat crops because of the blight, and has already been pledged three million dollars by agriculture-related industries. He hopes that Congress will vote his fund anything up to ten million dollars because of the "vicious, unprecedented, and unusual nature of the blight."'

There was a lengthy interview with Shearson Jones, looking like a fat white Moby Dick in the glare of the mobile television lights, and he spoke with jowl-trembling sincerity about the 'plain hard-working men who defy storm, drought, and disease to feed this nation of ours.'

Afterwards, John Magonick said, 'Other states have reported an unusually high incidence of crop failure this year. In California, whole vineyards of table grapes are rotting on the vine, and lettuces, according to the California Growers' Association, are looking very browned off. In northern states, too, it seems as if corn and soybean crops are suffering, and in Wisconsin some dairy farmers are complaining of rancid grass. The Department of Agriculture puts the blame on this year's humid conditions, but doesn't expect the country's nationwide food production totals to fall very much below eight per cent on last year's figure.

'In Canada, some wheat growers are suffering the same blight as our unfortunate Kansas farmers, and Parliament in Quebec will be discussing possible emergency measures tomorrow.'

Ed stood up and switched the television off.

'Did you hear that?' he said.

'Couldn't fail to,' said Willard.

'But did you hear the way it was all made to sound so goddamned *reassuring*? That was what bothered me when Shearson's assistant called me – what was his name – Peter Kaiser. Everything's fine. Everything's under control. Your crops have all been blighted in the space of forty-eight hours, we still don't have a goddamned clue why, but sit back and relax. Now they're talking about crop blights in California and Canada, and nobody seems to be worried. I mean, for Christ's sake, California produces a third of the vegetables for the entire country. And what are we going to do for wheat if Canada's harvest gets wiped out, too?'

'They said that grain reserves were pretty high.'

'Sure, but how long do they think they're going to last? I

don't know how many loaves of bread and hamburger buns get eaten in the United States in the space of a single day, but just think about it. There was something else that bothered me, too. Rancid grass in Wisconsin. What happens if dairy products get hit? And meat production?'

'Come on, Ed, you're letting this whole thing get you worked up,' said Dyson. 'If there was any real reason to panic, they would have said so on the news. There must be thousands of millions of tons of canned foods in the country to keep us going through a bad year, in any case. and what about all the frozen stuff?'

'And what about next year?' demanded Ed. 'What happens if our crops get hit again?'

'You heard what they said on the news. They've got the federal research laboratories working on it. They're bound to come up with something.'

'Well, I sure hope so.'

Ed didn't stay long at Willard's house. He was feeling too anxious and unsettled to sit down and have a drink with the boys. What's more, he hadn't yet heard from Season and Sally, and he wanted to go back to the farmhouse and wait for them to call. He finished his beer, said good night to Willard and Dyson, and walked back along the winding track that led to the main farmyard.

His mother was standing on the front verandah in a long white evening-dress with a high collar and batwing sleeves. She was holding on to the rail, and looking up at the full Kansas moon.

'Hello, Mother,' he said, as he mounted the steps.

She turned around, and nodded. 'Nearly harvest time,' she said. 'Or it should have been, at least.'

'I heard some news from Washington today,' Ed told her. 'It seems like we may be getting some extra compensation, on top of our usual crop insurance. We may be able to keep the farm going after all.'

'Well, that *is* good news,' said his mother. 'I was just thinking how sad it would be to see South Burlington die.'

He stood beside her, a few feet away. Her diamond necklace was sparkling in the moonlight, and he could smell her perfume, mingled with the wind-borne sourness of decaying wheat.

'Have you heard from Season?' he asked her.

She shook her head.

'Well, I'm going upstairs to have a bath and dress for dinner. Do you want a drink before I go?'

'No, thank you,' said his mother. Then, hesitantly, 'Edward?'

'Yes, Mother?'

'You're better without her, you know. South Burlington is better without her.'

Ed stared at her for a long time. Then he said, 'I love her, Mother. If I didn't think it would make matters worse, I'd quite happily sell this farm tomorrow, and everything on it, and go join her in California.'

'I'm glad your father can't hear you say that.'

'Daddy's dead, Mother. Don't keep waving his shroud at me. Now, if you'll pardon me for fifteen minutes, I could use a shave and a hot bath.'

Ursula Hardesty turned away, and struck a deliberately hurt and melodramatic pose by the verandah rail. Ed paused for a moment, wondering if he ought to say he was sorry, but then he opened the screen door and went inside. This was his house now, his farm, his marriage. Whatever charades his mother wanted to play under the harvest moon, well, let her do it. Charades were a luxury that few people were going to be able to afford for very much longer.

Nine

Half-way up Topanga Canyon, Carl Snowman turned the Mercury stationwagon into the steep and curving driveway, past the mailbox that carried a *Los Angeles Times* flag, and through the leafy gardens that eventually took them up to the house. He parked the stationwagon at an angle, and jammed on the brake tight, so that it wouldn't run back downhill.

'We've finished the extension now, you know,' he told Season, switching off the engine, and opening his door. The key alarm buzzed plaintively in the warm evening air. 'The playroom, the spare bedroom, everything. Sally can have a whale of a time.'

He opened the door for Season, and helped her out. Sally was in the back, covered by a rug, fast asleep after the flight. They had been delayed for three hours at Albuquerque, because of a refuelling problem and by the time they had reached Los Angeles, Season had been feeling distinctly frayed. Standing in the terminal at Albuquerque, staring out through the tinted windows at the sun-rippled concrete and the gleaming aeroplanes, she had been tempted to book a flight straight back to Wichita, and return to Ed.

It was only her urgent need to be herself, as well as Mrs Edward Hardesty, that had kept her away from the American Airlines desk. I have to give myself a try, she had told herself. If I don't try, then I'll never find out.

At the top of the cedarwood steps, the door of the house opened, and Season's sister Vee appeared in the lighted doorway. She was two years younger than Season, but their friends invariably thought she was older. Her hair was bleached Beverly Hills white, and she had a deep California tan. Apart from that, she wore the smocks and Gloria Vanderbilt jeans of a determinedly casual movie director's wife. Her hoop earrings swung as she kissed Season on both cheeks.

'You're so *late*! I expected you *hours* ago! I was beginning to think something *awful* had happened! Poor old Carl had to call the airline five times to make sure you weren't scattered all over the Grand Canyon!'

'It was something to do with the fuel,' said Season. 'I got to see rather more of Albuquerque air terminal than I really wanted to.'

'Well, don't you worry,' fussed Vee. 'You can rest up tonight, and sleep as long as you want tomorrow. I have your favourite dinner for you, and a bottle of champagne on ice, and you can take your shoes off and relax. Oh – and will you take a look at Sally! Hasn't she *grown*?'

Carl was just lifting Sally out of the back of the

stationwagon. He carried her across to the wooden steps in a careful and fatherly way – which wasn't surprising when you knew that he had four children of his own by a previous marriage, the youngest of whom was ten. He was a stocky, well-preserved forty-five-year-old, with cropped white hair and a square Polish-looking face. He made sensitive and not very successful movies about young kids dropping out from school – *Pursuit of Happiness*-type pictures.

Sally stood in the hallway rubbing her eyes as Carl went to carry up the cases. Season said, 'Don't worry, honey – we'll soon get you to bed. Would you like some milk and cookies?'

The inside of the Snowman house was built in natural, fragrant-smelling wood, with Navajo scatter rugs on the floor, and even an authentic cigar-store Indian presiding over the dining-area. The furniture was a self-conscious mixture of Italian stainless-steel and carved Mexican-Spanish, in red and gold. Already set out on the table, lit by trefoil candle-holders, were plates of salad and guacamole and taco chips.

'We're eating Mexican?' asked Season. 'That's wonderful. I haven't eaten Mexican in centuries. All we ever eat in Kansas is beef, and more beef, and for a change we have beef.'

'You're sure Sally doesn't want to join us for dinner?'

'No, no – ' said Season. 'She's tired. I'll take her straight to bed. I'd like to wash up myself.'

'Oh, before you go up – you must meet Granger. Granger – come and say hello to my favourite and only sister!'

From a corner of the living-area, carrying a large crystal tumbler of scotch, a lithe, blond-haired man appeared, wearing a black turtle-neck sweater, black trousers, and black shoes. He had a lean, ascetic face, with a hawkish nose. His eyes were very pale, as if the pupils had been bleached like a pair of blue jeans, from indigo to almost no colour at all. Around his neck was a massive silver crucifix, on which was impaled the body of Christ, in eighteen carat gold.

'This is Granger Hughes,' said Vee. 'Granger, this is my

dearly-beloved sister, Season Hardesty.'

Granger took Season's hand, bowed, and kissed it. 'I'm charmed,' he said. 'Coleridge wrote that "all seasons shall be sweet to thee," and how right he was.'

'Well, he's dead now,' said Season, slightly embarrassed.

'True,' said Granger, 'but I'm pleased to see that you're keeping his sentiments alive. You're a very pretty woman.'

'Thank you,' Season told him. She wasn't used to compliments, and she knew that he had made her blush. Out in Kansas, the nearest she had ever received to a compliment was that she was 'sassy'. She glanced towards Vee for some moral support, but Vee was simply grinning her toothy California grin and taking Granger's suavity for granted.

'Are you a priest, or something?' Season asked Granger. 'You seem to have all the necessary accoutrements.'

'I'm a priest of sorts,' said Granger, with a cryptic smile.

Vee said, 'He's more than a priest, Season. He's a *spiritual leader*. Carl and I met him through Dr Schauman – that's our analyst. We went to a wine-and-cheese party at Bobby Wanderelli's – you know Bobby Wanderelli who plays the cousin in *The Fortune Saga* on television? I mean, it's a terrible show but he's a wonderful person. You'd *have* to be wonderful to play that part for three series and stay sane! Anyway, Granger was there and Dr Schauman introduced us. He said he felt that both of our lives could do with some of Granger's religious solidity. Granger's very literal in his interpretation of the scriptures, you know. He believes that all the miracles that Christ performed actually happened – you know, like raising Lazarus and walking on water – and he thinks we can all achieve the same kind of miracles if we give ourselves to Christ.'

Season was watching Granger the whole time that Vee was talking. He had a slight smile on his face, but his eyes were giving away nothing. When Vee had finished, Season nodded as if to say, well, Mr Hughes, very impressive.

'I call my group "The Church of the Practical Miracle",' said Granger.

'And you really believe you can work miracles, the way Christ did?'

'You sound cynical,' said Granger. 'You don't believe in what the Bible tells us about Jesus?'

'Maybe I'm just tired,' said Season. 'You'll have to forgive me, but I've just flown here from Kansas, with a three-hour stopover in New Mexico. I don't think anybody would feel like performing miracles after that, or even witnessing one. You'll excuse me.'

'Wait,' said Granger, and the sharp way in which he said it made Season pause. 'Wait,' he said again, in a gentler voice.

Season looked at him. 'Mr Hughes – Granger – I really want to go take a shower.'

He stepped closer. His eyes stared into hers unfalteringly. She could smell the cologne he was wearing. It was dry, like Kansas grass. Vetiver, probably, or Monsieur Worth. Somehow it seemed rather odd for a self-styled spiritual leader to be wearing Monsieur Worth.

'You're feeling tense, aren't you?' he asked her. 'Your mind feels wound up like a clockspring, and you're exhausted.'

She looked at Vee again, but Vee was enjoying every minute.

Granger raised his hands. They were long-fingered, with professionally-manicured nails. He wore no rings at all, nor bracelets.

'Allow me to touch your forehead,' he said. 'I promise you that you will feel better.'

Season hesitated, but Vee said, 'Go on, Season, he's marvellous. You'll feel so much better.'

Season suddenly realised that she was reacting like an uptight Wichita farmer's wife. Don't you go tampering with them things you don't understand the nature of, young man. She smiled, and relaxed, and said, 'All right. I'm willing to try anything once. Provided it's moral, of course.'

'Of course,' said Granger, warmly. He extended his fingers, and with the cool tips of them, touched Season's forehead just above her eyebrows. 'Do you want to close your eyes?' he asked her. 'You don't have to.'

'Close them,' prompted Vee. 'You'll be amazed what

101

you see. You know, like the visions you get in back of your eyelids.'

'Now,' said Granger, 'I want you to feel the power that is flowing through my hands in the name of Our Lord Jesus Christ. It is the power of healing, the power of forgiveness, the power of purity. All those feelings which were troubling you, all those uncertainties, they will all resolve themselves. Jesus hears your troubles, and knows of your indecision and he understands. He will help you.'

Strangely, Season began to feel soothed. She could imagine some kind of gentle warmth radiating from Granger's fingertips, and smoothing out the knots and crumples that the day had made in her mind. She wasn't sure about Jesus, but the reassurance that someone understood how uncertain she felt, and how anxious about her marriage – that reassurance in itself was enough to calm her.

Granger murmured, 'You're a very lovely, magnetic person, Season. You have an aura about you which makes you both attractive and sympathetic. I don't think in my whole time in the service of Our Lord that I've ever come across anyone with whom I felt so close so quickly.'

Season opened her eyes. Granger was staring at her through the cage of his upraised fingers. The pupils in those washed-out irises of his were contracted almost to pinpoints.

'How do you feel?' he asked her, lowering his hands.

'I don't know,' she said. 'Better, I think.'

'Isn't he *marvellous*?' enthused Vee.

'Well, I certainly feel less harassed,' agreed Season, brushing back her blonde hair with her hand. 'Are you staying to dinner, Granger?'

Granger shook his head. 'I regret not. I have a meeting tonight. Even a church has to be run like a business these days. I have to fill out Form One-o-two-three for the IRS with my accountants.'

'Didn't Jesus throw the money-changers out of the temple?' asked Season.

'He certainly did,' agreed Granger. 'And one day, I hope I can do the same. That'll be a miracle worth praying for.'

They saw Granger to the door. Carl had already taken Sally upstairs to her bedroom in the extension, and they could hear her giggling and screaming as Carl chased her across the landing with a Cookie Monster glove-puppet. Granger stepped out on to the elevated wooden porch, and looked out over the warm twinkling Los Angeles night.

'Thank you for your hospitality, Vee,' he said. 'And thank you for introducing me to Season. You take good care of her while she's here. She's a very special person.'

'It was good to meet you,' said Season. Granger took her hand, and gave it a quick, affectionate squeeze.

They both stood by the railing as Granger walked around to the car port at the side of the house. A few moments later, he reappeared in a glossy black Eldorado, booped the horn a couple of times, and drove off down to the road. They watched his tail-lights disappear through the leaves.

'Well,' said Vee. 'What do you think of our spiritual leader? Quite miraculous, isn't he?'

'He's good-looking. Maybe a little theatrical.'

'Theatrical? Well, he may be theatrical by Kansas standards, but by Hollywood standards he's positively normal. You ought to see the guru that Marjorie Newman goes to see. Hairy, and yukky. and not too particular about the condition of his loincloth, either. I think Granger's a doll. If I wasn't so much in love with Carl, I think I might be tempted to test his spirituality for weak spots.'

They went inside, and the screen door banged behind them. 'You must come and see the extension,' said Vee. 'First we had fires, then we had a mudslide, but somehow we managed to survive long enough to finish it off. Thank God we don't have any more disasters on the slate.'

'I ought to call Ed and tell him we've arrived safely,' said Season. 'Is there a phone in my room?'

'Oh, sure. Listen – let's go upstairs and I'll show you around. Then you can come down and have something to eat. Mind you – the way prices have been shooting up around here, we're lucky to have half a tomato to nibble on.'

'There's been some kind of trouble with the vegetable

crop here, hasn't there?' asked Season. 'Some tomato grower was talking to me on the plane. *And* trying to make a pass, I might add. At least until Sally came walking along the aisle, calling me "mommy".'

'I don't suppose it's anything as bad as that wheat blight you've had in Kansas,' said Vee, leading Season up a curving wooden staircase to an oak-panelled passageway. 'But you have to do your marketing pretty early in the day if you want fresh lettuce and celery. By mid-morning, most of the stuff's gone. Still – they say it's just a "temporary shortfall".'

'You should have seen the farm,' Season said. 'The wheat was all black and drooping for miles. Poor Ed was absolutely heartbroken.'

'I expect Ursula was, too.'

Season raised her eyes to heaven. 'Don't talk to me about Ursula. She's like one of those terrible women in an Edgar Allen Poe story. She'd have me beheaded if she thought it would help South Burlington Farm.'

'This is your room,' Vee told her opening the door of a wide, airy, studio with a sloping dormer roof and a polished wooden floor. 'You wait till you wake up in the morning. There's a beautiful view of the canyon. Your shower's through there, and your telephone's right over on the desk.'

'Vee, it's beautiful,' said Season. 'I just know that we're going to feel right at home here.'

Vee held her arm. 'You're okay, aren't you? I mean, Ed didn't take it too bad?'

Season lowered her eyes. 'He didn't want me to go, if that's what you mean. He was more upset than he was saying. But he knows I have to get away from Kansas, even if it's only for a week.'

'What about your marriage?'

'Well, I don't know. I'll have to see how I feel. Ed doesn't want to give up the farm and I don't want him to give it up, either. If I took South Burlington away from him, just for my own selfish reasons, it would be like castrating him. He's a farmer, Vee, and when I married him I never even realised. But whether I can face up to going back to Kansas or not . . .'

104

Vee ran her hand through her sister's blonde hair. 'It's that bad, huh?'

Season nodded. 'It's wheat and it's sky and that's all.'

Vee kissed her. 'You wash up, get yourself ready. Carl will take care of Sally. And listen, Season, whatever happens, just remember we love you.'

Season's eyes filled up with tears. She held her hand over her mouth and the tears slid down her cheeks and clung on her fingers like diamonds. 'I'm sorry, Vee,' she said. 'I'm tired, that's all.'

'Sure,' said Vee, hugging her. 'I'll see you in a while.'

Ten

Della McIntosh walked through the terminal at Wichita Mid-Continental Airport at two thirty the following afternoon, dressed in a white cotton skirt and a midnight-blue T-shirt that had more than one of the good old Kansas boys on the baggage-collection carousels taking long and considered looks.

Her red hair was fresh-washed and shining, her sun-glasses were propped up in her hair, and if this had been any place in the world except the depths of the American Mid-West, she would have been taken for a very high-quality whore.

Ed was waiting for her outside, standing by his Caprice stationwagon, smoking a small cigar. When she came through the doors and hesitated, looking this way and that for somebody to help her, he stepped forward, tipped his hat, and said in an exaggerated drawl, 'Mrs McIntosh? Mrs McIntosh from Washington?'

She blinked at him, grinned, and then offered her hand. 'You must be Mr Hardesty. Well, how do you do? You're a lot smarter than I thought you were going to be. I expected somebody with chaff in their hair.'

'Oh, no, ma'am,' said Ed, taking her suitcase. 'Having chaff in your hair is illegal in Kansas these days. You can serve three-to-five for actually looking like a hick.'

'Senator Jones was right,' said Della. 'He said you'd make a good figurehead for our Blight Crisis Appeal, and I believe you will. Mind you, I haven't really heard you speak yet.'

'As long as I don't have to come out with all that sincere young farmer bit that Peter Kaiser was trying to lay on me, I don't mind what I do,' said Ed. He ushered Della around the car and opened the passenger door for her. She said, 'Thank you,' as she sat down, and he couldn't help noticing the way her skirt rode up over her long legs, and the full curves of her breasts. He closed the door, walked around the front of the car, and climbed in next to her.

'I told Dr Benson you were coming,' said Ed, as he pulled out into the airport traffic. 'He was out at Garden City last night, at the state experimental farm. Apparently they've been making some interesting progress on breaking down the blight.'

'Really?' said Della. 'You told him I wanted to meet up with him as soon as possible?'

'He says tomorrow evening. He has to go to Hays, too. That's where the agricultural experimental station is located. He doubts if he's going to be able to get back to Wichita until seven or eight.'

'He won't talk to the press before then?' asked Della. She pulled down the sun-visor in front of her, and inspected her face in the mirror.

'I don't think so,' said Ed. 'Is it important?'

'Senator Jones thinks it's important,' Della told him, fussing with her hair. 'He doesn't want anybody to panic about this blight.'

'Oh, no?'

Della glanced at him. 'The blight's serious, but it's not *that* serious. Senator Jones believes the most important priority is for Kansas farmers to get their compensation. If there's a panic, it won't help to bring in the contributions. That's all.'

'I see,' said Ed.

'I hope you do,' Della told him. 'Particularly since your whole livelihood depends on it.'

'You're trying to tell me what my livelihood depends on? If I gave up farming, I could quite easily go back to being an actuary.'

'An actuary? Are you serious?'

'Never more so. You used to be a newspaper reporter, didn't you?'

'I was until two days ago.'

'Peter Kaiser said that Senator Jones had won you over to the cause of helping us Kansas farmers by the sheer emotion of his appeal. Is that right?'

Della shrugged. 'You could call it sheer emotion.'

Ed brought the wagon to a halt at a red light. 'What else could you call it?' he asked her.

'Influence,' she said. 'Senator Jones is a very influential man.'

'Is he really serious about helping us? I mean – is this Blight Crisis Appeal genuine?'

'Oh, yes. It's genuine, all right.'

They headed out on Route 54 westwards, into Kingman County. The highway was almost deserted except for occasional trucks.

Ed said, 'You come from Kansas?'

'Oklahoma originally. I'm a one hundred per cent natural Okie.'

'How come you got yourself mixed up with a man like Shearson Jones?'

She smiled. 'Nobody gets themselves mixed up with Shearson Jones. If Shearson Jones wants to have you around, then he'll have you around. If he doesn't, you could no more get to see him than the Pope. Even the president doesn't get to talk to Shearson Jones whenever he wants to.'

'Sounds like a biggie.'

'Oh, yes,' grinned Della. 'He's a biggie, all right.'

The telephone rang in Peter Kaiser's office. Without taking his eyes off the reports he was reading, Peter picked it up and said, 'Yes?'

Karen's voice told him, 'It's Professor Protter for you, from the Federal Laboratories.'

'About time too,' said Peter. 'Put him through, will you?'

'Yes, Mr Kaiser,' said Karen, in a tone that only slightly reproved him for what had happened last night. She didn't want to make him feel too bad after all. But his clumsy attempt at seduction couldn't go completely without comment. He could easily have driven her back to her apartment, and tried to make a play for her there, instead of trying to scramble on top of her in the car. She had stopped petting in pull-offs when she was sixteen, and she had told him so.

She listened in to the telephone as Professor Protter said, 'Peter? I've got some preliminary results for you.'

'That's excellent,' said Peter. 'What kept you?'

'Nothing *kept* us,' Professor Protter retorted, testily. 'We've had a staff of ten people working on the samples all night. I don't think you quite understand what's involved in these tests.'

'I understand that Senator Jones asked for the results urgently.'

'Well, that's all very fine. But Senator Jones doesn't know one end of an electron microscope from the other.'

'He does know who pays your salary, Professor. He also knows who used to pay your daughter's salary. Now, what about these results?'

'They're not definite, by any means. Only conjecture, based on the broad outlines of what we've been able to discover so far.'

'In other words, you're not prepared to stand by what you say?'

'In other words, Peter, they're the best that scrupulous and conscientious scientists can do when they're put under pressure by a politician whose motives are mainly financial.'

Peter Kaiser sighed. 'All right, Professor. You can spare me the puritanical rhetoric. What have you managed to conjecture so far?'

'The samples we were sent by Dr Benson in Kansas have almost certainly been affected by a species of crop virus. The virus has been isolated under the electron microscope, and although we're not sure exactly what it is, or where it

108

comes from, there isn't any doubt that it's extremely active and extremely dangerous to cereal crops. It can spread as quickly as the most virulent of human diseases, and we're surprised that it didn't sweep through the wheatfields in Kansas more quickly.'

'You don't know how it originated? Whether it was natural or not?' asked Peter.

Professor Protter hummed for a moment in uncertainty. 'I'd hate to commit myself,' he said, 'but several of the wheat samples from Kansas had traces of some thin gelatinous substance on them – partly decomposed. Professor Gulaski has been running several tests on it, and he thinks it could be some kind of base material in which the virus was carried, and sprayed on to the crops. He's only guessing, of course, but one of his experiments indicates that the substance slowly breaks down under the influence of ultra-violet light.'

'What are you trying to suggest?' asked Peter. 'This virus was sprayed on to the crops on *purpose*?'

'That's a remote possibility, yes,' Professor Protter told him. 'Depending on how slowly the base substance was designed to deteriorate, it could have been sprayed sometime during the spring, when the first shoots of the wheat were coming up. Whoever did it could have easily prepared the gelatinous base according to the average number of hours of sunlight expected in Kansas, so that when the wheat was ripe, the virus broke out. It wouldn't even have been necessary to spray every farm at the same time to have the virus break out simultaneously. All they had to do was alter the composition of the gelatine to break down more quickly, or more slowly, or whatever they wanted. Anyone with a reasonably expert knowledge of virology and the preparation of photographic emulsions could have done it.'

Peter sat back in his seat. 'You know what this means, don't you? You know what you're saying?'

'I fully understand all the implications of everything I've suggested,' said Professor Protter. 'But I must repeat that so far it's only guesswork – and by my usual standards, pretty wild guesswork. We may still find that this gelatinous material is completely unconnected with the virus.'

'What about the samples from Iowa? The corn, and the soybeans? And all that stuff they were supposed to be sending you from California?'

Professor Protter paused for a moment, while he consulted his notes. 'We haven't run tests on everything yet. We just haven't had the time. But we've examined some grapes from Bakersfield, California, and there isn't any question at all that they've been attacked by a similar species of virus.'

Peter was silent. It seemed as if Dr Benson's first guess at the cause of the blight had been correct. It *was* a virus – and even more frighteningly, it *had* been spread deliberately.

Professor Protter said, 'It wouldn't have needed much spraying to start the virus off, you know. Just a couple of acres out of each farm. Once the virus gets going, it's almost unstoppable. We reckon it can ruin an acre of prime wheat in two to three hours.'

'All right,' said Peter, distractedly. 'Thanks for everything you've done. You'll complete those tests on the rest of that California crop, won't you? And you'll remember that you're bound to complete secrecy by federal law?'

'I won't forget,' said Professor Protter, sourly. 'Although how you're going to keep the lid on a nationwide blight for very much longer, I don't have any idea. I've already had the newspapers and the television stations calling me here.'

'We don't want panic,' Peter told him. 'If people start to panic, they're going to rush around to their local supermarkets and empty the shelves in an hour. Once the president knows what's going on, he'll probably want to issue rationing instructions.'

There was a silence, and then Professor Protter said, 'The president doesn't *know*?'

'Of course the president knows. He's aware of the blight, and he's aware that it's spreading, but he gets all his information from the Department of Agriculture, and so far we've tried to keep the blight in perspective.'

'In perspective?' asked Professor Protter. 'Don't you know what's going on out there? We may have lost fifteen per cent of our annual crops already!'

'Professor Protter,' said Peter, tersely, 'you're paid to find out what causes crop diseases, and to suggest antidotes – not to indulge yourself in wild political speculation.'

'Sometimes a job goes beyond what you're paid to do,' retorted Professor Protter.

'And sometimes a job can disappear under your feet,' snapped Peter. 'Shearson wants the wraps on this blight until he's ready to instruct the president himself, and if you try to blow it before then, you're going to find yourself cultivating your own backyard for a living.'

'I'll call you later,' said Professor Protter, and banged the phone down.

Peter sat at his desk for a while, pulling at the skin of his face in suppressed tension. Then he jabbed the button for Karen's phone.

'Karen? What's the latest on the fund?'

'I don't know exactly, Mr Kaiser. Do you want me to find out?'

'I wouldn't have asked if I hadn't wanted you to.'

'I'll check it right away. Oh – and by the way – *The New York Times* agricultural correspondent is holding on extension four.'

'Tell him I'm out.'

'This is the seventh time he's called today, Mr Kaiser. He's beginning to think you've got something to hide.'

Peter frowned. 'What do you mean by that?'

'Nothing, Mr Kaiser. They were his words.'

'All right. Put him through. Oh, and Karen – '

'Yes, Mr Kaiser?'

'Last night – '

'Don't even mention it, Mr Kaiser.'

'But I wanted to show you how sorry I was for my clumsiness. I got carried away, I guess. It's the strain of this blight crisis business. I thought maybe I could make up for it.'

'I don't know how, Mr Kaiser,' said Karen.

'You can stop calling me "Mr Kaiser" for beginners. My name's Peter. And for seconds, why don't you come to Kansas with me over the week-end to meet Senator Jones?

He's spending the week-end at Fall River, and we're bound to have a terrific time. When Senator Jones entertains, he really entertains.'

Karen hesitated. Then she said, 'I'll think about it. Okay? And don't blame yourself for last night. Everybody makes *faux pas* once in a while.'

Peter grimaced. 'All right, Karen,' he said. 'If you want to come, just book yourself a seat. I want to leave by nine o'clock Friday night. And don't forget to rent a car from Wichita to take us to Fall River.'

'Very good, Mr Kaiser. I'm just putting *The New York Times* through now.'

It was Bill Brinsky, a hoarse-voiced veteran reporter whom Peter had run up against more than once. Bill Brinsky's thirst for Chivas Regal was legendary, but as Peter had once discovered to his cost, it didn't matter how many whiskies you bought him, and how sozzled he appeared to be, he always sat down to his typewriter with a clear head and a very sharp way of setting out the truth.

'Bill,' said Peter, with a high note of false jollity. 'How are you doing?'

'I'm doing a lot of waiting and a lot of running around, Peter,' said Bill, in a harsh, barely courteous tone. 'I've been trying to get the facts on this blight of yours, and I'm beginning to feel like a Cherokee Indian riding round and around a circle of wagons. I know there are scalps in there, Peter, but I can't get at them.'

'Have you talked to the press office at the Department?'

'Oh, sure. Yesterday, and this morning, *and* early this afternoon. It's always the same story. "Yes, Mr Brinsky, there *is* a serious blight. Yes, Mr Brinsky, it *is* still spreading. Yes, Mr Brinsky, there *have* been outbreaks in other states apart from Kansas. No, Mr Brinsky, we *do* have the whole situation completely under control. And, no, Mr Brinsky, we *don't* expect a national shortfall of more than ten per cent."'

'That sounds fair enough to me,' said Peter. 'They're the facts as we know them.'

'They're not *facts*,' growled Bill. 'They're Department of

Agriculture bullshit. I've been calling stringers in Oregon and Washington and North Dakota and Wisconsin and California and all over. Sure, we've got ourselves a serious wheat blight in Kansas. But what about the sweet potato crop in North Carolina? What about the oranges and the tomatoes in Florida? What about the sugar-cane in the Mississippi delta, and the Louisiana rice? What about the grasses, too? Alfalfa, and timothy, and lespedeza?'

'Bill – ' interrupted Peter, 'before you give me a whole agricultural geography of the United States – let me tell you one thing. Every year, every single year, every crop in America suffers from losses through drought or blight or insect activity. A couple of years ago, we had an unusually high number of typhoons and storms. Orange groves in Florida lost thirteen point five per cent of their anticipated output. Wheat farms in North Dakota fell short by nearly twenty per cent. Far more than we're talking about today! But, all of a sudden, just because we have this very serious grain blight in Kansas, you and every other agricultural correspondent who's out looking for some page one limelight – all of a sudden, you look around and try to read a scare story into something that happens every single year!'

Bill Brinsky was silent for a second or two. Then he said, 'How much has Senator Jones's Blight Crisis Appeal Fund raised so far?'

'Three million, maybe a little more.'

'Only three million? I heard nearer ten.'

'Well, you know how people like to exaggerate.'

'I heard something else, too. I heard Senator Walsh from California was thinking of raising a similar fund for vegetable growers in *his* state and that Representative Yorty was planning on a compensation programme for soybean farmers in Iowa. I also heard that Senator Jones reminded both of those gentlemen that they owed him a favour for the help he gave them during that big commodity scam on the San Francisco stock market. And the result of that reminder was that Walsh and Yorty both agreed to delay launching their funds until Senator Jones's Blight Crisis Appeal reached pledges of twenty million dollars, with at least fifteen million dollars cleared through the bank.'

'You hear fairy tales,' said Peter, flatly.

'I do? Well, maybe I do. But what if I were to print those fairy tales exactly like fairy tales? "Once upon a time, there was a magic kingdom which was stricken down by a terrible blight . . . all of its crops died away on the branch . . . but the wicked viziers who ruled that land decided to make a whole heap of gold out of the disaster . . . they pretended that only three poor farmers had been stricken by the blight . . . and they asked everybody in the land to donate gold to these poor farmers . . . with every intention of keeping the gold for themselves."'

'You print anything like that and we'll sue you to death,' said Peter, in a totally cold voice.

'Are you going to try to stop me?'

'Listen to me, Bill, you don't have any substantive evidence and you know it, otherwise you wouldn't be talking fairy tales. I'll tell you what I'll do. If you give me your word that you'll hold back on all this innuendo you've heard – if you give me your word that you won't print any of it – then I'll guarantee you an exclusive copy of the federal laboratory report on the virus as soon as I get it. That'll be Monday morning, at the latest.'

'Virus?' asked Bill Brinsky. 'Did you say "virus"?'

Peter bit his tongue.

'Nobody said anything about a virus to me,' said Bill. 'Has somebody told you something I don't know?'

'All right, Bill,' said Peter. 'The federal laboratory has run some preliminary tests, and conjectured – only conjectured – that the Kansas wheat blight is a virus. You can print that if you like.'

'What about the other crop failures? Are they caused by a virus too?'

'Bill, the other crop failures are nothing more than natural wastage. I keep telling you.'

'All right,' said Bill, less aggressively, pleased with the tidbit of information that Peter had accidentally let slip. 'But don't forget that lab report on Monday, okay? I'll hold you to that.'

'You'll have it,' Peter told him. 'You know how straight we play the game here.'

'That's what I'm worried about,' said Bill.

By four o'clock that afternoon, the news media were beginning to smell a bigger story. Whatever reassurances the Department of Agriculture had been giving them over the past two days, it was inevitable that small-town reporters were going to visit the blighted farms all across Iowa and Nebraska and Kansas, and see the crops for themselves. From all over, they began to file human-interest stories about farmers who had been digging and tilling and ploughing for twenty years or more, only to lose everything they owned to the wildfire spread of the blight.

On the early evening news, there were pictures of blackened spinach crops, decaying corn, rotting oranges, and wilting lettuce. Later editions of *The New York Post* were running a front page which proclaimed: BLIGHT KOs CROPS – A LEAN YEAR AHEAD?

At six, the president called Alan Hedges, the chairman of the Agriculture Committee, into the Oval Office. Alan Hedges was a slow-speaking, white-haired, dignified old man from Alabama; while the president was short, clipped, and energetic, a liberal Democrat from New Hampshire.

The sun was falling across the White House lawns outside the Oval Office windows as Alan Hedges settled himself fastidiously into the studded leather chair facing the president's desk. The president stood with his hands clenched behind his back, staring out at the evening sky.

'Alan,' said the president at last, without turning around, 'I feel that you've been less than direct with me.'

'Oh?' asked Alan Hedges. He lifted a pair of wire-rimmed spectacles out of the breast pocket of his dark-grey suit, and wound them around his large red ears.

'The latest briefing that Shearson sent me about the wheat blight in Kansas suggested that the blight was restricted to the Mid-West, and that any outbreaks of blight in other areas were purely seasonal and usual. From what the newspapers and the television channels are now saying, it appears that you and Shearson have somewhat underestimated the extent of the blight. Wouldn't you say that was true?'

'Well, Mr President . . .' Alan Hedges began.

The president turned around. His iron-grey hair was cropped very short, and his face was as rugged as a boxer's. 'From what the newspapers and television channels are now saying, it appears that you and Shearson have been deliberately playing this whole thing down. Wouldn't you say *that* was true?'

Alan Hedges let a long sigh fall to the floor like a tired spaniel. 'Mr President, sir,' he said. 'It doesn't become any of us to over-react to the reality of a situation simply bacause the media see their chance to sell more newspapers or gain more viewers. Let me tell you something about agriculture. It's an up-and-down business. These days, we're used to having it up all the time. After the Second War, modern techniques improved farming beyond all imagination. Did you know that in nineteen forty-six this country couldn't expect more than twenty-six bushels of corn per acre? These days with hardier strains of crop and better techniques, we're getting ninety-seven bushels an acre, and more. And that's with only six man-hours, instead of one-hundred and eight. Did you know that in nineteen forty-six, the average US farm worker fed only eleven people with his efforts, but that nowadays he can feed fifty-two?'

'I know the agricultural capacity of my own country, Senator Hedges,' said the president, frostily. 'I just want to know how serious this blight situation actually is.'

'I'm trying to explain, sir,' said Hedges. 'What I'm saying is that by nineteen eighty expectations, we're going to suffer a loss of yield. But by nineteen seventy-two expectations, we're still going to do phenomenally well.'

'This isn't nineteen seventy-two,' snapped the president.

'No, sir, it isn't. But our food supply commitment isn't so much greater today that we can't cope with it. If you want, I have all the figures here. You can see for yourself that everything is under control. Unpleasant, yes, and very unfortunate for many farmers. But under control.'

The president made no move to take the buff-coloured

folder that Hedges offered him. After a few moments, Alan Hedges placed it carefully on the edge of the president's desk.

Hedges said, 'I'd very much appreciate it, Mr President, if you could make a statement tonight or tomorrow morning that places the whole blight question into its proper perspective. Otherwise we're going to have the newspapers full of scare stories, and we're going to find that all the reserves of food which ought to be carefully held back to keep the situation under control for next year – well, you know what people are like – they're going to panic and those reserves are going to dwindle away in front of our eyes. We wouldn't want to have a famine on our hands, would we?'

The president stood silently beside his desk for a long while. Then he said, 'Are you sure of what you're saying, Alan? You don't have any ulterior motives for playing this blight down?'

Alan Hedges blinked at him. 'Ulterior motives, Mr President?'

The president gave a quick, humourless smile. 'I want the Department of Agriculture to keep an hour-by-hour check on this blight, Senator. I want daily reports on any new outbreaks, and I want constantly updated estimates of this year's agricultural production. I'm also going to direct a special team to give me an assessment of the nation's grain and frozen food reserves, as well as canned and dried products. You know that Canada's suffering the same blight, don't you?'

'Yes, sir. I've already had reports from their agricultural people in Winnipeg.'

'Good. Make sure that any research materials are pooled, and that we keep a close eye on what they're doing.'

'Very good, Mr President. Will that be all?'

'Not quite, Alan. One of the reasons I called you in here alone was because this spectre of food shortages raises a very delicate issue. But I want to tell you that if any hint of what I have to say to you now were to leak out of this office, the consequences would be grave in the extreme.'

Alan Hedges said nothing, but took off his spectacles

and sat upright in his chair, listening.

'It's part of a president's duty to act with unnatural foresight,' said the president. 'Now, from what you've told me this afternoon, it seems as if there won't be any severe problems with food shortages during the coming months, provided everybody keeps his head. I'm going to commandeer a few minutes of television time tonight to do what you've suggested, and explain to the public at large that we don't have anything to worry ourselves about, at least for the time being. But there's one thing else I want you to do, and I want you to do it in complete secrecy.

'If things go wrong, and we do find ourselves drastically low on food, I want to make sure that the administrative centre of this country is well stocked with supplies. I want you to arrange for enough canned and dried foods to be shipped into Washington during the next two weeks to keep the senior executive staff of our major departments at a nutritional subsistence level for six months. Do it discreetly, by a variety of different methods of transport – train, airplane, ship, truck. And if anybody asks you what the supplies are for – just tell them they're for federal quality control tests. Something like that.'

'Am I going to see an Executive Order?' asked Alan Hedges, softly.

The president looked at him without any expression on his face at all. 'Take it as an Executive Understanding. The same way Hoover took Roosevelt's wire-tap instructions.'

'You think I'm deliberately underestimating this blight?' Alan Hedges wanted to know.

The President inclined his head in a gesture that could have meant anything at all. *I believe you, I don't believe you, what does it matter anyway?*

'Let me put it this way, Alan,' he said. 'If this nation is going to be threatened by severe shortages, it's going to need a vigorous, active, and healthy government. That's all I'm going to say on the matter.'

'Very well, Mr President,' said Alan Hughes, getting up from his chair. 'If that's the way the management of this theatre wants it, that's the way it's going to be.'

Out at South Burlington, Ed had been giving Della McIntosh a tour of the blighted crops. It was almost dark as they drove back to the farmhouse, and the headlights of the Jeep jounced and flickered across the devastated fields.

'Have you noticed something?' said Ed, pointing to the beams of the headlights. 'No moths.'

Della looked at him. 'Do you think the virus might have killed them, too?'

'It's possible. Maybe they just don't like dank, decaying wheatlands.'

The lights were shining in the house with deceptive normality as they parked outside on the red asphalt yard and stepped down from the Jeep. Della untied the scarf from her red hair, and said, 'I guess I'd better be getting back to Wichita. What's the time?'

'Eight-thirty. But you don't have to go all the way back into the city. You could stay here.'

'I have a room booked at the Mount Vernon Inn.'

'So what? I'll call and tell them you couldn't make it. It's a hell of a boring drive back into Wichita at this time of night.'

'Well . . .' said Della. 'I'm supposed to be preparing an objective assessment of your suitability as a figurehead for Shearson's fund.'

'What's non-objective about staying for dinner and sleeping overnight? Dilys is a great hand at fresh pecan pie.'

Della laughed. 'In that case, you have utterly persuaded me. Pecan pie is my third greatest weakness.'

They walked across to the farmhouse, and stepped up on to the verandah. 'I don't suppose I dare to ask what your first two greatest weaknesses are,' smiled Ed.

She paused, her red hair wild and curly in the light of the verandah lamp, her big breasts emphasised by the slanting shadows. She was just the opposite of Season in so many ways – direct, relaxed, and noticeably at home in rural surroundings. Ed had noticed the way she had run an appreciative hand over a hand-made saddle that had been lying in the back of the Jeep.

'My second greatest weakness is the country,' she said.

'You see that moon up there? That big harvest moon? That's a real Kansas and Oklahoma moon. You don't see anything like that in Washington, or New York City.'

They were just about to go inside when Jack Marowitz drove up in his yellow Pinto, climbed out, and slammed the door.

'Ed?' he asked. 'You got a moment?'

'Sure, Jack. Della – this is Jack Marowitz, my technical genius. Jack, this is Mrs Della McIntosh. She's working with Senator Jones on the Blight Crisis Fund.'

'Pleased to know you,' said Jack, shaking Della by the hand. 'Listen, Ed – can you give a minute of your time? No offence meant, Mrs McIntosh – but alone?'

'No offence taken,' said Della. 'Maybe I'll just go right along inside and introduce myself to your mother.'

'That's a nice idea,' said Ed. 'I won't keep you long.'

Della went inside, and the screen door banged behind her. Then Ed said, 'What's the problem, Jack? You look like you've seen a ghost.'

'It's a theory,' said Jack. 'That's all it is. But somehow it seems to make a whole lot of sense.'

'Go on.'

'Have you been into Willard's house lately?'

'Sure. I was there last night. We had a drink together, Willard and me and Dyson Kane.'

'Okay – then you can remember what's on the wall.'

Ed frowned. 'What's on the wall? What do you mean – wallpaper?'

'No, no. Pictures. Think of what pictures he's got on his wall.'

'I don't know . . . he's got a picture of Nanette . . . and that oil painting of Mount Sunflower . . . I can't think of anything else.'

'An aerial view of South Burlington, right?'

'Yes, that's right. Yes, that's over the fireplace.'

'Well – who took that aerial picture?'

'I don't know. It was taken earlier this year, wasn't it? I think I was away in New York, clearing up some business. I remember Mom mentioning it to me . . . she was real pleased with it . . . but that's all.'

120

Jack was very intense and excited. 'Listen,' he said, 'that aerial photograph was taken by a company called Your Spread From The Sky, Inc. They operated out of the airfield at Salina for about a year, touring Kansas and taking aerial pictures of people's farms and houses.'

'How do you know that?' asked Ed.

'Their name's printed on the bottom of the photograph. Your Spread From The Sky, Inc., Salina, Kansas. I talked to Willard about it, and he said that what they did was fly over your spread in a light plane – bright red, it was, with something like Aerial Photographs written on the side of it in white. They took a whole lot of colour pictures, and then sent you a sheet of proofs in the mail. If you wanted to buy a blow-up picture of your farm, you sent them back fifteen dollars, and they printed it up for you.'

'So? I've heard of that kind of thing before.'

'Sure you have. It's very common, very ordinary. It's so common and ordinary that nobody's going to take any notice of it. But it's the only way I can think of that somebody could overfly this farm at a very low altitude and spray the kind of virus that Dr Benson seems to believe this is.'

Ed stared at him. 'Jack,' he said, 'you've got your head in the right place. You're damn right that's the only way that anybody could do it. All the time I've been trying to think of surreptitious ways somebody could have poisoned the crops – night spraying, or flying the stuff in on kites – and all the time they did it right out in the open. Or could have done, anyway. You're sure they're not legitimate?'

'I called their number at Salina. The operator told me they were gone. Then I called the agency in charge of leasing hangars, and they said that Your Spread From The Sky, Inc. had operated out of Salina for three months and then moved out. All rent paid up to date, everything cleaned up, and no forwarding address. They had a telephone number in Chicopee, Massachusetts, but when I called it this afternoon, it turned out to be the College of Our Lady of the Elms.'

'Have you told anyone else about this? Dr Benson?'

'Not yet, Ed. I wanted to talk to you first. And I didn't

like to make too much of a song and dance about it, in case I turned out to be wrong. I did call Walter Klugman, though, at Penalosa; and John Cafferty, out at Ninnescah Creek; and they've both had aerial pictures taken by the same people. All straight, all efficient, everybody got their photographs and everybody was satisfied. Whoever set it up was a real professional.'

Ed rubbed his chin. He had shaved in a hurry that morning, and it was rough with stubble. 'Keep this to yourself for the moment, Jack,' he said. 'But do me a favour and call the Wheat Growers' Association in North Dakota tomorrow. See if they'll give you the names and telephone numbers of a couple of farmers up there, and check whether they've had aerial photographs taken or not. And you could do the same for a couple of corn and soybean farmers in Iowa while you're at it.'

'You're not going to try playing detective?' asked Jack. 'I mean – once we're fairly certain, I think we ought to turn this all over to the Department of Agriculture, don't you?'

'In time,' nodded Ed. 'But right at this moment, I'm just finding out one or two things about the Department of Agriculture, and I think I'd like to wait a while before we blithely hand them everything we know.'

'What do you mean?'

'I'm not sure. But I can't quite make up my mind what Senator Shearson Jones is up to. I can't believe he's organising this appeal fund for our benefit alone. Not just a few Kansas farmers with the seats out of their pants. And why has he played down this blight so much to the media? I can look out there tomorrow, when the sun comes up, and see nothing but ten miles of blackened fields. It's the same all over Kansas, and it's probably just as bad everywhere else. How come nobody seems to be excited? How come Shearson Jones can talk about a shortfall as low as eight per cent? The wheat harvest's dead, Jack, in the space of a few days, and in my book that's one hundred per cent shortfall. That's disaster.'

Jack nodded towards the house. 'You think this Mrs McIntosh is going to tell you anything?'

'I don't know. She's an Oklahoma lady, so maybe she might.'

'Good luck,' said Jack, tipping his hat in semi-serious respect. 'From the looks of her, I think you may need it.'

Eleven

Over dinner, Ursula Hardesty warmed to Della McIntosh very quickly. Ursula had been a farmer's wife, after all, and she liked plain speaking and she liked to talk about the land. She even found that she and Della had friends in common – remote friends, the Shaughnessys of Kansas City – but friends all the same.

Ursula wore a powder-blue dress with silver stitching – a dress about which Season had always said, 'It's terrific taste if you're planning on taking a time machine back to nineteen fifty-eight.' Della had taken her suitcase up to the wide back-bedroom which overlooked the meadow where they usually landed the helicopter, and she had changed into a simple low-cut dress of bottle-green satin. She had bought the dress especially for this week-end, to impress Shearson.

Perhaps Ursula wasn't aware of Della's shining red hair and her big, firm breasts. Perhaps she wasn't aware of the way Della's lips glistened moistly in the candlelight, and the way that she spoke to Edward in such a careful, modulated voice. But Ed doubted it. He knew that his mother liked Della a lot. She was a country girl, for all her involvement in Washington; and South Burlington Farm, in Ursula's opinion, badly lacked the attention of a country girl.

At nine-thirty, Ursula declared her intention of going to bed. She was going to return to her house in Independence in the morning, and 'leave Edward in peace.' Ed had never seen her retire so early, or in such good humour. He kissed her evasively, and said, 'Good night, Mother,' and she smiled at him as she left the room.

'You want a brandy?' he asked Della, as he led her into

the living-room. 'It's quite a civilised label. I didn't distil it myself.'

'I'd love one,' she said, and watched him as he went to the drinks cabinet to pour it. 'This is a very attractive house, you know. Dignified but friendly.'

'Well, that's us Hardestys all over,' smiled Ed, handing Della her drink. He sat down beside her on the sofa.

'Shearson Jones seems to be very taken with you,' said Della. 'He thinks you'll make an excellent figurehead for this Blight Crisis Appeal.'

'He does? And what do *you* think?'

'I think he's right. Now I've seen you, I can vouch for his intuition. He was a little worried you might look like Quasimodo, but since you clearly don't – well, I think you're just the man.'

'What are his plans?' asked Ed, sipping brandy, and looking at Della over the shining rim of his glass.

'He wants you to make a live TV broadcast from Fall River on Saturday afternoon. As far as I know they've written the script already. It won't be anything ridiculous or schmaltzy. All they'll ask you to say is that you're a young Kansas wheat farmer, that you've dedicated your life to cultivating your farm, and that through no fault of your own you've now found yourself flat busted. That's it.'

Ed sat back. 'That sounds simple enough. Is it going to be networked?'

'Coast-to-coast, as far as we know.'

Ed nodded. 'That sounds okay.'

There was a silence, and then he said: 'What's a pretty girl like you doing with a character like Shearson Jones anyway? He's a major-league heavy, isn't he? And not just politically, either. From what I've seen of him on television, he's not exactly the world's skinniest man. How come you're working for someone like that?'

'I wasn't, until Wednesday.'

'But why? I don't know much about him, but from what I've heard he's pretty hard to get near. The only way I got through to him in the first place was because my daddy helped him with some wheat-dumping deal. I don't understand why you're hanging around a man like that.'

Della shrugged. 'It's the power, I guess. The influence. It's very intoxicating.'

'Even more intoxicating than good country air?'

She looked up at him. 'What does that mean?'

'I don't know,' he said. 'Whatever you want it to mean.'

'You're a married man, aren't you?' she reminded him. 'A married man with a young daughter of six.'

'You want to talk about families?'

Della held her glass of brandy up to the light. An amber reflection curved across her cheek. 'No,' she said. 'Not particularly.'

They sipped their drinks in silence for a few minutes and then Ed said, 'What does Shearson Jones want out of this fund? Can you tell me that?'

'Prestige,' said Della. 'Votes. It's all very good for the public image.'

'Is that why he's working so hard to suppress the truth about this blight? How serious it is, and how wide it's spread?'

Della blushed. 'I wasn't aware he'd done anything like that.'

'Wouldn't you, if you were in his position? Let's face it, the moment the public realises how many crops have been destroyed, they're not going to worry about Ed Hardesty and Walter Klugman and all the other poor jugheads of Kingman County, are they? They're going to start worrying about themselves.'

Della said, 'I think this blight's spread much faster than Shearson expected it to. He thought he'd have two or three clear weeks at least. Now it looks like a matter of days. But he's collected something like eleven million dollars already, and if you do well on the television on Saturday – well, that could jump to twenty or thirty million.'

Ed set down his glass. 'He's got eleven million already?'

'That's right.'

'Well, that explains a lot,' said Ed.

Della leaned over towards him. 'Don't think too badly of Shearson, Ed. He's all kinds of things, but he's also a very professional and dedicated politician.'

Ed found himself looking into Della's eyes, very closely.

'You're an interesting woman,' he said. 'I didn't know they bred them as interesting as you in Oklahoma.'

'We're not all hayseeds,' she said. 'And my mother was Miss Oklahoma City, nineteen fifty-one.'

'You're aiming higher than that, huh?'

'I could be.'

They had known what was going to happen from the moment Ed had invited her to stay over. All through dinner their conversation had been leading inevitably to this one moment. Ursula had helped it to happen, too, by her active approval of everything that Della had said and done. She had smiled at Della with a toothy expression that could only be interpreted one way: wouldn't I have loved to have *you* as a daughter-in-law?

Ed said, 'You must be tired.'

'Not too tired,' said Della, throatily.

Ed stood up, walked across to the drinks cabinet, and poured himself another brandy. 'Like you said,' he told her, 'I'm a married man with a young daughter of six.'

'I'm not forcing you to do anything you don't want to do,' Della said.

He turned, and looked at her, and then gave her a wry smile. 'No,' he said, 'I know you're not. But you must have guessed where my marriage is at, right now. And at times like this, I guess everybody's looking for a little reassurance, and a little consolation, and maybe a little excitement, too.'

'You think I'm exciting? Miss *Kansas City Herald-Examiner*, as was? Shearson Jones's private messenger lady?'

'Yes,' he said.

'What about your mother?'

'She takes enough sleeping-pills to knock out a rhinoceros. Apart from that, she likes you.'

'She likes me that much?'

He walked back to the sofa, and stood close beside her. 'Does it matter?' he asked her, quietly.

'No,' she said. 'It doesn't.'

Ed leaned forward and kissed Della on the forehead, just below the line of her bright coppery hair. It started off as a

126

chaste kiss; as a kiss of friendly affection and nothing more. But she put her arm around his neck, so that he couldn't break away from her, and she raised her lips to him, very soft and very moist and very willing. He hesitated for a moment, and then he kissed her again, and this time it was a long, searching, devouring kiss, a kiss that meant I want you, however wrong it might be. A kiss of lust, and shared frustrations, and sheer excitement at making love to someone new.

'Let's take a bath,' whispered Della. 'I've been flying, and taking a look around your farm and I've been looking forward to a bath all afternoon.'

'All right,' said Ed. 'A bath it is.'

They went upstairs together, Ed leading Della by the hand up the galleried staircase, until they came to the rococo bedroom. Della said, 'Quite a place,' as Ed showed her through to the bathroom.

'Season designed it. She visited the Palace of Versailles once, on a trip to France, and I think it made a lasting impression.'

They went into the bathroom. The tub itself was midnight blue, and the wallpaper was an Osborne & Little design from England, blue peacocks strutting across a white background, like a Rorschach print of stately elegance. Ed ran the faucets, and sifted Swiss herb salts into the water. Della stood before the mirror, tidying her hair.

'I'm surprised you took this farm on,' said Della.

'Oh?' asked Ed. 'Why?'

She turned away from the mirror. 'You seem to like classy living as much as the next man. You're not dumb. So why maroon yourself out here in Kansas, away from civilisation, and theatres, and anything that's anything?'

Ed unbuttoned his shirt. 'Land, and growing things, they're as much a part of what makes this country worth living in as theatre and smart restaurants. And, in any case, I guess every actuary's a dumb hick at heart.'

'Oh, yeah?' she asked, raising an eyebrow. 'Well, I hope you're not too dumb and hickish to unzipper my gown for me.'

She turned around, lifted her hair up from the nape of

her neck, and presented her back to him. He stood right behind her, watching both of their faces in the bathroom mirror. The steam from the hot water was already misting the edges of the glass so that it looked like an old and romantic photograph.

Ed tugged the zipper right down the curved small of her back. Then he gently slipped the straps off her shoulders, and pulled down the front of her gown, baring her breasts. In the mirror, he could see how large and rounded they were, and how wide her pink areolas spread. He watched his hand reach around her, and clasp her left breast as if it were a heavy, ripe fruit.

Della stretched her neck back, and kissed him. He pulled her gown right down, and she was standing in front of the mirror naked. The shape of her pale body was punctuated only by the petal-pink spots of her nipples and the gingery plume of her pubic hair.

They said nothing. There was nothing for them to say. Ed stripped off his shirt, and took down his pants. Then he sat on the edge of the tub and clasped Della around the waist, pulling her towards him, so that at last she lowered herself on his lap. As the steam from the running water gradually hazed up the bathroom mirror completely, they were able to see Della opening her thighs wide, and straddling Ed's legs, so that the dark hard head of his penis could slide its way between the rose-coloured lips of her vulva, right up as far as his black-haired balls; but then they could make out nothing more than two blurred impressionistic figures, two different patterns reflected in a surface like breathed-on mercury.

Ed clutched Della's soft, big breasts, resting his cheek against her back and thrusting and thrusting until he felt that it wasn't humanly possible to thrust any deeper. Della threw her head from one side to the other, gasping and shuddering with the feeling of what Ed was doing to her. And when Ed at last ejaculated, she bent forward and said, 'Oh, that's beautiful,' even though she hadn't reached a climax herself.

Afterward, they sat in the bedroom, wrapped in huge soft yellow towels, watching each other with new awareness. Della hadn't told him yet, but she didn't want to sleep with him in his marital bed. The act would only have been symbolic, but it was more than she felt he was prepared to give her, and more than she was prepared to take – at least until they knew each other better.

Ed said, 'Was I better than Shearson Jones?'

She looked at him wide-eyed. 'How do you know I've ever made love to Shearson Jones?'

'Have you?'

She smiled at him. Not too broadly. She didn't want to antagonise him. 'Would it matter to you if I had?'

'I don't know,' he said. 'Maybe I'm being ridiculously jealous, the way most new lovers are.'

'Well,' she said. 'Shearson Jones has plenty of enviable things in his life. Money, power, influence, and scores of women. But you have plenty of enviable things, too. A farm, and a beautiful wife, and a lovely daughter.'

'What are you trying to do?' Ed asked her. 'Make me eat ashes for what we just did?'

'How could I? We both wanted it and we both enjoyed it. And that's as far as it has to go. No guilt. No recriminations. No nothing.'

'Are you really that blasé?' he wanted to know.

She shook her head. 'I'm not blasé at all. If I was blasé, I'd cling on to you for all I was worth. I wouldn't care about who you were, and what your farm meant to you. I wouldn't care about your wife or your daughter.'

'You don't care now. Don't give me that.'

'I do care, as a matter of fact, because I think you're somebody special. You're a nice man. Good-looking, hard-working, and prepared to fight for what you believe in. I wanted to make love with you because I wanted to please you and I wanted to please myself. Now, it's over.'

'You mean we're never going to make love again?'

'How do I know? I thought it was up to the man to do all the chasing.'

He frowned, and rubbed the back of his hair with his towel. Then he grinned, and chuckled.

'You know what you are, don't you?' he asked her.

'What am I?'

'You're beautiful. That's all. Just beautiful.'

On Friday morning, the president called a delayed news conference and informed the White House Press Corps that he had been holding 'urgent and concerned meetings' with the Department of Agriculture, and that he had also talked directly on the telephone with the governors of nine states, including Kansas, Iowa, Montana, Washington, California, and Florida. The damage to crops caused by various blights and diseases was 'difficult to assess in terms of the nation's foreseeable lunchpail' – a phrase which he would later have cause to regret he had ever spoken, and not just for grammatical reasons, either. But most of the governors had believed that the blight situation was 'containable' and that food stocks were generally high enough to see them through until next year's spring crops.

What none of the governors realised was that the blight crisis was already well beyond disaster level. Most of their state agricultural departments had sent samples of the mystifying disease to Washingon for assessment, but Washington had so far given them nothing in return except the words of Shearson Jones – that the federal researchers were 'on the brink of solving the problem' and that 'the agricultural cavalry is on the way.'

By Friday, the truth was that the blight had spread so terrifyingly quickly over crops of all kinds that some kind of antidote treatment would have to be applied by the following Tuesday at the latest to save even fifty per cent of the nation's expected food production. And despite the reassuring words of Shearson Jones – on which the state governors had based their opinion that the situation was reasonably under control – there was no chance at all that an antidote could be manufactured in sufficient quantities to meet that deadline, even if an antidote were discovered at all.

The media, too, had been lulled into thinking that the blight story was nothing more than a passing problem – like a hurricane, or a snowstorm. It was beyond the imagination of most newspaper and television editors to interpret American life as anything more than a series of

130

transitory crises – headlines that were fresh one day and stale the next. They still hadn't been able to grasp that the blight could irrevocably alter the whole structure of western society in the time it usually took for the average American to work up an appetite for his next meal. Shearson Jones said nothing to disabuse them, and for lunch on Friday he ate turtle soup, two roasted squab, and a peach crab lantern.

On Friday afternoon, CBS News reported in a special bulletin that the president was now 'carefully optimistic' about the national shortfall in food production. Senator Shearson Jones was going to Kansas for the week-end, and he would make a full broadcast about the crisis on Sunday night, when he had been able to judge the effects of the blight first-hand.

Early on Friday evening, a California wine grower went out into his blighted vineyard in the Napa Valley and blew most of his own head off with a 12-bore shotgun. His distraught wife told police that they had struggled for fifteen years to cultivate their own distinctive wines, and that this year had been 'make or break' year for their winery.

In Washington, the Federal Crop Insurance Programme announced that 'very careful screening' would have to be given to claims for blighted crops. It was possible that claims would be so heavy this year that the programme would not be able to meet all of them out of its own resources.

In Washburn, North Dakota, a farmer called his local radio station to say that the crop blight was caused by 'bacteria from the moon rocks.' All the moon rocks should be gathered up at once and fired back into space he insisted.

In Georgetown, shortly after six o'clock, Shearson Jones's telephone rang, and Billy, his manservant, went to answer it.

It was Peter Kaiser. He wanted to know if Shearson was still on schedule for the nine o'clock flight from Dulles to Wichita Mid-Continent Airport. Shearson had just come out of the shower, and he was wrapped in a silk Chinese robe with an electric-blue dragon twisting its way around it. He was smoking a large cigar and he smelled of Signoricci II.

'I'll be there,' he told Peter Kaiser. 'Barring an act of God, or an unforeseeable disaster.'

'What about a foreseeable lunchpail?' asked Peter Kaiser.

Shearson chuckled. 'Wasn't that the worst speech ever? I'm surprised the TV people haven't picked it up already. If we didn't have this Blight Crisis Appeal going, I'd have gone right in there and torn it to shreds myself. A chicken in every pot, and a mirage in every lunchpail. How that stuffed dummy ever got to be president is beyond me.'

'He was voted in,' said Peter.

'No, he wasn't. His opponents were voted out. Anyway, I don't want to talk about him. Tell me how the fund's going.'

Peter paused as he shuffled through his accounts. Eventually, he said, 'As of this afternoon, when the banks closed, we had seven million dollars already credited to the Blight Crisis account by special clearance. There were still two million dollars outstanding, and the bank doesn't expect that money to be through until Tuesday or Wednesday.'

'What about the Michigan Tractor contribution?'

'That could take longer. You know what they're like. Their board hardly ever agrees to meet in emergency session; and when they do, they've got five major subsidiaries to take into account. We'll be lucky if we get their cheque for a week, maybe longer.'

'But they've offered us two million.'

'I know, Senator. That's why they're taking so long about it.'

'Damn,' breathed Shearson. 'I don't know how much longer we can keep this whole balloon flying. Seven million is a hell of a lot less than I was counting on. And we're going to lose a million at least in administrative expenses and commissions.'

'I'm sorry, Senator,' said Peter. 'I'm doing my very best

to get the money cleared promptly. But I've only had three days, and it's a miracle we've gotten so much already. There were twenty-eight corporations involved in raising that seven million. Most of them were already on my list of over-profitables, and they couldn't get rid of the money fast enough. But from now on in, we're going to have a far tougher time.'

'To be quite frank, Peter, I don't think there's going to *be* any "from now on in",' breathed Shearson, puffing at his cigar. 'I've done what I can to keep this blight in the right kind of perspective, but if the media don't realise what's going on by the middle of next week, then they're even dumber than I always thought they were.'

'The president seems to think it's all under control,' said Peter.

'The president's scared shitless, and he's clinging on to any and every optimistic statement that anybody comes up with,' retorted Shearson. 'How can he possibly turn around to the people of the greediest nation on the face of this earth and say, "I'm sorry, folks, but you're going to have to do without bread, or corn, or french fries, or Post Toasties"? He'd be dragged out of the White House and publicly crucified.'

'What about Protter?' asked Peter. 'Has he come up with anything yet? I asked him to call you direct if he did, in case I was out.'

'No. No word from Protter,' said Shearson. 'Listen – I'll meet up with you later. Right now I have to get myself dressed. But start thinking up ways to get that two million out of Michigan Tractors before mid-week.'

'Okay, Senator. I'll see you at the airport.'

Shearson put the phone down, but almost immediately it rang again. Billy walked across the parquet hallway with metal-tipped heels that methodically clicked, and picked up the receiver. He listened, and nodded, and finally he said to Shearson, 'It's Professor Protter. He says priority.'

'All right,' said Shearson. 'I'll take it. Bring me a tankard of Dom Perignon, will you? I'm as dry as a hog.'

Professor Protter sounded strained. 'Senator? I believe I may have some good news for you.'

133

'Good news?' asked Shearson, suspiciously.

'That's right. We've made some excellent progress on the virus. It was very fortunate. Almost an accident. But the net result is that we may be able to clear most of it up.'

Shearson sucked silently at his cigar.

'Are you there?' asked Professor Protter.

'I'm here,' said Shearson. 'Tell me what you've found out.'

'It was Dr Egan's idea, as a matter of fact. He sent a sample around to the Pentagon's bacteriological warfare centre, and asked if they could possibly identify it. They spent twenty-four hours going through ten different samples, and then they called us back and said there wasn't any doubt about it.'

'Well?' said Shearson, impatiently.

'It's an artificially cultivated virus which bears a strong resemblance to one of our own viruses called Vorar D. It was originally developed as a defoliant for Vietnam, but since then it's been taken through several different variants. It has the same effect as powdery mildew – it arrests photosynthesis in growing plants – but it also causes very rapid decay and breakdown of the cells. It's aerobic – which means that it's transmitted through the air – and it's not very easy to kill.'

'I thought you said we could clear most of it away.'

'I did. The Pentagon already have a formula for sterilising crops that have been infected by Vorar D, and they're pretty sure they can adapt it to clear away this particular variety. The only problem is that it's going to take some time.'

'I see,' said Shearson.

There was a lengthy silence. Then Professor Protter said, 'You don't sound as if you're particularly pleased.'

'Pleased? Of course I'm pleased,' said Shearson.

'Then what will you do? Will you call the president, and get the authorisation for the sterilising compound to be manufactured right away? Or what?'

'I hope you're not trying to dictate my course of action, Professor,' said Shearson, testily. 'I need to see a written report on this Vorar D before I can advise the president.

And what do we know about this sterilising compound? Federal restrictions are very tight on what we can spray on our crops and what we can't. Supposing it has dangerous side-effects? Supposing it pollutes water? Supposing it can cause malformation in unborn children?'

'It's been thoroughly tested,' said Professor Protter.

'Maybe it has, but you're talking about a variant of it. Come on, Professor, the lives and safety of millions of Americans are at stake here. You can't treat them like guinea-pigs in one of your laboratories.'

'Senator – it will take *weeks* to produce sufficient supplies of sterilising compounds and even longer to spray them over all the affected areas. If we don't set something in motion now, we may be too late. That's if we're not too late already.'

Billy arrived with a half-pint silver tankard of cold champagne, which he set down beside Shearson's telephone. Shearson snapped his fingers at him to bring him a taper for his cigar.

'What I want you to do, Professor – ' said Shearson, puffing at his cigar again, ' – what I want you to do is prepare me a complete file on what you've discovered so far. Then, when I come back from Kansas on Monday morning, I'll call a special meeting of the Agriculture Committee, and we can discuss what action we're going to take.'

'But Senator –'

'Don't "but Senator" me, Professor. Just do what you're told.'

'Senator, this is one time when I'm going to say no. The situation is urgent, we have the means to do something about it. Two days could make all the difference. I'm going to go way over your head with this information, and if I still don't get anywhere, I'm going to the press.'

'Professor,' rumbled Shearson, gently. 'I very much advise you against doing that.'

'Try and stop me,' snapped Professor Protter, and slammed his phone down.

Shearson held his own receiver in his hand for a few seconds, staring at it thoughtfully. Then, almost inaudibly, he said to Billy, 'Get me Peter Kaiser again.'

At eight forty-five p.m., Karen Fortunoff was still waiting by the gate at Dulles Airport for Peter Kaiser to join her. She was wearing a smart camel-coloured suit, and she had bought herself a new week-end case especially for the trip. The flight had already been called twice, and she didn't know if she ought to board the plane, with the risk that Peter wouldn't make it in time, and that she would have to fly to Wichita alone – or if she should wait for him to arrive, and risk missing the flight altogether.

Outside, in the darkness, the Tri-Star's engines were already whining, and she could see the last of the service vehicles driving away. She checked her watch. Maybe she should just forget the whole thing. She didn't particularly like Peter anyway. If she hadn't already told her friends that she was going to spend the week-end in the million-dollar vacation home of Senator Shearson Jones, and if she hadn't been so worried about keeping herself up-to-date on the blight crisis, she would have gone back to her apartment and resigned herself to another Saturday and Sunday doing the same old things. Reading, drawing, watching TV.

She went to the window and stared out at the aeroplane. Most of the passengers were already in their seats, and she could see the stewardess counting heads for cocktails. Reflected in the dark glass, she could see her own face, too, like a silent and inquisitive stranger.

She heard someone talking in a loud, harsh voice, and she turned around. With relief, but with apprehension, too, she saw Peter hurrying along the carpeted corridor. He had to hurry because he was trying to keep up with one of the airline's electric carts, on which in huge and weighty splendour sat Senator Shearson Jones, in a white suit as large as a circus marquee.

Peter gave Karen a quick half-smile when he saw her, and said, 'Hi. You made it, then?'

Karen said, 'Yes,' but she was more interested in the spectacle of Shearson Jones easing his bulky body from the cart and waddling sweatily towards the gate. She felt as if

136

she were in the presence of a political and physical phenomenon; a being who defied gravity and governments, both.

She didn't think at first that Shearson had noticed her, but as they followed him down the walkway to the aeroplane, the senator said loudly, without turning around, 'Who's the girl, Peter?'

'Karen Fortunoff,' said Peter. 'My head girl. Very efficient.'

'Good,' rumbled Shearson. 'I like to have pretty girls around me. I congratulate your taste.'

Peter took Karen's elbow as they boarded the plane. 'See?' he whispered. 'He likes you.'

Karen gave him an uneasy grin. 'As long as he doesn't *want* me, I don't mind.'
•

Dr Benson yawned as he walked along the corridor to his office in the Kansas Agricultural Research building. He could hear his telephone ringing but he wasn't going to hurry. He was too tired after driving all the way back from the experimental agricultural station near Hays, and all he wanted now was a cup of hot coffee, a bath, and six hours' sleep.

The phone was still ringing as he pushed open the door of his untidy office and threw his dogeared briefcase into a corner. He took off his car-coat, hung it up on the back of the door, and then shuffled through the heap of papers on his desk to see if the telephone was anywhere within easy reach. He found it at last, sniffed, and picked it up.

'Yes?' he asked, non-committally.

'Is that Dr Nils Benson?' asked an intent voice.

'Who wants him?'

'Professor Protter, from the Federal Agricultural Research laboratory in Washington.'

'Oh, I see. Then this is he. How do you do, Professor. I'm glad you called.'

Professor Protter sounded anxious. 'I'm glad you answered,' he said. 'I was just about to hang up.'

Dr Benson lifted his eyeglasses with his left hand and pinched the bridge of his nose to relieve the pressure of tiredness. 'I went out to the state experimental farm at Garden City, and then over to the experimental agricultural station at Hays. It's been a pretty exhausting couple of days. I only just walked into the office.'

'Have your state research people found anything out?'

'Not a lot,' said Dr Benson. 'But they confirmed the blight is a virus of some kind – which is what I originally guessed it to be. They're running more tests over the weekend.'

'Listen,' said Professor Protter, 'they're absolutely right when they say it's a virus. We took it to the chemical warfare people, and they identified it almost straight away as a new strain of Vorar D.'

'Vorar D? I read about that. So, I wasn't so far off target after all. I told one of our farmers here that the blight was probably started deliberately.'

'I'm not hazarding any guesses about how it was started,' said Professor Protter. 'That's up to the FBI. But I *am* worried about the lack of concrete help I'm getting from the Agriculture Committee in general and Senator Shearson Jones in particular.'

'You've told Jones about Vorar D?'

'Of course. I told him that the Pentagon have a suitable sterilising compound, too.'

'And he didn't seem interested?'

'He wanted written reports, and tests on the sterilising compound, and God knows what. There's no question at all that he's trying to slow this whole thing down.'

'Can you think of any reason why he should?'

'Only one,' said Professor Protter. 'He's opened this Blight Crisis Appeal for Kansas wheat farmers, as you obviously know. So far I think it's brought in three or four million dollars, although the news tonight said he was aiming for a target of twenty-five million dollars or more. Now – I may be unjust in thinking this – but it occurs to me that if the government announces they've found a way to arrest the blight, then interest in compensating the poor unfortunate farmers is going to take a downward curve. It's the same with the way that Jones keeps telling the media that the blights in other states apart from Kansas aren't very serious. In my opinion, he's trying to maintain a completely distorted impression of what's going on, simply to rake in as much contribution money as he possibly can.'

Dr Benson threw a copy of the Kansas paper off his chair, and sat down. 'That's a pretty heavy accusation,' he said. 'Do you think you can substantiate it?'

'I'm not interested in substantiating it right now,' said Professor Protter. 'All I'm interested in is getting through to the president, and making sure that production starts on sterilising compounds right away.'

'Why don't you make an announcement to the press? That's what I always do when I want to tug a few executive earlobes.'

'I'm not in a position to do that,' said Professor Protter.

'Why not? If you're right, what can they do to you?'

'Senator Jones can do a lot to me, and to my family. That's why I'm sharing this information with you. I was wondering if you could leak the story for me – get things moving. You could always say that it was your own people in Kansas who had identified the virus.'

Dr Benson cleared his throat. 'You want me to be the fall guy?'

'You can call your research people – have them check on the virus. I can assure you that everything I'm telling you is true. Six CW experts can't be wrong.'

'Well . . .' said Dr Benson.

'It's not just important,' Professor Protter told him. 'It's crucial to the survival of this whole nation. I wouldn't have asked you otherwise.'

'All right, then,' said Dr Benson. 'I'll call Mike Smith at the local radio station. He's good on handling this kind of thing.'

'I'm sure you won't regret it,' said Professor Protter.

'No, Professor, I don't think I will,' Dr Benson told him. 'If I'm going to go down, I might as well go down with all guns blazing.'

Dr Benson put the phone down, and rummaged around his room for his telephone directory. He was searching for the number of the Wichita news station when there was a light rapping sound at his door. He looked up, and there was a pretty red-headed woman in a grey raincoat, with a pocketbook under her arm. She smiled at him, and said, 'Hi. Am I disturbing you?'

'I, er – well, no, I don't think so,' said Dr Benson.

The woman stepped confidently into the office. 'I was waiting for you to come back from Hays. I saw the light go on in your office so I came up. My name's Della McIntosh, by the way. I'm the new projects manager for Shearson Jones's·Blight Crisis Appeal.'

Dr Benson shook her hand hesitantly. 'That's quite a coincidence,' he said. 'I've just been talking about the Blight Crisis Appeal to a colleague of mine.'

'That's nice,' said Della, perching herself on the edge of Dr Benson's desk, and giving him more of her warmest grin. 'Was it anybody I know?'

'Oh, I shouldn't think so. You're not an agronomist, are you?'

'No, but I'm over the age of consent.'

Dr Benson let out a grunt of amusement. 'Is there anything I can do for you?' he asked. 'Apart from ask your consent?'

'I flew in from Washington yesterday,' Della told him. 'I spent last night looking over Mr Hardesty's farm at South Burlington, and now I'm interested in talking to you. Have you discovered what causes the blight yet?'

'No . . . not exactly. We're still working on the theory that it might be a form of powdery mildew.'

'I thought you believed it was a virus.'

'Did Mr Hardesty tell you that? Oh, well, I was only generalising. It could be any one of a dozen things. It's going to take our people at Hays and Garden City a long time to find out which.'

Della stood up. 'We're sending out a television statement on Sunday evening from Senator Jones's home at Fall River. If you can spare me an hour or so, I was wondering if you could give me some scientific background. We want to make it all sound authentic.'

'Well, er – I have a quick call to make – then maybe I can spare you a little time. Would you excuse me for just a minute or two? You could sit in my secretary's office across the hall.'

'Sure,' smiled Della, and stepped out of the office, closing the door behind her. She quickly crossed the corridor to the office marked 'Enquiries', switched on the light, and went across to the grey steel desk. The tell-tale light on the telephone was already lit up, so she carefully lifted the receiver, and listened in.

' – *called me urgently and confidentially, and said that the Pentagon's chemical warfare people had identified it as Vorar D – that's right – well they used to use it for defoliation work in Vietnam – but he doesn't want to leak the story himself – no – well, as far as I understand it, Senator Jones can put some sort of a squeeze on his family – that's right –* '

When the light blinked off again, Della quietly replaced the receiver, and tippy-toed across to the window. By the time Dr Benson came in, shrugging on his car-coat again, she appeared to be absent-mindedly staring out at the light of Wichita's Civic Centre.

'I thought we'd go down to the coffee shop,' said Dr Benson. 'I haven't eaten in hours.'

'Personally, I could do with a drink,' smiled Della. 'Is there a good cocktail bar near here?'

'Well, I guess so – but the truth is I don't usually –'

Della linked her arm in his. 'Oh, come on. Surely work's over for the day, even for you busy agricultural scientists.'

Dr Benson shrugged. 'I guess I'm all right as long as I stick to Coke.'

'Coke?' asked Della, as they walked along the corridor to the elevator. 'What kind of a scientist drinks Coke?'

Dr Benson didn't answer, but pulled her an uncomfortable smile as they descended to the lobby. Della cuddled his arm, as if he was an affectionate old white-haired sugar-daddy, and when the security guard opened the downstairs door for them and let them out into the cool night air, he gave Dr Benson such a significant wink that Dr Benson felt like Humbert Humbert on his night off.

'Is that the bar?' asked Della, looking across the neon-lit plaza. 'The Silver Star?'

'That's the bar,' said Dr Benson, in a resigned voice.

The rented chauffeur-driven Lincoln Continental skirted the trees on the southern side of Fall River Lake and came out at last into a clearing. The driver had done this run before, and he turned up the driveway which led to Shearson Jones's house without having to be directed. He stopped at the white-painted wrought-iron gates, let down his window, and said, 'Senator Jones and party,' into the driveside microphone. There was a pause, then a click and a hum, and the gates swung open.

Sitting in one of the jump seats, Karen couldn't see the house very well until the chauffeur turned the Lincoln around on the gravelled front apron, applied the brake, and opened the door for her. When she climbed out, though, and stood waiting for Peter and Senator Jones in the wind that blew off the lake, she realised just how much one and a half million dollars could buy, especially out in rural Kansas.

Lake Vista – a name which one of Shearson's mistresses had chosen – was a modernistic two-story house built out of natural stone, timber and glass. It was set in the rock overlooking the lake, with two balconies actually overhanging the dark and glittering water. But its most striking feature was the triangular timber roof which rose from the centre of the house like a stylised Indian tepee. Shearson kept at Lake Vista one of the country's most valuable and important private collections of primitive Indian art, including a Pottawatomie painting on buffalo hide that had been valued at six million dollars.

'Quite a place, huh?' asked Peter, taking Karen's arm and leading her towards the front door. 'You wait until you see the inside.'

'It's unbelievable,' said Karen. 'It's just like something out of the movies.'

The featureless wooden front doors of the house opened up, and two tall blue-jawed men in plaid shirts and mushroom-coloured stetson hats came out to help Senator Jones across the gravel. One of them tipped his hat to Karen and said, 'How are you?'

'They're the Muldoon brothers,' explained Peter, leading Karen up the steps and into the polished wood hallway. 'They used to work a farm in Elk county, until they were bought out by an oil company. They're pretty wealthy in their own right, but for some reason they've always attached themselves to Shearson as unpaid side-kicks. Don't ever ask me why. You'll have to find out for yourself.'

The inside of Shearson's house was even more spectacular than the outside. The interior of the pointed wooden roof was lined with zig-zag galleried steps, so that a visitor could climb upwards from level to level, admiring Shearson's Indian paintings and artifacts all the way up to the very tip of the house. Under the stressed-concrete beams which supported the 'tepee', there was a spacious conversation area; and off to the left, towards the lake, there was a sitting-room with Cherokee rugs and leather furniture and genuine Canadian totem poles.

'I'm impressed,' said Karen.

Behind her, the Muldoon brothers were almost carrying Shearson into the house. Grimacing, they supported him through the doors, across the conversation area, and into the sitting-room, so that they could deposit him at last in a sturdy studded library chair, with a view through the sliding-glass windows of the darkling lake.

'Travel grows less and less desirable every day,' grumbled Shearson. 'Did Della get here yet?'

'She called and left a message,' said one of the Muldoon brothers. 'She said she was talking to someone called Dr Benson at the Silver Star cocktail bar in Wichita, and that she didn't expect to be late. Things were going just fine, she said.'

'I'm pleased to hear it,' said Shearson. 'Now, will one of you boys bring me a bottle of champagne, and some glasses? I think we ought to celebrate our safe arrival.'

Peter nudged Karen towards a large couch, covered in rough-brushed hide. 'Go on,' he said. 'The senator won't eat you. Will you, Senator?'

Senator Jones took out a large linen handkerchief and mopped sweat from his face and his jowls. 'It's possible,' he

143

said. 'I'm so damned hungry I could eat anything, and she looks pretty tasty.'

It didn't take Ed long to find them. The security guard at the agricultural research centre had seen them leave the building, and walk across the plaza towards the Silver Star bar. When he pushed his way through the Dodge City-style doors, he saw them at once. Dr Benson with his white-haired head in his hands, Della with her arm around him, and Mike Smith from the radio station, short and crewcut and stubby, standing beside them with a helpless look on his face.

Ed crossed the bar and laid both of his hands on Dr Benson's back. 'Dr Benson?' he said. 'How are you feeling?'

'Drunk,' said Dr Benson.

Ed looked at Della with an expression like cracked ice. 'Did you bring him in here?' he demanded.

Della said, 'He wanted to come. He said he felt like a drink.'

'Goddamit, you knew he was an alcoholic!'

'How was I supposed to know that?' asked Della. 'I've never met him before in my life. All *I* wanted to do was talk about the blight, and all *he* wanted to do was drink. Is that my fault?'

'I don't know,' Ed said, bitterly.

'He called me,' said Mike Smith. 'He said he had some news about the blight.'

'Did he tell you what it was?' asked Ed.

'Well, he did,' said Mike. 'But I'm not sure what I'm supposed to believe now. I mean, the guy's stewed. Whatever he says, it isn't going to make a lot of sense.'

'It's a virush,' said Dr Benson, rearing up from his barstool.

'You see what I mean?' put in Mike Smith. 'It just doesn't make sense.'

'It's a *virush*,' insisted Dr Benson. 'A damned terrible virush I can't remember the name of. Vorar D. That'sh it. Vorar D. You look it up. Vorar D.'

'That's what he told me on the phone,' said Mike Smith.

'He said that somebody called Professor Protter in Washington had called him up, and spilled the beans on the whole blight situation. The blight was caused by some virus called Vorar D, some kind of defoliant they developed for Vietnam.'

'He's drunk,' said Della. 'He's been rambling like this ever since I met him. Earlier on, he was saying that the blight was an act of God.'

'God?' enquired Dr Benson, loudly. 'Has God decided to grace us with His presence?'

Mike Smith pulled a face. 'I can't broadcast anything from a source as pickled as this,' he said.

Ed kept his arm protectively around Dr Benson's shoulders. 'I know you can't,' he told Mike Smith. 'But when I first talked to Dr Benson about this blight, he wasn't drunk. And he did believe it was caused by a virus. Presumably somebody in Washington – Professor Protter, or whoever – presumably they've discovered what virus it is.'

'I can't send out a story on evidence like this,' said Mike Smith, shaking his head.

'So what are you going to do?' asked Ed. 'You've seen the crops for yourself, the condition they're in. Are you going to ignore them, and run the same news stories as everybody else?'

'It's under control,' said Mike Smith. 'Everybody from the governor downwards tells me it's under control.'

'Sure it's under control,' said Ed, hotly. 'It's under so much control that I've just lost eighty-five thousand acres of wheat without being able to stop it, or even slow it down. Under control, crap.'

Mike Smith spread his arms apologetically. 'I don't see what I can do. Here's a scientist giving me all the answers I want, and the only trouble is that the scientist is blind drunk. Sober him up, and then I'll talk to him. But it's more than my reputation's worth to interview him now.'

Della said, 'I'm afraid he's right. You can't believe a man in this condition, even if you want to.'

Ed lowered his eyes. 'No,' he said. 'I suppose you can't. Dr Benson – I'm going to drive you home.'

Dr Benson shook his head. 'One more drink. One more, and then I'll come. Bartender – one more drink!'

Ed looked at Della with a feeling of bitterness that he could hardly control. 'I should have known better,' he said. 'I should have known a whole damned sight better.'

'Once a hayseed, always a hayseed,' Della told him, and grinned.

Ed slammed the flat of his hand on to the bar, and the barman looked around warily.

Twelve

She was lying on the cedarwood pooldeck in back of the house, stretched out on an airbed. A light breeze rustled in the trees, and the sunlight danced in dazzling spots on the surface of the water. She felt soothed, and relaxed, and calm. All the tensions of Kansas had eased their way out of her mind, until there was nothing inside her consciousness at all but summer heat, and fragrant wind, and peace.

She knew it would take far more than a couple of days sunbathing to replace the tensions that she had lost, but for the time being the peace was enough.

Carl and Vee had taken Sally to Universal this morning for the studio tour. Season had preferred to stay behind. She had lingered over her breakfast, drinking four cups of black coffee. Then she had undressed and sat naked on the edge of the pool, slowly kicking her legs in the water and smoking a joint. The glittering ripples had cross-hatched her imagination with bright reflections, and she had meditated for almost a half-hour, feeling one with the sun and the water and the trees.

Now, shiny with Coppertone, aromatic as a pina colada, she was lying with her eyes closed getting an all-over tan.

A little after eleven, she heard a knocking at the french doors which gave out on to the pool deck. She was almost asleep, and she stretched herself like a cat.

'Vee?' she called. 'Is that you?'

There was an awkward throat-clearing noise. 'Mrs Hardesty? Season? Am I interrupting you?'

Season reached across for her beach-wrap, and covered herself. Then she pushed her wide pink-tinted sunglasses on to the end of her slippery nose, and peered towards the house. It was too shadowy inside to see who was there.

'Who is this?' she said.

'It's me. Granger Hughes. I just stopped by to see how you were. But if it's inconvenient –'

'Oh, Granger. Not at all. Did Marie let you in? Come on out here, and I'll have her fix us some drinks. It's good to see you.'

Granger stepped out through the french doors into the sunlight. He was dressed in white today – a crisp cotton suit and white shoes. He wore aviator sunglasses, and his blond hair looked spiky, as if he had been swimming. The sun momentarily caught his huge crucifix, a flash of religious light.

'How are you?' said Season. 'I won't shake your hand. I'm smothered in suncream.'

Granger drew up one of the white wrought-iron chairs, and sat beside her. 'I'm very well,' he said. 'And I'm pleased to see that you're still here in LA.'

'I think I'll be staying for quite a while.'

'You're going to need some time, huh?'

Season nodded. 'I'm beginning to feel better in myself. I'm beginning to understand that I didn't actually lose my personality when I was out there in Kansas. I'm still me. But I've been in hiding for so many months inside of my head – well, it's going to take me a while to coax me out again.'

Granger crossed his legs. 'Do you think I could help? That's what my church is all about.'

'I don't know. I've never been particularly religious. I believe in God, but that's about all.'

'That's all you need. We're not one of your heavy, upright, believe-it-or-else organisations. We're not a bunch of religious kooks, either. We're just a group of friendly, concerned young people who believe that the power of our

Lord Jesus Christ was, and is, a *practical* power. As practical as a garage mechanic's wrench, or a housewife's food blender.'

'The Church of the Holy Cuisinart?' asked Season, sarcastically.

Granger grinned. 'You can make fun. A lot of people do. But the whole thing makes human sense and spiritual sense too. Our Lord has power, and nobody in the whole world can convince me that he won't let us use that power for good. Why do you think Jesus demonstrated his miracles in public? So that the people around him would realise that *they* could heal people too.'

'Well, I don't know,' said Season. 'Right now I feel like emptying my head right out, not filling it up.'

Maria came to the doors in her black dress and her white apron. Season called, 'Maria? Could you bring us out two glasses of white wine, please? The Christian Brothers' pinot chardonnay.'

Granger said, 'I'm not asking you to fill your head up. Keep it as empty as you like. I just believe that I could help you come to terms with yourself again. And I know that you'd enjoy one of our meetings. Why don't you come tomorrow? I could call by and pick you up.'

'I'm not sure,' said Season. 'We have friends coming over for lunch tomorrow.'

Granger looked at her winningly. His eyes were as pale as opals. 'It won't take more than a couple of hours of your time. I mean that. And it could be the turning-point in your whole life. Apart from that, you'd be the most beautiful woman in the whole congregation, and I'd love to have you there.'

'You're flattering me again, Granger. Last time I was tired. Now I'm not.'

'You're still beautiful.'

Maria came flip-flapping out from the house in her plastic sandals, carrying two large glasses of freezing-cold pinot chardonnay on a tray.

'Mr Hughes staying for lunch?' she asked. 'Avocado salad.'

'That's a nice idea,' said Season. 'Carl and Vee won't be

back from the studio tour until later. Can you spare the time?'

Granger grinned. 'For you, I could spare the rest of the day. Maybe the rest of the month.'

Season lifted her glass. The sun sparkled on the meniscus of the wine. 'I'll drink to that,' she said, with an exaggeratedly flirtatious smile.

Morris Hunt, the governor of California, was presiding over an outdoor picnic lunch that afternoon under the shady oaks of Mrs Irwin J. Harris's garden in Santa Barbara. There was music from a small band on the verandah, all of them dressed in red-striped blazers and 1920s skimmers, and there were more flowers on the ladies' hats than there were in the flower-beds. Across the immaculate lawns, sprinklers left a rainbow carpet of fresh dew. The picnic cost fifty dollars a plate, in aid of spina bifida children. Nine years ago, Morris Hunt's own child had been crippled, and finally died, from spina bifida.

A few minutes before Morris Hunt was expected to speak, a harassed-looking aide in a rumpled grey suit came hurrying across the grass and whispered in his ear. Morris Hunt frowned, and asked the aide something which nobody else could hear. The aide whispered in his ear again. Morris Hunt leaned over towards Mrs Irwin J. Harris, a strawberry-blonde lady in a huge fruit-bedecked hat, and it was clear that he was making his apologies.

Inside the house, under an oil painting of the late Irwin J. Harris himself, the telephone was waiting on a polished walnut table. Morris Hunt, a dark-haired, serious-looking man of forty-five, with a striking resemblance to Douglas Fairbanks Junior, picked up the receiver and said, 'Morris here. What's wrong, Walter?'

It was Walter Oppenheim, the chairman of the State Agricultural Committee, calling from Sacramento. He sounded breathless and harassed.

'Morris, I've got some real disturbing news. I told my staff yesterday to call on every fruit and vegetable producer of any reasonable size throughout the state, just to check how they were coping with the blight. The news is, it's very bad. The report was completed ten minutes ago, and believe me, Morris, we're going to lose eighty per cent of our produce this year unless we can halt this blight by the end of next week. It's spreading so damned fast! One day there's a field of lettuce, and the next day there's nothing but brown splotches.'

'Walter, I don't believe what I'm hearing,' said Morris Hunt. 'Yesterday everybody was full of optimism. Oh, we might lose a quarter of our produce at the very worst! What's happened since then?'

'Nobody foresaw it spreading so fast,' said Walter. 'Jesus Christ, Morris, it didn't even begin to appear at all before Monday or Tuesday. Now it's Saturday, and already it's wiped out a third of our fruit and vegetable produce.'

'Has anybody got close to analysing it yet?'

'Well, my own people at Fresno have been working on it pretty hard, but so far they don't have any ideas at all.'

'Have you kept in touch with Washington?'

'Sure, I put in a call early this morning, and I'm going to call them again now. All I get is "we think we've nearly cracked it, and we'll let you know." They've been saying that since Wednesday.'

Morris Hunt lowered his head. 'You're sure it's going to be as serious as eighty per cent crop loss?'

'Morris, it may be worse. We may lose everything.'

'You know what that's going to do to the state's revenues, don't you? Total bankruptcy. And that's quite apart from the human problem we're going to face.'

Walter said uneasily, 'What do you want to do?'

'I'm going to fly back to Sacramento straight away. Tell Roger to call an emergency meeting for five o'clock, and to make sure that everybody attends. No exceptions. I want an assessment of the state's food supply situation on my desk by four. Frozen foods, dried foods, canned foods – both private and military stocks. For God's sake, though, don't tell the media. Nobody at all. If it gets out that we're thinking of rationing food there's going to be anarchy.'

'Okay, Morris,' said Walter. 'Will do.'

Morris put down the phone and walked outside again. He crossed the lawn to the top table, and leaned over to

150

Mrs Irwin J. Harris.

'Mrs Harris,' he said, 'I'm afraid that some really ridiculous crisis has come up. I'm going to have to leave you straight away.'

'Oh, no,' said Mrs Harris. 'You haven't even eaten your pâté de foie!'

Morris looked down at his plate, where a fresh-cut slice of pale pâté was waiting for him, dotted with truffles.

'I'm sorry, Mrs Harris,' he said. 'But I think I just lost my appetite.'

Karen Fortunoff sat on the upper balcony of Lake Vista, drinking champagne, eating dry-roasted cashew nuts, and watching a portable television which one of the Muldoon brothers had silently placed on a small table for her. It was hot on the Kansas plains, almost insufferably hot; but up here by the ink-blue waters of Fall River Lake, there was a refreshingly cool wind. Karen wore a one-piece swimsuit in electric blue satin, and a loose white summer wrap which she had bought especially for the week-end.

A chubby, intent-looking man on the television was holding up a pack of indigestion tablets, and saying: '*Acid indigestion? Over-eating? There's only one sure way to feel better fast.*'

How right you are, thought Karen. All you have to do is let the worst crop blight in America's history run riot – just long enough to gather in as much money as you possibly can from a spurious help-the-farmers appeal fund. That's the sure way to cut out over-eating, particularly other people's, and that's certainly the way to feel better fast.

She felt strangely confused emotions about Shearson Jones this afternoon. Last night, once everybody had showered and changed into formals, the staff of Lake Vista had laid on the kind of meal that Karen would have classified as a banquet, but which Shearson had simply dismissed as 'supper.' They had started off with soft-shelled crabs on toast, followed by chicken croquettes, lamb cutlets with tartare sauce, beef tongue in aspic, salads, fresh fruits, ices, cheeses, and liqueurs. She had watched in sheer amazement as Shearson Jones crammed his mouth with course after course, swilling his food down with mouthfuls of vintage French wines, and only a gentle kick under the table from Peter Kaiser had reminded her not to stare too intently at her host's gastronomic enormities.

Early this morning, wandering around the house on her own, she had asked one of the Muldoon brothers, as innocently as she could, if Lake Vista was stocked with sufficient food to see them through a period of shortage. The brother had grinned and taken her on a tour of the kitchens, where two Chinese chefs were kept constantly busy while Shearson was in residence. He had taken her, too, to the cold store, where beef and lamb and venison carcasses hung in hundreds; and to the wine cellars, which had been excavated almost a hundred and fifty feet into the rock.

'We could live here for six months without ever going to a market once,' said the Muldoon brother. 'Even if we had the senator here, eating his usual five meals a day.'

As Saturday wore on, though, Karen had grown increasingly restless and disappointed. Although she was impressed by the wealth and vulgarity of Shearson's house, and by the greed of his lifestyle, she had expected him to invite at least one or two minor politicians to share his week-end in the Mid-West, or a movie star at the very worst. Instead, Shearson spent hour after hour closeted with Peter Kaiser, talking money and politics, and if anybody else was coming, there wasn't any sign of them yet. Last night, Peter hadn't come up to their balconied bedroom until way past three in the morning, and even though Karen had been reasonably encouraging, for the want of anybody else, he had fallen straight to sleep, and snored. He had been out of bed at six, and dressed, and his only amorous gesture had been to peck Karen on the cheek before he went downstairs to breakfast.

Now he was back in conference with Shearson, and she didn't expect to see him until dinner. She yawned, and in technological response, the television started a re-run of *The African Queen*.

A voice said, 'Hi.'

She looked around. Stepping out on to the balcony came

a tall, loose-limbed man in a short-sleeved white shirt and cream slacks. His hair was thick and wiry and black, his eyebrows shaggy, and his eyes as green as pistachio ice, with mint chips. He smiled at Karen, walked to the rail, and looked out over the lake.

'Quite a romantic view you've got yourself up here,' the man said.

Karen shaded her eyes against the sun so that she could look at him. 'It depends how romantic you're feeling.'

The man glanced at the television. 'You sound as if you don't feel romantic at all.'

'I'm *potentially* romantic,' she said. 'It's just that, around here, romance doesn't seem to be written into the schedule. It's either eating, or politics, or both.'

'That doesn't sound too much fun,' said the man. 'I only just arrived here. My name's Ed Hardesty, by the way.'

Karen held out her hand, and said, 'Karen Fortunoff. Say – aren't you the farmer? The one who's supposed to be heading up the Blight Crisis Appeal?'

'That's right.'

Karen sat up straight. 'Listen,' she said, 'would you like a glass of champagne? I'll have one of the Muldoons bring it up for you.'

'Why not?' said Ed. 'I've got nothing on my hands but time. Della said I had to come out here this afternoon for a video test, but it looks like the TV people have gotten delayed.'

'Well, that's show business,' said Karen. 'Have you ever seen this house before? Isn't it something else?'

'I don't know,' said Ed. 'I'm kind of a traditionalist myself. My ideal home is one of those white antebellum mansions in Virginia, with the darkies singing sweet and low in the cottonfields.'

Karen frowned at him. 'You weren't originally a farmer, were you? I mean, you don't *talk* like a farmer.'

'I was born on a farm, right here in Kansas. But I guess I've spent most of my intelligent life in New York City. I only came back here to take over the farm when my father and my older brother died.'

'Oh. I'm sorry.'

Ed looked away. 'It was a pretty hard knock. But at least I still own the land they gave their lives for. I guess it probably sounds sentimental to anyone else, but it's given me the chance to build them some kind of memorial.'

Karen pressed the buzzer on the table for one of the Muldoons to come up. She scrunched up her eyes against the sunlight, and said, 'That doesn't sound sentimental at all. This blight must be hitting you pretty hard. Emotionally, as well as financially.'

Karen watched Ed carefully. She didn't know him at all, and she supposed that it was quite possible he was a friend of Shearson's, or Peter's, or even a hired informer. But somehow he didn't sound like it, or look like it. In the time that Karen had been working for Peter Kaiser, she had come to develop a nose for anybody who snuffled around the same political sty as Shearson Jones. They always had some of Shearson's piggish characteristics – which Ed Hardesty plainly didn't.

'You know this blight's going to turn out a whole lot worse than the news media have been giving out,' Karen volunteered.

Ed turned away from the railing, and regarded her curiously.

'What makes you say that?' he asked.

'Well, the television news has been saying it's serious. A third of the wheat crop lost already, and a quarter of the soybean crop. But I don't think anybody realises quite how serious it really is.'

'What do you mean?'

'There's been a whole lot of hushing up. Some of it's been deliberate, some of it hasn't. Some of it's been well-intentioned, because the government doesn't want anybody to panic. But the truth is that almost every crop in every state has been affected – some badly, some not so badly – and it's going to get a whole lot worse.'

'How much worse?' asked Ed, stiffly. He was as suspicious of Karen as she was of him.

'Worse to the point where there may not be any fresh cereal, fruit, vegetables, or grazing crops – none at all. Worse to the point where the United States agricultural economy for one whole year may be totally wiped out.'

'Why are you telling me this?' asked Ed, in a wary voice.

Karen brushed back her hair. 'I don't know who else to tell, except you. I thought of calling the newspapers anonymously, or CBS News or somebody. But who's going to believe me, when the Department of Agriculture in Washington is quite freely *admitting* they've got crop problems. *Sure,* we've got crop problems, but they're all under control. The way things are at the moment, it's all a question of interpretation, you know? And the Department of Agriculture has been interpreting every single outbreak of blight optimistically. They haven't been *denying* anything to the media. They've just been adjusting the truth to make it all look happy. They even shot a special public-relations film out in Nebraska yesterday, showing a smiling farmer in the middle of a whole lot of unblighted wheat.'

Ed said, 'Surely someone's going to start playing Deep Throat before long. Look how fast the damn thing's spreading. It's wiped out the whole of my farm – well, eighty per cent of it – in something like four days.'

'I think you're underestimating Senator Jones,' said Karen. 'When it comes to agriculture, he's a very heavy number. He has the Department of Agriculture's press office right under his thumb. It's his personal mouthpiece. And there are plenty of newspapers and television stations – particularly out here in the Mid-West – that rely a whole lot on Shearson Jones's sponsorship, or the sponsorship of his companies, at least.'

'Agreed. But he can't suppress this thing for ever.'

'He doesn't have to. He doesn't even want to.'

'Then why is he letting this happen? Why is he trying to make out that it's only us poor unfortunate Kansas wheat farmers who are seriously hit?'

Karen said, 'It's this Blight Crisis Appeal, that's all. Shearson Jones wants to scoop in as much money as he possibly can before anybody realises how catastrophic this blight is really going to be. I don't know how much you've been told, but he's already cleared nine million dollars through the appeal, and he's trying to spin things out for just two or three more days so that he can make sure of a two-million dollar offer from Michigan Tractors.'

'And the media are actually going along with it?'

'Of course they are. They've got what they think is a story. Didn't you see *Time* magazine, with all that cliff-hanging stuff about the last-minute race to develop an antidote? They quoted a couple of state agricultural specialists who stepped out of line and said that Doomsday was on the way. But what's that, compared with somebody like Shearson Jones saying that the blight is a supreme test of American agricultural technology, and that it's going to revive the fighting spirit of the dustbowl days?'

Ed blew out his cheeks in disbelief. 'This is just fantastic,' she said. 'How can one man influence a whole country so much, right on the edge of a crisis? And what does he think he's going to get out of it? If the blight gets completely out of control, it's going to sink the whole country's agricultural economy for years – and how can that be worth it, even for him, and even for nine million dollars? If the whole country goes down the tubes, the money won't be worth anything anyway.'

Karen stood up, and walked over to join Ed at the railing. She was already freckled from the day's sunshine, and the irises of her dark brown eyes were as soft as medieval velvet.

'I'm only guessing,' she said. 'But I'm Peter Kaiser's personal secretary, and when Peter Kaiser talks to Shearson Jones on the telephone, all the calls are routed through my desk. That means my information is limited, but good. Right from the swine's mouth, so to speak. The way I've pieced it together, from what I've heard Peter and Shearson saying, the blight's turned out to be a whole lot worse than Shearson first expected it to be. He thought it was going to be regional. A few crops here and there, nothing disastrous. But instead of that, it's spreading all over the country. Even the media don't know how wide it's spread, because Shearson's made sure that the state agricultual people keep quiet about it. He doesn't want to start a nationwide scramble for food, that's the standard excuse. And you have to admit that it's a sensible and justifiable excuse, as well as a self-serving one, so it's hard to turn around and say he's gotten hold of a pussycat that's turned out to be a tiger – and he's pretty anxious to claw in as much money as quickly as he can and then let go. That's why he's got you here. A last magnificent fund-raising effort before the lid blows off of the whole thing.'

'But the damage he's going to do to the country – ' said Ed.

Karen shook her head. 'He believes it's going to be minimal. Peter Kaiser and I and all the rest of the staff have been working on assessments of the country's food reserves. Canned foods, dried foods, frozen food, military dumps, that kind of thing. There *are* going to be shortages, sure, and we're all going to have to look forward to a few months without adequate supplies of fresh fruit and vegetables, until the next crops can be forced. But it's not going to be that bad. I mean, it's going to be *bad*, but nobody's going to starve. There's always the danger they won't be able to find an antidote to the virus in time for next year, I suppose, but Shearson's been leaning pretty heavily on the federal research people to come up with something.'

'So,' said Ed, quietly. 'You really believe that Shearson Jones isn't doing anything worse than flim-flamming the news media for a few days while he rakes in a few shekels? Just playing the same old game that politicians have always played – making money out of inside information?'

'Do you know very much different?' asked Karen, disturbed.

Ed leaned his elbows on the railing. 'I believe I do. I'm not saying that what you've just been telling me isn't right. I'm sure it is. But he's been playing the game a whole lot closer to the edge. Or at least I think he has. You know this blight is caused by a virus?'

'Yes,' she said. 'I heard that.'

'Well – I've been working alongside of Dr Benson at the Kansas Agricultural Research Centre, and Dr Benson was told last night that the federal laboratories in Washington have already found a way of killing the virus off.'

'You're serious?' asked Karen. 'They've actually done it?

But that means Shearson's been deliberately holding it back.'

Ed nodded. 'The way Dr Benson heard it, Shearson Jones doesn't want to announce that the blights are all caused by the same virus, because that would take away the special status he's been trying to give to the wheat farmers in Kansas. Apart from that, the virus has turned out to be something very much like Vorar D, which was developed by the Pentagon for use in Vietnam, as a replacement for Agent Orange. Vorar D eats its way through plant life like you wouldn't believe, and the media will know that. The whole thing will bust wide open.'

'But you say they've got an antidote.'

'They have the technology to develop some sort of sterilisation compound. It isn't magic, and we'd probably still lose most of our crops. But the sooner it's manufactured and sprayed, the better.'

'Why didn't the federal research people go to the media?' asked Karen. 'That would have sunk Shearson Jones on the spot.'

Ed shrugged. 'Dr Benson said that Shearson had some kind of half-nelson on their top researcher. That's why they called Dr Benson in secret, and asked him if *he'd* leak the news about Vorar D instead.'

'So why didn't he? And come to that, why didn't *you*?'

'Dr Benson tried to. But Della McIntosh wanted to get some background for the Blight Crisis Appeal, and she made the mistake of taking him into a bar. You probably don't know Dr Benson, but he's a reformed alcoholic. At least, he was until last night. He'd arranged to meet a radio reporter, but he was so stoned that he was incoherent. I didn't even understand what he was talking about myself until this morning, when I went around to see him at his apartment. I don't suppose it was Della's fault. She just didn't know. But the radio guy just thought he was raving.'

'My God,' said Karen.

Ed frowned at her. 'What's the matter?'

'What you've just told me about Dr Benson is the matter. Della McIntosh is Shearson Jones's latest mistress. Did you know that? Well, you obviously guessed it. But she was

158

sent here ahead of Shearson to size you up for the Blight Crisis Appeal, just to make sure you weren't some kind of Mickey Mouse, and also to have a quiet word with Dr Benson.'

There was a long, tense silence. Ed said: 'Are you kidding me along?'

'Mr Hardesty – Ed – why do you think I'm here at all? Peter Kaiser is hardly the last of the red-hot lovers, and I certainly didn't come for the fun and the games and the laughter. Do you see anybody laughing around here? I'm not. I'm worried about what's going on, for myself and for my relatives and for America in general, and I don't want Shearson Jones and Peter Kaiser plotting the end of the world behind my back.'

Ed said, 'If there's enough stored food to last the winter, and the federal laboratories have found an antidote, it's hardly going to be the end of the world. And we can make damned sure that Senator Jones gets what's coming to him.'

'All right – maybe I'm exaggerating about the end of the world,' said Karen. 'But there's one thing – and I probably shouldn't be telling anybody this, but Peter Kaiser has already made his own personal arrangements to stock up with emergency food in case of a shortage, and Shearson Jones has enough eatables here to last him for a century. Worst of all, I listened in to a telephone conversation from Alan Hedges, the chairman of the Agriculture Committee, and I can't be exactly sure of this, but it sounded like the president himself has ordered extra stocks of food to be shipped into Washington, in case the administration has to go short.'

Ed looked at Karen tight-lipped, and then back towards the house.

'Isn't that great?' he said, hoarsely. 'That's how close and patriotic this nation becomes in a crisis. Oh sure – we all get to feel like buddies when the Russians invade Afghanistan, but what happens when we're faced with a disaster at home? The politicians go on screwing the rest of us like they always do, and the powerful make plans to save their own hides while the average John and Jane Doe can go hang.'

Karen said, 'What are you going to do? Are you going to tell the newspapers?'

Ed reached along the railing and laid his hand on top of hers. 'I'm going to do more than that. I'm going to tell America myself. Just for today, I'm going to play along, like the poor young farmer who's lost all his crops. But tomorrow evening, I'm going to be on live coast-to-coast television, and even if I only get ten seconds before they pull the plug on me, I'm going to use that broadcast to tell the real truth about what's going on here, and tell it out loud.'

Karen looked at him. 'I'm glad I talked to you,' she said. 'I was afraid you were one of Shearson's people. I can trust you, can't I?'

Ed smiled. 'You and I, we don't have any choice. If we don't trust each other, just for this one day, then we won't be able to trust anybody ever again.'

At that moment, Della stepped out on to the balcony, carrying a silver tray with an ice-bucket of Dom Perignon. She was dressed in a tiny gold satin bikini which scarcely covered her nipples, and which was drawn up revealingly tight between her legs.

'Drinks, children?' she smiled.

Karen glanced quickly and interrogatively at Ed to see if he thought that Della had been listening to their conversation, but Ed gave her a brief shake of the head. Della came up close, and stood between Ed and Karen, with her back to Karen and her breasts touching Ed's shirt-front. Dramatically, she laid her hand on top of Ed's and Karen's hands, and said, 'Isn't this romantic? All for one, and one for all.'

All of his neighbours in that quiet and slightly shabby part of Washington recognised Professor Protter. He was small, and bald, and he walked in a busy, bustling way, like a wind-up clockwork toy. He always wore the flashiest of sports coats, too, with grey flannel pants that were baggy at the knees. They often wondered how a man who looked like that could have found himself such a pretty, exuberant wife, but then they didn't know how tender and charming he could be to the ones he loved, and they didn't know how much passion he showed her in the big brass-railed bed that dominated their pink-painted bedroom.

His wife was brunette, plump, but startlingly good-looking, particularly if you had a taste for Czech women. On Wednesdays and Fridays she gave piano lessons to the neighbourhood children, and on warm evenings, when the Protters' windows were raised, you could sometimes hear her playing a Kempff piano concerto, with her husband accompanying her on his violin.

That Saturday afternoon, almost at the same moment that Della stepped almost naked on to the balcony of Lake Vista in Kansas, but an hour later because of the time zones, Professor Protter closed the door of the old Federal-style house behind him, and descended the five steps to the sidewalk, jingling his keys on the end of their chain. Overhead, the sky was grey and heavy, and there was a feeling of summer rain in the air. Three black children were playing football in the street.

As he walked away, Professor Protter turned for no reason at all and looked up towards the second-storey window. It was open, because of the heat, and his wife was leaning out, framed by the flowers in her window-box. She saw him, and gave him a little finger-wave, and blew a kiss.

A tall black man passing by in a crumpled linen suit said, 'How you doing, Professor?' and Professor Protter nodded and smiled.

He usually went out about this time on a Saturday to buy a bottle of Hungarian wine from Schwarz's liquor store two blocks down. Then, he took the bottle home, and he and his wife would sit listening to long-playing records until it was time for an early supper. Saturday was usually goulash. Goulash and Liszt.

As he crossed the street at the end of his block, a dark-blue Cutlass abruptly started its engine, and moved out from the opposite kerb. Professor Protter didn't give it a glance. He was thinking about Vorar D, and about Dr Benson; and he was hoping that Dr Benson would call him at home this evening.

The Cutlass U-turned, with a squeal of tyres, and nosed in beside him, keeping pace with him as he walked. It was only when he was passing the delicatessen, the one with all the fondants in the window, that he caught sight of its reflection in the glass, and turned towards it.

He saw the man's face, in dark glasses, and he saw the shotgun. It didn't even occur to him to take cover. He stopped in surprise, and the car stopped, and for a moment the killer and the professor faced each other in that humid afternoon atmosphere, with the normal noisy life of the streets going on all around them.

'Are you – ' Professor Protter started to say, and took a step forward. The man in the car, owing to a nervous reaction, fired. Professor Protter was hurled backwards into the delicatessen window, into the glass which smashed but hung magically suspended for a moment before slicing down on him, nearly one hundred pounds of razor-sharp plate, right into his open mouth, and severed his head from the upper jaw upwards.

The noise of the shot, *whaabaammmm*, and the terrible clanging of the broken glass, those didn't seem to be audible until minutes and minutes afterwards, when the Cutlass had long since swerved away into the Saturday afternoon traffic, and the proprietor of the delicatessen had rushed forward, *rushed*, clutching his apron only to stop utterly still when he saw the top half of Professor Protter's head lying bloodily amongst his fondants, its red-smeared upper teeth looking as if they were biting into a tray of lemon creams.

'God,' was all he could say.

She reached up and tugged the cord that closed the bedroom drapes. The warm afternoon sunlight shone through the thin white cotton of her kaftan, and revealed her gentle curved silhouette. Lean, triangular back. Small rounded bottom. Long, lean legs.

Granger Hughes, on the far side of the room, beside the frondy potted palm, said, 'We don't have to do this, you know.'

'Don't you want to?' she asked him. 'Or is it against your religion?'

He smiled. 'My religion is practical miracles,' he said.

'And if there was ever a practical miracle, it's you.'

She walked across the polished wooden floor, and the kaftan flowed all around her. She approached him as quickly as a train, almost as if she wasn't going to stop, and she had unbuttoned his shirt in a matter of seconds, four quick twists of her long-fingered hands. She pulled the shirt open, and bared his chest, with its huge silver-and-gold cross. He was very tanned, as if he had been stained in walnut-juice, the way boys disguised themselves in childhood adventure stories. His nipples were as dark as berries.

She kissed his chest, and then took one of his nipples gently between her teeth. 'I could bite it off,' she said. 'Would one of your miracles glue it back on again?'

He kissed her hair. He could smell the sun and the coconut oil on it. He kissed her blonde eyelashes, her nose, her lips. Then, as if he was a sculptor unveiling his latest work, he gathered her kaftan in his hands, and lifted his arms, so that she stood in front of him naked.

'I'm looking for myself, you know,' she said simply. 'I'm not necessarily looking for you.'

He said, 'I don't care,' and bent his head forward so that their foreheads touched, blond hair against blonde hair. they could have been twins, erotic gemini. His hands ran down the length of her back, clasping the rounded cheeks of her bottom, and then he held her very close to him, so close that for a moment she wondered if she was going to be pressed into him completely, and become part of his body. Her friends, looking for her, would stare into his eyes, and see something that was elusively her for ever after.

She unbuckled his belt, and he stepped out of his slacks. His plain white undershorts showed the rigid outline of his penis, the cupped curve of his balls. She pulled them down, and his erection rose red into the diffuse sunlight.

'I never imagined priests could be like this,' she said. 'I never even imagined *men* could be like this.'

'I'm not ordained,' he told her.

'No,' she whispered, as she lay back on the bed. 'But you're holy.'

The sheets were soft pink. She felt as if she were melting amongst them. Lying on her back, with her thighs slightly

163

apart, and her knees slightly raised, she closed her eyes and imagined she was travelling through time and space, to a world where nothing mattered at all but rest and flowers and laughter.

The first lick of his tongue on her bare clitoris came almost as a shock. But then he licked again, and again, and gradually she opened her eyes. She couldn't believe the sensation of it. It made her body thrill as if she was watching something terrifying and exciting and stimulating all at once, and her muscles suddenly tensed in spite of herself. She raised her head and looked down, and there was Granger's fair head moving rhythmically between her parted thighs, his tongue lapping at the flesh of her vulva, pink tongue between pink lips.

She watched him in utter fascination as he licked her faster and faster. Sometimes he would play on her clitoris for half a minute at a time, stirring her deeper and deeper towards an orgasm. But then he would guide his tongue into her vagina, or around her urethra, playfully changing the tempo until she longed for him to return to her clitoris again and give her the deeper feelings she needed.

It was strange. It was all technique. She wondered whether it made any difference to him what woman he did it to. After all, one cunt must be very much like another. She watched him lick, and lap, and tickle her, and the more she watched the further away her feelings of excitement receded.

Three or four minutes passed. He kept on licking at her. She lay back, and stared up at the ceiling. She felt like another joint. Perhaps that was her problem. She wasn't relaxed enough. Wasn't spaced out enough. She idly wondered what would happen if Vee were to walk in through the door, and see Granger kneeling between her legs. Nothing, probably. She would say, 'How was the studio?' and Vee would say, 'Okay. Do you want a glass of wine?'

She was just wondering how long it would be before Sally got back when Granger slapped her. *Crack!* Across the face – so hard that it jerked her head to one side.

She stared up at him, wide-eyed, shocked, her cheek

blazing crimson and her ear throbbing with pain. He was glaring down at her fiercely, his eyes furious, and his jaws were working as if he was about to throw a fit.

'You bitch!' he hissed at her. 'You high-and-mighty languorous boring bitch!'

She whimpered, and tried to roll away from under him. But he clamped his hand on her shoulder, and shoved her forcefully back on to the sheets.

'You hit me,' she said, and her voice was trembling. It sounded like someone else's voice altogether. 'For no reason at all, you hit me. You total bastard.'

'I hit you and I'll hit you again,' he said. He seized her shoulders and shook her violently. 'You think you can send your tedious mind off on some spiritual errand while the rest of your body lies around here and spends its time with me? I took you to bed, you bitch, not half of you. I took you to bed, and I want all of you!'

She shrieked, a high, off-key shriek. He slapped her again, on the other cheek, harder.

'You dare!' she screamed. 'Oh, god, you dare!'

He turned her over on to her face, and twisted her arm behind her back. She could feel his heavy crucifix swinging against her shoulder. He was lean, but he was so much stronger than she was that she could scarcely move, and when his brown muscular knee wedged itself between her thighs, opening up her legs, there was nothing she could do to prevent it.

Panting, cursing under his breath, he roughly parted the lips of her vulva with his free hand. Then he leaned forward, giving her arm another savage twist to prevent her from squirming away, and pushed the head of his erection up against her.

'Granger!' she begged. 'No, Granger! Not like this! No!'

He grunted once, and his thick penis forced its way up inside her. She felt the prickly curls of his pubic hair up against the bare cheeks of her bottom, and his tight balls deep between her legs.

He thrust into her relentlessly, harder and harder. Her twisted arm was agony, and he was hurting her vagina with every thrust. But he went on and on until she couldn't resist

165

the feeling of having him right up inside her again and again and again; and though she swore into the pillow in the filthiest language she knew, there was a moment when she could feel him approaching the edge of his climax, and when she was certain that it was going to be impossible for her to suppress an orgasm of her own.

He came. She felt him fill her. And then her face was squeezed and her fingers were clenched and her nipples were rigid with overwhelming sensation. She said: 'Ah!' and then '*Aaaah!*' and then she screeched out loud and shook like a woman in some nightmare convulsion. It took whole minutes before she could be still, before her nerves stopped jumping, before she could open her eyes.

She was aware of birds singing outside in the garden. She raised herself on one elbow and looked blearily across the bedroom. Granger was standing a little way away, buttoning up his shirt. His penis, limp now, was still shining.

'Granger?' she questioned him, softly.

He watched her without answering.

'Granger?' she repeated. 'What happened?'

He stepped into his undershorts, and found his slacks. 'A miracle,' he said, sharply. 'A practical miracle. Something which you should have experienced a long, long time ago.'

Mary's Drive-In Diner was a small green-painted building with a sun-bleached shingle roof and a hand-painted cut-out sign above the door that showed a smiling dark-haired woman holding up a plateful of amateurishly rendered sausages and beans. It was situated just off Highway 60, in La Lande, New Mexico, and it had originally been built in the 1930s to take advantage of the automobile trade that drove past on its way to see Billy the Kid's grave.

Mary, the dark-haired woman on the sign, was still running the place, although she was grey-haired now, and her husband had long since gone to join William Bonney under the hard-packed soil of De Baca County. On the Saturday evening that Ed Hardesty was preparing to give his broadcast from Shearson Jones's house in Kansas, and Season Hardesty was sitting at the kitchen table at Vee's house eating an early supper with Sally, Mary was wiping over the top of her red laminate counter, opening up catering-sized cans of hot dogs, and setting out catsup bottles, salt, pepper and ashtrays, in readiness for her 'Saturday evening rush.'

Her 'Saturday evening rush' might be no more hectic than a single truck driver, stopping on his way to Fort Sumner for a cold Miller and a cheeseburger. Or it could be a bewildered California family in a Winnebago Chieftain, already unnerved by the wildness of the countryside, and now trying to find their way back to Route 66 and eventual civilisation. At best, it could be six or seven airmen from Cannon AFB near Clovis, all neat and polite and hungry as hell. Mary had switched on the juke-box, and it was playing *The Very Thought Of You*. Outside, the sun had just gone down, and the sky was the rich dusty purple of blueberries. There was a soft breeze blowing from the south-west, from Lincoln County and the Capitan Mountains, and the air carried that distinctively Western smell of dry aromatic weeds, and history, and dust.

Shortly before nine o'clock, an ageing lime-green Cadillac pulled off the blacktop and circled around Mary's stony front yard. It stopped, and out clambered a family of five – Mr and Mrs Donald Abbott, of Portales, New Mexico, and their three young children – all on their way back from a visit to Mrs Abbott's mother in Santa Fé.

Mr Abbott was slight, stooping, and bespectacled. He had celebrated his forty-second birthday a week ago, and he worked for the Roosevelt County health department. At his age, he should have been a district supervisor, except that the county's chief health executive didn't particularly like his face. What's more, he had held out for better medical facilities for underprivileged families at a time when it was politically embarrassing.

Mrs Abbott was plain and friendly, with a face that was as forgettable as a single bagel in a bagel bakery. Their children – Duane, ten; Norman, eight; and Betsy, six – were no more memorable than little bagels. A police officer later described them as 'Mr and Mrs Average, and Average Kids.' But it was better, in a way, that they were. Fewer

167

people would have been shocked if it had been a Spanish family, or a black family, or a family of Mescalero Apaches.

Mr Abbott opened the screen door of Mary's Diner and held it back while his family trooped in. Mary said, 'How are you, folks?' and came around the counter in her blue checkered apron, carrying the dog-eared menus that her six-foot nephew Stephen had Xeroxed for her at his used-car office in Las Vegas. The Abbotts sat a corner table, and ordered hotdogs all round, with onion rings.

While they were eating, Mr Abbott told Mary that they were hoping to take the children to Los Angeles later in the year, so that they could see the ocean and Disneyland. Mary told them that her late husband, Morton, had lived in New Mexico all of his life, and had never once seen the ocean. He had seen John Slaughter once, in 1919, when he was a small boy, but that was all.

Mr and Mrs Abbott drank two more cups of coffee, while the children played Osmond songs on the juke-box. At a quarter to ten, the family left, and Mary stood at the diner door to watch them drive off towards Clovis. Then she went back inside to clean up.

Shortly after dawn on Sunday morning, a trumpet-player who had been entertaining the previous evening at a party at the air base came across the lime-green Cadillac parked beside the road about a mile and a half east of Floyd. He would have driven past it in his Volkswagen without stopping, except that he badly needed a first cigarette, and his car had no lighter. He could see that the Cadillac was occupied, so he pulled in just in front of it, and walked back. It was a cold morning, and the windows of the Cadillac were partially misted up.

The trumpet-player knocked on the driver's window. There was no response so he knocked louder. They were probably all asleep. He shivered in the morning air and chafed his hands together.

It was only when he knocked a third time that he realised something had to be wrong. Twice, he shouted, 'Hey in there! Hey, open the door!' but there was no answer. He could vaguely make out a man and a woman and three

168

children, but they were all lolling back in their seats as if they were dead.

Frightened, the trumpet-player ran back to his own car and took out a tyre-iron from under the seat. He took it to the Cadillac's door, and tried to prise it open, but the lock was too strong for him. He stood panting beside the car, unsure what to do, and he was still there when an air force truck came past. He flagged it down, and it crunched to a halt a little way down the road.

'There's something wrong!' he shouted out. 'It looks like they're dead in there! I can't open the door!'

A tall young airman in a peaked cap and fatigues jumped down from the truck and walked over to take a look for himself. Then, without a word, he loosened a shovel from the truck's side panel, swung it back, and smashed the Cadillac's side window.

The children in the back appeared to be dead. They were curled up like fumigated baby mice, their eyes closed, and their faces white. The broken glass lay on them like splinters of ice. In the front, the driver was alive, but barely conscious. His wife was face-down on the seat.

'*Doctor . . .*' whispered the driver. '*For God's sake . . . doctor . . .*'

The young airman loped back to his truck, and unclipped his radio microphone. The trumpet-player heard him saying, '. . . whole family, that's right . . . no, I can't see what's wrong with them . . . just about a mile or two outside of Floyd . . . you know the road?'

A white-painted fighter-bomber thundered above them as it came in from a dawn exercise. The trumpet-player shielded his eyes against the sun, and then turned away, his hands on his hips in a gesture of helpless resignation. The driver of the Cadillac had closed his eyes now, and was lying back breathing harshly through his mouth. The trumpet-player didn't know whether he ought to take the man's spectacles off or not.

The young airman came back and said, 'They're sending an ambulance from the base. They said not to touch them, in case they have something contagious.'

The trumpet-player nodded. He was glad he had decided

169

against taking off the spectacles. 'The kids, too,' he said, indicating the back seat of the car. 'Whatever it was, it really must have hit 'em hard.'

The airman said, 'Suffocation, maybe. They could have had a leak in their muffler. When that carbon monoxide gets into the car, boy, you don't even realise what's happening to you. A friend of mine killed himself that way. You know, with the rubber hose.'

The trumpet-player held his hand over his mouth. There was no sound out here except for the whining of the wind in the Cadillac's antennae, and the laboured breathing of the driver. There were a few brief rumbles of jet engines from the air force base, but they died away as quickly as summer thunder.

'Some place to die, huh?' said the airman.

The trumpet-player nodded. He was beginning to feel very cold now, and he was wishing that he had never stopped. It was so incongruous and so tragic to see this family sitting in their car that it brought tears to his eyes.

'Do you have a light?' he asked the airman.

The airman shook his head. 'Don't smoke. Easier not to, you know, with all that airplane fuel around.'

'*Doctor* . . .' whispered Donald Abbott.

'A doctor's coming,' said the airman, loudly. 'Don't worry, old buddy, you're going to make it.' Then he looked at the trumpet-player and pulled a face, as if to say, what does it matter? The poor guy's going to die anyway.

Under the tepee-like roof of Shearson Jones's hallway, the television lights had been set up, and the cameras fixed into position. The whole morning had been chaos, with television people rearranging the furniture and reeling out hundreds of feet of cable and leaving styrofoam cups of coffee wherever they went. Shearson, in his mahogany-panelled study, had stayed well out of their way, except to talk for a half-hour to the director about how he was going to present his appeal, and how the broadcast should look. 'Quiet and simple, with folksy dignity, that's what I want,' he had insisted. 'There's no way we should look like we're rattling a tin cup under anybody's nose.'

Peter Kaiser had spent five harassed hours mapping out contingency plans for handling all the money the appeal was going to bring in, and he had taken up so much of Karen's time with typing and telephoning that she hadn't even been able to get away for a swim. The fund had now been sub-divided into geographical regions – east, central, and west – so that contributions could be handled more efficiently. It would also make the money more difficult to trace, when accounting time came. Karen had spent most of the morning calling San Francisco, Chicago, and New York, briefing Peter's regional office staff. None of them had been particularly helpful and happy about being disturbed on a Sunday, even this Sunday.

Ed had felt tense all day. He had woken just before it was light, and he had sat out on his balcony, wrapped in his bathrobe, smoking a cigar and watching the grey waters of the lake. Behind him, in his bedroom, Della McIntosh had lain sleeping on his bed, her red hair spread out over the pillow, her knees drawn up like a child. She had knocked on his door at midnight, and he had let her in without a word. They had said nothing to each other at all – nothing about motives or betrayal or politics. They had made love three times, and the last time she had sat on top of him, while he had reached up with his hands and cradled her heavy breasts. They had kissed once, almost a chaste kiss, and then slept.

After breakfast, Ed had watched the television technicians for a while. Then he had swum up and down Shearson's triangular pool. He had thought of calling Season in Los Angeles, but somehow he had felt disinclined. There was too much on his mind. Della was no substitute for Season, but Season was so much more complicated. The day was sunny but cool.

At three o'clock, after everybody had sat around the lunch table for a gargantuan lobster salad, and Shearson had retired to his suite of rooms to doze and belch for an hour in private, the TV direcror had introduced Ed to his make-up lady and his continuity girl and the silent, elegantly-dressed black prompter who was going to hold up his short speech for him on large idiot boards. Then Ed

171

had been given a plaid shirt and a pair of jeans to put on, his hair had been washed and blow-dried, and a small touch of blush had been rubbed along his cheekbones.

'We want you to look healthy and rural,' said the director.

'Even though I'm destitute, and my crops have been wiped out?' asked Ed.

'Listen – people don't want to be reminded of *The Grapes of Wrath*. They don't want haggard sharecroppers. They want a healthy, friendly, young fellow who's been hit by a tragic bolt from the blue.'

'Would you like me to endorse somebody's breakfast cereal at the same time?' Ed had asked, sarcastically.

'Just read what's on the cards and sound as if you mean it,' retorted the director. 'And for Christ's sake don't smile.'

Ed was placed against a background of bare wooden floorboards and walls with only Andrew Wyeth's severe painting of Dil Huey Farm behind him. The director had asked him to run through his words, and he had haltingly obliged. What had made it worse was that he had known all along he was never going to say them.

I'm a Kansas wheat farmer. You've just heard Senator Shearson Jones asking for help on our behalf. All I want to say is that in Kansas we're not the kind to go begging. We wouldn't be asking for your assistance if we hadn't been struck by the worst natural crop disaster for nigh on forty years. It's hit us hard, and it's hit us fast, and there was no way in the world we could have stopped it.

I want you to contribute to the Kansas Blight Crisis Appeal because my fellow wheat farmers and I want to go on growing wheat for this great country of ours. Every dollar you give will be sowed in the Kansas soil like a seed, and out of it we'll be able to harvest a new economic strength and fine cereal foods for future generations of Americans.

I give you this personal promise. We're tough, hard-working people. We don't normally ask for handouts. And with the donation you send us, we'll work ten times as hard as usual to make sure that we get back on our feet again fast. Thank you for listening. My name's Ed Hardesty.

'This is gibberish,' said Ed, as the lighting technician came across the floor and tilted his head slightly to one side.

'Face that way,' said the technician. 'If you face the way you were, your nose looks shapeless.'

'If I face the other way, I can't read the gibberish.'

'You may think it's gibberish,' said the director. 'But if you write sense for television, it comes out sounding weird. The first criterion is it has to *sound* like sense. Whether it *is* or not, that's irrelevant.'

'All right,' said Ed. He had promised himself that he wouldn't create any difficulties. If he created difficulties, they might not ask him to speak on the broadcast. The lighting technician switched off the spots, and he saw swimming coloured shapes in front of his eyes.

A few minutes before air time, Shearson Jones appeared, wearing a dark grey suit that would have swamped Orson Welles. He lowered himself carefully into a leather-backed throne of a chair, and the make-up lady fussed around him and mopped away the perspiration which had popped out on his forehead and around his mouth.

'These lights are goddamned hot,' he complained. 'I feel like I'm losing pounds, just sitting here.'

Ed waited in the cool and the shadow behind the lights. He watched quietly as the television people straightened Shearson's lapels, and shifted a potted yucca a few inches to the left, so that it wouldn't look as if it was growing out of Shearson's head. He was so tense and intent on what was going on that he didn't notice Della approach him from behind until she put her arm around him.

'Hi,' she said. 'Are you nervous?'

He looked down at her. She was dressed in blue jeans, a pink T-shirt, and no bra. Her nipples showed through the thin cotton.

'There's no reason to be nervous,' said Ed. 'It's all written out on the cards for me. All I have to do is read it.'

'But you're still nervous?'

'A little.'

She glanced around, to see if there was anybody standing close. Then she said, 'I overheard you.'

'You overheard me?' he asked her. 'What are you talking about? When?'

'I overheard you talking to Karen on the balcony.'

Ed looked at her closely. She didn't look away. Her eyes searched into his just as deeply, and with just as much intensity, as his were searching into hers.

'What did you hear?' he asked her.

'Everything,' she said.

'You heard what I said about this broadcast?'

She nodded.

'You haven't told Shearson? Or have you?'

'No,' she said.

'Why not? You si'enced Dr Benson quick enough. I called him this morning and he's been taken into a clinic to dry out again.'

'I know. I'm sorry.'

'You're *sorry*?' Ed said. 'That guy spent years weaning himself off the bottle. Now you've probably ruined his life, as well as his career.'

'Yes,' said Della. 'But you can believe me when I tell you he's going to be fully compensated.'

'By whom? Blue Cross doesn't cover you for alcoholism.'

Della reached out and held Ed's wrist, the gentle but persuasive way that a friend does. 'I'm sorry about Dr Benson,' she said. 'But there's something a whole lot more important at stake here. In fact, it's so important that I have to ask you not to say anything today except what's on the cards.'

'Are you kidding me?' demanded Ed. 'Do you have any idea what's going on? What Shearson Jones is doing? Do you have any idea what kind of a disaster we're facing here? I mean – every crop in every state is blighted. Can you understand what that's going to mean?'

'The news is going to break out anyway,' said Della. 'But right now, I want to keep this Blight Crisis Appeal going for just two or three more days.'

'For what? For Shearson Jones to make himself two or three million dollars richer?'

'Precisely.'

Ed lifted her hand away from his wrist. 'In that case, you

can count me out. I wouldn't give that fat slob a subway token.'

'Ed,' said Della, 'I work for the Federal Bureau of Investigation.'

Ed slowly turned his head and stared at her. 'Now I *know* you're joking,' he said. 'You just want me to go out there and speak my words like a good little boy, so that Shearson and you can get away with as much loot as possible.'

'You don't believe me?'

'Why should I? You certainly don't *look* like an FBI agent. Do you have a badge?'

'Back in Washington, yes.'

'Well, that's convenient,' said Ed.

'Ed,' insisted Della, 'you have to believe me. We've been trying to catch Shearson Jones red-handed for nearly two years. Now, we've got ourselves a chance.'

'So why did you silence Dr Benson?' asked Ed.

'I had to. I didn't want to, but I had to. None of the appeal money has been transferred to Shearson's private accounts yet, and until that happens, he isn't guilty of anything. He told me to keep Dr Benson quiet and that's just what I did, in the most harmless way I could think of. I had to keep his confidence.'

Ed looked at her again. At the curly red hair, and the soft shining lips, and the huge breasts.

'You're an FBI agent?' he asked her. 'I don't believe it. Eliot Ness always wore pinstripe suits.'

'I was chosen for my looks. I worked on the Miami pornography scam a couple of years ago. It's the kind of work I do best.'

'I'll bet.'

'Ed,' said Della, 'you don't have to believe me. But if you don't, Shearson Jones could escape from this whole set-up scot-free.'

Ed closed his eyes for a moment. He knew what his urgent duty was: to stand up in front of those television cameras and tell as many people as possible what was going on. They were voters, and citizens, and human beings, and they had a right to know. Yet if Della was telling the truth and she did work for the FBI, it was equally important that he didn't blow her carefully-arranged scam and warn Shearson Jones off. After all, she had actually given her body to Shearson Jones for the sake of a watertight arrest, and Ed wasn't the kind of man who thought that was an easy or an offhand thing for a woman to do, even a woman like Della McIntosh.

He opened his eyes. Della was still looking at him intently.

'I don't know,' he said. 'I don't know whether to believe you or not. If you're really an FBI agent, why didn't you tell me this last night?'

She gave an ironic smile. 'I was always told that it was impolite to talk with your mouth full.'

'I mean seriously.'

'Because I wasn't sure of you,' she said. 'I wasn't sure how you were going to react. And because I was making love to you. That's all.'

Ed said, 'I don't know if that's enough. Not to convince me of what you are, anyway, and what you're doing here.'

Della gave him a long, level look. 'In that case, you'd better go out in front of those cameras and say just what your conscience dictates.'

Ed said quietly, 'I think I'm going to have to.'

Surprisingly, Della had tears in her eyes. Ed could see them sparkling in the back light from the television floods. 'The goddamned wretched thing about it is, I've fallen in love with you,' she said. 'That's the goddamned wretched thing about it.'

Ed said, 'Della – ' but she turned quickly away and walked back across the television cables, and out through the door that led to the side verandah. Ed felt tempted to follow, but he could hear that Shearson was almost finished with his introductory speech, and he knew that the television people would be calling him forward in a minute or two.

The director twisted around in his folding-chair, caught Ed's eye, and pointed towards the place where Ed was supposed to stand. Ed nodded, and tippy-toed across the floor. As if in a dream, he could hear Shearson Jones saying, '. . . and now . . . I want you to meet one of the farmers I've been talking about . . . one of the hard-working, strong-willed Kansas wheat growers who have had to fight against this terrible and unprecedented disaster alone and single-handed . . . with only their guts and their know-how to rely on . . .'

It was discovered by chance. It could have remained hidden, and nobody would ever have known, not until it was far too late. Although, by the time it was found, it was far too late anyway. The damage had been done.

The grain ship *City of Belleville* was docked at St Louis, Missouri, taking on a cargo of hard wheat for Europe. It was Sunday afternoon, a few minutes after five o'clock, and Ed Hardesty had already started speaking on the television. Not that the stevedores at Jefferson Docks cared very much – they were too busy on overtime, loading thousands of tons of grain from the wharfside silos into the *City of Belleville*'s holds. The shipment was already a week overdue and the men had been promised double time if they caught up on the lost seven days.

The ship's first mate was a tough, bullet-headed little man from Milwaukee. His shore friends called him 'German'. His ship friends called him 'Square', because of his shape. His real name was Herman Heller, a second-generation immigrant whose only surviving relative, his dotty father, now sang off-key *Lieder* in a Wisconsin nursing-home.

Herman Heller was standing at the ship's rail smoking his pipe and watching the pale brown river roll by. Here in St Louis, the weather was humid and uncomfortable, and there was a dark stain of sweat down the back of Herman's light blue T-shirt. He was thinking about a woman he knew in New Orleans – a quiet, jolly woman with a big nose who ran a delicatessen on the south side of the city. She had a husband who was confined to a wheelchair, and she didn't ask anything of Herman but vigorous humping when he was there and suggestive letters when he wasn't. Herman was good at suggestive letters. The woman's *blutwurst* was unsurpassed.

Herman was deep in his reverie when Dan Bashnik came

up to the bridge in his red woolly hat and held up what appeared to be a black metal baton. 'Square,' he said. 'Take a look at this.'

Herman took out his pipe. 'What's that? Where'd you find it?'

'Number One hold. It was just lying there on top of the grain.'

Herman held out his hand for it. Dan Bashnik passed it over, and watched while Herman inspected it. Herman hefted it in his palm, then twisted it around, and finally sniffed it to see if it smelled of anything.

'What do you make of it?' asked Dan.

'I don't know. Never seen anything like it. Maybe it's part of a grain sorting machine, got itself loose.'

'You going to hand it in?'

'Sure, it's no use to me.'

Dan wiped his nose with the back of his hand. 'Well, if there's any kind of reward for it, don't forget who found it.'

'I should forget my friend, Dan Bashnik?'

'You'd forget your own mother if it meant the difference between two bucks and ten.'

Herman jammed his pipe back between his pecan-coloured teeth. 'Just fuck off, Bashnik. If there's anything in it, I'll make sure you get your share.'

He opened the door to the bridge and laid the black metal baton on the varnished shelf beside the maps of the Mississippi. It stayed there all afternoon and all evening, until Herman went ashore to check the cargo inventory and the bills of lading. Then – almost as an afterthought – he shoved it into the pocket of his windbreaker.

It was dark as Herman made his way down the gangplank to the dockside. There was the whinnying of cranes, and the clatter of fork-lift trucks, and the odd cold echoing sound of warehouses and water and ships. Herman walked across to the offices with the steady plod of a man who has been doing the same thing for twenty years at somebody else's expense. He looked neither right nor left.

One of the St Louis safety inspectors was in the office when Herman walked in, a white-faced young man with a John Denver haircut and an immature moustache. He was smoking a cigarette and flicking through a girlie magazine. Errol Marx of the grain company was there too, a shaven-headed black man with heavy-rimmed eyeglasses.

'You ready to leave?' asked Marx.

'Just as soon as we clear the paperwork,' Herman told him.

Marx reached for his clipboard, took out a ballpen, and sniffed. 'It took you long enough to get that goddamned grain on board,' he said.

Herman didn't answer. He did his job at one pace and one pace only, and that was Heller's pace. If anybody objected, that was tough tits. He reached into his pocket for his matches.

The safety inspector said, 'It's unfair, you know. All these magazines are full of white girls. Only one or two black girls. Don't you think that's discrimination?'

Marx ticked off a column of figures. 'They don't have black girls because black men don't need to read magazines,' he said. 'Black men get all the tail they want for real.'

'Oh, bullshit,' said the safety inspector. 'Just because I fancy looking at some black ass now and again.'

'Well, here's something else to look at,' said Herman, taking the black metal baton out of his pocket. 'One of my guys found it in the wheat. A real toothbreaker, huh?'

The safety inspector peered at the baton for a moment, frowned, and then slowly put down his magazine.

'Put it down,' he said, in a cautious voice.

'Why? What's it going to do? Blow up? It hasn't blown up yet.'

'Put it down,' insisted the safety inspector.

Herman, puzzled, laid the baton down on the desk. Errol inspected it through his spectacles, poked it with the end of his pencil, and said, 'What the hell is it?'

'I should be asking *you* that,' said the safety inspector. 'It came out of *your* wheat. Now, just you wait here for a while. I want to go get something. And make sure you don't touch that thing any more.'

Herman shrugged at Errol, and told the safety inspector, 'Okay. You're the boss.'

They waited in silence for nearly five minutes. Herman

179

packed his pipe again, and lit it, and the small office was clouded with aromatic smoke. Errol Marx sneezed twice, and then blew his nose on a Kleenex. 'You don't object to my smoking, do you?' asked Herman, rhetorically.

Eventually, the safety inspector came back. As he came through the door, he was unzipping a black plastic carrying case, and taking out a grey rectangular instrument with a white calibrated dial.

'What goes on here?' asked Errol. 'What the hell's that thing?'

'You never seen a geiger counter before?' asked the safety inspector.

'Geiger counter? Like, for radioactivity? You mean that thing could be radioactive?'

'I don't know. That's why I'm checking.'

The safety inspector switched the geiger counter on. Immediately, without him having to hold it anywhere near the black baton, it began to click as loudly and wildly as a migration of locusts.

'Jesus Christ,' said the safety inspector, switching it off.

'What's wrong?' demanded Herman. 'What is that thing? What goes on here?'

The safety inspector didn't answer him. Instead, he picked up Errol Marx's telephone and dialled a number. Errol glanced at Herman and shrugged as the safety inspector waited to get through. They both watched him biting his lips in anxiety.

At last, someone answered. The safety inspector said, 'Fred? It's Nelson. Listen, I'm sorry to call you now, but I've got myself a red alert down here. No, nothing like that. We've got the *City of Belleville* here, loading up with wheat from number seven silo, and some from number eight. Well, one of the crew members came into Errol Marx's office a few minutes ago with something they'd turned up in the wheat. I kind of recognised it – I mean, I've seen something like it before in science magazines so I checked it over with the geiger counter. Yes, right – and it went way off the scale. I'm sure of it, Fred, no mistakes possible. Right. Well – we're going to need the fire department down here, I guess, and an ambulance, and someone who knows something about radiation. Sure, I'll have the ship and the dockside sealed off right away.'

Herman interrupted him. 'Listen,' he said, 'what are you talking about, radioactive? You can't seal my ship off. I have to sail in an hour.'

The safety inspector held his hand over the mouthpiece of the telephone. 'There's no way. No way at all. Your ship, your cargo, and most of your crew – especially *you*, because you've been handling that thing – you're all highly radioactive. You're not going any place tonight but hospital.'

'Then what the hell is that thing? And what the hell's it doing in the wheat?'

'The second question I can't answer,' said the safety inspector. 'As for the first question – well, I believe it's some kind of radioactive isotope.'

'Isotope?' queried Herman, looking at Errol Marx.

Errol said, 'Search me.'

During the evening, Donald Abbott and the bodies of his family were flown from the sanitarium at Cannon AFB to an isolation hospital on the outskirts of Phoenix, near Scottsdale. Donald Abbott was scarcely alive, and the medics at Cannon had given him only a one per cent chance of survival. 'I never saw anyone so close to death without actually being dead,' one of the docters said later.

The first diagnosis was food poisoning, and when it was discovered that the Abbotts had spent the past two days with Mrs Abbott's mother in Santa Fé, police and health officials were urgently sent to her home to check on the food that the family might have eaten – and on the safety of Mrs Abbott's mother herself.

For two or three hours – until it was given a full medical clearance – the chief suspect was a tub of chocolate maple ice-cream, which only the Abbott family had eaten. Then the coroner's report came in on the contents of Mrs Abbott's stomach, and it was clear that she had consumed a frankfurter sausage and a quantity of bread sometime during Saturday evening. The coroner's comment was bald and devastating. 'The frankfurter sausage was analysed, and found to contain sufficient botulin to poison a horse.'

The New Mexico Highway Patrol located Mary's Diner within twenty-three minutes of being called from Phoenix. Mary, bewildered and shocked, confirmed that the Abbott family had eaten hotdogs there on Saturday evening. Eight airmen and a truck driver had also eaten there, but they had all chosen hamburgers, cheeseburgers, or reubenburgers. The Highway Patrol officers took away all the fresh meat from Mary's Diner, sealed it in plastic, and sent it to Phoenix for tests.

On Monday morning, at 10.3 a.m., Donald Abbott died of botulism.

The death of Donald Abbott and his family had yet to make news, however. What *was* news, as Sunday became Monday, was that a Kansas wheat farmer had stood in front of the cameras on live coast-to-coast television and announced that Americans were facing a whole lot more than 'a noticeable percentage of inconvenience' from the crop blights which had struck all over the country. They were facing nothing less than the total destruction of their agricultural economy, and possible starvation.

The television people hadn't pulled the plug on him, as Ed had expected them to. The director had recognised good hard news material when it was handed to him on a plate, and Shearson Jones had wrathfully decided it was better not to intervene. If he had ordered the transmission to be killed, he would only have given Ed's comments more public credibility. But he had sat on his throne and glared in fury at Ed with a face like a malevolent blancmange.

Ed had been chilled but sweating as he faced the dark, polished, noncommittal lens of the television camera. He had been aware of Shearson Jones, smouldering in his chair; and of Della, who had returned from the verandah to listen to him. In some ways, though, the most disconcerting face of all had been that of the elegant young black prompter, who had continued to hold up his idiot cards regardless of what he was actually saying. There had been moments when he had almost slipped into his pre-written speech, simply because he was groping for words, and there they were, up in front of him.

'I was supposed to stand here today and tell you how much we Kansas wheat farmers need your help,' he had said.

'The trouble is, I can't do that. My conscience won't let me. Because the truth is that every one of you is going to need help just as badly as we do. This blight that you've been hearing about – these isolated crop diseases – well, they're neither as slight nor as isolated as you've been led to believe.

'What's happening is that every major fruit, vegetable and cereal crop in the entire continental United States is being quickly destroyed by a virus. They're not totally destroyed yet, by any means, but unless an antidote can be sprayed on the worst of them within a matter of days, this country is going to be facing shortages like you've never seen before, and that's quite apart from the prospect of complete economic collapse.

'I want you to know that an antidote to the virus was recommended to the federal agricultural research laboratories two days ago by the Pentagon's chemical warfare experts. They've looked at the blight, and they believe it's quite close to something called Vorar D – which was artificially engineered for defoliating the jungle in Vietnam. They think it's curable, and they've already told that to Senator Shearson Jones.

'Senator Shearson Jones, however, has kept that information to himself, just like he's kept every fact about this crop blight to himself – even when it started to become clear that it could possibly herald a major disaster. And why? Because he wanted businesses and private individuals and Congress itself to contribute lavishly to his crisis fund. He didn't want us all to be worried about our own problems, or the prospect of nation-wide catastrophe, because we wouldn't dig so readily into our pockets if we were.

'I believe you ought to know that Senator Shearson Jones and some of the senior members of his staff have made provision to keep themselves supplied with food during the coming lean months; and I believe you also ought to know that the President himself has ordered the administration in Washington to be provided for. That's how real the danger has already become.

'This is the truth as far as I know it. There may be worse things happening which I don't know about. The prospects for the fall and the winter may be better than I've been led to understand. I don't know. All I can say right now is that this nation is faced with the prospect of a famine, and that every man, woman, and child has the right to know.'

When Ed had finished speaking, the lofty triangular room had fallen totally silent. Then the elegant young black prompter had let one of his cards fall, and it had skated across the floor.

Shearson Jones had lifted himself out of his chair, and waddled to the centre of the hall. His bulk had been dark, imposing, and immovable.

'Hardesty,' he had said, harshly, 'you have just brought down the temple. The art of politics, quite apart from feathering one's own nest, is to preserve the public's sacred ignorance. The public, far from having a right to know, have a right to be kept in the dark. It is for their own good, their own safety, and their own survival. You don't shout "fire!" in a crowded auditorium, even if there *is* a fire. You tell the audience that there has been an infestation of fleas, or that the leading actor has fallen sick, and then you usher them quietly out.

'I admit quite freely, that I might have exploited some aspects of this blight to my own personal ends, although you will never get me to say so in front of a judge, or a Senatorial committee.

'But you have seriously misjudged my capabilities as a politician in keeping this crisis low-key. I have been trying to save this country's neck. And now, with your one foolish broadcast, you have guaranteed its strangulation.'

Ed had stayed where he was.

'I shouldn't let it worry you, Senator,' he had said, loudly. 'You'll be okay, won't you? You have plenty of food, and plenty of wine, and enough money to last you through the next few months. Why should you be upset?'

'Because the United States of America is my country,' growled Shearson. 'And because you have effectively undone with two hundred ill-advised words the work of Thomas Jefferson, Abraham Lincoln, Franklin Roosevelt, Dwight Eisenhower, John Kennedy, Richard Nixon, and hundreds of Americans a hundred times abler and more dedicated to this country than you are.

'Graft is one thing, Hardesty. Suicide is another.'

Book Two

One

It was the sound of breaking glass that woke Nicolas up. Not downstairs, in his own delicatessen, but all over the city. Glass breaking, in street after street, with a terrible wintry jangle like sleighbells.

Nicolas sat up, and listened. He was Greek, round-shouldered, with fuzzy grey hair all over his chest and back, although his head was bald and blue. Next to him, his wife Dolores was still sleeping, her heavy eyebrows drawn together with all the intensity of mating caterpillars. Nicolas laid a cautious hand on her shoulder, as if silently advising her to remain asleep.

Outside, the noise grew louder. The cracking and smashing of huge plateglass storefronts. Then, suddenly, a series of malicious, slushy crashes, as glass display cases and cold-beer cabinets were attacked with hammers and bricks and bars. Sombody screamed – really screamed, as if their fingers were being torn off. There was a whole lot of garbled yelling, and then the distant scribbling sound of ambulance sirens.

'Dolly,' whispered Nicolas, but now she was awake. The danger in the night air was as strong as a smouldering mattress – too strong for anyone to stay asleep. She stared up at him, the back of her hand pressed to her forehead, and said 'Nick? What is it? What's the matter?'

'Listen,' he told her, as if he was going to tell her something interesting. But he meant: listen to the noise outside.

They sat in their dark wallpapered bedroom in that rundown section of Milwaukee where the elevated highways leave you blotted in shadow in the summer, and blessed with nothing but dirty second-hand slush in the winter; and the two of them, both fifty-five years old, heard the chiming of glass that heralded the end of their life's labours, and their small ambitions, and the mutual love which they had nursed through two delicatessen stores, one bankruptcy, five children, two deaths, and more freezing Christmases on the shores of Lake Michigan than they could remember.

The smashing noises were coming closer. They were in the next street now. And they could hear something else: the pattering of running feet. Nicolas thought: *they sound like rats, hurrying through the night*. He had heard rats running across the floor of a flour warehouse once, and that was just what they sounded like.

He hesitated for a moment, but then he gave a decisive sniff, and swung his legs out from between the sheets. He walked around the end of the bed, where his pants were neatly hung with their maroon suspenders still attached, and crossed the bedroom to the window.

Dolores watched him as he held aside the floral drapes and peered down into the street. There must have been a fire burning not far away, because she could see the reflected sparkle of orange in his eyes. On the top of the varnished bureau beside him were the bits and pieces of his hobby – the modelling knives and tubes of glue and carefully-cut sections of balsa wood which he devotedly assembled into tiny ships. The sad gilded face of the Virgin looked down on him from a plastic icon.

Dolores said, 'What do you see?'

Nicolas frowned. 'Nothing so far. But it looks like something's burning on the next block. An automobile, maybe. Or a van.'

'They're burning a *van* on the next block?'

'It's hard to say. I can't see anyone around.'

'Not even a cop?'

Nicolas shook his head. They were both sensitive about the police, the Prokopious. In this neighbourhood, they were regularly shaken down and robbed, and the police patrols did very little to protect them. There were always plenty of police around at Thanksgiving, or at Christmas, when Nicolas gave away bottles of retsina and Keo brandy. But when the kids came around with their knives and their zip guns and raided the cash register, you could scream 'Police!' until you were purple in the face and nobody would come.

190

'What do you think's happening?' asked Dolores. 'All that glass breaking. It sounds like a war.'

'Maybe it's something to do with the food shortages.'

'You mean that television programme? I don't understand.'

Nicolas let the drapes fall back into place. His face was sweaty and serious. 'You heard what they said on the news. They said keep calm, don't try to stock up on more food than you need. But you think people are going to take any notice of that? They panic when there's a shortage of gas. They panic when there's a shortage of bread. In my opinion, that's what they're doing now. Panicking. Breaking into food stores, looking for supplies.'

Dolores said anxiously, 'They'll come here.'

Nicolas nodded. On the bedside table just behind Dolores's black wavy hair, his luminous alarm clock read three in the morning, almost to the minute.

'What are you going to do?' asked Dolores. Her question was punctuated by a loud crash from across the street, and the sound of a woman shouting. Nicolas turned and regarded the drapes as if he expected them to fly apart of their own accord.

'I'll call the police,' he said.

'The police? And what will they do?'

'I'll call Sergeant Kyprianides.'

'You really think he's going to worry? Just because he's Greek? He's as rotten as all the rest of them.'

Nicolas unbuttoned his striped pyjamas, peeled them off, and folded them up. He was a short, heavy man, with a girdle of fat around his hips. He found a clean pair of jockey shorts in the bureau drawer and then stepped into his pants. In the stained-pine wardrobe he found a clean red shirt.

'I'm going downstairs,' he said.

Dolores said, 'What for? What can you do on your own?'

Nicolas pointed towards the window. 'What *for*? Do you hear what they're doing out there? You want the store wrecked?'

She climbed out of bed. She was wearing the pink baby-doll nightdress he liked, with the frilly panties. Her sagging breasts showed dark-nippled through the nylon, and her thighs were creased with fat.

'I don't want *you* wrecked,' she said, and she really meant it. 'Who cares about a few bowls of taramasalata?'

Nicolas held her wrist, and kissed her on the forehead. 'The day I let some bum walk in off the street and tear my store to pieces without lifting so much as one finger to stop him – that's the day I'm going to be laid out in my coffin. You got me?'

She bit her lip.

'I'm sorry,' he said, and opened the door to go downstairs.

It was then, right then, that the front window of their own store was smashed in. It was so loud and violent that Nicolas said, '*Hah*' in involuntary shock. Dolores crossed herself, and whispered 'Mother of God.'

Nicolas was angry now. He could hear people shouting downstairs as they clambered into his store through the broken window. Looters, in *his* store, trampling over *his* displays and *his* counters, and helping themselves to all the things he had worked for years to buy. Helping themselves to the cans and the bottles and the home-cooked pastries. Destroying *his* life and *his* livelihood.

The .38 police revolver was on top of the wardrobe. Nicolas stalked over, reached up for it, and brought it down. Dolores said, 'Nicky – for God's sake – leave them – '

'Leave them?' he asked her. His mouth was tight and he had that bitter, hard, sorrowful look in his eyes, the same look he always had when they were robbed or ripped off. 'In this country, you have to fight for what's yours. You understand me?'

He pushed his way down the landing to the stairs which led to the store. Dolores came after, trying to pull his sleeve, but he shook her loose with one impatient twist. He knocked askew a picture of fishing boats off the island of Serifos. Blue skies, bleached boats.

Dolores said, 'No, Nicky, please.'

Nicky, halfway down the stairs, turned and looked back at her. The revolver was raised awkwardly in his left hand.

From downstairs, there was another splintering crack as the looters broke into his refrigerated display cabinet, and someone shouted, 'Get that canned food at the back – all that canned stuff!'

Dolores said nothing, but walked quickly back along the landing in her pink baby-doll nightie to where the telephone hung on the wall by the stairs. Nicolas heard her dialling, and knew that she was calling Sergeant Kyprianides. He felt short of breath, and afraid, but there was no point in waiting until the police turned up. They might not turn up at all, what with all the smashing and looting that was going on tonight throughout Milwaukee. They'd be busy taking care of the breweries, and the big department stores. What would they care about one small Greek delicatessen in the grittier part of town?

Nicolas went down the dark stairwell, unbolted the brown-painted door at the bottom, and pulled it cautiously open.

He was dazzled straight away by car headlights, directed right into the smashed-open store from a station wagon that had been pulled up across the sidewalk. There was a sharp smell of burning paint, and the night air was warm and electric with fright. He drew the door open a little further, and he could see the outline of a man in a plaid jacket, leaning over the frozen-food cabinet with a large plastic trash bag in one hand, helping himself to broccoli and asparagus spears and mixed vegetables and TV dinners. He could hear feet crunching on broken glass in back of the store, too, but from where he was standing he couldn't see anybody.

'Are you through with that frozen food yet?' a voice demanded.

The man bent over the freezer cabinet said, 'Give me a minute, will you?' as he gathered up boxes of Hungry Man dinners by the armful.

Nicolas cocked his revolver, and stepped out into the store. He said, 'Put up your hands,' but at first nobody heard him.

Louder, he said, '*Put up your hands!*'

The man at the freezer cabinet turned around, slowly

lifting one arm up, but keeping a tight hold on his plastic bag of frozen food with the other hand. He was young, maybe thirty-two, with a moustache and horn-rim eyeglasses. He looked like an ordinary suburbanite, not at all like a robber.

Nicolas edged his way along the shelves, keeping his back to the serried cans of tuna and eggplant, his revolver held high in both hands. As he moved around, he was able to catch sight of a blonde woman in a fawn tracksuit, standing beside his display of bottled fruits, and another young man, unshaven and dark, a Greek possibly, or an Italian, in army fatigues.

Nicolas said, 'You lay down the stuff and you get out of here. You understand me? I'm used to dealing with bums.'

The man by the freezer cabinet said, 'Mister – there's no way we're bums.'

'You're not bums? What are you doing looting my store, if you're not bums? Now, get out of here.'

The woman said, 'We're sorry. But it's the food crisis.'

'Just get out,' said Nicolas, waving the revolver towards her.

'You don't understand,' the man by the freezer cabinet told him. 'There's hardly any food left. This is the last place, just about. How are we going to feed our kids? We've got kids.'

Nicolas looked from one face to the other. It wasn't hard to see that they were as frightened as he was. These weren't the hard, amused faces of shakedown artists, or street hoodlums. These were just ordinary people caught in a desperate and unfamiliar act. He felt sorry for them, almost. But he felt protective towards Dolores, and himself, too; and, after all, the food in this delicatèssen was his, not theirs, no matter how many kids they had.

'Go,' he admonished them.

There was an uncomfortable pause, but then the Greek-looking man in the army fatigues reached down behind the bread rack and lifted up a shotgun. It wasn't the kind of shotgun you saw on the streets, sawed off, with hardly any stock. It was a long-barrelled hunting gun, still shiny with oil.

Nicolas veered the revolver across the store. 'Drop it,' he said. 'Put it down, or I'll shoot you.'

The Greek-looking man said, 'This food in here – you think that you're going to keep it all to yourself? All of it? Just because you're a storekeeper you think you've got some God-given right to survive while everybody else starves?'

Nicolas didn't even want to think about it. He said, 'I'm giving you three. You understand me? Three, and then I shoot.'

The Greek-looking man, still holding the shotgun, looked across at the man by the freezer. A question passed between them, unspoken but obvious. Nervously, instantly, Nicolas fired.

The first shot missed. The revolver bucked in his hands, and he heard the bang of broken glass at the back of the store, followed by a sudden rush of green olives from three broken jars. He fired again, before he could allow himself to think, and the Greek's shoulder burst apart in a spray of gory catsup. The girl shrieked, a silly short shriek that made Nicolas frown at her as if he couldn't believe anything so ridiculous. And then there was a deep, deafening *bav-vooom*! and Nicolas realised with strange slow horror that the Greek had fired back at him with his shotgun, and that he'd been hit, badly hit, in the belly and the thighs. He was shocked, off-balance, hurt. He felt as if someone had splashed blazing kerosene between his legs, as if he was burning and burning and would never stop.

In perceptual slow-motion, he looked down towards his legs, and saw that his pants were in bloody ribbons, that his thighs were as black and raw as hamburger meat, and that the remains of his penis were dangling from a thin shred of skin. He collapsed, both physically and mentally. His mind folded in on itself like a Chinese conjuring trick, and he pitched to the floor. He was aware of somebody shouting, and bright lights, and the feel of the plastic floor-tiles against his cheek, but that was all.

Dolores came down the stairs and into the store as the

three looters were climbing out through the shattered window. She saw Nicolas lying doubled up against the shelves that ran the length of the middle of the store, and the blood that was sprayed all around him. She could hardly make out the looters at all, because she was half-blinded by the car lights, but the looters saw her.

She screamed, 'Stop! Stop!' although she didn't want them to stop at all. One of them hesitated, holding a shotgun one-handed, its stock tucked under his arm. Dolores stared at him for a moment, at his almost invisible silhouette, and then marched formidably across the store towards him, clambering through the shattered window in her baby-doll nightie, her feet slashed by broken glass, until she was out on the sidewalk. The car meanwhile was backing off the sidewalk, bouncing on to the road, and getting ready to take off.

Dolores said to the Greek-looking man with the bloody arm and the army fatigues, 'You've killed my husband.'

The man said tensely, 'Back off. You hear me? Just back off.'

'You've killed my husband,' said Dolores, simply. It seemed important to tell the man what he had done. 'He came from Serifos. There are blue skies there, and blue sea. Now look.'

She turned back towards the darkened store. She couldn't see Nicolas in the shadows, but she knew he was there. 'His name was Nicolas Andreas Prokopiou.'

A hoarse voice from the car shouted, 'Gerry! For Christ's sake!' And somewhere in the air, far away, Dolores could hear the whoop of a police siren. She took two or three steps forward, and the man with the shotgun took two or three steps back.

'Gerry!' screeched the blonde woman's voice from the back of the car.

There was one more second of uncertainty, and then the Greek-looking man raised his shotgun, and shot Dolores at almost point-blank range in the face. He had meant to blind her, so that she could never recognise him again, but before tonight he had only used his shotgun for hunting rabbit. He had never seen what it could do to a human being from only two feet away. It almost blew her head off, in a fountain of blood that jumped five feet in the air. She teetered around, spun and then fell.

The Greek-looking man ran to the car, threw the shotgun in through the open window, then tugged open the door and climbed in himself.

The woman said, 'You're out of your mind! If I'd known you were going to do something like that, I wouldn't have come! Do you hear me? You're crazy!'

'Just shut up,' snapped the man in the plaid jacket, as he pulled away from the kerb, with the car tyres shrieking like strangled chickens.

They tried to make their way towards Lisbon Avenue, so that they could escape from the centre of Milwaukee through Wauwatosa, and eventually out on Appleton Avenue to Menomonee Falls, where they had come from. But even though Sergeant Kyprianides hadn't been around to answer Dolores's call for help, the Milwaukee Police Department had surrounded the city in force. There were road blocks on all the major highways out of town, and as they reached the intersection of Lisbon and North, they saw police lights flashing up ahead of them, and the spotlights of police helicopters flickering from street to street like August lightning.

The man in the plaid jacket jammed on the brakes, and the station wagon slithered to a halt.

'What do we do now?' he demanded. 'They've blocked the road.'

'Either we leave the food and walk, or we try to break our way through,' the Greek man told him.

'How can we leave the food?' asked the woman. 'We *need* that food. If we don't have food, we're going to starve. For God's sake, Chris, we even killed for it.'

'Gerry killed for it,' said the man in the plaid jacket. 'I didn't. I didn't want any killing.'

'Oh, no?' said Gerry. 'I seem to remember it was your idea to bring the shotgun along.'

'As a deterrent,' said Chris angrily. 'I didn't mean for you to *use* the damned thing.'

'What do you think I was going to do with it?' shouted

Gerry. 'A gun is a gun. If you don't use it, there's no point in taking it along.'

'Will you two *stop* it,' said the woman, as if they were two bickering nephews.

The police helicopter spotted them sooner than they expected. Chris was just about to get out of the car and check that the tailgate was properly closed when the night was suddenly roaring with noise, and a piercing blue-white halogen lamp filled the station wagon with unearthly *Close Encounters* kind of light.

The helicopter circled the rooftops above them for a few minutes, and then an amplified voice commanded, 'You people – get out of the vehicle – make sure you get out slow and careful – and lay your hands on the roof.'

Chris looked across at Gerry, who was sitting in the back seat with his shotgun across his knees. The flackering of the helicopter rotors was so loud that they didn't even attempt to speak. They just looked at each other and the whole of their high school beginnings were in that look, the friendship that had lasted through business college, and military service, and settling down in Menomonee Falls – Chris at the University of Wisconsin, and Gerry at Michigan & Muskego Insurance. The friendship that had brought them here together tonight, in this reckless adventure that had been conceived out of fear, and bravado, and a suburban dread of going short. Some families may starve, friend, but not mine.

Chris looked at Gerry's bloodstained shoulder. 'We're going to have to surrender,' he said.

'And abandon the food?' asked Gerry. 'Meekly step out, with our hands up, and abandon the food?'

'What else can we do?' asked Chris, as the blue-white light fogged the interior of the station wagon, and the racketing bull-horn demanded yet again that they should step out of the vehicle.

'We can fight,' hissed Gerry.

'Fight? Against a helicopter? Are you nuts?'

'Don't you believe it,' said Gerry. 'A helicopter is the most vulnerable thing you can imagine. Didn't they teach you that in the service? One shotgun blast in the rotor, and you'll bring them straight down.'

'I'm not sure I *want* to bring them straight down.'

'Either you bring them straight down, or we starve, *and* go to prison,' said Gerry.

There was a moment in which none of them spoke. The helicopter roared lower, circling around the station wagon, and Gerry's face, already white from shock and loss of blood, appeared as livid as a phantom in the spotlight, with hair that flared blue as a devil's.

The woman said, 'We'd better get out. If we don't get out soon, they'll start shooting, and the last thing I want to do is die by default.'

Chris held out his hand towards Gerry. Without hesitation, Gerry hefted up the shotgun from the back seat of the station wagon, and handed it over. The woman's name was Madeleine Berg, and she was the divorced mother of three children. She said, 'Chris, we've been neighbours for a few years now. Let's call this thing quits.'

Chris broke the shotgun open, ejecting the spent cartridges. He reloaded it, and then he said, 'Maddy, if you want to get out now, then get out. This food's going back to Menomonee Falls.'

Madeleine turned around and looked at Gerry. None of them knew what they really wanted to do. They were dazzled by light and deafened by noise, and the amplified voice from the helicopter was telling them to get out of their vehicle now! – you get me? – now! or face the consequences.

'Aim to one side of the light,' Gerry suggested. 'That way, you'll be certain to hit the rotors.'

Chris glanced at them both. 'Wish me luck, then,' he said. He unlatched the station wagon door.

He didn't even have time to aim. He had already waited too long, and as the minutes had passed by, the police marksman on board the helicopter had been growing edgy. As soon as the car door opened, and Chris showed his face, a small blizzard of machine-gun bullets banged into the metal roof. None of them hit Chris directly, but one of them drove a shard of metal as long and thin as a ballpoint pen straight into his right eye. Chris felt his eye burst, and he dropped to the sidewalk in sheer horror at what had happened to him.

The helicopter raged around the station wagon in a circle. Then the marksman opened fire again, and raked the vehicle's roof and hood with over a hundred racketing shots. One of the last bullets hit the gas tank, and as Gerry and Madeleine were cowering in their seats, a hungry wave of superheated air, mixed with blazing gasoline, rolled through the length of the car. Gerry's last vision of anything was Madeleine, with her hair frizzed by fire, the skin of her face already blackened, staring at him in agony and fright. Then his own world was consumed in excruciating pain, and he breathed in fire.

The helicopter hovered around the blazing station wagon for a few minutes, and then angled away over the rooftops. This was the ninth party of looters the police had stopped tonight, and now they were searching for more.

In his smashed-open store under the elevated highway, Nicolas Prokopiou lay half-conscious and bleeding. He heard the helicopter as it passed overhead, but it was just one more blurry noise in a night of chaos. Fire sirens whooped in the distance, and there was a crackle of shooting from the direction of Marquette University.

He closed his eyes and thought of Serifos. The dense blue skies, the dark blue seas. The fishing boats with their sun-faded paint, tied up with salt-faded ropes. The days when he had stood by the harbour, his hair ruffled by the wind, and dreamed all kinds of dreams.

A few minutes before dawn, he died. He suffered very little pain, and his death was like falling asleep. It wouldn't have comforted him to know that Dolores was already dead, with half of her head blown away in crimson spatters and her body lying exposed on the sidewalk in her pink baby-doll nightie. Nor would it have comforted him to know that Chris, the looter, had survived; and was shivering under heavy sedation in hospital, blinded and burned, while his wife and children waited apprehensively at home for the food that he was going to bring.

Two

That same night, at the Hughes Supermarket on Highland Avenue in Hollywood, Mike Bull was organising his defences. Mike Bull was the supermarket manager, and the medium-sized twenty-four-hour store at the intersection between Franklin and Highland was his first important appointment. Before he had been promoted, three months ago, he had been fruit and vegetable manager of a branch further downtown. Now, at the age of thirty-one – a stocky, terse, but good-humoured bachelor with a face as pudgy as Mickey Rooney – he was running his own ship, and he was determined that night that the rats weren't going to clamber aboard.

He hadn't seen Ed Hardesty's television appearance – nor the frantic and frightened news programmes that followed. But within twenty minutes, a laconic customer with long greasy blond hair and frayed denim shorts had advised him to blockade the store. 'You should hear the TV, man. Walter Cronkite reckons we're all going to be starving by Thanksgiving. And you know what that means, don't you? Folks are going to start stocking up on every damn thing they can get.'

Mike had looked around the store. It was his business to sell what was in it, and if people came in and cleared his shelves, then no matter what the reason, he should be pleased. But the prospect of a food panic made him uneasy. The tough and the young would clear the place out, and leave the weak and the elderly without supplies.

He beckoned his under-manager, Tony, across to his office. Tony was Italian, young, and combed his hair a lot. Tony wanted to make it in the movies, and as far as he was concerned, retail selling was a total pain in the ass. But he liked Mike, and he didn't like being yelled at, and so he came and stood in Mike's office with an expression that was almost co-operative.

'Have you heard the news?' Mike asked him, rolling up his shirtsleeves

'News?' asked Tony.

'Yeah. It seems like these crop blights we've been hearing about – all those excuses why they couldn't deliver the grapes and the tomatoes and the celery and all of that stuff – well, it seems like we're in for some kind of a national famine.'

'That bad, huh?' asked Tony.

'That's what I hear,' said Mike.

Tony scratched the back of his neck. It was quite obvious that he didn't understand the implications of what Mike had told him at all.

'I'm going to close the store,' said Mike.

Tony frowned at his digital watch. 'It isn't time yet.'

'I know. But it may soon be too late, unless we close this place up.'

'Too late?' asked Tony, baffled.

'Sure. I mean – what would you do, if you heard that there wasn't going to be enough food for you and your family during the coming months?'

'I don't know,' said Tony. 'Stock up, I guess.'

'Exactly. And that's what people are going to start doing tonight, as soon as they realise how serious this situation's going to be. Take a look at it now – have you ever seen so many people here on a Sunday evening? And look at those people there – those shopping carts are filled to the top.'

Tony peered through the window of the office into the store. 'I guess you're right,' he said, slowly. 'Look at that woman there – she's got herself a train of three carts tied together.'

'That settles it,' said Mike. 'I'm going to close the place up.'

'What for?' Tony wanted to know. 'If things go on this way, we could make ourselves three times the weekly turnover, all in one night.'

'You don't understand,' Mike told him. 'We've got a responsibility to the whole community around here – not just the first fifty people with enough wit and enough money to clear the place out. And even if we do sell

202

everything tonight, there's no guarantee that we can restock until next week. If at all.'

'Well, I'm sorry, but I think you're wrong,' said Tony.

Mike looked at him sourly. 'You can think what you like, but right now I'm the manager and I say we close. So get to it. And make sure you put up the steel shutters.'

Tony saluted him. '*Jawohl, mein Führer*,' he said, with no pretence of a German accent.

Mike had only just gone back to his desk when his buzzer went. He returned to the window, and saw that there was a scuffle going on in one of the aisles. He quickly opened his office door, and made his way beside the cold meat counter to the scene of the disturbance.

'All right,' he demanded. 'What's going on?'

The woman with the three shopping carts tied together was jostling with an elderly man in mirror sunglasses and a pale-blue shirt. She was loud, and rinsed with strawberry blonde, and Mike could see at once that she was going to be difficult. One of his assistants was trying to hold her back, while another one was picking up boxes of cereal that had scattered all across the aisle.

'This lady thinks she can corner the cereal market,' protested the elderly man. 'All I want is a couple of packs of cornflakes, but she's got every single box in the store.'

'They're all out of cornflakes, that's all,' snapped the woman. 'Is it my fault if they're all out?'

'I think I have more cornflakes in the stockroom,' said Mike. 'How many did you want?'

'Two packs, that's all,' said the elderly man. 'I'm not an hysterical hoarder, like this lady.'

'Who are you calling a hoarder?' the woman wanted to know. 'Do you have a family with six kids to feed? Do you have to worry about a husband who's paralysed on one side? My family's supposed to starve, so that a dusty old geriatric like you can have breakfast?'

'Come on, madam,' said Mike. 'Nobody's going to starve for the sake of two packs of cornflakes.'

'Oh, no?' the woman demanded. 'Did you see that Kansas farmer on the television? He says we're all going to starve, and that the President's stocking up with food at the

White House. Well, let me tell you, friend – if the President can do it, then sure as hell so can I.'

'Listen, madam,' Mike said patiently, 'nobody's going to starve. We have plenty of supplies right here in the store, and even more in the stockroom, and still more on order from our central depot. So don't go panicking, huh? If you panic, you're only going to help to create an artificial shortage.'

'You're trying to tell me how much I can buy?' demanded the woman.

'I'm just asking you to cool it, that's all. Walking around the store with these three trolleys all tied together, that's a hazard to other shoppers. Now, I'd appreciate it if you'd pay for your groceries and leave.'

'You *make* me leave,' the woman challenged him. 'You just lay a finger on me and see what happens.'

Mike was about to answer with another of his soothe-the-angry-customer routines, when he heard shouting and scuffling at the front doorway of the store. Tony was shouting, 'We're closed! Don't you understand me? We're closing up!'

Somebody yelled back, 'You can't close! We've got a right!'

Mike left the lady with her three trolleys and her piles of cornflake boxes, and pushed his way through the crowds of customers to the doors. Tony had managed to lock two of the doors, but the last one was being forced open by a press of angry people. There must have been two or three hundred of them outside, all jostling to get in.

What goes on here?' Mike shouted. 'Hey, mister – we're closed! We're closing up now!'

A tall young man with shoulders as broad as a surfboard and floppy sun-bleached hair was gripping Tony's shirt and trying to push him out of the way. Behind him, a husband and wife in matching pink T-shirts that read GOODBYE J. P. SARTRE were struggling to force a shopping-cart into the store. Behind them was a wrestling turmoil of anxious and angry men and women, already panicked by the warning that America was going to starve.

'You can't close!' shrieked a woman with frizzy hair.

'Your sign says twenty-four-hour store and you have to keep that! It's the law!'

'In this store, I'm the law!' Mike shouted back. 'Now go home, cool down, and come back in the morning! There's no crisis, we have plenty of supplies, but I can't endanger you or my staff by letting all of you in right now. You got me?'

'Just shove it up your ass,' snarled the tall surfer, and roughly elbowed Mike aside. Mike tried to grip the chrome handrail by the door, but he caught his back against a stray shopping-cart, lost his balance and fell against the liquor counter. The next thing he knew, the doors were being forced open again, and crowds of whooping and shouting people were pouring in to the store.

'For Christ's sake, let's have some order!' yelled Mike. 'Just take what you want, but don't panic!'

He tried to stand up on the handrail so that he could make himself heard over the hideous shrieking and gabbling of the crowd, but a fortyish-looking man in sunglasses grabbed him by the shirt and pulled him down again.

'I ought to beat your brains out!' Mike screamed at him.

The man shrugged. 'I was doing you a favour. You're wasting your breath, trying to stop the great American public from panicking. It's their favourite occupation.'

'Just get out of my way!' Mike told him. 'Tony – let's get back to the office! Gina, Wendy – clear out of your cash registers and lock them up!'

'Asshole,' said the man in sunglasses, unaccountably.

Mike helped his checkout girls take the cash boxes out of their registers, and then he and his staff fought their way through the aisles back to the office.

All around them, the store was surging with hysterical shoppers – fighting and scrambling and tearing at each other as they attempted to cram their baskets and their shopping-carts and even their pockets with anything they could lay their hands on. A five-foot display of baked-bean cans clattered to the floor as Mike and Tony led the checkout girls past, and Mike was hit on the side of the face by a falling can. Right in front of him, a woman in stretch ski-pants and curlers was kneeling on the floor, gathering up packs of bacon in her arms and whimpering.

There were shouts and splintering crashes as shelves collapsed under the weight of people climbing up on to them to reach the topmost boxes of food. A woman screamed, 'I'm pregnant! For God's sake don't push me! I'm pregnant!'

People were taking everything. Not just cans of vegetables and meat; not just staple supplies; but pet foods and bottles of lavatory cleanser and fluorescent plastic sandals. They seemed to have forgotten why they were there, and what they had come for. Now they were even ripping the plastic edging from the shelves, and smashing the refrigerator cabinets. Mike, as he managed to usher everybody into his office, saw one man in a flowery Hawaiian shirt beating his fist against an empty spice rack until his fingers were spattered with blood; and another sight that was to stay with him for days afterwards – a pretty young girl in khaki jeans clutching five or six crushed French loaves, and wetting herself, all down her thighs.

Mike pushed Tony into the office ahead of him, slammed the door and locked it.

'Jesus Christ,' shuddered Tony. 'Have you ever seen anything like that in your life? They've gone bananas!'

Mike went over to the telephone, and dialled 625 3311, for the police. The telephone rang for a long time before it was answered, and outside the office window the screaming and the smashing grew louder and even more frightening.

'Come on, come on,' breathed Mike 'What's the matter with these people? We've got a riot on our hands.'

At last, a dry voice said, 'Police. Is this in connection with tonight's emergency?'

Mike hesitated. 'It's a riot, if that's what you mean. Up at the Hughes supermarket on Highland.'

'Okay,' the voice told him. 'Hold on for a moment, and I'll have you connected with the emergency squad.'

Mike held his hand over the receiver while it rang on a special extension. Through the office window, he could see a middle-aged woman trying to climb up on to the cookie shelves, to reach three or four scattered bags of Pepperidge

Farm ginger-nuts. Another woman leaped on her back, clawing at her T-shirt, until it ripped apart. The two women fell into the aisle, fighting and scratching, and knocking over two other women as well. Mike saw blood and torn-out hair and bare breasts scored with livid red furrows.

'For God's sake,' he said into the telephone. He loosened his necktie, and unbuttoned the first couple of buttons of his short-sleeved shirt. One of the checkout girls, Wendy, was starting to sob.

At last, a snappy police sergeant said, 'Yes? Emergency squad.'

'I'm the manager of the Hughes supermarket on Highland,' said Mike.

'Okay,' said the sergeant, 'Hughes supermarket. I've made a note of that. We'll get there when we can.'

'When you *can*? We have a riot here! People are getting hurt!'

'Listen, mister, we have a riot in every supermarket in the city. Four supermarkets on Santa Monica boulevard are burning. All I can say is that we'll get there when we can.'

'But what am I supposed to do? They're stripping the place!'

'You'll just have to let them strip it. I'm sorry, mister, but we simply don't have the manpower. I'm sorry.'

Mike didn't know what else to say, how else he could plead. He held the phone in his hand for a moment, listening to the sergeant say, 'Hello? Are you still there? Hello?' But then he laid it back in its cradle.

'What did they say?' Tony asked him.

'They said they'd do their best. It turns out that every supermarket in Los Angeles is being torn apart the same way. Four supermarkets are burning.'

'Mother of God,' said Tony, in a hushed voice.

Gina, the Mexican check-out girl, looked up from comforting Wendy. 'Isn't there anything we can do? Those people out there, they've gone crazy.'

Tony went close to the window. 'They haven't reached the stockroom yet. But I guess it's only a matter of time.'

'Is the stockroom locked?' asked Mike.

Tony nodded. It was always locked. He made sure of

that, personally. He combed his hair a lot, and yawned a lot when he was making out shelf inventories, but he never failed to obey instructions.

Mike joined him at the window. They couldn't quite see the stockroom door from the office, but they could see the corner of the frozen dairy foods cabinet next to it. There was a pushing waltzing scrum of people there, and the floor was plastered with pink yogurt.

They heard a rattling noise, and they knew that the crowds were trying to pull down the stockroom door.

'If we want to keep that food intact, we're going to have to do something fast,' said Tony. 'That's a pretty good lock on there, but it won't hold them out for ever.'

Mike covered his mouth with his hand. Halfway up the hardware aisle, a woman lay doubled-up on the floor, bleeding and sick. Another woman was walking unevenly through the crowds that still milled around the supermarket, her hair awry and her eyes staring.

'I have an idea,' said Mike. 'Gina – pass that sack of waste-paper, will you?'

An hour ago, Mike had been irritated to find that the cleaner hadn't taken the plastic bag of trash away. It was nothing more than crumpled-up wrapping paper, out-of-date invoices, used carbon paper, and string. But it would suit his present purpose just fine. He carried it to the office door, propped it up against his legs, and then reached in his pocket for matches.

'You're going to set fire to the place?' asked Tony.

'Just a limited fire, I hope,' Mike told him. 'Enough smoke and enough yelling to get these people out of here.'

He struck a match, and paused for a while to let it burn up. The rattling of the stockroom door grew increasingly ferocious, and he thought he heard a hinge tearing. Then he dropped the match into the bag of waste-paper, and watched it flare.

'Are you ready?' Mike asked Tony. 'When I give the word, we open the door and go out yelling fire. And I mean *yelling*.'

'I'm game,' said Tony. He reached into his shirt pocket, took out his green plastic comb, and ran it with a stylised flick through his hair.

'You look like a prince,' said Gina, with friendly sarcasm. Tony realised what he had done, and grinned sheepishly.

'It's kind of a habit,' he said.

The bag of trash was blazing hot and smoky now. Mike said, 'You set?' and before Tony could answer, he tugged open the office door, and kicked a shower of fiery paper into the store.

'*Fire!*' he screamed. '*Fire! Fire! The place is on fire!*'

'*Fire!*' yelled Tony, right behind him.

The effect on the crowds was immediate; and even more dreadful to Mick than the way in which they had first surged into the store. They let out a low quavering moan, like a wind on a seashore, and then that moan rose into a scream. Then, there was nothing but scrambling and pushing and a chopped-up shrieking which made him turn away towards the smoke and the burning paper with a grimace of disgust.

He didn't feel holier-than-thou. He knew that if his own life was at risk in a fire, he'd be struggling to get out along with everybody else. But somehow the way that the crowds in his supermarket were tearing at each other to get to the exits, the way that women were wrenching at each other's clothes, the way that men were screaming like small children, that all turned his stomach.

In a matter of a few minutes, the supermarket was almost empty. Two or three of the customers were too dazed or too hurt to walk. One man was lying face-down in the poultry freezer, his face against the ice, and it was plain that he was dead. Mike lifted him out, and laid him down on the floor. The man flopped back with his eyes open and the side of his cheek the colour of chilled turkey.

'You think you should say some words?' asked Tony, stepping beside him and looking down at the body.

Mike shook his head. 'I'm a supermarket manager, not a priest.'

'The doors are all locked now,' said Tony. 'I put the shutters down, too.'

'Thanks, Tony,' said Mike.

Curls of black burned paper drifted across the floor in the silent draught from the supermarket's air-conditioning. There was a sharp odour of smoke in the air.

'Did they go far?' asked Mike. 'Or can we expect them back?'

'It's hard to tell,' said Tony. 'There were still quite a few of them gathered around outside when I put the shutters down. Twenty or thirty, maybe. They know the stockroom's still untouched, so I guess they'll be back.'

Mike laid a hand on Tony's shoulder. 'If you want to leave now, slip out while the going's good, I won't hold it against you. I'd like to send Gina and Wendy home.'

Tony shook his head. 'What do I want to go home for? To watch all this on the TV?'

'Okay, but we should get the girls out.'

Gina was standing at the open office door. 'We'd rather stay,' she said. 'At least until it's quiet.'

Mike said, 'You know the crowds may come back; and they may be a damn sight more vicious than they were just now.'

Gina nodded. 'All the same, we'll stay, if that's okay by you.'

Mike looked around the wreckage of his store – the collapsed shelves, the smashed freezer cabinets, the food that was strewn all over the floor and trodden into a surrealistic salad of Cheerios, baked beans, loganberry jelly, bootlaces, cat food, and plastic doilies.

He said to Tony, 'Go to the liquor cupboard, will you, and bring me a bottle of bourbon. Make sure you charge it down to me. I think I could use a drink.'

Three

All over the United States that night, fires were burning. From the top of the Hancock Building in Chicago, a CBS News reporter described the dark and fiery scene beneath him as 'a preview of hell . . . like something by Hieronymus

210

Bosch.' Not many of his listeners knew who Hieronymus Bosch was, but the vision on their screens was unmistakable. Block after block of garish fires, hideous shadows, and running people.

Thousands of stores, restaurants, hotels, warehouses, and hamburger stands were broken into, all over the country. Anywhere there was food, there was violence. At a branch of McDonald's in Darien, Connecticut, seven looters were shot dead by police as they tried to break into the restaurant's cold store. One of the dead men was found to have tucked dozens of free McDonald's airplanes into his windbreaker, presumably to take home for his children.

At the Iron Kettle restaurant, on Cape Cod, Massachusetts, the seventy-two-year-old proprietor was crushed against a brick wall as she attempted to stop looters escaping from her restaurant in a pick-up truck.

And in New York City, at Macy's, hundreds of screaming men and women broke the windows of the delicatessen hall on 33rd Street and poured into the store, leaving amidst the shattered glass two dead women and one man with his left cheek sliced off. The crowds looted all the fresh and canned food they could tear from the shelves, and then they rampaged through the rest of the store, oblivious to the shrilling alarms and the policemen with nightsticks who patrolled the counters with orders to 'contain, but not arrest.'

One of the managers of Macy's who witnessed the looting said, 'It was terrifying. It was like sale time in Hades.' And New York's Commissioner of Police, in a hurriedly-called television interview, explained, 'It's a disaster. But, it's way beyond our power to prevent looting and theft on such a grand scale. We have neither the men nor the facilities. All we can do is try to ensure that the looting is carried out with the minimum of risk to life and property.'

During the night, Manhattan was a hideous nightmare. Ambulances and police cars whooped and screamed through the echoing streets, and there was the sporadic crackling of gunfire from Harlem and the West Side. The South Bronx, already devastated by arson, became an

211

inferno whose glow could be seen as far away as New Rochelle. In Brooklyn, fifteen women were trapped and burned to death in a Woolworth store as they tried to escape with hair dryers, bicycles, garden furniture, and cosmetics. Their bodies were twisted up 'like little black monkeys' and their loot was melted in their claws. Almost all the food had been pillaged now from restaurants and stores, and people were helping themselves to whatever was left.

The Mayor of New York said on television, 'What we're seeing here is consumer anarchy. We've led people to expect certain privileges if they live here in the United States, and one of those privileges is an abundance of food. Now that privilege is threatened, and people won't let it go lightly. They'll tear this city apart first.'

In New York, more than anyplace else, the looting quickly took on distinctive social patterns. Up in Harlem, and down in the slums, the break-ins were usually violent, indiscriminate, and often ended in fire. Reports that reached the Police Commissioner's desk by early Monday morning showed that most of the break-ins in poorer districts netted less than half of the available loot. The rest was smashed, abandoned, or burned. In the better-off parts of the city, however – in the east 80s and around Gramercy Square – the looting was systematic, and efficient, and effected with far less violence. Police surprised eight residents of Olympic Tower working as a co-ordinated looting team, with six station wagons, all legally rented from Hertz, and a truck. They had broken into a Safeway depot on 10th Street, breaking open the gates with bolt-cutters, and by the time a police patrol car came by, they had already loaded their vehicles with a quarter of a million dollars' worth of foodstuffs. The officers counted two hundred cans of pâté de foie gras, at forty-five dollars a can, and a *New York Post* reporter remarked, 'People aren't taking what they think they're going to need. They're taking what they think they're entitled to.'

By dawn, Detroit was burning. A heavy pall of white smoke hung over Hamtramck and Harper Woods, and they could smell destruction out at St Clair Shores. The night had been wild with helicopters and police patrols and shooting, and when the grimy sun rose over Lake St Clair, there were burned-out vans littering the Detroit Industrial Freeway and the Renaissance Centre was encircled by Michigan National Guard.

The Mayor of Detroit told the newspapers, 'This was the worst night of my life. Black Sunday. And that isn't any kind of a joke. This was the night the black people of Detroit let me down.'

The looting and the destruction had been so widespread that the news media hardly knew how to deal with them. From midnight, when the first horrified bulletins began to pour into CBS and NBC and ABC, each television channel had made the decision to stay on the air all night, with almost hysterical first-hand reports from San Francisco, New Orleans, Denver, Chicago, Washington, and New York.

It was easier to tell the individual stories. From Florida, Harold Kane Kaufman-Vorbrüggen of the Cordon Bleu restaurant in Dania, Broward County, hesitantly explained to newsmen how looters had broken into the kitchens and ransacked the larders and refrigerators. They had taken only the steak and the fish, and left thousands of dollars' worth of truffles and escargots. One of the diners told the news cameras, 'I guess we have to count ourselves lucky that looters have very little taste.'

In Elizabeth, New Jersey, a supermarket manager and his wife went down to their store as soon as Ed Hardesty's programme was shown, taking with them a vacuum flask of coffee, two packs of sandwiches, two Colt AR-15s, and eleven boxes of 7.62 ammunition. Two local residents came and rattled the supermarket doors to see if they were open, but when the manager's wife fired at them from the roof, they quickly retreated. The supermarket manager said, 'I guess you could rightly say that I've always believed in overkill.'

In San Francisco, a Chinese couple opened the doors of their store on Sacramento Street and put up a sign saying, 'Bad Times Are Coming. Help Yourself.' Hardly anybody did, despite the fact that five blocks away, a mob was looting a Save-U supermarket, and setting fire to a drugstore.

But although the individual stories were easier to tell, it was the widespread mood of panic and betrayal that swept over the whole country that was the real story. The country had been through thin times before. The Depression had been a thin time, and plenty of people had had to go without. But now, *everybody* was going to have to go without, rich or poor, lucky or unlucky, unless they made damn sure they had a huge stockpile of canned and frozen groceries. Because of that, the frustration and resentment that boiled up on Sunday night were more explosive than any public feeling that had ever boiled up before. This wasn't an upsurge of morality and conscience, like the protests over Vietnam. This wasn't the rattling of political and ethical sensibilities, like Watergate. This was hysteria time, and if you didn't grab you didn't eat.

As Sunday night passed over the continental United States like a devouring and apocalyptic shadow, it left behind a trail of destruction and smoke and wrecked buildings. The whole country had changed overnight, from a buoyant and self-assured society with its first feelings of confidence about the 1980s, to a shattered and haunted land where hope seemed to be as scarce a commodity as food.

The National Guard were enforcing martial law in all but seven states. Everywhere you drove that Monday morning there were uniforms and jeeps and personnel carriers, and if you didn't have a good reason for being in Rupert, Idaho, or Maple Shade, New Jersey, or any place at all that wasn't home, then you were liable to immediate arrest. At 7.30 a.m. Central Time, on all channels, the President made a live television announcement about the events of the night.

'What has happened across our nation during the past twelve hours has been the most agonising example of self-destruction we have ever inflicted on ourselves. We have had some hurtful and tumultuous times before. I believe it is the destiny of this nation to test its belief in itself time and time again, no matter how painful those tests may be. In the

214

Civil War, we tested our belief in the sanctity of individual freedom . . . In the Civil Rights marches of the 1960s, we faced up to the reality of black citizenship . . .

'Then there was Watts, and Kent State, and the assassination of President Kennedy and his brother Robert . . . and Watergate . . .

'But last night was not a test . . . neither of our pride in being American nor our confidence in what we can achieve. Last night was a horrifying exposure of the weaknesses inherent in our whole society. Last night showed that we have set personal wellbeing above national survival. Last night showed that we have become a nation of weak, self-interested, corruptible consumers.

'It isn't easy for me to say these words. As your President, I have to take ultimate responsibility for the shape our society is in, and I do. I take responsibility for failing to understand that our recent years of economic recession were warnings of a major shift in our national psychology. Instead of believing in work and its profitable rewards, we now believe in profitable rewards whether we work or not.

'Well, I'm going to make an appeal right now . . . an appeal to sanity and an appeal to reason. I'm going to appeal to all of you to carry on your normal everyday lives . . . to go to work as normal . . . and to try to restore the best part of the life we lost last night . . .'

The President was asked if it was true that he had made provisions to hoard food for the administration.

He said, 'Hoard is an emotive word. Let me just say that there have always been contingency plans to protect the administrative arm of government in the event of a national emergency, and it would not be accurate for me to say that some kind of contingency plan had not been considered in this case.'

'Yes – but does the administration have its own secret supply of food?'

'That's all I'm prepared to say,' the President answered. 'It's a question of national security and I don't wish to breach national security by shooting my mouth off.'

The *Washington Post*'s next edition carried the banner:

PRESIDENT ADMITS GOV'T FOOD HOARD.

By midday Monday, the first panic was over. But the cost of the night's destruction was estimated to run into hundreds of billions of dollars. In Los Angeles, seven downtown blocks had been burned into empty shells, and more than eight hundred people were homeless. After a tour of all the looted supermarkets, warehouses, and restaurants, the LAPD estimated that more than fifty people had died in the looting, and that several hundred had been seriously injured.

A pall of black smoke drifted northwards across the Hollywood hills, and the residents came out on to the streets to stand in silence and watch their city smoulder.

In Denver, the Brown Palace Hotel had been burned down, and it was almost impossible to see the mountains for smoke. In Las Vegas, rioting guests had stripped Caesar's Palace, smashing windows and overturning gaming tables, and gutted seventeen restaurants. In Santa Fé, National Guardsmen had fought a three-hour gun battle with local vigilantes who had attempted to break into one of the city's largest food depots. Eight people had been killed.

The Mayor of Chicago announced a twenty-four-hour curfew. Nobody was to leave their home until the National Guard and the emergency services had been able to clear wreckage and contain the fires. Anybody seen on the street would be shot. When she was asked on television if her orders weren't too extreme, the Mayor snapped, 'If you want to talk about extreme, go see what these animals have done to my city.'

Washington, DC, was comparatively unscathed, although there had been severe looting in several of the black neighbourhoods. At the first sign of trouble, the Army had been called in to surround the city centre, and by midnight there had been tanks and armoured personnel carriers positioned at Washington Circle, all the way along Constitution Avenue, and around the Capitol and the White House. One cynical news reporter, filmed beside a Sheridan tank which was parked at the intersection of 17th Street and Constitution Avenue, remarked, 'The military must be congratulated for the speed and efficiency with which they took up a defensive posture to protect the American President from his own people.'

City life was allowed to continue in New York. The Mayor considered that curfews or military restrictions would not be 'conducive to normalcy.' The streets were appalling. There was broken glass littered everywhere, overturned automobiles at almost every intersection, and a fog of foul-smelling smoke. National Guardsmen patrolled Fifth Avenue in pairs, and M723 troop carriers sped across town, positioning guardsmen at potential trouble spots. But thousands of New Yorkers went to work as usual. They had coped with blackouts, transit strikes, Arctic snow, and torrential rain. What had happened during the night was only one more grotesque inconvenience.

At eleven-thirty a.m., after consultation with the governors of the worst-affected states, the President declared 'a temporary state of National Emergency.' He ordered special legal provisions for punishing looters, and immediately put into effect an aid-and-recovery pro-gramme out of federal funds. The *New York Times* was to call his actions 'shutting the larder door after the food was bolted.'

But the national sense of shock was one of the strangest of Monday's phenomena. It was expressed almost entirely on television, since very few people were prepared to confess to their friends that they, too, had been out looting the night before (in spite of the number of heavily-laden station wagons that had returned to the suburbs at dawn). In any case, most of the looters were law-abiding people who had acted completely out of character, and as Monday brightened, they began to feel ashamed and bewildered, and to look over the odd selection of food they had managed to scavenge, and ask themselves if it had been worth the hair-raising fright of smashing windows and burning stores and trying to elude the police.

Dr William Abrahams, of the Seattle Institute of Motivational Research, expressed his conviction on television that Americans had reached 'that inevitable moment when their psychological model of themselves has

217

been projected into reality – with disastrous consequences. Americans have always seen themselves as possessed of a divine right to affluence; blessed with a heavenly dispensation to go out and get whatever they want regardless of law, ethics, or basic humanity. Now they've put that vision into practice, and may God preserve us.'

At one p.m., the President appeared briefly on television again, and pleaded for 'calm, constructive thinking, and prayer.' He announced a forty-eight-hour amnesty for looters, 'in the sure knowledge that most of you have repented of your actions', and he asked that all stolen foodstuffs and goods should be returned to designated 'loot points' throughout the United States. The loot would be sold at clearance prices, and the money used to compensate city administrations, storekeepers, police departments, and supermarket chains.

By eleven o'clock that evening in the Central Time Zone, Busch Stadium in St Louis, Missouri, which had been signposted as a 'Loot Amnesty Centre', had been visited by only five uncomfortable-looking citizens, who returned between them two cases of corned beef, a leatherette swivel armchair, a broken portable television, sixty cans of petits pois, and a box of half-thawed soya-burgers.

By seven o'clock Pacific time, the Hollywood Bowl was stacked with 250 boxes of taco chips, bags of smashed cookies, and a truckload of garden hose.

The President later admitted that he may have made a 'motivational misjudgement' in announcing that the goods would be sold to compensate police and supermarket chains. Most people thought of the police as more felonious than the average man in the street; and most people believed that supermarket chains could easily sustain their losses. Apart from that, the supermarkets' 'help-yourself' technique of selling had convinced most people that the goods on the shelves were pretty much theirs already.

A special NBC film report at mid-afternoon showed a small country store in Forty Four, Arkansas. Looters had ransacked it during the morning, and had beheaded the proprietor with an axe as he tried to stop them. The whole store was splattered with blood, even the light fitting that hung from the ceiling. In an outraged interview, the President's adviser on National Security said that the United States no longer had any normal right to condemn the barbaric practices of any other country, because the Americans who had committed this crime were 'Neanderthals.'

Strangely, though, as the sun went down over the eastern seaboard, and the nation settled down for another night, the first shock and the panic began to subside, and were almost immediately replaced by boredom with the subject of looting, and irritation. Viewers began to call the major TV networks to complain that the extended evenings news bulletins were interrupting their regular viewing. A re-run of *The Sting* had been promised for Monday night's NBC movie, and many television viewers were afraid they were going to miss it.

So by eight o'clock, most channels returned to normal schedules, except PBS, which doggedly kept on with interviews and analyses of the Sunday night riots. For most people's attention-span, however, it was probably more than time to change over to something fresh. By eight o'clock, almost every available political commentator had been able to put in his ten-cents' worth, and the news programmes were reduced to interviewing Naderites, John Birchites, and disaffected evangelists.

Only one major protagonist in the events of the previous night had yet to speak. Senator Shearson Jones, the senior senator from Kansas. He had been unreachable all day, even to Presidential aides. They had tried to telephone him from the White House sixteen times on Monday morning, but each time they had been told that he was 'still *en route* to Washington.' A message was left that the President wanted to speak to him the minute he stepped through his office door.

In fact, Shearson Jones was making no attempt to return to Washington. He judged that, politically, now was not the time. He told his security people to lock the gates of Lake Vista to keep newspapermen and curiosity seekers at bay, and then he closeted himself in his suite of rooms with

219

Peter Kaiser. They had more urgent work to attend to than making excuses to a confused and angry President. In the panic of the night, nobody in the administration had thought to freeze the Blight Crisis Appeal, and Peter Kaiser was arranging for as much money as possible to be transferred to a charitable holding trust. It was difficult and complicated work, and it needed all of Peter Kaiser's skill and all of Shearson Jones's bludgeoning. By three o'clock that afternoon, however, they had extracted more than three million dollars extra out of the fund, and Peter was busy dispersing it from the holding trust to scores of ready-prepared subsidiaries. It would take the IRS years to discover that 250,000 dollars which had been invested in Roseville Hearing Aids, St Paul, had come from Kansas Charitable Investments, Inc., of Kansas City, and that when Roseville Hearing Aids had gone out of business, with no protesting creditors, the money had then been paid directly into the account of Ernest Thompson, of San Diego, California, who was really Senator Shearson Jones.

Shearson had been infuriated by Ed's revelations, and mortified by the savagery and looting that had followed. But he was flexible enough to adapt himself to a changed situation, and not to cry over spoilt opportunities. The Blight Crisis Appeal had done famously well, considering the few days that it had been open, and Shearson wasn't going to complain about twelve million dollars or more. He had lost the contribution from Michigan Tractors, and he was sore about that, but twenty or thirty lesser donations had cleared the bank during the Monday morning, before any of the companies involved had thought to act, and these payments had more than compensated Shearson for what he had lost. They could ask for their money back now until they were black in the face. It was too late, because the money had vanished.

Shearson had said nothing at all to Ed after his first angry outburst, but as Monday wore on it became clear that Ed was not going to be permitted to leave Lake Vista until Shearson decided to let him go. Ed was also kept incommunicado. Every time he picked up a telephone and tried to place a call, the house operator told him gently but firmly that 'all outside lines are busy right now, Mr Hardesty.'

Ed spent the day in his bedroom, drinking beer and watching on television the scenes of violence that his own words had helped to unleash. He didn't yet know what to feel about what he saw. Should he feel angry? Sad? Indifferent? Was it really his fault that all this disaster had happened? Or would it have happened anyway?

He crumpled an empty Coors can in his hand and tossed it into the waste-basket. He wanted very badly to talk to Season right now, and not just to make sure that she and Sally were all right.

He needed more than a friend or a lover right now. He needed his wife.

Four

Peter Kaiser came into his room shortly after eight that evening, and stood watching the television, his hands stuck deep in his pockets. He looked waxy, and sweaty, and there were dark rings under his eyes; but he had an air of satisfied tiredness, as if he had pulled off something really difficult.

'Well?' he asked Ed. 'What's the latest?'

Ed was sitting on his bed, in a buff-coloured shirt, jeans, and bare feet. He eyed Peter without answering, as if the question wasn't worth his time.

'Now you know what it's like to wield power,' smiled Peter, sitting himself uninvited on the end of the bed. 'A few words from you, and the whole country goes crazy. Makes you feel pretty good inside, doesn't it? Pretty damned important.'

'There's only one reason those people went crazy,' Ed told him, in a harsh voice. 'They went crazy because they're afraid.'

'Well, isn't that what national politics is all about?' grinned Peter. 'The calculated exploitation of fear? Don't tell me anybody does anything at all out of brotherly love.

221

Do you pay your taxes out of brotherly love? Do you anything at all out of brotherly love?'

'Maybe not,' said Ed, 'but at least I don't exploit the country's misfortunes for the sake of a few million lousy dollars.'

'It's very easy to call a few million lousy when they aren't yours, Mr Hardesty. Or may I call you Ed? You are a celebrity now, after all.'

'I don't particularly care about that,' said Ed. 'I'd like to telephone my wife.'

'Haven't you tried already?'

'All day. But the operator keeps telling me the lines are busy.'

Peter pulled a consoling face. 'Well, that's true, they are. But you can try again in the morning. Maybe Shearson will begin to cool off a little by then. He's pretty mad at you right now.'

'Isn't he going back to Washington?'

'In a while. We have a few unexpected problems to clear up before we go. You know, tidying up the Blight Crisis Appeal, things like that.'

Ed climbed off the bed, and walked across the bedroom to the french windows that led out on to the balcony. He dry-washed his face with his hands, and then let out a long breath of exhaustion. He'd been watching the television news bulletin all night, and he was bushed.

'Would you tell me something about Shearson Jones?' he asked Peter.

Peter shrugged. 'Why not?'

'Would you tell me what it is that makes it possible for a man to serve as an elected representative of a country he professes to love, and at the same time to make profits on the side? To me, the two sides of a man like that just don't fit together.'

Peter glanced towards the television. The sound was turned off, but it was easy to make out what was happening. There were lines of people at Los Angeles International Airport with hurriedly-packed suitcases, all trying to leave the country before the looting and the rioting grew any worse. Los Angeles had been through one of the most horrifying nights of all. The *Los Angeles Times* had called it 'Walpurgisnacht.'

Peter turned back to Ed. 'I don't know why so many people believe that politicians ought to behave like priests. They're not elected to bring us all to the kingdom of Heaven. They're elected to look after our interests at city hall, or in the state senate, or Congress, or wherever. So provided they look after our interests properly, what does it matter if they make a little money on the side? As long as they don't sell out the people who voted for them, who's to criticise? And besides, it's a time-honoured American tradition, going back to Thaddeus Stevens and James G. Blaine.'

Ed stared at him. 'Do you really believe that?'

'Would I work for Shearson Jones if I didn't?'

Ed slowly shook his head. 'You people amaze me.'

'We're professionals, working in a professional environment, that's all,' said Peter. 'So long as we keep the balance between public ignorance, political power, and financial leverage, then we're fine. It's like one of those diagrams you used to have in your trigonometry books at school. But as soon as someone starts tilting the balance – as soon as we get some amateur interference . . .'

'Like me,' suggested Ed.

'Well, that's right, like you – well, *then*, the whole balloon goes up with a rush; and, boy, didn't it go up last night.'

'They said on the news they're going to mount a Congressional inquiry,' said Ed.

'Sure they will. They have to. You don't expect the nation to tear itself to pieces in the space of one night without someone having to carry the can. And really that's the reason I've come to talk to you.'

'Oh, yes?' asked Ed, suspiciously.

Peter got up off the bed, walked across to Ed, and laid a confiding arm around his shoulder. Peter must have been tired and out of condition, because there was a red pustular spot on the side of his nose. Ed didn't know whether to look at him or turn away.

'The point is,' said Peter, 'that within a week or two,

you're going to have to stand up in front of some very inquisitive Congressmen, and answer some very difficult questions. One of those questions is going to be – what led you to believe the Senator Shearson Jones was diverting money from the Blight Crisis Appeal Fund into his own pocket? And can you produce any substantiating evidence? And what are you going to say to that?'

Ed didn't answer. He wanted to hear what Peter had in mind first. If there was one lesson he had learned since he had arrived at Lake Vista, it was that you kept your mouth closed until you knew what the hell was going on.

'Well,' said Peter, as if he hadn't really expected any kind of reply anyway, 'what you're going to say is, nothing.'

'Nothing?'

'That's right. You're going to say that you made a mistake. That you overheard a telephone conversation, and misunderstood the implications of it. You thought that Senator Jones was arranging to divert some of the money from the Blight Crisis Appeal, when in fact he was making special arrangements to get it out to Kansas wheat farmers even more quickly than he originally planned.'

'I see,' said Ed, cautiously. 'And why should I say something like that?'

Ed pulled an expression of surprise that was almost comical. 'Why? Because it's true. Or at least, it will be by the time you appear in front of a Congressional committee.'

'What's going to make it true? The philosopher's stone?'

'The what?'

'The philosopher's stone. A mythical catalyst that was supposed to be able to turn lead into gold. I'm amazed at your ignorance.'

'I'm amazed at your pettishness.'

Ed, with great care, lifted Peter's arm away from his shoulders. 'I don't care to be hugged by political hoodlums,' he said.

Peter stood back, his hands on his hips, and then laughed. 'I admire your nerve,' he said. 'You may be an amateur, by God, but I admire your nerve, Unfortunately, nerve isn't going to be enough. Your wife and daughter are

224

staying with the Snowman family on Topanga Canyon, aren't they?'

Ed's muscles tensed up like an overwound clock. 'Yes,' he said tightly. 'What of it?'

'Nothing,' smiled Peter, circling the room with his hands still propped on his hips. He looked very pleased with himself. 'Nothing that needs to worry you at all if you say what we want you to say at the Congressional inquiry.'

Ed stalked across and grabbed Peter's shirt, twisting it around in his fist. 'Don't you tell me nothing,' he said, fiercely. 'Not where my wife and daughter are concerned.'

Peter lifted his face with complete arrogance, as if he were challenging Ed to hit him.

'All right,' he said. 'Your wife and daughter are being watched by a private detective.'

'Why? What the hell good will that do?'

'It will make you say what we want you to say. That's all.'

'Why? Come on, Peter, spit it out! Why?'

Peter tugged his shirt collar free. 'Because whenever Shearson says so, the private detective will do just a little more than keep an eye on your wife and daughter. He'll follow them to a conveniently quiet spot, and blow their brains out.'

Ed gave Peter a disbelieving frown. 'Now you're kidding,' he said. 'Now I definitely know that you're kidding.'

'You think so? You want to try me?'

'For Christ's sake, you're talking about murder! Even Shearson Jones isn't into murder!'

'You think I'm joking? You want to try me out? You're always welcome. Your wife and kid don't mean anything to me.'

Ed seized Peter's shirt again, and this time he ripped it down the front. 'By God,' he said, 'if you're serious, if you really mean what you're saying, I'm going to take you apart!'

Peter pushed him away again. He was still smiling. 'I'm serious all right,' he said. 'I made all the arrangements last night, as soon as you'd blurted out that broadcast of yours.

You managed to outmanoeuvre Shearson Jones just once, my friend, but you can be damn sure you'll never be able to do it again.'

Ed felt as if his chest was the inside of a steam-kettle, scalded with high-pressure emotions that he couldn't let out. His fists were clenched, and he could have happily, needfully, punched Peter Kaiser straight in the nose. But he was beginning to learn that it didn't pay to assault Peter Kaiser face to face. Peter Kaiser was made out of nothing but obedient shadows, and devious turns of phrase. It was Shearson Jones that Ed was after, and if you wanted to play it tricky with Shearson Jones you had to be smart, and quick, and you had to make doubly certain that you'd arranged yourself a way out, as well as a way in. This wasn't the little league any more.

Ed walked across to the drinks cabinet and unscrewed the Johnny Walker. Through the wide-open french windows, he could see Fall River Lake glittering with evening phosphorescence. The smattering of stars that hung suspended above the hills gave no astrological clues at all to the violence that had swept across America in the past twenty-four hours; nor to the violence that would follow. The breeze stirred the drapes, and chilled the sweat on Ed's forehead.

'Well?' asked Peter Kaiser.

'Well?' repeated Ed. 'What do you want me to tell you? That from now on, I'm going to toe the line? That I love Shearson Jones?'

'You want to talk to your wife and kid on the telephone?' asked Peter. 'You can if you like.'

'What do you want me to tell them?'

'Tell them whatever you want. This is a free country.'

'Can I tell them they're going to be shot?'

'They won't be. Not if you do what you're told.'

Ed tipped back his whisky in one swallow. Peter watched him with a fixed expression of false good humour. 'Getting yourself drunk won't solve anything,' Peter said.

Ed wiped his mouth with the back of his hand. 'I'm not drinking this to get drunk. I'm drinking it as an antiseptic.'

Five

At five o'clock CBS News began to bring reports from London that all passenger flights from the United States had been held on the runways at Heathrow Airport without the passengers being allowed to disembark. There had been four hours of 'crucial discussions' between Her Majesty's Foreign Office and the State Department, and eventually the passengers had been allowed to leave the aircraft, but only to assemble in the departure lounges, and not to pass through Customs.

By nine o'clock, all flights to England from the United States had been cancelled, and by seven o'clock all flights to destinations in Europe, Scandinavia and the Middle East had been wiped off the board, too. In London, more than 2000 Americans were reboarded on to their aircraft, and sent straight back to the United States – despite the fact that many of them had left America before the riots of Sunday night.

Lord Carey, the British Foreign Secretary, said that 'much as I regret the course of action we have had to take in relation to United States citizens arriving in the United Kingdom, it is apparent that the tragic events of the past twenty-four hours would have led many of them to seek to stay in the United Kingdom indefinitely . . . And while I wish to the bottom of my heart that we had the facilities and the finance to cope with a massive influx of American refugees . . . the fact remains that we have not . . . and therefore with the understanding of the President, we have regretfully been obliged to turn away, for the time being, any United States citizen who arrives at a British port of entry.'

Germany, France, Holland, and the rest of the EEC countries quickly followed the British example. They were all sorry. They all spoke of their regret. But even 'special relationships' could not overcome the impossibility of accepting refugees who might eventually arrive from the United States in their tens of millions.

Watching the television in his room, Shearson Jones said to Peter Kaiser, 'Don't you ever wonder why we fought for those sons-of-bitches at all? I mean, don't you wonder?'

But as Monday drew to a close, there were more important questions than that, and they were still unanswered. The looting and the arson had been so devastating that most of the networks had forgotten why they started at all, and nobody was asking if the threat of a famine was real, and how serious it was, and what the President was going to do about it.

Of course, nobody in the administration had yet been told about the Abbott family, of Portales, New Mexico. And nobody had yet been officially told about the isotope that Square had found in the grain elevator in St Louis.

And that was one of the reasons why the Duncan family, of Willingboro, New Jersey, sat around their kitchen table that evening for a supper of canned salmon and salad without any feelings but feelings of family closeness and good appetite, and gratefulness to the Lord for providing their daily sustenance. There were four of them – Emmett Duncan, a telephone engineer, his wife Dora, and their two daughters, Jenny and Kate. If you had asked any of them what *Clostridium botulinum* was, they wouldn't have been able to tell you. But the salmon they ate that night was swarming with it.

Six

It was two o'clock on Tuesday morning when Ed was awakened by someone shaking his shoulder. He thought he was still dreaming at first – a strange airless dream of waiting in a funeral parlour for the body of his father to arrive – and he struck out with his left arm and hit Della on the side of the head. She seized his wrist and said, 'Quiet. I don't want to wake up the Muldoons.'

Ed rolled over and sat up in bed. He'd been drinking for most of the afternoon, and his mouth tasted as if he'd been chewing alfalfa seeds. Della was wearing an emerald green silk wrap, and she smelled of Paco Rabanne. 'What's the matter?' Ed asked her, frowzily. 'Couldn't you just have slipped into bed?'

She smiled in the darkness. 'I don't have time for that tonight, I'm afraid. I need your help.'

'Help? What kind of help?'

'Shearson and Peter Kaiser have been forced to clear out the Blight Crisis Appeal faster than they wanted to. That's why you haven't seen them around today. They've been diverting as much money as possible into false-bottomed trusts and phoney accounts.'

'Well? What do you expect me to do about it?'

'Ed – all the telexes and the memos and the accounts are still downstairs in Shearson's office. All the documentary evidence I'm going to need to bring him before a Grand Jury. But if I leave it until tomorrow, Peter Kaiser's going to have time to spirit them all away, and file them where they can't be traced.'

'You're going to break into Shearson's office and steal his papers?' asked Ed, incredulous.

'It's the only way. I can't get through to the FBI office in Wichita and order up a search warrant. Shearson's keeping a check on every single telephone call. But I can get in there and take the paperwork I need.'

'What's Shearson going to do if he catches you at it?' Ed wanted to know.

'I think I know the answer to that better than anyone,' Della replied. 'Shearson Jones is suspected by the FBI of implication in at least five killings, and probably more.'

Ed frowned, thinking of Season and Sally, and Peter Kaiser's threat to kill them. 'Do you mean that?' he asked.

'Of course I mean it. He's a very wanted man.'

'Somebody in the FBI actually has proof?'

Della sat up straight. 'What do you want, Ed? One minute you're publicly tearing the man apart, and now

229

you're doubting he's a potential killer. Do you want to see blood?'

'Not my own, thanks. And not yours, either.'

'Well, in that case, why don't you give me some help? The sooner I can lay my hands on some incriminating paperwork, the sooner Shearson Jones is going to find himself in the federal penitentiary. That's if they can find him a cell large enough.'

'This is crazy,' said Ed. 'I'm a farmer, not a burglar.'

'You used to be an actuary, though, didn't you? There'll be scores of accounts and bank drafts to sort out down there, and if I'm going to get it done quickly, I'm going to need some expert assistance.'

'How the hell are you going to break in there?'

'Just leave that to me. I've been trained. All you have to do is keep quiet and do what I tell you.'

Ed ran his hand through his scruffy hair. 'This is a heck of a way to spend the night,' he said, but he climbed out of bed, and reached for his pants and his red sweatshirt, the one with *South Burlington Farm* emblazoned on the front.

As he was pulling the sweatshirt over his head, Della asked him, 'Did you manage to call your wife?'

Ed's head appeared through the circular neck-hole. 'Not yet. Why?'

'No reason. I wondered if they were still giving you that busy switchboard routine.'

'I haven't tried since seven o'clock last night.'

Della stood up, and tightened the silk tie around her waist. 'I guess Shearson's trying to keep us all out of public circulation until his money's been safely salted away.'

Ed said, 'The truth is that Peter Kaiser said I could call Season if I wanted to.'

Della looked up. 'He did? And you didn't? Don't tell me you didn't want to.'

Ed stooped down and picked up his sneakers. When he stood straight again, he simply gave Della an unhappy smile.

'It's not because of me, is it?' asked Della. 'You mustn't ever think of abandoning your wife because of me.'

'No,' said Ed, quietly. 'Peter Kaiser says there's a private detective following Season and Sally around. Well – I don't have any way of telling whether he's bluffing or not. But the twist is that unless I suffer severe loss of memory whenever anybody asks me about Shearson Jones and the Blight Crisis Appeal, that private detective is going to get orders to kill both of them, right away. I'd like to call them, but I think it's safer if I don't. Not just yet, anyway.'

Della came slowly over to Ed and laid her hands on his shoulders. Her hair gleamed coppery-gold in the faint light from the open windows. 'So that's why you wanted to know if the FBI had any proof that Shearson was really a killer.'

'Yes,' said Ed, quietly. He hesitated, and then he said, 'I know that things haven't been too good between me and Season lately . . . We've bickered over the farm, and we've argued over living in Kansas, and we've had enough rows about my mother to send up the Goodyear blimp. But I don't want anything like this to happen . . . not in a thousand years.'

Della kissed him, gently and lingeringly, on the lips. It was a kiss of affection and understanding, rather than a kiss of passion. 'Do you want to back out of this break-in?' she asked him. 'I'll understand if you do. Your wife and child are far more important to you than Shearson Jones.'

Ed shook his head. 'If we can find something to lock Shearson Jones up in the pen, then I'm ready to help.'

'You're sure?' she said.

'Just tell me what to do,' he replied, 'and make sure that the FBI send me a case of bourbon at Christmas for the next twenty years.'

Della checked her watch. 'Let's go, then. The Muldoons are usually awake at the crack, and it's going to take us at least a half-hour to get what we need.'

The upper landing outside Ed's bedroom was silent, and illuminated only by a low-voltage bracket lamp. Della paused for a moment, and looked carefully along the landing towards the double doors of Shearson's personal bedroom suite. They were closed, as usual, and probably locked. One of the Muldoon brothers had told Ed that Shearson had once been attacked in a hotel in New York by

231

a prowler, and ever since then he had been neurotic about the idea of being surprised in his sleep.

'Don't they have anybody patrolling the house during the night?' whispered Ed.

Della shook her head. 'The Muldoons check on all the doors and windows before they go to bed, and switch on an outside alarm; and there are a couple of Dobermanns loose in the grounds. For tonight, they've closed down the switchboard, too. The only telephone that works is Shearson's private line. Maybe Peter has a phone, too. But that's all. They don't need much else in the way of security, out here in the wilds.'

She gripped Ed's sleeve, and led him swiftly along the length of the landing to the angled cedarwood staircase. The stairs were so well constructed that not one of them creaked as they padded down to the main living area. They waited for just a second, listening, to make sure that they hadn't been heard; and then they crossed the wide living-room floor, and approached the passage to Shearson's study.

A portrait of a sour-faced trooper by George Caleb Bingham observed them from the passage wall; and a little further along, they were stared at fiercely by a Kwakiutl Indian mask in green and scarlet, fringed with real human hair. The cold magnetic light of the moon fell across the passage from a triangular wood-framed window, and pointed to the door of Shearson's study as if it were a mystic sign.

Della said, 'Keep an eye open, will you? This shouldn't take long.' And while Ed loitered at the corner of the passage, wishing that he'd thought of going to the bathroom before he ventured out on this bag job with Della, she reached into the pocket of her emerald green bathrobe and took out a plastic envelope, which, by the clinking sound it made, probably contained lock-picks.

'They teach you to burglarise people's houses?' asked Ed, in a breathy whisper.

Della raised one finger to her lips. 'They call it "gaining essential access". It's only called "burglarisation" when you get caught, and the agency disowns you.'

She peered at the lock closely. 'It's nothing special,' she told him. 'A five-lever armour-plated deadlock.'

'Is that all?' asked Ed. 'In that case, you should be able to open it with your hairgrip.'

'Will you keep a look-out, and shut up, and trust me?' hissed Della.

Ed waved a hand at her to calm her down. 'Just open the door. I trust you.'

He kept a watch on the silent living area as Della worked at the lock. The polished tables, the empty chairs, the long-case clock that ticked away the small hours of the morning with tired reluctance. From where he was standing, he could see the stairs and most of the upper landing, too, and there was no sign yet that anybody was stirring. He looked at his watch and it was eleven minutes after two. He wondered why he felt so unreal, so detached from everything that was going on. Maybe it was this stylish and stylised house, with its Indian art treasures, and that indescribable aura of sheer wealth and political power which surrounded Shearson Jones. Maybe it was the terrible events of Sunday night, the looting and the burning – events which he felt responsible for starting, but which he had only been able to experience at second-hand, on television.

Another oddity, too, as far as his feelings of reality were concerned, was that the television news programmes kept informing him that 'Kansas farmer Ed Hardesty, who publicly exposed the threat of a nationwide famine, is now in hiding in Washington, DC, along with Senator Shearson Jones, the man he claims is responsible for the crisis.'

The gates of Lake Vista had been firmly locked against the press since eleven o'clock Sunday evening, and two attempts by CBS News to land in the grounds by helicopter had been thwarted by Shearson's yapping dogs and by the Muldoon brothers, waving scatter-guns and threatening all kinds of murder. Through his office in Washington, Shearson had announced that he was returning to the capital, in due course, and that he would make 'a full and uninhibited statement' later – but first he felt it his duty to

233

make several 'private and confidential' visits to friends and political associates in Kansas. That had lent him the time to empty the Blight Crisis Appeal of anything that wasn't nailed to the floor, while reassurring the President that he was quite prepared to return to Washington and face the music.

What Ed didn't know was that Season had called Lake Vista five times during Sunday night and Monday morning, and that Willard Noakes had called, too, just to leave a message that 'we're right behind you, and if you need us, call.'

Della, wrestling with the door of Shearson's study, said, 'I can't get to grips with this fucking lock. What the hell does he need with a five-lever deadlock?'

'I thought you said it was easy,' said Ed.

'It should be,' she told him, irritably. 'It just so happens that it isn't.'

'Do you want me to try?' Ed asked her.

'Are you an FBI agent? Or a professional thief?'

'No, I'm not.'

'Well then, keep quiet, and let me get on with it.'

'All right. I'm sorry. I was only offering to help.'

'Don't.'

Ed turned away from Della, and checked the living area again. It was 2:21 a.m., and the house was still silent. He thought he could hear someone snoring, but he couldn't make out who it was.

The events of Sunday night had created an extraordinary kind of tension in the house. Ed had seen hardly anything of Karen since Sunday morning: Peter Kaiser had been keeping her away from anybody who might be considered an enemy of the Lake Vista establishment. Peter wasn't sure yet if Karen had been responsible for tipping Ed off about the extent of the crop blight, but he wasn't taking any chances. His mother had once told a new and rather sophisticated girlfriend of his that he had wept as a child in *Bambi*, especially in the scene where Bambi wanders through the fiery forest calling 'Mother! Mother!', and Peter had never trusted any woman since.

The tension had been heightened by Shearson's silence.

Instead of storming and raging about the house as Ed had expected him to, he had closeted himself away, and spoken to nobody but Peter and his servants. Several times during the day Ed had felt tempted to ask to talk to him, if only to clear the air. But Shearson had stayed out of sight. He wasn't interested in Ed's apologies, or explanations, or even his pledges to see Shearson roasting in hell. Shearson had several millions of dollars to rake off, and that was all that mattered.

'That's it,' said Della, with surprising suddenness. Ed turned, and the door was already ajar.

'You're a genius,' Ed told her. 'A five-lever, armour-plated lock?'

'They give us a pretty thorough training,' Della explained, with unconvincing modesty.

'You bet your investigative ass,' said Ed, flippant, but also impressed. He'd tried to pick a padlock once, on Season's diary, and he knew just how damned difficult lock-picking could be. He'd had to wait until Season had gotten around to telling him about her affair with Clive Harris of her own accord, and by then he hadn't been really interested any more.

'Come on,' whispered Della. 'And make sure you close the door behind you.'

They stepped into the office. It smelled of wine and cigar-smoke, and Shearson's underarm sweat. Della switched on the green glass desklamp, and directed it away from the window, in case it cast any light across the gardens outside which could be seen from a balcony upstairs.

The wide oak desk was in chaos, heaped with scratch pads and graph paper and accounts books. It looked as if Shearson and Peter had finished their day's work and then left everything exactly where it was, without bothering to clear up. There was even a half-smoked cigar in Shearson's ashtray, and a congealing cup of coffee beside Peter's chair. Ed picked up a yellow legal pad that Shearson had carelessly dropped on to the floor. On the top page, he had doodled an animated dollar-sign, with a broad smile, a big nose, and two little legs.

'It seems like even dollars can walk,' said Ed, throwing

the pad down again.

'Sure they can,' said Della, who was busily leafing through the papers that Peter Kaiser had been working on. 'They walk right out of the Blight Crisis Appeal fund, around the block a few times, double back around the next block, and then dodge in to Shearson Jones's bank when nobody's looking.'

'I call that smart,' said Ed.

'I don't,' said Della. 'I call it embezzlement.'

Ed looked around the office. The walls were clad with knotted pine, sanded and varnished. There were five or six photographs of Shearson making presentations to smiling wheat farmers in Kansas, and a misty early-American landscape by George Catlin. On the oak bookshelf beside the desk reclined a Victorian alabaster sculpture of an idealised Indian maiden, Pocahontas out of Wonder Woman, with feathers in her hair and bare breasts.

Della threw Ed a heavy pile of loose papers. 'You can start on those. You're looking for any financial movement out of the Blight Crisis Appeal fund. You're looking for where it goes, who handles it, which banks are involved, account numbers, possible pseudonyms, that kind of thing. You're looking for double entries and obvious laundering jobs. You think you can manage?'

'Sure I can manage,' said Ed, taking the papers across the room and spreading them out over a small side-table. 'I mean, pinning down two expert embezzlers out of a whole mess of memos, that can't be difficult.'

'You don't have to find anything specifically criminal. All we need is names, or account numbers. Anything that looks remotely unorthodox.'

'Okay,' said Ed. 'This is your party.'

They worked their way through the papers for forty minutes. Most of the notes and jottings were indecipherable, crowded with notes about tax law – such as 'Arizona acct exempt under Code Sec 501(c)3??' and 'trnsfr to cemetery company poss?' – and then there were columns and columns of figures, hardly any of them annotated or explained.

But after a while, Ed began to detect a distinct flow of

correlated figures from one page of all these scribbled accounts to another. He pulled the desk lamp nearer, and switched on Peter Kaiser's print-out calculator, and after five minutes of intensive button-punching, he said, 'That's it. I think I'm on to something.'

Della came across and looked over his shoulder. 'See here,' he told her, 'this figure of 1.72 million dollars has been ostensibly transferred into a holding fund, to accrue interest while the Blight Crisis Appeal fund management decide how best it's supposed to be spent. It's been split six ways, and invested under the perfectly legal terms of the holding fund into six different agriculture-related industries. But if you look at the figures on this page *here*, you'll see that a real-estate development company in Fort Myers, Florida, has been lent by six different sources a sum of money that amounts to 1.548 million dollars, which is 1.72 million dollars less ten per cent. There are only two names jotted down here – "Olga" and "Jimmy" – but God knows who they are.'

Della quickly looked through the accounts. 'It's not much,' she said. 'But maybe it's enough to point the FBI fraud people in the right direction. At least it's something. Shearson Jones is usually so good at dusting over his tracks.'

She collected up the papers, folded them, and tucked them in the pocket of her robe.

'Supposing Shearson notices they're missing?' asked Ed, replacing the desk lamp, and tearing the strip of paper off the calculator.

'It won't matter if he does. As soon as the Muldoons are up, and the alarms are switched off, I'm getting out of here, and fast.'

'Where does that leave me?'

'It leaves you right here. You'll be safer that way. If Shearson thinks you're implicated in stealing his personal papers, he'll hang your guts on the outhouse door.'

'You FBI agents have such a delicate turn of phrase.'

Della checked the office to make sure that everything was back where it was supposed to be. But she was about to switch off the desklamp when the door opened. Just like that, unannounced. And there, in a plaid cowboy shirt and BVDs, his eyes still blinking with sleep, was one of the Muldoon brothers.

For a moment, Muldoon stared at them both in total surprise, and they stared back at him, and nobody said a word. But then Muldoon turned back towards the passage and yelled out: '*Calvin! Calvin, c'mere! And bring the gun!*'

Ed made a rush for him. He managed to seize Muldoon's right arm, and pin it behind his back, but Muldoon twisted around and punched him very hard in the ear. Ed said, 'Shit!' and lost his balance, banging his head against the door-frame.

Della unceremoniously pushed Ed aside, and struck Muldoon on the collar-bone with her elbow. Then she jabbed him straight in the throat with her rigid fingers, and he pitched backwards across the passage with a high whining sound, like a vacuum cleaner with its bag full.

'Now – quick, for Christ's sake!' panted Della, and seized Ed by the hand.

Ed's ear was still singing, but he jostled his way out of Shearson's study, and down the passage, and across the living area. He barked his shin against a chrome coffee-table, and swore under his breath, but Della reached back and tugged at his sweatshirt to get him moving.

Calvin Muldoon popped out from a door beside the staircase, his pump-gun raised, his face white with surprise. Della snatched at the barrel of the gun, missed her grip, but chopped Muldoon in the kidneys with a short, vicious stroke of her right hand. Muldoon folded, and Ed hit him again, straight in the mouth. The gun dropped to the wooden floor with a clatter, and Ed reached down to pick it up.

'Shearson!' gasped Della. 'He's our only way out!'

Ed wasn't sure what she meant, but he hauled himself up the staircase after her, and pelted along the landing just behind her, and they skated along the last few feet together and collided with Shearson's double door at the same moment.

Della jiggled the door handle, but the doors were locked. 'Shall I blow the lock off?' asked Ed.

238

Della snapped her head around and stared at him as if he was mad. 'Are you crazy? You can't shoot locks off with a rifle! All you get is noise and smoke and bullets flying in all directions.'

'Oh,' said Ed, disappointed. 'They always do it in the movies.'

'In the movies they don't have solid cedarwood woors.'

Behind them, Calvin Muldoon was already up off the floor and coming up the stairs. Ed turned around and pointed the pump-gun at him, along the length of the landing.

'You come any nearer and I'll blow your head off!' he shouted, in what he hoped was a convincing tone of voice. Muldoon raised his hands, but still kept on coming, in a slow and sidling kind of a walk.

Just then, across on the other side of the landing, Peter Kaiser's bedroom door opened, and there was Peter himself, in a white T-shirt with PK embroidered on it, and white shorts.

'What the hell goes on here?' he said, irritably.

Ed swung the pump-gun around and fired. There was an ear-splitting bang, and an Indian tapestry that was hanging only two feet away from the open door of Peter's bedroom was ripped into black ribbons. Peter slammed his door shut instantly, and locked it.

While Ed was distracted, Calvin Muldoon tried to make a silent rush up the landing on tippy-toes, but Ed whipped the gun back around just in time, and levelled it at Muldoon's head with an expression of such fierceness that the poor man was brought up short, teetering on his toes.

'I warned you,' Ed told him, harshly. Muldoon backed off, his hands raised high.

'It's okay,' he said. 'It's okay. Take it easy. I was only doing my job.'

Della meanwhile had been trying to pick Shearson's lock. She was hunkered down in front of it, her teeth bared in a grimace of concentration, her fingers trembling as she tried to sense the levers inside.

Ed said, 'Hurry up, will you? They're going to go off and

get guns of their own before we know where we are.'

Calvin Muldoon was already backing down the staircase, and Ed heard his brother call from the living area, 'Are you all right, there, Calvin? Didn't get yourself hurt, did you?'

Della said nothing, but reserved her attention for the lock.

Peter Kaiser's door opened again, only an inch or so. There was a pause, and then Peter said, 'Is that you Hardesty? Can you hear me?'

'I can hear you,' Ed told him.

'I don't know what you think you're doing, Hardesty, but whatever it is you won't get away with it. This house is locked up tighter than a prison.'

'Let me worry about that,' Ed called back.

Peter thought for a moment, and then he said, 'If you harm Senator Jones in any way – and I mean this – you'll have every police force in the country after you.'

'He won't be harmed, unless he's stupid,' said Ed.

'You won't get away with it,' Peter repeated.

Della said, 'Come on, you pig of a lock. Come on.'

'For Christ's sake,' Ed exhorted her.

Now, Calvin Muldoon was climbing back up the staircase, crouched low on knees and elbows. Ed couldn't see too clearly through the carved wooden banisters, but he glimpsed a nickel-plated .45 automatic in Calvin's right hand. He was frightened now. There wasn't any doubt that the Muldoons were as well armed as the Marine Corps, and that they wouldn't hesitate to shoot if they thought it was part of their job. He wondered if he ought to fire a warning shot along the landing, but he didn't know how many shells were left in his pump-gun, and so he decided not to.

Della said, 'Done it,' in such a quiet voice that Ed didn't hear her. But then she pushed Shearson's door open, and Shearson's alarm bells went off, and amidst the shattering, blinding noise, Ed realised that she had saved their skins at the last possible moment. Holding the pump-gun in his right hand, he pushed Della through the open door with his left, and then backed in after her.

'I hope you know you scared the pants off me just then,'

240

Ed told her, and he was so genuinely frightened that his voice sounded strangled and high. The bells kept on shrieking, so they could scarcely hear each other speak.

'Let's go get Shearson,' shouted Della.

They locked the double doors behind them, and then strode purposefully down the short corridor that led to Shearson's bedroom. Ed kicked open the louvred door, and pounced into the room with the pump-gun held high, like something out of *Starsky and Hutch*. He needn't have bothered. The huge king-sized bed with its puffy white coverlet was empty, and Shearson Jones was standing instead on the far side of the room, next to a small cocktail cabinet, dressed in a vast white nightshirt, and lighting up a Partagas cigar.

The alarm bells were so shrill in here that Ed didn't even attempt to speak. He simply waved the rifle at Shearson, and inclined his head towards the door.

Shearson puffed at his cigar, and shook his head. He mouthed the words, 'no way.'

Della, in her bright green wrap, walked directly over to Shearson and yelled something in his ear. He stared at her for a moment, and then thoughtfully laid his cigar down in a silver ashtray. He opened a louvred wardrobe door, and tugged out pants, shirt, and a dark blue sweater that must have taken the wool of two dozen sheep. Without another word, he gave the clothes to Della, and led the way out of the bedroom.

'What did you tell him?' shouted Ed.

'I told him we only had one shell left in the gun,' Della told him. 'I also told him what part of his anatomy was going to get hit first.'

Ed raised his eyebrows. 'He believes that I'd do that? I mean, maim him that way?'

'No. But he believes that *I* would.'

They reached the doors of Shearson's suite, and Della quickly unlocked them. Shearson stood by, as fat and white as an apparition of Falstaff. Della shouted at him, 'Do what you're told. That's all. No jokes, no tricks, no nothing. I don't have much of a sense of humour tonight.'

Shearson made a *moue* amidst his four double chins.

241

Gradually, Della drew the door inwards. As she did so, the alarm stopped ringing, and there was an extraordinary silence, still crowded with ghostly after-images of clangorous bells.

They waited. Ed glanced down, and saw the sweep hand of his watch counting out more than thirty seconds. The landing outside was utterly silent, and yet the Muldoons had to be there, and maybe Peter Kaiser, too, if he'd summoned up the nerve.

'We're coming out now!' called Della.

There was no reply. Only silence, and darkness.

'If you try to stop us, Senator Jones will be seriously wounded,' she said. 'Not killed, but wounded in a way which is going to cause him agony and distress for the rest of his life. Do you understand that?'

Still no reply. Della looked back at Ed, and then at Shearson Jones, and from the expression on her face she was obviously trying to calculate the risks of taking an enormously fat senator and a nervous farmer-cum-actuary on a run for freedom that could get them all killed.

'Ed,' she said, 'you could still stay behind. I'm not saying that Shearson would give you a particularly nice time, but it could be better than dying.'

Ed shook his head. 'I'm coming, and that's all there is to it. Don't worry about it, Della, I won't hold you back. Just say the word and we'll go.'

Della looked at Shearson. 'You hear that, my darling? You're coming on a little trip.'

Shearson sighed. 'My father always told me to stay clear of women with oversized breasts,' he replied. 'Their sense of loyalty can always be assessed in inverse ratio to the measurement of their bazumbas.'

Ed prodded Shearson's fat side with the muzzle of the pump gun. It was like prodding a pillow. Shearson looked round at him, offended, but Ed gave him what Sally had always called his 'nice alligator' smile in return.

'Are you going to tell me who you are?' Shearson asked them. 'Do I get to know why you're kidnapping me? Are you Symbionese Liberation Army? Are you Israelis? Not that it really makes a great deal of difference.'

Della ignored him. 'I want you to step out of this door with your hands up,' she instructed him. 'And I'm just going to warn you that if you attempt to get away, or do anything at all except what I tell you to do, then Ed here is going to take your balls off as fast as you can say Vatican choir.'

'Well, you can't be Israelis,' said Shearson. 'Israelis never have such a colourful turn of phrase.'

'Move!' said Della, and pulled him towards the door.

Shearson grinned at her as he stepped out on to the landing. 'Whatever happens, my dear,' he told her, 'I'd like you to know that you were a great lay.'

With Shearson ahead of them, Ed and Della walked out of the bedroom and along the landing. There was no sign of Peter Kaiser or of either of the Muldoon brothers. The house was so silent they could almost hear the dust falling.

Ed looked nervously from one side to the other as he escorted Shearson down the staircase. Shearson was humming to himself under his breath, and that unsettled Ed even more. It sounded as if Shearson knew something that he and Della didn't.

They crossed the living area. Shearson remarked loudly, 'I wish you'd tell me what devious political purpose this kidnap is supposed to serve.' And almost instantly, every light in the living area was switched on, and both Muldoon brothers stepped out from passages at the side, with automatics raised in both hands.

Later, Ed remembered what happened in such detail that he couldn't believe it had all been over so quickly. He had thrown himself forward, right on to Shearson's back, and toppled the senator to the floor. As he did so, he had twisted himself around and seized Shearson's neck in the crook of his arm, wrenching it back, so that Shearson's head protected his chest. Della had dived behind one of the sofas.

Calvin Muldoon had dodged down beside a chair, squinted along the sights of his Colt .45, and fired twice. One shot had shattered a white porcelain lampshade base into a blast of snowy shrapnel. The second had echoed its way down one of the passages.

There had been a second's silence, and then Calvin's brother had fired a wild shot that broke a window on the other side of the room. There had been another second's silence. Neither dared to shoot again in case he hit the senator. There had been a sharp smell of gunsmoke in the air.

'Muldoon!' Ed had called out. 'Muldoon – there's nothing at all you can do.'

'You just try to move and I'll get you,' Calvin Muldoon replied. 'Either that, or I'll get the woman.'

Ed had thought about that, in one of those vivid, jumbled, instant flashes of processed information. Then, without hesitation, he had lifted the pump-gun and fired.

The shot had blown the stuffing out of the cushions in the chair which Calvin Muldoon had been using for cover. The room had suddenly been filled with smoke, and echoes, and hundreds of floating duck feathers. Calvin Muldoon had been hit in the neck, and he had suddenly appeared with his hand held around his throat, kneeling bolt upright, his face as horrified as one of Shearson's Kwakiutl masks. Thick red blood had been jetting out from between his fingers across the floor, spurt after spurt after spurt. His brother had shouted, 'Calvin! Calvin, my God! Calvin!'

Next, they were out of the door, out into the night, and running. Della was way ahead, crossing the wide front drive to the travelled stand where the cars were parked. Ed trailed fifty or sixty feet behind, trying to drag Shearson along by the sleeve of his nightshirt.

'I can't run! I can't run!' wheezed Shearson.

'I don't give a damn!' Ed shouted at him. 'Run, or I'll blow you to big fat pieces!'

There were three cars parked by a windbreak of red pines – Ed's own Caprice Classic station wagon, in which he had driven up to Lake Vista with Della; a Chevy Suburban wagon which the Muldoons used to drive around the grounds; and Shearson's rented Lincoln Continental. The chauffeur, a quiet and serious man with a permanent frown, had been put up in the guest cottage close to the main gates.

'Keys!' said Della, as Shearson and Ed caught up with

her. 'Did you remember your car keys?'

'I didn't even know I was going to have to drive tonight,' said Ed.

Shearson gasped, 'No more running. Please. I beg you. No more running.'

Della opened the Suburban's left-hand door, and felt around for keys. 'No damned keys,' she said. 'Why couldn't they be careless for once?'

Ed, one-handed, the pump-gun still waving at Shearson Jones, opened up the Lincoln. It smelled of leather and car-freshener. 'No keys here, either.'

Della looked back towards the house. Peter Kaiser appeared briefly in the open front doorway, and then disappeared again. All around them the night was windy and strewn with stars. They could hear Muldoon shouting, and Peter calling, 'Don't do that, you'll choke him, for Christ's sake!'

Della bit her lip. 'They'll be after us in a minute. You wait until Peter Kaiser finds those papers are missing. Listen – get in the car.'

'What's the point? We can't get it started.'

'Just get in the car. It's downhill all the way to the guest house. If you can give it enough of a push to start with, we can coast to the gates, and then get hold of the keys from the chauffeur.'

Muldoon appeared in the doorway of the house now, and unexpectedly fired a shot. Ed saw the flash of the .45's muzzle, and heard the bullet drone away into the pines.

Shearson said, 'You'd better make up your tiny minds, because they're quite liable to shoot us all.'

Ed tugged open the back door of the Lincoln. 'Get in,' he ordered Shearson. Shearson beamed smugly, and wedged himself inside with a great show of puffing and blowing.

'I hope you realise this is all futile,' he said, as Ed slammed the door on him.

Della opened the passenger door. 'Give me the gun,' she told Ed. 'I'll try to give you some cover while you get us started.'

Ed looked at her for one questioning second, and then tossed the pump-gun across the roof of the car. Della

245

caught it in one hand, without effort, as if she'd been trained in gun-handling all her life. Even Ed couldn't have caught it like that.

Releasing the Lincoln's parking brake, Ed gripped the steering wheel in one hand and the door frame in the other, and started to push. At first, the car wouldn't move at all. He grunted, and pushed again, and it swayed forward about a half-inch. Behind him, Shearson Jones said, with mock concern, 'You don't want me to get out again, do you? Would that be of any help?'

Ed gasped, 'You stay – where you – are. I need – the ballast –'

There was another loud shot from the house, and a bullet pinged off the Lincoln's rear bumper. Ed shouted to Della, 'They're trying to hit the tyres!'

'That's another fallacy,' said Della. 'You can't burst a tyre with a bullet. They're aiming for the gas tank, more likely.'

'Whatever,' panted Ed, and heaved at the Lincoln again.

Gradually, with a slow gravelly crunching sound, the limousine began to creep forward. At first it wasn't rolling at any speed at all, and Ed was worried that it would come to a stop as soon as it came to a gentle rise in the driveway. But he kept on heaving at it, and it picked up more and more momentum, until Della had to run along beside it.

There was a crackling fusillade of pistol-shots from the house. One of them ricocheted off the Lincoln's trunk, with a noise like a complaining seagull. Another struck the gravel close to Ed's feet.

'Peter Kaiser's shooting as well,' said Della. She stepped up on to the sill of the Lincoln's open passenger door, rested the pump-gun across the roof, sighted it, and fired one loud booming shot towards the doorway of the house. Shearson, inside the car, grimaced and said, 'Jesus.'

'All right,' said Ed, 'let's get the hell out of here.'

The large black Continental bounced silently along the sloping driveway. It was eerie, travelling without an engine. There was no sound but the crunching of the tyres on the ground, the squeaking of the suspension, and Shearson's thick panting in the back seat.

246

'There's the guest cottage,' said Della, pointing to a small white-washed house set back amongst the silhouette of the trees. It was almost three o'clock in the morning now, and the sky had faded a little, to a pale shade of oyster, but the ground was still thick with the shadows of the night.

Ed steered the Lincoln around the curve which took the driveway to the main gates. Then he applied the brake, and opened his door.

'Give me two minutes,' he said. 'If Shearson tries anything, shoot him. Anywhere you like.'

'I hope you realise that the gates are locked, and that you don't have a key to them, either,' smiled Shearson, fatly.

Ed said nothing, but walked briskly across the driveway to the brick steps which led up to the guest cottage. He skirted around the shadowy wooden verandah, his feet echoing on the boards, until he came to a window with floral drapes pulled across it. He listened, and he thought he could hear the chaffeur snoring inside. He banged loudly on the window with the flat of his hand.

The bedside light went on straight away, with almost comical speed. A voice said, 'Who's that? What's happening?'

'Everything's okay,' said Ed. 'I just need the keys to the car. Someone locked it by mistake, and Senator Jones has left some important documents in it.'

A long silence. Then the chauffeur said, 'Do you know what time it is? It's three o'clock in the morning.'

'Sure it's three o'clock in the morning. But the President's called on Senator Jones for some urgent information, and we have to have those keys. Come on, pal, just pass them out, and then you can go back to sleep.'

Ed heard a cot creaking, and a loud sniff. 'I'm not supposed to hand them over to anybody, you know.'

'Senator Jones isn't just anybody, and neither is the President. So will you give me the keys?'

Up at the house, Ed heard the whistling roar of the Chevy Surburban's engine starting up. He stepped back from the cottage window, and peered up the hill. He could make out the wagon's lights as Peter and Muldoon circled around the front of the house in pursuit.

'Will you hurry up, please?' Ed called out. 'Senator Jones is real impatient.'

'Hold on a minute,' said the chauffeur, from behind the floral drapes. 'I'm trying to remember if I left the keys in my uniform pants or my Levis. I did some work on the car earlier on, you know. The brakes were squealing like hogs. Do you know what it was? Dust, that's what it was. This perishing Kansas dust, in the linings.'

Ed stepped back again. The lights of the Muldoons' wagon were already halfway down the hill, flickering their way through the pines. He could hear the whine of the four-wheel drive, and the crunching of the tyres on the gravel.

He thundered on the chauffeur's bedroom window with his clenched fist. 'Are you going to give me those fucking keys or do I have to tear down the wall and get them myself?'

The drapes abruptly parted. Then the sash window came rattling up. The chauffeur was standing there in pink striped pyjamas, solemn and frightened, with his hair sticking up from sleeping. He was holding out the keys like a small boy who's been caught stealing candies.

Ed snatched the keys out of the chauffeur's hand, and ran back along the verandah. As he hurried down the brick steps, he could see the Chevy wagon only two hundred feet away, and he was caught in the glare of its lights. He threw himself into the open door of the Lincoln, stabbed the wrong key into the ignition, wrestled it out again, stabbed another key in, and then twisted the engine into screaming life.

Dazzling headlights crowded his rearview mirror. There was a shot, and the back window turned to milk. Della screamed at Shearson Jones, 'Get down! They'll take your head off!'

Ed tugged the gear shift into reverse, and then pressed his foot on the gas pedal. Another bullet banged into the Lincoln's trunk, with a hollow echoing sound.

The limousine's rear wheels slithered and shrieked on the gravel, spraying up dust and stones. Then it shot backwards, straight into the oncoming Chevy wagon, and there was a loud *kabbosssh!* of colliding metal. Ed felt his neck wrenched from the impact, and Shearson tumbled against the back of his seat with all the elegance of two hundred and fifty pounds of Idaho potatoes. But Ed pulled the gear shift right down to second, shoved his foot on the gas again, and the Lincoln roared forwards towards the main gates with its rear end sliding sideways and its suspension bouncing wildly.

The car collided with the wrought-iron gates, and stopped, its engine bellowing in frustration. Della was clutching the back of her seat, her eyes wide, her pump-gun ready for a last quick shoot-out with Peter Kaiser and Muldoon. Shearson was lying sideways now, and puffing in pain.

'They're coming again!' shouted Della, her voice shrill.

Ed threw the Lincoln back into reverse, stepped on the gas again, and for a second time the long black car hurtled backwards into the battered Chevy wagon. For long seconds, both vehicles were locked together in a crunching, grinding tangle of bumpers and crushed lights, their tyres whinnying and their engines outraged. Then Ed changed back into drive, and the Lincoln surged forward into the gates with another resonant crash of metal.

They wouldn't have made it through if it hadn't been for Muldoon's powerful wagon, right up behind them. Muldoon gave them an extra shunt as they hit the gates, and the force of both vehicles together was enough to burst open the locks. The Lincoln slewed out into the road, its trunk lid flapping up in the air, its radiator grille twisted and broken, but still roadworthy and going at full speed.

'Now, hit it!' screamed Della, in excitement. 'Get your foot down and really hit it!'

'What the hell do you think I'm doing?' Ed demanded, juggling with the steering wheel as the Lincoln skidded sideways around a ferociously tight curve. 'This isn't a sports car, for Christ's sake. This is a two-ton limousine!'

The road from Fall River Lake leads down to Fall River itself, and joins up with the east-west highway which runs through Keighley and Augusta and back into Wichita. But it's a wiggling series of hairpins, through rocks and pines and deceptive tunnels of light and shade, and the thin strip of blacktop is patchy, uneven, and often cambered the wrong way.

Ed glanced in his mirror as they sped beside the lake. Through the frosted rear window, he could see the flash of headlights as the Chevy wagon came after them. He said to Della, breathlessly, 'They're right in back of us. Why don't you try to pick them off when we take the next right-hand curve?'

Della shook her head.

'Why not?' yelled Ed. 'They're trying to kill us!'

'Maybe they are, maybe they're not,' said Della. 'They're trying to catch us, more than anything. But I don't like to shoot at people unless I really have to.'

Ed lost his concentration for a moment, and the Lincoln barely made it around a long left-hand curve, its tyres screaming in a falsetto harmony that went on and on, until Ed couldn't believe that he was going to be able to hold on to the car any longer. He was plastered in sweat by the time the road took a twist in the opposite direction, and they were driving downhill through a shadowy archway of pines.

He checked the mirror again, and the lights of the Chevy Suburban were still behind him, although further away now. Nobody in their right mind would have taken a curve at that speed on purpose.

'Listen,' said Ed, as he piloted the Lincoln down a fast slalom of alternating bends, 'They're chasing us, they're shooting at us, and you don't think you really have to shoot back?'

'I want Peter Kaiser alive,' said Della. 'He's going to be a material witness to this fraud, and he's more susceptible to legal pressure than Shearson Jones.'

In the back of the car, lolling from side to side as the Lincoln howled around curve after curve, Shearson Jones said, 'So that's who you are, my gingery angel. The Federal Bureau of Investigation, incarnate. No wonder they gave me such a cock-and-bull story about you when I asked them to check you out.'

Della twisted around in her seat. With her loosely-tied emerald-green bathrobe and her upraised pump-gun, she

250

looked like some kind of comic-strip Dragon Lady, all silk and cleavage and sawn-off rifle. As he glanced across at her, it occurred to Ed, not for the first time that night, that she must be naked under that wrap.

'You know something,' he said, as he spun the Lincoln through a steep-sloping S-bend, 'this must be the craziest night of my life.'

'You're wrong,' breathed Shearson, leaning forward and resting his arms on the back of Ed's seat. 'Last night was the craziest night of your life. The night you announced to 250 million Americans that they were probably facing imminent starvation. That was the craziest night of your life.'

Ed said nothing. He still hadn't mentally got to grips with what had happened last night, and right now, pushing this 7-litre Lincoln down a tortuous mountain road, he didn't have the time to. He flicked his eyes across to the mirror again, and the Chevy's headlights were still there, still dancing and jiggling close behind him, occasionally obscured by the flapping lid of the Lincoln's trunk.

They flashed past a sign, and Della said, 'Fall River, two miles. We've almost made it.'

Shearson said, 'I'll have your scalps for this. I hope you understand that. You, Hardesty; and you, my dear; and that pontificating Charles Kurnik at the FBI. Three scalps, to add to my collection.'

'Shut up, senator,' said Ed, and at the same moment one of the Lincoln's front tyres burst. There was a loud, flabby report, followed by the slap-slap-slap of torn rubber on the road, and then the huge limousine was swerving and sliding from side to side, with Ed spinning the steering-wheel in a desperate struggle to keep the car out of the trees.

'Hold it!' shrieked Shearson, in an unnaturally feminine voice. 'For God's sake, hold it!'

The Lincoln's trunk swung around to the left, and sideswiped the trunk of a roadside pine. Then the car screeched around in the opposite direction, its front wheels banging and shuddering over a line of rocks. Ed, gripping the wheel, saw trees, darkness, sky, and more trees, and then his whole world tilted sideways and he was hit on the bridge of the nose by something as hard as an iron bar.

A whole minute of silence passed by. Ed raised his head. His nose felt as if it had swollen three times its normal size. He looked painfully around him and saw that the limousine had dropped down an eighty foot slope, and was now resting at an angle of forty five degrees in a narrow rock-strewn gully. There was no sound but the ticking of the engine as it slowly cooled down, and the whistling of black-capped chickadees in the trees.

Beside him, Della was holding her head in her hands. The pump-gun had dropped to the floor. In back, Senator Jones suddenly started moaning, and saying, 'My finger. God damn it, I've broken my finger.'

Ed said, 'Della, are you okay?'

Della nodded dumbly. Ed turned to Senator Jones and asked, 'Is it just your finger? Nothing else broken?'

'Isn't a finger enough?' snarled Shearson.

Behind them, up on the road, the Chevy's lights had stopped. Ed picked up the rifle, and tried to open his door, The impact of the crash had wedged it back in its frame, so he had to kick it twice with his heels before it would budge. then he climbed out into the sharp early-morning air.

Peter Kaiser and Muldoon were already on their way down the slope. It was still too dark to see clearly, but Ed caught the glint of Muldoon's nickel-plated automatic as he came down through the trees.

'I don't know why you don't give up now,' said Shearson, from the back of the car. 'You don't stand a chance in hell.'

'Just shut up,' said Ed, and crouched his way along the length of the Lincoln's fender. Then he lay down on the ground, on a slope of pine needles and pine cones, and positioned himself so that he could take a shot at Peter Kaiser or Muldoon as soon as they were in range.

Della slipped out of the driver's door behind him, and wriggled her way up close.

'Whatever you do, don't hurt Peter Kaiser,' she said. 'He's going to be a number-one plea-bargaining witness. Especially when we put some pressure on his mother.'

'I'll do whatever I have to do to keep us alive,' said Ed.

252

Soon, Peter Kaiser and Muldoon were less than twenty feet away, and their faces were clearly visible against the black shadows of the pines. This is going to be like shooting coconuts at a fair, thought Ed, as he squinted along the rifle. The front sight of the pump-gun appeared as a dark notch in Muldoon's pale head.

'Senator Jones? Are you there?' called Peter, anxiously.

They could hear the car's suspension squeak as Shearson moved his bulk towards the opposite window.

'I'm all right,' Shearson called out, hoarsely. 'I've broken my damned finger, but that's all. It's Hardesty you've got to watch out for. He's around the car somewhere, with the girl.'

There was a pause, and then Peter shouted, 'Hardesty? You there?'

Ed looked around at Della, but Della shook her head. Don't answer, not yet. See what they have to offer first.

'If you can hear me, Hardesty, you'd better listen good,' said Peter. 'You're guilty so far tonight of burglary, theft, criminal damage, kidnapping, and homicide. You hear that? Calvin Muldoon is dead, and you shot him. You're holding a US senator against his will. You're in a pretty sticky position, Hardesty, and you'd better understand it.'

'Why haven't you called the police?' Ed shouted back, before Della could stop him. He could see Muldoon quickly jerk his head around to see if he could make out where the voice was coming from.

Peter Kaiser took a couple of steps closer. 'I haven't called the police because the police are too busy with all the rioting and the looting you started off with that broadcast of yours. Apart from that, you've ransacked some pretty sensitive papers there. I wouldn't like them to get into the hands of somebody who might misinterpret them.'

'So what's your offer?' asked Ed. 'You want to make a deal?'

'The offer's simple. I'll let you out of here alive, as long as you let Senator Jones go free, and as long as you never mention anything about the Blight Crisis Appeal again.'

'One more thing,' said Ed.

'What's that?'

'You take the tail off of my wife and my daughter. Because I warn you, if anything happens to them, I'll hunt you down and take your head off.'

'That's all right,' Peter nodded. 'I can agree to that. Now, do you want to come out, with your hands where we can see them?'

Ed turned to Della again. 'What do you think?' he asked her.

Della said, 'I don't trust him. My reason says he's probably on the level, but my instinct says beware.'

Ed squeezed her hand. 'Well, I've always been the kind of person to follow my instinct. Let's give them a test. Remember the old cowboy films?'

He handed her the gun to hold, and then, twisting on the needly floor of the woods, he tugged his red sweatshirt off.

'Striptease, at a time like this?' she asked him.

'Just give me the gun,' he told her.

Quickly, he wrapped the sweatshirt around the barrel of the rifle. Then, hesitantly and jerkily, he raised it up above the protective fender of the Lincoln, as if it was someone coming out of cover.

'*There!*' said Peter.

The silence of the woods was cracked by three pistol shots in rapid succession. Ed's sweatshirt was flapped up into the air by one bullet, and they felt the wind of a second as it passed narrowly overhead. The third pinged off the Lincoln's trunk.

Ed snatched down the rifle, rolled around to the slope which he had chosen as his firing position, snuggled the butt against his cheek and looked for Peter and Muldoon.

Muldoon, crouched as low as an arm-swinging baboon, was only a few feet away, running in fast to finish off the red sweatshirt. Peter was already round the other side of the limousine – presumably intent on rescuing Shearson. Della was right behind Ed, her head buried beside his thigh.

Muldoon didn't have a chance. He was so close that Ed shouted, 'Muldoon! Drop it!' just to give the man a break. But Muldoon made a dive for the ground, and fired off another thunderous shot from his .45, and Ed squeezed the

254

trigger without allowing himself to think anything else but *kill him*.

The shot echoed and echoed, and then there was silence again. Ed cautiously rose to his feet, and walked around the Lincoln with the pump-gun held up and his eyes alert.

Muldoon was lying on his back on the stony ground, his eyes wide open, his automatic thrown aside, his plaid cowboy shirt dark with blood.

Peter appeared, holding a revolver, but Ed swung the rifle towards him and said, 'Drop it,' and he did.

'You've killed him,' said Peter, in a shaky voice.

Ed nodded. 'I didn't want to. Believe me. But it was him or us.'

'What are you going to do now?' asked Peter. 'Are you going to shoot the rest of us, too? Or what? One way or another, we're going to have to report this to the police.'

'The police already know,' said Ed, quietly. 'At least, the federal authorities do.'

'What do you mean?'

'Della works for the FBI. The reason we broke into your office was to find evidence of what you've been doing with this Blight Crisis Appeal to take you to court.'

'You're joking. Are you joking?'

'You think I go around shooting people for fun? I never hurt anybody in my life before, until tonight,' Ed snapped at him. He was shaking, and if he could have done, he would have slung the pump-gun right off into the trees.

Shearson Jones pushed open the passenger door of the wrecked Lincoln. 'Would someone help me out of here?' he demanded. 'And would someone tell me what the devil's going on?'

Della came up, brushing pine needles from her robe. 'We're getting out of here, that's what,' she said, in a clear voice. 'We're going to leave Muldoon here for the moment, and we're going to drive into Wichita and turn in these papers to the FBI. And if you're innocent enough to think that *we're* in trouble, Mr Kaiser, just think what kind of trouble *you're* in. Fraud, embezzlement, tax evasion, carrying unlicensed firearms, attempted murder of a federal agent. You'll be lucky if they let you out to see the turn of the century.'

'Is there room in that wagon for all of us?' wheezed Shearson, plodding up the hill towards them.

'There should be, with Muldoon gone,' said Peter. 'I have Karen with me, too, though.'

'You brought Karen? Why?'

Peter Kaiser looked embarrassed. 'Kind of insurance. In case we had to do a trade – her freedom for Shearson's.'

'My, my,' said Della, shaking her head. 'You *do* get your money's worth out of your girlfriends, don't you?'

With Ed staying a little way behind to keep Peter covered, they slowly made their way up to the road again. Karen was standing by the wagon in bare feet, jeans, and the white puffy-sleeved shirt she usually wore in bed. When she saw them coming – Peter and Della, Shearson and Ed, she couldn't work out what had happened at first – who had captured whom. But when Ed said, 'It's okay, Karen. Everything's fine,' she came walking across the blacktop bare-footed with tears running down her cheeks.

'Oh, God, I was frightened,' she said, holding Ed's arm. 'Oh, God, I can't tell you how frightened I was.'

Ed put his arm around her and held her close. Della, beside the wagon, gave him a mocking little raise of her eyebrows, and a smile that could have meant anything at all.

Seven

During the weekend, an intensive search by fifteen volunteers from the St Louis Fire Department had revealed five radioactive isotopes in grain elevators along the waterfront, and 'perceptible' radioactivity in almost every grain and flour store within a six-mile radius of the city. The isotopes had been taken to the National Nuclear Research station in Kokomo, Indiana, where tests showed by late Monday afternoon that each of them contained over 4000 curies of radioactive cobalt-60.

At 11.43 p.m. on Monday night, the President was informed of the discovery, and he issued immediate instructions for the contaminated cereals to be destroyed. They were to be taken out to sea and jettisoned in deep water off Miami, under the supervision of experts from the Navy, the Bureau of Atomic Energy, and the FBI. The President emphasised that it was 'essential, at this time of threatened shortage, not to let these radioactive foodstuffs go astray, or to fall into the hands of those who might not be so scrupulous about where they go to.'

Geiger-counter searches of grain elevators and flour warehouses all over the country were put into motion a few minutes after midnight, and by seven o'clock on Tuesday morning, officials had discovered isotopes in Chicago, Duluth, Milwaukee, and Seattle. Whoever had planted the isotopes had shown no discrimination. They were found in grain stores at breweries, amongst oats and bran in animal-feed factories, and in flour warehouses at kosher bakers. The nuclear laboratories were unable to tell where the isotopes had come from, since their casings bore no serial numbers or manufacturer's marks, but three out of the seven analysts working on them expressed an opinion that the cobalt was of European origin.

'We are being attacked from without, rather than within,' said the Director of the FBI, Charles Kurnik. 'I don't think we need more than three guesses to answer the question *by whom?*'

With instructions from the President to use the utmost diplomatic discretion, the Secretary of State began to put out feelers in Japan, in China, in Soviet Russia, in Iran, in Germany, and in Britain. Without revealing the seriousness of the isotope crisis, he was supposed to vibrate the web of international diplomacy, and see if he could detect in which corner the spider was sitting.

By noon on Tuesday, the President and his cabinet were faced with the question of what to do about the billions of bushels of highly radioactive grain still stored in elevators all around the country – grain which was still being happily used to bake bread, brew beer, feed animals, fill out

257

hamburgers, and to make anything and everything from children's cereals to bourbon whisky.

Five nuclear experts were brought to the White House just after lunch as special advisers, but as Tuesday afternoon wore on, they were unable to agree amongst themselves how dangerous the radioactivity in the grain and the flour was actually going to be. Certainly, the levels were way above those which the FDA would normally consider acceptable, but these weren't normal times. Almost all of this year's crops were dying of blight, and now it looked as if the stockpiles from last year were going to be contaminated beyond use.

Dr K. E. Salkeld of Minneapolis stood before the President – a tall, ascetic man with a reputation for facing up to the bitterest scientific facts – and took off his spectacles in a gesture of defeat. 'Mr President,' he said, 'this radioactivity is of sufficient strength to have the same effect as a nuclear bomb, without an explosion. Our children will eat it in their diets, our adults will drink it in their beer, and it will work its evil way into the very bones of our population. Many millions will almost certainly die in terrible agony. Those who are left will face pain, loneliness, and the horror of living in a society where a very high percentage of the population is outrageously deformed.'

What worried the President more than anything else, however, was the immediate prospect of another night like Sunday, with more rioting and burning. It was quite possible that millions of Americans might be affected by radioactive poisoning if he were to keep the crisis quiet for a few more days, until he had worked out some kind of contingency plan. But the effects of the cobalt-60, although threatening, were still largely hypothetical, whereas it was almost inevitable that thousands of people would die tonight if he were to announce at once that there was a total ban on bread, cereal, cake, cookies, beer, spirits, and pastries – and if Dr Salkeld was right, meat as well, since so many American animals were fed on grain. The Cabinet had already left most of their turkey sandwiches untouched, and at six o'clock the President had turned down the offer of a steak.

At nine, a report was brought into the Oval Office from the State Department. At an emergency meeting of the European Economic Community in Brussels, all the member countries had guaranteed to supply to the United States, as much surplus meat, cereal, dairy produce, and vegetables as they could muster, They realised that whatever they could supply would fall 'far below the day-to-day needs of a country of 250 million inhabitants', but they appreciated the President's co-operation in halting emigration from the United States to Europe, and they believed that 'one-thousandth of a loaf is better than no bread.'

With the help of hundreds of officials from state capitals and county seats all over the United States, who had industriously filed reports on how much canned and frozen food was being held in commercial warehouses and supermarket storerooms, the calculation was that America could 'just about survive the winter, at subsistence level.'

The President read out the report to his Cabinet as twilight fell across the White House lawns outside. 'In the space of a few days,' he said, 'this nation of plenty has been reduced to the economic level of a country as poor as Cambodia; and all those pitiful scenes which we have witnessed in Cambodia are going to be witnessed here.

'There is no question that the blight which has so swiftly destroyed our crops, and the radioactive material which has so effectively contaminated our stores of essential foodstuffs – there is no question at all that these have been deliberately introduced, with the single intention of destroying our country.

'We do not yet have adequate evidence to pin the blame for these criminal actions on any known adversary. Our first suspect, of course, must be the Soviet Union, but the Director of the Federal Bureau of Investigation tells me that it would have been possible for as few as a hundred agents to have blighted our crops and to have planted those isotopes. Our unknown adversary could have been Iran, or Palestine, or even an unknown political pressure-group from an ostensibly friendly power.'

Just before dark, the President left the Oval Office, and

went for a walk in the White House gardens by himself. He smoked two cigarettes, although nobody apart from his wife and his closest friends knew that he was a smoker. After his walk, he closeted himself in his small side office and placed a telephone call to Alan Hedges, the chairman of the Agricultural Committee.

'Alan,' he said, 'I want you to give me an update on the emergency supplies you've been shipping in for the administration.'

Alan Hedges said, 'Pardon me one moment, Mr President . . . the figures are right here. That's it . . . we've completed all the shipments of canned goods and stored them in three separate warehouses around the city, as well as five truckloads of special emergency rations out at Anacostia Naval Annex. The rest of the refrigerated goods are arriving by rail just after nine o'clock tonight.'

The President ran his hand tiredly through his thatch of grey hair. 'That's okay, Alan, you did well. But I'm afraid we may have an extra problem. You're going to have to check through those rations and make sure that none of them were produced within the last three weeks.'

There was a short silence, and then Alan Hedges said, 'Is this on the level?'

'I'm afraid so. I can't give you all the details yet, but it appears any food containing any kind of cereal ingredient which was prepared and canned within the last three weeks may have to be considered a hazard to human health.'

'You can't tell me anything more than that?'

'I'm afraid not. But I can assure you that when the time comes to make a public statement, you'll be the first to know.'

'Well,' said Alan Hedges unhappily, 'I appreciate your confidence in me.'

'Thank you, Alan. Now will you check out those supplies for me?'

'Yes, Mr President. Whatever you say.'

Neither the President nor Alan Hedges heard the extra click on their telephone line as Alan Hedges' secretary Wanda Kaminski put her receiver down, too. And neither of them knew that directly afterwards she dialled the

260

Washington bureau of *The New York Times* and asked to speak to Bill Brinsky.

The news on early evening television on Tuesday was grim, but less hysterical than before. The networks had all been personally requested by the President to 'Keep the tone down.' The crop blight was still spreading, although 'great and urgent efforts' were being made in Washington to prepare an antidote. The research had been seriously hampered by last week's violent killing of Professor Protter, who had carried most of the information he had gleaned from his analysis of Vorar D in his head. Nonetheless, the Department of Agriculture hoped to be able to issue farmers with their first supplies of some kind of antidote 'within two or three weeks.'

Most major cities in the United States were still under the watchful eyes of the National Guard, the Army, and the Marine Corps. So far, over five thousand men and women had been arrested for looting or for breaking curfews, and twenty eight had been shot dead. Food was being sold only from certain major supermarkets, and each customer was being rationed to twenty-five dollars worth of food at the checkout, although there were no strict checks on how many supermarkets any one customer went around to visit, or even how many times he went through the same supermarket's checkout in one day.

The front-page photograph of the *New York Daily News* had shown a two-mile line of shoppers waiting outside the A&P on Third Avenue at 51st Street, some of them with camp-stools and even sleeping-bags. The headline read FOOD LINE BLUES.

At seven o'clock, the President appeared on television again to 'thank the American people for their calm, their dignity, and their brave acceptance of one of the greatest natural disasters of our time.' He explained that America's allies were airlifting food which would be stored all around the country, and sold to the population on ration 'when the time for such extreme measures eventually comes.' He was giving out no hints yet that the crop blight had been started on purpose – despite what Ed Hardesty had said on Sunday night – and he deflected questions from the press that the approaching famine might have been caused by Soviet sabotage.

Another question he ducked was, 'Where is Senator Shearson Jones? Have you talked to him yet? Has he answered Mr Ed Hardesty's allegations that the blight was allowed to spread so that he could line his own pockets? And, come to that, where is Mr Ed Hardesty?'

The President left the lectern, with its Presidential seal and its screen of bulletproof plastic, and waved to the press as he left the room without even turning back to look at them.

George Bannon, of the *Washington Post*, said, 'Something tells me we're being strung along for some reason or other. My nose itches, and when my nose itches, that means trouble.'

'When my nose itches, it means hay fever,' replied Bill Brinsky, tucking his notebook back in his pocket. Then he left the press room to go back to his typewriter, and his half-finished story for tomorrow morning, which began, 'Sources close to the President have revealed that the nation's food crisis, already worsening by the hour, may be exacerbated by yet another problem . . . apart from the continent-wide crop blight. It appears that for reasons yet unexplained, any food containing cereals that was prepared in the last three weeks may be dangerous to human health. This leak, although still unconfirmed, comes from a highly reliable quarter; and if the White House does confirm it, the nation will be facing not only the total destruction of its crops and livestock, but anything up to forty per cent of its existing food stocks.'

That Tuesday evening, ignoring the imposition of a curfew at sundown, thousands of ordinary families, both black and white, marched along St Paul Street in Baltimore to City Hall. They carried burning torches and home-made banners which read SURVIVAL OF THE FITTEST? and OUR FIRST CIVIL RIGHT – FOOD. The National Guardsmen who watched them shuffling silently through the warm darkness, men and women with confused but determined faces, babies in strollers, old people in wheelchairs, had been ordered not to shoot until the parade had dispersed. One of the Guardsmen, interviewed by a roving television camera, appeared on the screen with tears running down his cheeks. 'They can order us not to shoot our people,' he said, 'but they can't order us not to cry for them.'

In New York, where the Mayor had been making every effort to keep the city as quiet and as normal as possible, there were new fires in Queens and in Harlem, and nearly three hundred black youths broke into the Four Seasons Restaurant on 52nd Street, bludgeoning police and security guards and stabbing two waiters. They rampaged across tables, splashed in the ornamental pool, and strewed oysters and roast game and wine bottles all over the floor. 'It was like something out of a Fellini movie,' said Norman Cramer, the movie producer, whose wife suffered a dislocated shoulder. 'There were all these savages out of the streets, dancing on plates of veal and asparagus in filthy sneakers, and sluicing themselves with Dom Perignon.'

In Muskogee, Oklahoma, twenty men and one woman tried to break into a supermarket and steal boxes of canned meat, vegetables, and fruit. They were almost through loading when they were surprised by a National Guard patrol who machine-gunned all of them without warning. Their bodies were littered across the supermarket parking lot, and a reporter for the *Tulsa Herald-Bulletin* said, 'There was so much blood it was gurgling down the storm drains like crimson bathwater.'

One of the most vicious firefights of the night was in Los Angeles, where nearly 100 residents of the Palms district banded themselves together into an armed 'food-looting force.' They successfully raided two supermarkets with a convoy of seventy station wagons and trucks, and they were about to attack a large Quik-Serv store on Culver Boulevard when they were ambushed by 150 officers of the Los Angeles Police. Fifteen of the looters were shot dead, twenty-eight wounded, and nine policemen suffered serious bullet-wounds. At one time, the crackling of gunfire across the front of the supermarket was so loud that it could be heard in Westchester.

There were plenty of profiteers, of course. In San

Francisco, where the Mayor had so far only imposed a midnight curfew, stores were brightly lit and wide-open, and selling cans of corned beef at six dollars and fifty cents a can. Canned vegetables were at a premium, with a single can of spinach selling at anything from four dollars upwards, and fresh vegetables, from the few farms which had been left unscathed by the blight, were 'like diamonds.' One fresh lettuce, at a supermarket on Stockton Street, was selling for twelve dollars and fifty cents. A middle-aged man was shot dead by San Francisco policewomen when he tried to escape from a small neighbourhood store with three cans of lima beans in his pockets.

As Tuesday turned to Wednesday, the confusion and the terror grew. Only the President's continual reassurance that 'everything will work out', along with the forced optimism of the television news programmes, kept the nation from total hysteria. Shortly after midnight, though, the President issued an Executive Order that all banks and savings banks would be closed until further notice, and that the public sale of silver and gold bullion was to be suspended. No financial assets could be sent out of the United States in any form whatsoever, except to meet previously-contracted debts. On the stock exchange in Tokyo, where the time was already 2.30 p.m. in the afternoon of Wednesday, the dollar collapsed against the Yen to 102.30, and it was only after 'limitless guarantees' from the Federal Reserve Bank and the International Monetary Fund that it steadied at ¥ 120.25.

A thoughtful and dignified editorial in the *New York Times* balanced the frightening story from Bill Brinsky on the front page by saying, 'We are all about to live through this nation's most testing days. Let us show the world at least what our courage is made of, what our resolve is made of, and how the great ideal of a free democratic society can meet up to the most tragic and disastrous circumstances that Nature or Man can devise.'

As those words were flying off the presses in a special late exclusive edition at two o'clock Wednesday, a friend of the Duncan family in Willingboro, New Jersey, was returning home from a late shift at the telephone company when he passed by the Duncans' house and noticed that the Duncans' kitchen light was still lit. At first he thought that maybe Emmet had sneaked downstairs to raid the icebox, especially the way that everybody was rationing out their food now, and he thought nothing of it. But two hours later, he looked out of his own bedroom window across the street and saw that the light was still burning.

In green pyjamas and a blue towelling bathrobe, he crossed the street, walked up between the laurel bushes by the Duncans' path, and rang the doorbell. He rang five times, but there was no reply. After a few minutes, he went around the back, and tried to look into the kitchen, but the drapes were drawn across. Eventually, he shook the handle of the back door. To his surprise, it was open.

He saw them almost immediately. Emmet Duncan was lying curled up on the floor, in a sticky sea of vomit. His wife Dora had managed to drag herself through to the living-room, but had collapsed behind the sofa. Jenny and Kate were both sitting with their faces against the kitchen-table, as if they had fallen asleep. Only the whiteness of their faces and the diarrhoea caked on their legs showed that they had died.

The stench in the kitchen was hideous, and when Emmet's friend took one step forward, a seething cloud of blowflies rose up from the bodies and battered around the kitchen like some kind of nightmarish hailstorm.

Eight

Up in the hills, in Topanga Canyon, Wednesday morning was as quiet and sunny as any other day. Only when Season stepped out through the french doors to join Carl and Vee on the pooldeck could she see the distant dark plumes of smoke which hung over Los Angeles like the black feathers of an old-fashioned funeral. And there was the smell, too – like burning cushions.

Carl was dressed in a white safari suit, and he was

already halfway through a large tumbler of tequila, with salt around the rim. Vee was wearing a pink sun-dress and sandals, and she looked as if she hadn't slept.

'No calls?' Season asked. 'I didn't think I was going to get to sleep at all, until you gave me those pills. They're amazing.'

'You feel better?' asked Carl. Then he glanced at Vee, and said, 'No, there were no calls. They mentioned Ed on the news once, but only to say that there wasn't any sign of him yet. I should think the police have got their hands full without looking for people who can usually take care of themselves.'

'Well, that's Ed all right,' said Season, rubbing her elbow as if she were cold, and giving Carl an uncomfortable smile.

'Do you want breakfast?' asked Vee. 'I'll have to cook it myself. Maria hasn't arrived yet.'

'Has she phoned you? I mean, she's all right?'

Vee shook her head. 'I don't know. There was a whole lot of shooting last night, especially around Palms and Culver City. I just hope – well, I just hope I didn't make a mistake, letting her go see her mother.'

'Have you called the police?' asked Season.

Carl took a mouthful of cold tequila, and grimaced. 'The police lines are permanently busy. We've been taking turns dialling Maria's mother's house, too, but we can't get any reply. I expect she's okay. She's a sensible girl. But, my God, I never thought I'd live to see the world like this. Just look at those damn fires.'

Season walked across to the breakfast table and sat down. There were two burned-down joints in the ashtray, and two empty plates with the greasy remains of bacon and scrambled egg on them. She looked up at Vee, and she had to half-close her eyes against the winking reflections from the pool.

'Vee,' she said, 'I'm thinking of trying to make it back to South Burlington.'

Vee stared at her. 'Are you *crazy*? What do you want to go back to South Burlington for?'

'For Ed. If he's going to go anyplace at all, he'll go to his farm.'

'But *why*, Season? You came out here to get away from Ed. You came out here because you couldn't take Kansas any longer. Don't tell me you've forgotten how bad you were just a week ago? You were in *pieces*! And now you want to go back?'

Carl put in, 'Apart from that, Season, think of the danger. There's no way you could possibly take Sally along with you, for starters. And you couldn't fly. They said on the news this morning that all flights out of LAX and Burbank have been cancelled, at least until the weekend, and private flying has been restricted to essential flights only. Come on, Season – the freeways are jammed solid by day, there are curfews in almost every single state at night – you'd never find anyplace to stay, or anyplace to hide.'

'Carl –' began Season, but Carl raised his hand to quieten her.

'There are vigilantes out there, Season. Looters, hoodlums, rapists, you name it. And if *they* don't get you, the police or the National Guard probably will. I'm telling you straight, you wouldn't only be ill-advised if you went, you'd be *dead*, and I don't want to see Sally without a mother or Vee without a sister. Or me without a sister-in-law, if it comes to that.'

Vee squatted down beside her and said earnestly, 'He's right, honey. You can't even think of going. If Ed wants to get back to you, you're going to have to leave it to him.'

'I feel like I've deserted him, just when he needed me most,' said Season. 'Didn't you see the way he looked on television on Sunday? He looked so sincere, so straight. He was saying what he believed was right, and that's the way he's always been.'

'I know he has,' argued Vee. 'But think about it. Sincere and straight may be the breakfast of champions, but they may not be what *you* really need in your man. There is *so much else* required in a one-to-one relationship apart from sincere and straight. What about alluring? What about devious? What about irritating? Provoking? Expansionising? Season – you can't stand there like some suburban housewife from San Fernando and tell me that you and

267

your female identity don't require more out of a marriage than sincere and straight? Can you?'

Season lowered her eyes. She looked at the joints in the ashtray and the egg scrapings on the plates. 'No,' she whispered. 'I guess I can't. I guess I do need more than Ed can give me.'

'So you'll stay?'

'What about food? Things are going to be pretty lean from here on in. I can't take the food out of your mouth. Nor yours, Carl, whatever you say.'

'We're pretty well stocked up here,' smiled Carl. 'Vee never did like marketing, so I guess we've got ourselves enough steak to last us through till Christmas.'

'We've even got a turkey for Thanksgiving,' said Vee. 'I bought two last year, and froze one of them.'

'Let's hope we still have something to give thanks for,' Season said, and the tears that blurred her eyes were only partly provoked by the sunshine that skipped and dazzled on the pool. She was thinking of Ed, too, and even though they'd only been apart for a week – even though she'd begun to find a strange new energy in herself through the sexual and emotional stimulation of Granger Hughes – she missed Ed badly. She could just picture Ed raising his eyes from a copy of one of his tedious agricultural magazines and smiling at her with that amused, warm expression that meant *I love you, and nobody else*.

She wiped her eyes with the heel of her hand. 'I guess I'd better go see what Sally's doing,' she said. She attempted a smile. 'You're very good to me, both of you. I don't know what I'd do without you.'

'You're family,' said Carl, as if that explained everything.

Season went back inside the house. Carl had switched off the air-conditioning, in response to a plea from the Mayor to save as much energy as possible, but there was a crosswise wind blowing that morning from the ocean, and it was tolerably cool. She called, 'Sally? Are you dressed yet? Auntie Vee wants to know if we'd like some breakfast.'

There was no answer. She called, 'Sally? Sally, are you upstairs?'

Again, there was silence. She frowned. She had seen Sally only a few minutes ago, taking off her pyjamas and laying out her new blue-chequered sun-dress. She said, 'Sally?' more quietly this time, and walked slowly towards the stairs.

She was just about to put her foot on the first stair when Sally's voice from the kitchen said, '*Mommy!*' in such an odd and off-key way that Season froze. She felt as if someone had slowly poured a carafe of ice-cold water down her back. Her hair tingled and even her nipples rose.

'Sally?' she asked, in a trembly voice. Then she was rushing along the corridor into the kitchen and screaming, 'Sally! Sally – what's wrong?'

She burst through the white louvred kitchen door and there they were. Five of them – tall, greasy-haired, dressed in black leather jackets, with chains and studs and pointed insignia – all of them except for the one who was holding Sally, who was blond and almost angelic-looking, and who was wearing a pale blue denim two-piece suit, and a white shirt, and a pale blue bootlace tie. He was twisting Sally's arm around behind her back, and gripping his forearm against her throat, and he was smiling.

'Don't do anything silly, Mommy,' he grinned. 'I shouldn't like to have to waste your baby. She's too pretty to die, don't you think?'

Season stood where she was, shuddering, cold. 'My God,' she said, in a voice as splintered as pieces of broken mirror. 'My God, if you hurt her – '

One of the angels snorted in amusement. 'Kind of touching, hunh, Oxnard?'

'Oh, *very*,' said Oxnard. His face was white, much whiter than any of the others, and so the grime on his cheekbones where his motorcycle goggles had been was far more pronounced. 'A really moving example of motherly love.'

Season stared at Sally in horror. The wide-open eyes, the same straight nose as Ed's, the softness around the mouth that was hers. In her blue-check dress she looked as innocent and vulnerable a a baby bird.

'Mommy,' appealed Sally. 'Mommy, he's hurting me.'

Season looked at the Angel called Oxnard. 'What do you

269

want?' she asked, in an intense whisper. 'What is it you want?'

Oxnard kept on smiling. Another Angel, with frizzy hair and a faceful of red zits, started to mime the actions of playing a violin, and humming a sentimental tune. The others shuffled their feet and laughed.

Oxnard tugged his forearm a little closer under Sally's chin. 'What I *want* and what I *need* are two different things,' he said, in that sly, smiling voice. 'I *need* food. That's what I need. You see, most of our friends have left LA, all lit out and left nothing. And there isn't a single café or diner or hamburger stand left open in the whole festering city. So, I'm hungry; and so are my associates here, and we need food. That's what we've come for, and that's what we'll be satisfied with. But ... if you're talking about what I *want* ... that's different. What I *want* is to shove seven inches of stiff intellectual pecker right down your gorgeous throat.'

Season stood rigid, the muscles in her cheeks pronounced, her thin fingers clenched into narrow fists.

'My sister and her husband are outside,' she said. 'In a minute or two they're going to miss me. They're going to come looking, and what are you going to do then?'

Oxnard looked around at the rest of the Angels and then snorted. 'You think we're cowards? You think we're scared of your sister and her husband?'

'You're cowardly enough to frighten a little girl,' snapped Season.

'Oh now, come along,' said Oxnard, softly. 'You know festering well why we've got your little girl. Nothing to do with cowardice. Just practicality, seeing as how every smug middle-class canyon dweller who's afraid of being molested by real people has gotten himself a gun these days. And the best protection against the wild shooting of canyon dwellers is a child hostage, don't you agree?'

Season said, 'You'll have to talk to my sister's husband. He's got the key to the freezer. If you want food, that's where it is.'

Oxnard, still holding Sally tight against him, held out his free hand towards the Angel standing on his left. The Angel, unshaved, with the oddly flat face of a boxer, reached into his leather jacket and dragged out a huge black revolver. Oxnard took it, hefted it in his hand, and then pointed it directly at the top of Sally's head.

'Call him,' he said. 'Call your sister's husband. Go ahead. And tell him that if he jumps, or rushes, or does anything sudden at all, then it's going to be cortex omelette all round. You got me?'

Season stared at him, feeling as chilled as an ice queen. 'Why are you doing this?' she asked him. 'You're educated, aren't you? Why?'

Oxnard grinned, 'Education, as they always used to tell me, is nothing more than a tool for getting what you need out of life.'

He paused, and then he said, '*And* what you want.'

Season asked him, in a quivering voice: 'You want me to do something for you? Would you let her go if I did that?'

'Oho,' laughed Oxnard. 'Now we're getting into it. Can I hear you actually *offering*?'

'If it means you'll let my daughter go, yes,' said Season, simply. 'Let her go, and make sure she doesn't see what happens, and then you can do whatever you want.'

Oxnard looked down at the small girl he was pressing against his chest. 'I need the food as well,' he said, carefully. 'Why don't you call your sister's husband first, and your sister, too.'

Season was silent for almost half a minute. Then she said, 'That's a deal, though, is it? Can I trust you that much?'

The Angels giggled, and Oxnard slowly shook his head. 'You can't trust me at all, honey buns. I've never made a commitment yet and I'm not about to make one now. But, sure, if that's what you want to believe, then go right ahead and believe it. Now, call your sister's festering husband, before I start to lose my patience. You don't want to see this kitchen redecorated with the inside of your pretty little daughter's head, do you?'

Season backed slowly across to the kitchen door. She didn't take her eyes of Oxnard for one moment. She turned her head slightly, without turning her eyes, and called, 'Carl! *Carl!*'

Carl and Vee came together. They could hear something

271

was wrong but they didn't know what, and by the time they walked into the kitchen it was too late to do anything about it. Carl looked around at the Angels lounging against his pine table, and his Neff oven, and his red custom-enamel sink unit, and said, 'What the hell do you animals think you're doing?'

Oxnard carefully and deliberately cocked his revolver. 'You just watch who you're calling an animal, you half-assed canyon dweller. I've already explained to Mommy here what it is we need, and what it is we want, and I think we're pretty close to a deal.'

Season said, 'Carl – they need food – they want cans and frozen stuff I guess – I had to tell them that you had the key to the freezer.'

Carl nodded. He went to the kitchen cupboard, hesitated and raised his hands so that Oxnard could see that he wasn't playing games, and then opened the cupboard up. He took out a keyring with two small chrome keys on it, and tossed it over. The Angel with the boxer's face caught it, and winked in appreciation. 'Thanks, mister.'

'That's it, then,' said Carl. 'Take the food and let the girl go. Just take whatever you need.'

'Well, that isn't everything,' said Oxnard, slowly. 'The deal was that we take the food because we're hungry. But we let the girl go because we're going to have some fun with Mommy here. Not to mention Mommy's sister.'

Carl lunged forward, red-faced. 'You lay one filthy finger on – ' he started, but Oxnard thrust his revolver right up against Sally's head and shrieked, '*You want me to kill her? Right in front of you? Is that what you want? Jesus Christ!*'

There was one split second when they were all mad with the fear and tension of what was happening – when Season could see nothing in front of her eyes but boiling scarlet and feel nothing in her nerves but total fright. Then, with a slow breath, Carl backed off, one step at a time, until he was standing beside Vee and Season, and breathing like a man who's run a mile in five minutes.

'What do you want to do?' he asked, in an ashy voice. 'Season? Vee? Can you live with any of this?'

Season said, 'Carl, I'm going to have to. If I don't

272

live with it, then Sally's going to die with it. And that's all.'

She hesitated, and then she said, 'Vee wasn't any part of the deal, though. You hear me, Oxnard? My sister wasn't any part of the deal. You can't ask anything of her.'

Oxnard frowned. 'I don't understand you, ' he said. 'It seems to me that as long as I'm holding a loaded Magnum up against your sweet little daughter's head, I can ask anything of anybody who cares about her.'

Another cold pause. And then Vee turned pale-faced to Season, and said, 'Season – we can't let them kill her. For God's sake.'

Carl growled, 'You morons will die for this. I mean it. Every last one of you will die.'

'He's very dramatic, don't you think so, Oxnard?' one of the Angels asked, and Oxnard grinned and nodded.

'He's a thespian,' said Oxnard.

'A *thespian*?' asked the Angel with wild hair and zits.

'That's right. That's intellectual talk for over-aggressive, over-acting, worn-out, used-up, suburban asshole.'

'Your gun makes you strong, that's all,' quivered Carl.

'That's right,' agreed Oxnard. 'It's a good thing I've got it, don't you agree? Now why don't you go sit on that breakfast stool over there, and keep quiet, and why don't you two ladies start stripping off ready? Huh?'

Season said, 'Not in front of the child. You promised. I'm not doing anything in front of the child.'

Oxnard snapped, 'Lady – unless you perform in front of this child – then this child is going to perform in front of you. And let me tell you one thing from personal experience – only *one* personal experience, mind you, but one is quite enough – dying is a very much less pleasing performance than fucking.'

'You've killed someone before?' asked Season, coldly.

Oxnard nodded. 'That's right. Now, strip off.'

Carl said, 'Listen, you, whatever your name is. There's no way. You hear me? There's absolutely no way.'

Oxnard said, 'They call me Oxnard, if you must know, on account of the fact that I come from Oxnard. My real name is Charles.'

'Isn't he too much?' giggled one of the Angels. '*Charles,* for Chrissake.'

There was a fraught silence. Then Season, with complete dignity, unbuttoned her white broderie anglaise sundress and shrugged it off her shoulders. Underneath, she was naked, her skin still that bright bronze colour of a fresh suntan. Oxnard smiled, and the rest of the Angels whistled and laughed.

'You can do what you want,' said Season, tightly. 'But you'll have to take my daughter out of here.'

Oxnard thought about it for a while, and then said, 'Okay. It's a reasonable, clean, one hundred per cent American request. Carlo – you want to take the gun, and Shirley Temple here, and keep her out of the living-room until I call you? But one thing. If I tell you to waste her, you *waste* her, and quick. Let's not make any mistakes about that.'

The Angel with the frizzy hair took the Magnum, gripped Sally's wrist, and pushed her out of the kitchen. He grinned at Season as he passed by, and said, 'Nice tits, lady. Real nice tits. I'll catch you later.'

Sally, swallowing in fear, said, 'Mommy! Mommy – what are they going to do?' but Season simply shook her head, and tried to smile. There were too many tears choked up in her throat for the words to come out.

Oxnard rapped to Vee, 'Come on, honey. You too. Get it all off.'

Vee hesistated for a moment, but then she tugged her pink sundress over her head, and dropped it to the floor. She was even skinnier than Season, with a dark mahogany suntan from years in California. There were faint semi-circular scars under her breasts where she had them had lifted.

Oxnard looked appreciatively from one sister to the other. 'Well, now,' he said, 'isn't that the neatest pair of canyon-dwelling women you ever saw?'

Carl held his hand across his mouth as Oxnard stripped off his jacket, unbuckled his belt, and kicked off his pants. Oxnard nodded to the tallest Angel, who wore a soiled red rag around his head, and said, 'Hold that flake. Hold him tight. And if he tries to make trouble, break his festering fingers.'

Then Oxnard suddenly reddened, and shouted, 'Okay! Okay! We're going to have ourselves some fun here! You know what I mean? Fun! You come here, Mommy, and stand in front of this fancy sink. That's right. Facing the window. Now, spread 'em. That's right, spread 'em. You hear me! I want to see your ass!'

Chilly with fear, Season stood by the sink, gripping the draining-board, and staring sightlessly out of the window at the flickering palm trees in the front garden. Oxnard, wearing nothing now but his shirt, his bootlace tie, and a pair of dirty white moccasins, grasped the cheeks of her bottom and fondled them with hard, searching fingers.

'Think you're going to get out of this easy, huh?' he whispered loudly in Season's ear. His breath smelled of Scope. 'Think you can just close your eyes and pretend that nothing's happening, that it's just another pecker in life's never-ending parade of peckers? That's what you think, huh? Well – let's make it more difficult for you, shall we? Let's make it a little more *memorable*.'

He turned around, and strode across the kitchen, absurd in his shirt and his sneakers, but somehow even more menacing because of his absurdity. Carl tried to push his way forward, but the tall Angel's muscular grip pulled him back.

'You're crazy!' shouted Carl. 'You know that? You're out of your polluted little brain!'

The tall Angel knocked him hard in the side of his head with his pointed knuckles, and Carl staggered. Vee, naked and defenceless, said, 'For God's sake, leave him alone!' But the Angel simply bared his teeth at her in a mock-animal snarl.

Oxnard pulled open one kitchen cupboard after another, and dragged all the spices and cans and cups and bottles on to the floor, in a clattering cascade. Red pepper was sprayed across the tiles, along with sugar and coffee and broken china and scattered spoons.

'Oil! That's what I want! Oil!' raged Oxnard. 'Good, slippery, lubricating oil!'

In the end cupboard, by the ovens, he discovered a plastic bottle of Mazola. 'There!' he said, staring wildly from one Angel to the other. 'A good clean US product for a good filthy unAmerican purpose!'

He turned around to Vee, and said: 'Come here! Come on, you can have the privilege of joining in this little erotic stunt!'

'*Bastard!*' howled Carl. '*Maniac!*' But the Angel punched him again, in the mouth this time, and knocked out one of his teeth. Carl spat strings of blood, and went down on to his knees. One of the other Angels was giggling so much by now that he sounded as if he was going to choke.

Seizing Vee's wrist, Oxnard forced her to crouch down on the floor in front of the sink, right between Season's wide-apart thighs.

'Now, you're sisters, aren't you?' breathed Oxnard. 'You should get on well together, in every possible way. You can start giving her a tongue job, sweetie, while I start doing what I want to do.'

Vee blinked up at him in fright.

'You understand what I'm saying!' shrieked Oxnard. 'Do it, or I'll have that niece of yours blown to pieces!'

Shaking uncontrollably, Vee raised her face.

Above her, Season whispered, 'Do it, Vee. It's not going to harm us. I love you, and I always will.'

'That's right,' smiled Oxnard. 'Sisterly love, incarnate. Or should I say carnal?

'Come on. Let's see some enthusiasm down there. Let's see you get your mouth round it!'

Vee began to weep, silently, but as she wept she did what she was told, and thrust her tongue deeper between her sister's thighs. Oxnard watched her appreciatively for a while, then he asked Season under his breath, 'You know what I'm going to do? That's right, you guessed it. I'm going to do it, and I'm going to need your help, so when I start to push you'd better start pushing back.'

Season nodded dumbly, her eyes still closed. All she was thinking was: do it, do it, for the love of everything in the whole world do it, and then let me alone.

'Push!' commanded Oxnard. One of the Angels whooped, and said, 'That's doing it, Oxnard! That's really doing it!'

'*Push!*' Oxnard shouted, even louder.

Season pushed, but her muscles were too clenched, and she couldn't admit him even a half-inch. He furiously grabbed a handful of her hair, and wrenched it so hard that she could hear the roots tearing.

'Push,' he told her. 'And this time don't fight me. Because if you fight me, I'm going to kill your little girl, and you, too, and everybody in the whole festering house! You think the cops are going to care? The whole of LA is littered with dead people! You think they're going to care about one or two more?'

Season fought back the panic which was rising in her chest. 'Okay,' she said, in a barely audible whisper. 'If that's what you want.'

Gradually, gritting her teeth, she opened herself up to him. He grunted with effort as he worked his way up inside her. She could feel nothing but intense, wincing pain, as her mind said *yes, you have to*, but her body resisted.

For a few seconds, the three of them were twisted and locked together in a painful tableau of mutual hatred and physical stress.

'Isn't this *it*!' panted Oxnard. 'Isn't this *it*! Don't you dumb screwed-up canyon-dwelling broads do *anything* for kicks? Don't you know that a woman with any class would rather *die* than do this? You cheap cunts!'

From outside the house, without warning, there was a dull, echoless thump. Oxnard raised his head. 'What was that?' he said. 'Gene – what the hell was that?' Immediately, without any conscious effort, Season expelled him.

There was another thump, louder than the first. The Angel called Gene opened the kitchen door and went out on to the white-painted wooden landing outside. Season, clenched-up and shaking, backed away from the sink, and Vee climbed slowly to her feet.

'Oxnard – it's the bikes, dammit!' yelped Gene. 'Somebody's blown up the bikes!'

Oxnard shouted, '*What?* What the hell do you mean?' and stormed across to the door. Outside the house, on the driveway, the Angels had parked their five motorcycles; and now two of them were blazing fiercely.

'That's my bike!' yelled Oxnard. 'That's my BMW, for God's sake!'

He started to scamper down the wooden stairs, his shirt-tails flapping in the breeze. The Angel called Gene followed closely behind him. Together, they ran across the driveway until they reached the fiery motorcycles, shielding their faces against the flames. But it was far too late: the motorcycles' polished chrome was already brown from heat, and the fuel tanks were spouting blazing fuel all over the cylinders. The air rippled, and there was a strong smell of burning rubber.

Oxnard turned around. 'If those people did this – ' he raged. 'If any one of those people did this – '

He didn't get the chance to say any more. There was a sharp, distinctive crack, which any expert would have recognised as the report of a powerful hunting rifle. Oxnard's shirt was blasted with a pattern of bright red blood, and he toppled backwards as if someone had given him a shove in the chest.

The Angel who had been holding Carl said, 'What goes on out there?' and took two or three steps towards the door. Carl lunged for the cutlery drawer, tugged it right out on to the floor with a crash, and scrabbled for a knife. The other Angel tried to stop him, but Carl shoved him away with his elbow. The Angel missed his footing, reached for the edge of the sink, and steadied himself. But then Carl was on top of him with maddened ferocity, both arms upraised, and a twelve-inch carving knife in each hand. The Angel raised one hand to protect himself, but Carl's first carving knife chopped right through the palm of his hand and out through the back. The second knife caught the Angel in the side of the neck, and crunched almost six inches through solid muscle. The boy reeled, bleeding, and trying uselessly to shake the first knife out of his hand.

The tall Angel at the door had gone by now, running down the outside stairs and trying to reach his bike. There was another brisk rifle shot, and he staggered, tripped, and toppled sideways into a flower-bed, dying noisily amongst the azaleas.

Season, almost blind with fear, ran through to the living-

278

room. She said, '*Sally! Sally!*' in a voice that didn't even sound like her own. But as soon as she saw what had happened, she slowed, and lowered her arms, and walked the rest of the way across the floor as if she were being filmed in slow-motion. She was suddenly aware of the sunlight, and the breeze, and billowy drapes that rose and fell.

Granger Hughes was standing in the centre of the room, smiling and holding Sally's hand. The only sign that the Angel called Carlo had been there was his black Magnum revolver on the glass-topped coffee table, and a broken lampshade. As Season knelt down in front of Sally and reached out her arms for her, quivering with the fright of what had happened, her eyes glistening with tears, Granger laid his hands on both of them in what was almost a benediction.

A young man in a clipped brown beard and a black T-shirt came in through the french windows, holding a rifle over his arm.

'That's all of them,' he reported, quietly.

Season hugged Sally closer, and cried. They both cried. Then Carl came in with Vee, dabbing his mouth with a bloody kitchen towel.

'Are you okay?' asked Granger.

'Thanks to you, yes,' said Carl. He looked down at his safari suit and realised it was splashed in squiggles of the Angel's blood. 'My God, I don't know what happened. How did you get here?'

'I was coming up this morning to see if you wanted to join us down at the Church of the Practical Miracle,' said Granger, gently and almost absent-mindedly stroking Season's hair. 'When we drove up from the road, we saw the bikes. That's all. We were suspicious about what was going on, so Helmut here went around the back to the pool-deck and saw one of the Angels in the living-room with Sally. The dull bulb had laid his gun down on the table; I guess he didn't think he was going to get any trouble from a nine-year-old girl. So Helmut crept in behind him and gave him the benefit of five years' karate lessons.'

'Is he dead?' asked Carl.

Helmut, the bearded one, rubbed his knuckles. 'If he isn't,' he grinned, 'he'll be lying there wishing he was.'

'Now then,' Granger admonished him. 'Love thine enemy, even in defeat.'

Carl pulled a Mexican blanket off the sofa, brought it across, and draped it around Season's shoulders. Vee had already pulled on her sun-dress again, although it was back to front.

'We're all pretty shocked,' Carl told Granger. 'I guess Season and Vee are both going to feel like a good hot soak in the tub, and we're all going to need a brandy. You'll have to forgive us if we act a little odd. I thought we were all going to die for a moment there, and what these girls have been through doesn't bear thinking about.'

'I'd like to stay and help, if I can,' said Granger. 'But won't you think about coming down to join us? From what I hear, there are mobs attacking private houses all over. We saw five or six houses burning along Topanga Canyon alone.'

'Is it really that serious?' asked Vee, unsteadily.

'Oh, it's serious all right,' nodded Granger. 'And by the looks of it, it's going to get a whole lot worse. Have you heard the news about all food less than three weeks old being contaminated? And I mean, *all* food.'

'We heard it on the news,' said Carl. 'They said it was only a rumour – unconfirmed.'

'I don't think so,' said Granger, shaking his head. 'I wish it were.'

Carl said: 'So what's your congregation going to do? Pool their food? Try to survive by sticking together?'

'That's right,' said Granger. 'From what I hear, groups of people are getting together all over the country for their mutual protection. I mean, Carl, there aren't just Angels out there now, there are organised mobs of looters. And our particular advantage at the Church of the Practical Miracle is that one of my oldest friends is Mike Bull, who runs the Hughes supermarket on Highland. He has a whole stockroom of food down there which he managed to keep out of the hands of the looters. He called me last night and asked if I could get together about a hundred really trustworthy and responsible people, so that we could barricade ourselves in with all that food and try to weather this whole crisis through.'

'What about the contaminated food?' asked Vee.

'That's easy. Mike's a supermarket manager, so he knows all the dating codes. He won't feed us with anything risky.'

Season stood up. She was very pale, and for the first time she felt the acute muscular pain of what Oxnard had done to her. Reality was just beginning to jangle through the soundproofing of shock. 'Can we really justify shutting ourselves in with all that food, while other people starve?' she asked Granger. 'Is that really what Christ would have advocated?'

Granger stared at her for a long moment. 'Christ said, There is no man that hath left house, or parents, or brethren, or wife, or children, for the kingom of God's sake, Who shall not receive manifold more in this present time, and in the world to come life everlasting.'

He reached out his hand for her, but she did not take it, or acknowledge it. She said simply, 'I was violated today by a man who seemed to believe that the only moral he had to observe before taking anything, or assaulting anyone, was that he should want to. The effect that his behaviour had on other people didn't matter, as far as he was concerned. Shock them, frighten them – so what? Well, I'll tell you so what. He hurt me beyond belief, and humiliated my sister in front of her husband. And I'm afraid the way you're talking now, Granger, and the way you've acted towards me since I've been here – well, they're both nothing more than less obvious and less offensive examples of the same moral attitude.'

She laid her arm around Sally's shoulders, and said, 'You saved Sally's life, and you saved the rest of us, too. I'm very grateful, and it's a debt I won't ever be able to repay you. But as far as your Church is concerned, and as far as your own personality is concerned, I think I've seen them today for what they are – or at least for what they could be. I don't like people who take what they want by force, Granger, and I don't like people who believe that they are

281

chosen by God, and free of the rules of kindness and sharing that are supposed to govern the rest of us. Now, if you'll excuse me.'

Granger gave Helmut a backwards glance to see if he was listening, and then turned back to Season. 'Quite a preacher yourself,' he told her, with unexpected sourness. But then he smiled, remembering himself, and said solicitously, 'Well – you've been through a bad time. I can understand that you're feeling kind of off-balance. So the offer's still open. You can come down to the supermarket and join us if you want – provided you get there before midnight tonight, because that's when we're going to start barricading ourselves in.'

'Thank you,' Season whispered.

'As for that other stuff . . .' went on Granger. 'Maybe you'll feel better when you've washed the stench of that animal off of you, and forgotten the stink of his breath.'

Season stood up straight, and the blanket slipped down her shoulders a little, baring her neck. 'Actually,' she said, almost hysterically, 'he used Scope.'

Granger watched her lead Sally towards the staircase, walking awkwardly as an automaton and climb the stairs. He blinked at Carl and Vee in perplexity, and said: '*Scope?*'

Carl said: 'Thanks for the rescue, Granger. I mean it, sincerely. You saved us. And you too, Helmut. And, Granger. Don't worry too much about Season. If you went through what she's just been through, and talked half as much sense, then you'd be twice the preacher you are now.'

'Carl,' said Granger, 'I'm not sure that anybody's talking sense. The whole darn world's gone out of its head.'

Nine

In a special newsflash on Wednesday evening, at nine o'clock Central Time, the President of the United States confirmed that 'all food produce containing cereals – and that includes processed meats, breads, cookies, pastas, beers, and spirits – must now come under suspicion of having been contaminated with heavy cobalt radiation. As a general rule, foodstuffs produced more than three weeks ago can be considered safe – provided, of course, they are canned, or frozen, or still fresh. But if you are in doubt, a more detailed explanation will be broadcast immediately after this message on your local television station, and on your local radio. You will also be able to obtain leaflets from your City Hall or local citizens' centre.'

The President, looking twenty years older than he had the previous week, and with a pronounced stutter, went on to say that 'everybody should stay at home unless essential business takes them out.'

He was asked if he could now confirm that there was a Communist plot to overthrow the United States by 'starving us out.' He said tiredly: 'I can neither confirm nor deny such a plot at this stage of the crisis.'

After the newsflash, the President was called urgently back to the Oval Office. A top-secret report had just arrived from the office of the Secretary of Health and Scientific Affairs. The President read the report slowly, watched by his two closest friends and personal aides. When he had finished reading it, at 10.13 p.m., he said: 'I – ' and collapsed. He was rushed at once to the Walter Reed Army Medical Centre where he was confined to an oxygen tent. His doctors agreed that he was suffering from 'overwork, high blood pressure and severe stress.'

The health report revealed that there had been thirty-five cases of fatal botulism throughout the preceding forty-eight hours. They had occurred all over the continent, from New Jersey to Arizona, from Texas to Alaska. In each case, the carrier had been a canned food product – not necessarily from the same manufacturer, and not necessarily the same variety of foodstuff. But every can that had been inspected by government health researchers had been punctured by a tiny hole – so small that the contents did not even leak – and in some cases the hole had been resealed by a dab of candle-wax.

The Secretary of Health concluded that 'it must be

beyond serious doubt that some malevolent agency has deliberately and in a calculated manner introduced *Clostridium botulinum* into a random variety of canned foods throughout the nation. Therefore – as grave as I realise the implications of such a recommendation must be – I have to put forward the urgent suggestion that the sale of all canned foods in the United States be immediately suspended pending more detailed investigation.'

Acting alone, the Vice-President sent desperate appeals for canned, dried, and frozen foods to the EEC nations, to Japan, China, and even to the USSR. The first response, even from our allies, was guarded. If the United States was really on the verge of economic and social collapse, then it was almost inevitable that the future of world politics would be heavily centred on the Soviet Union, and few nations were keen to mortgage their future by helping the United States too enthusiastically.

The Soviet Union 'regretted the crisis in the United States of America, but unfortunately had no surplus foodstuffs to spare.' The Vice-President ripped up their telegram, but conceded that at least they had shown the good grace not to mention the Afghanistan grain embargo.

At seven o'clock on Thursday morning, the Vice-President announced on television that the sale of all canned foodstuffs was banned, although he was humane enough to suggest that 'those who have no other food whatsoever', and who were obliged to eat canned foods, should 'exhaustively inspect the exterior of any can for pinholes, possibly concealed by wax.' Over seventy-six new cases of botulism had been reported during the night, all of them fatal.

For the first time in its history, *Time* magazine was published that week with a black border around its cover, instead of its traditional red. It was probably appropriate, because it was the last-ever edition. Its cover story: Famine, USA.

Federal experts now estimated that even the best-stocked American homes had only sufficient usable foodstuffs to carry their families through three more weeks. Most poorer urban families, however, were down to their last few cans – and now cans were under suspicion, too, they virtually had no food to eat at all.

Heavily-guarded food distribution centres were set up in the major cities, giving out packages that had been flown into New York, Boston, Washington, Los Angeles, Houston, Seattle, and Chicago from Britain and Denmark. American families who just two weeks ago had been eating steak, sweet potatoes, corn, fresh fruit, and any variety of ice-cream they wanted, now found themselves reduced to dried eggs, British chocolate, malt extract, margarine, and small cans of Danish processed pork. In Houston, three men were shot by National Guardsmen when they tried to break into the food distribution centre on Harrisburg Boulevard with machine-guns.

Time said, 'This week, Americans are feeling their first real pangs of hunger. After only two weeks of blight and catastrophe, they are actually beginning to understand what it means *to go without.*'

During the three hours that followed the Vice-President's announcement of a ban on canned foods, there were more than 17,000 suicides or attempted suicides throughout the United States. The Harvard psychologist Dr Leo Wolpers called it 'the Total Despair syndrome.' He said: 'People have lost their confidence in tomorrow.'

Hundreds of thousands of Americans tried to escape the country by boat and a harrassed Coastguard spent hours trying to turn back dinghies and catamarans and fishing smacks, all overloaded with desperate people with suitcases. Many of the boats were so overcrowded that they sank as soon as they reached the open sea. The *Boston Globe* printed on its back page, without caption and without comment, two photographs side by side – one of the Vietnamese boat people and one of the American boat people.

In the House, Representative George Meacher of Tennessee asked in an emotional speech how this 'magnificent democracy of ours, founded on liberty, freedom, and honour, could be brought low in two weeks by a virus, an isotope, and a disease of the gut?' Nobody could answer him.

Looting, homicide, arson, rape, and cases of 'crazy and suicidal driving' were reported 'by the thousand.' Most police forces could do nothing more than patrol the streets and try to keep their cities and suburbs as quiet as possible. A woman died in childbirth on the sidewalk outside the Waldorf-Astoria in New York because there were no doctors available, no ambulances, and most of Park Avenue was blocked with abandoned cars. In San Quentin prison, eighty-six inmates who attempted to escape because they were mad with hunger were shot dead. Two half-naked teenage girls from respectable Back Bay families were found wandering around downtown Boston in a state of shock after being kidnapped from outside their homes and raped more than twenty times each by marauding white hoodlums.

Thursday was the day that most newspapers stopped printing, that the last few gas stations closed down, that power blackouts began to darken thousands of square miles of the eastern seaboard. There was a terrible wildness in the air, a terrible panic, that nobody who lived through the first days of the famine could ever forget. One journalist remembered climbing Coit Tower in San Francisco and staring out for hours over a city that 'flowered with fires, and echoed with shots, and howled with the sirens of the helpless police.' Above everything, though, he said 'I could hear the cries and shrieks of a people who felt as if they had been abandoned by democracy, abandoned by capitalism, abandoned by peace, and abandoned by plenty . . . a people who more than anything else felt they had been deserted by God.'

During Thursday, the phone rang again and again at the Snowmans' house on Topanga Canyon. Nobody answered it until late on Thursday evening, when a motorcycle cop who had been checking houses for squatters and looters picked it up and said, 'They've all gone. This is the police.'

'Are they all right?' asked the voice at the other end.

'Who knows, friend? We've got chaos here, a bad brush fire burning. They could be anyplace at all.'

'Nobody's left a forwarding address?'

The cop gave a cursory look around. 'Not that I can see,'

he said. 'It looks like they just lit out. They didn't even lock the doors.'

There was a pause, and then the voice said, 'Can you do me a favour?'

'Sure, you name it.'

'Can you write on the wall someplace that Ed Hardesty called, from South Burlington Farm in Kansas, and that I'm going to try to make my way to LA?'

The cop took out his pencil and jotted the message down. 'South Burlington?' he asked.

'That's right.'

'Okay, then, I got you. I'll do that.'

'Thanks a whole lot. If this situation ever mends itself, come around to the house you're at and claim yourself a case of whisky.'

The cop grinned. 'To tell you the truth, I'm a vodka man.'

Ten

Ed carefully set the telephone back in its cradle, and looked across the living-room at Karen. Then, while she watched him, he stood up and walked to the window, staring out at the front yard of South Burlington Farm the same way he used to when he was a boy.

'Well?' asked Karen. 'Weren't they there?'

'That was a cop,' Ed told her, taking out a cigarette and lighting it slowly. He breathed out smoke. 'He said the house was empty. Even the doors had been left unlocked.'

'They've probably gone to stay somewhere safer,' Karen suggested. 'The way I heard it on the news, a whole lot of people are banding together to protect themselves from looters, and Hell's Angels, and people like that. Maybe they've found some kind of sanctuary.'

Ed leaned against the window-pane. Outside, the sun was gradually eating its way into the roof of the stables opposite, and the sky had flushed the colour of ripe

287

strawberries. To a city dweller, an evening like this on a Kansas wheat farm would have looked idyllic. To a farmer, the overwhelming silence, right in the peak of the early harvesting season, was ominous. The tractors were all parked and covered with tarps; the stables were empty and quiet. A single door banged and banged in the warm breeze that had risen on the prairie.

'I used to believe that this was God's own country,' said Ed. 'Now I'm not so sure.'

Karen said nothing, but came across to stand beside him. She was wearing a pale blue blouse that belonged to Season, and a pair of Season's baggy denim jeans. Her hair was drawn back, the way Season often drew hers back, and tied with a ribbon.

'You'll find them,' she said, gently. 'You know you will.'

Ed looked at her. 'Yes,' he said, unconvinced.

At that moment, Della came down from the bathroom, showered and smelling of Goya talcum. She had dressed herself in one of Ed's green gingham shirts, with the sleeves rolled up, and the front unbuttoned right the way down to her navel. She had washed her hair, and it was wet and combed Sha-Na-Na style.

'I just looked in on Shearson,' she said. 'He's sleeping.'

'Again?' asked Karen.

'I think he's trying to retreat from reality,' Della remarked. She went to the cocktail cabinet and, uninvited, poured herself a bourbon. Ed said, 'Help yourself to a drink,' but his sarcasm didn't faze her in the least. She came to the window and possessively curled her arm around his waist, and kissed him on the cheek. Karen gave them both a tight lemon-at-the-party kind of a smile.

'Shearson can't imagine a world without food,' said Della. 'Therefore, he's decided to withdraw from it completely until it all gets back to normal. If this famine goes on, he'll probably sleep like a baby until he dies of starvation in his bed.'

'How's Peter?' asked Karen.

Della swallowed bourbon. 'Peter's okay. I think he's got used to the idea that he's going to be better off if he co-operates. Peter's enough of a political manager to know

288

what kind of a jam he's in. In his case, I think a little plea-bargaining is going to go a long way.'

'You still think you're going to be able to bring Shearson to court?'

'I don't know,' said Della. 'But until I get orders to the contrary, he's under arrest charged with fraud and misappropriation of funds and more federal bank offences than you can mention. And that's the way it's going to stay.'

Peter Kaiser appeared in the doorway, dressed in an ill-fitting short-sleeved shirt in bright orange, and a pair of creased khaki slacks that were too wide around the waistband and three inches too short around his ankles.

'Well, well,' said Karen. 'How's Waikiki beach today?'

Peter didn't even answer. He sat himself on the end of the sofa, clutching himself as if he was beginning to feel the cold, and looked steadfastly miserable.

'You want a drink?' asked Ed. 'There's some bourbon left, or a little sherry.'

'No. No, thanks,' Peter told him.

Della said, 'You're not in cell block eleven yet, Peter. Don't look so unhappy.'

Peter looked up. 'You think I'm unhappy because of that? You think your half-assed threats of arraignment mean anything at all? You can stick your arraignment, right where the camel stuck his dates. I'm worried about my mother, if you must know. I tried to call her this morning, but all the lines to Washington are out.'

'I got through to LA just now,' said Ed. 'Maybe they're only out for an hour or two.'

'What do you care?' asked Peter.

Ed stared at him. 'I care because I have people of my own to think of, just the way you're thinking about your mother. Now, have a drink, for Christ's sake, and stop looking so damned depressed.'

They had been staying at South Burlington Farm since early Tuesday afternoon, and the tension between them hadn't been improved by the rapidly-worsening famine bulletins on the television. There was sufficient canned and frozen food at the farm to keep them going for another week or two, if they were lucky, but after that they knew they were going to be out on their own. They had hoped to be able to stay for a month, but the President's announcement on Wednesday evening had meant that over sixty per cent of their food had had to be thrown away. Ed had opened all the suspected cans and dug the food into the ground, in case they were tempted to open them later, when they were hungrier, and far less anxious about the risks of botulism.

On Tuesday morning, after capturing Shearson, they had stopped just outside of Fall River at a roadside diner, where Della had put in a call to the FBI office in Wichita. There had been no reply, she said; so she had tried calling Kansas City. The bureau chief there had told her not to risk bringing Senator Jones across country to Kansas City until the famine situation had 'normalised itself'. He had warned her not to try handing him over in Wichita, either since there had been fierce demonstrations and looting in the centre of town, and the Mayor had declared an area bounded by 13th Street to the north, Hillside Avenue to the east, Pawnee Avenue to the south, and the Highway 81 bypass to the west, totally under 24-hour curfew and a shoot-on-sight regulation for anyone found on the streets.

Ed had painstakingly bypassed Wichita by driving south on 77 to Winfield, and cutting across home to Kingman County through Wellington and Harper. Shearson had sat in the back, sweating and complaining; Karen had fallen asleep with her head against the Chevy wagon's window. Peter Kaiser from time to time had said, 'This is completely illegal, you know. We have the right of *habeas corpus*. Even derelicts have the right of *habeas corpus*.'

Della, still holding the pump-gun across her knees, had said, 'I hope you're not trying to tell me that you're as good as derelicts. Even derelicts live their lives by some kind of a moral code.'

Shearson had grumbled, 'Don't women make you ill. A rotten woman is as bad for your stomach as a rotten steamer.'

Ed had been nervous, approaching the ranch again. He had wondered for one hopeless moment if Season and Sally had made it back to Kansas, but he knew damned well that there were no flights from California, or anywhere else for that matter. He had also wondered, more realistically, if the farm had been looted while he was away, or burned by vengeful neighbours who had seen his Sunday-evening broadcast and assumed that he had somehow been involved in Shearson's Blight Crisis scam himself; or if Willard and Dyson and Jack Marowitz had decided to abandon the farm and head for the city.

He had stopped at the gates to South Burlington. A large, crudely-scrawled notice-board had been erected by the farm insignia, proclaiming: PRIVATE LAND – TRESPASSERS SHOT. He had driven the Chevy Suburban a short way along the dusty entrance-road, and then stopped, flashing his headlamps and sounding his horn.

Slowly, keeping the wagon covered with a shotgun, Dyson Kane had emerged from behind the nearby fence.

'Dyson!' Ed had shouted out. 'It's me! Ed! I brought a few friends along with me!'

'*Friends*, he calls us,' Shearson had remarked, with heavy irony. 'They're very *droll* these farmers, aren't they, as well as mischievous.'

Dyson had taken a few suspicious steps nearer. 'They really friends?' he had asked. 'None of those people are holding a gun on you, are they?'

'It's all okay,' Ed had answered. 'Look – this is Mrs Della McIntosh. She came around at the weekend.'

Dyson had walked right up to the side of the wagon and taken a look inside. 'Well, now,' he had said, reaching across to shake Ed's hand. 'And isn't that Senator Shearson Jones you've got in back?'

'That's right,' Ed had told him. 'I'll tell you all about it up at the farm. You want a ride?'

'It'll have to be later,' Dyson explained. 'I'm on guard duty right now. We had two or three pretty nasty bunches of looters around yesterday afternoon. They're looking for anything they can lay their hands on – particularly livestock. They're all armed, too, and if things get any worse I reckon they're going to start killing people.'

'Okay,' said Ed. 'You've got something to drink out here? Do you want me to send some sandwiches down?'

'I could go a couple of BLTs,' smiled Dyson. 'Unfortunately, we don't have any L and we're all out of Ts. But you can send one of the kids down with a round of B.'

'You've got it,' Ed had said, and driven the wagon the rest of the way up to the farmhouse, with red dust trailing from the wheels.

Apart from occasional bands of scavengers, South Burlington Farm hadn't seen much of the disastrous rioting and burning that had scarred America on Sunday evening and Monday morning. Kansas wheat farmers, those who lived on their spreads, were quiet and reserved and dogged, and they met disaster with quiet God-fearing bitterness, rather than hysteria. Out here in Kingman County, there had been too many droughts and too many lost crops for folks to panic when they heard there were tough times up ahead.

Still, Willard had taken sensible precautions. As well as arranging a guard-duty roster, he had brought in some of the farmworkers from outlying houses, and given them temporary accommodation in his own cottage, and in the apartments over the stables and the garages which used to be occupied by stable-boys, in the days before motor-tractors and Jeeps. He had put Jack Marowitz in charge of rationing, and Jack had divided up the remaining food supplies on the farm according to their nutritional value and the size of the farmworkers' families. Four families had chosen to leave, and join their relatives in Hutchinson and Emporia and Lehigh; and since most of the acreage was blackened now, and rotting, and there wasn't the slightest prospect of a harvest, even a drastically reduced one, Willard had given all of them permission to go. In all, South Burlington Farm had been left with twenty-three men, women, and children, apart from Ed, Della, Karen, Peter Kaiser, and the obese and slumbering senior senator for Kansas.

Ed had called his mother in Independence five times, hoping to get her to join them, but each time the phone had rung and rung and nobody had answered. He had had to give up.

Peter Kaiser said, 'You can't hold us here for ever, you know. Sooner or later you're going to have to do something positive.'

'That's for Della to decide,' Ed told him. 'She represents the law around here.'

'It doesn't matter to me if she represents the International House of Pancakes. She can't legally hold us without formal charges and without giving us the chance to call a lawyer.'

Ed crushed his cigarette out in an ashtray that had been given to him in New York by Donaldson, Lufkin & Jenrette. 'Where else are you boing to go?' he demanded. 'Out *there* – where people are tearing each other to shreds for the sake of a few cans of baked beans?'

'I have to get back to Washington,' Peter protested, sulkily. 'I have to get back and there isn't a damn thing you can do to stop me.'

'Talk sense, for Christ's sake,' Ed told him, 'If there was any kind of law and order out there – don't you seriously think that someone would have come looking for Senator Jones by now? A senator disappears, nobody knows where he is, and it's hardly even mentioned on the news. It's a jungle outside of this farm, Mr Habeas Corpus Kaiser, and a bright young man like you ought to have the sense to realise it.'

Peter abruptly stood up. 'I'm going,' he said. 'I'm going to walk out of here and you can't stop me.'

Della stepped forward, her hands on her hips, her big breasts swaying under her shirt. 'If you so much as take one step out of this room, Mr Kaiser, I'll blow your head off.'

'You wouldn't dare,' said Peter.

'Wouldn't I? This state is under martial law. You're a dangerous suspect attempting to escape FBI custody.'

Peter shook his head. 'I think you misunderstood me. You wouldn't dare because, without me, you wouldn't have a case. I'm your evidence, apart from those papers you stole, and you know it. So I'm not frightened of you, Mrs J. Edgar Hoover. Not one bit.'

293

He turned, and walked determinedly towards the door in his flapping khaki pants. Della, almost casually, reached for the pump-gun which she had left propped against the bureau in the corner. She raised it, pumped the action, and said softly, 'Freeze, Mr Kaiser. You're under arrest, and if you attempt to get away I'm going to have to shoot you.'

There was a formality in the way Della spoke to him that made Peter hesitate. Halfway through the door, he paused, and looked at her over his shoulder. She was standing with the gun raised to her shoulder, the sights marking his head. He licked his lips, as if he had just finished drinking a bowl of particularly nasty tomato soup.

He stood where he was for what seemed like a whole minute. Then he turned around, and went back to the sofa. 'The day they started hiring whores for cops, that was when the whole legal system went down the tubes,' he said. 'Can you believe this hooker, being a cop?'

Della kept the gun levelled at him, but Ed stepped forward and laid his hand on the barrel. 'That's enough, Della. You may be an agent of the law, but this is my house, and that's my sofa, and I don't particularly want to have holes blown in it.'

He raised the barrel of the pump-gun until it was pointing at the ceiling, although she tried to resist him. He looked her straight in the eyes and said, 'You understand? Because this is the time when people are going to start making their own laws, like they did in the frontier days.'

Della didn't answer, and lowered the gun. Peter Kaiser, from his place on the sofa, watched them both closely, but said nothing at all.

That night, Thursday, Ed was woken up by the deep, distant coughing of shotguns. He sat up in bed, and listened. There was another shot, and another. He shook Della's shoulder, and said, 'There's a firefight going on out there. Can you hear it?'

She raised her tousled head from the pillow. 'It sounds like it's coming from the main gate,' she said.

Ed swung out of bed, and switched on the light. He tugged on his jeans and a T-shirt, and opened the top drawer in his rococo-style bedside table. Della, pulling on an old red sweater of Season's, watched him sharply as he took out a Colt .45 automatic, and checked the magazine.

'What's that?' she asked. 'A family heirloom?'

'That's right,' he told her. 'My father bought it to keep my mother in line. Now, let's get out there and see what's going on, shall we?'

Peter Kaiser was already on the landing when they opened their door, in a large pair of blue undershorts with green flowers splattered all over them. Blinking at Ed, he said, 'I heard shooting. Did you hear shooting?'

'Just keep your head down,' said Della. 'Don't forget you're a valuable witness.'

'For God's sake,' said Peter.

Ed ran ahead of Della downstairs, and opened up the front door. They crossed the verandah under a sky that was dark and windy and heavy with cloud, and Ed led the way across to the farm's Wagoneer. He swung himself up into the driver's seat and started the engine without even waiting for her, or opening the passenger door to let her in.

'There's no mistaking that you're the boss around here,' she complained, as she clambered up, and laid her pump-gun down on the Jeep's floor.

Ed twisted the Wagoneer around the asphalt in a squittering curve, and then roared off towards the entrance road and the main gates.

'They're threatening my farm,' he snapped, thrusting his hand into his hair and brushing it back off his forehead. 'Don't you understand that? Or have you never owned anything you cared that much for?'

Della said, 'I've never owned anything. There never seemed to be any point to it.'

Ed wound the window down. They could hear the shooting quite clearly now – sharp, argumentative bursts of machine-gun fire, countered by the deep blasts of shotguns. The night air was warm and dusty, but it was dark too, with clouds covering the moon, and it was difficult to make out what was happening up ahead. They could smell gunsmoke drifting their way on the fresh easterly wind.

In the light of his headlamps, Ed saw somebody lying in the roadway. He pulled up, opened the Wagoneer's door, and jumped down. Della said, 'What is it? What have you stopped for?'

Ed didn't answer, but crouched his way forward beside the Jeep's front wheel, and then scuttled out to where the man was sprawled out in the dust. There was blood everywhere, most of it dried in dark Rorschach prints, but some of it still wet and globular. Ed carefully eased the man over on to his back, and then he saw who it was.

'Oh, Jesus,' he said, through his teeth.

It was young Jack Marowitz, dead. He looked as if he had been hit five or six times in the chest by a machine-gun, because the front of his yellow college sweatshirt was mushy with blood. As Ed turned him over, a strange sighing noise came from his perforated lungs.

Ed heaved the body over to the side of the road, and then crouched his way back to the Jeep. The firing was much closer now, and he could hear unfamiliar voices shouting something which sounded like, *'Get behind them! Circle around them, George! Get behind them!'*

Della said, 'What's happening? Who was that in the road?'

Ed slid into the driver's seat, slammed the door, and revved up the Wagoneer's engine. 'Jack Marowitz, my crop adviser. One of the best in the business, as far as I was concerned.'

'But what's going on? Who shot him?'

'I don't know. It sounds like some kind of a raiding party. They're over there on the right, most of them. At least it sounds that way, from the gunfire.'

'Where are your people?'

Ed drove cautiously ahead for three or four hundred yards without lights. As he drove, he pointed to the fence which ran alongside the entrance road on the left-hand side. 'That's where Dyson was hiding himself yesterday, so I guess that's where they are tonight. It was Willard, Jack, and one of the garage hands on guard duty until three o'clock.'

There was a brief snatch of firing, and a sudden rattling

of bullets against the side of the Jeep. Ed immediately swerved off the track, and stopped the vehicle beside the protective camouflage of a clump of stunted bushes. He pushed open the driver's door, and scrambled quickly out into the grass, followed by Della.

A shotgun banged loudly off to the left, and Della raised her head a little to see if she could pinpoint where the shot had come from.

'Those are your people, aren't they, with the shotguns?' she asked.

Ed nodded. 'It sounds like it. Did you see where they were?'

'I think so. Down behind the fence there, about five or six uprights along. The other people are using M3A1s.'

'You can tell just by listening?'

'Every gun has a distinctive sound of its own. And remember I'm trained.'

Ed said, 'How many of them do you guess there are? Six, maybe?'

'It's hard to tell,' said Della. 'More, probably, by the way they're firing.'

Ed thought about that, Then he said, 'In that case, I think we'd better go back and get some reinforcements. There's no way that four of us are going to be able to hold off that many of them.'

'I think it's time to back off,' said Della. 'We don't have any proper cover here or any spare ammunition. Can you call Willard, and see if you can get him to hear you? Tell him to make his way back to the farm.'

'Listen,' said Ed, 'who's giving the goddamned orders around here?'

'Have you got a better idea?' Della demanded.

There was another burst of light machine-gun fire, off on their right. The raiders were encircling them now, trying to cut off their escape back to the house.

'If we don't get out of here now, they've got us,' said Della. 'So what are you going to do? Call your friends, or die gallantly?'

Ed looked at her intently, trying to make out her face in the darkness. 'If any of us come out of this famine alive,' he

297

said, 'what the hell are you going to *do* with your life?'

Della said, '*Call* them! If we don't run, we're going to have to fight.'

'I asked you a question,' insisted Ed.

'Do you really think I've got the time or the inclination to answer you? But if you must know, I'm going to give up the FBI and do what I always wanted to do. Marry, settle down, live in Bluefield, West Virginia and raise children and flowers.'

Ed said, 'Bluefield, West Virginia?'

He was going to say something else, but he was interrupted by a fast, sharp burst of bullets. Six or seven of them struck the Jeep Wagoneer. They heard the side windows crack, and the high, squeaky hiss of a punctured tyre. Then they heard someone calling, '*Get over that fence, George! Along the back!*'

A man came running past the Jeep, doubled-up, holding a grease-gun, and panting as he ran. He came so close to Ed and Della that he almost kicked Della in the face – but he overshot them by two or three paces before his mind registered that what he had seen on the ground could have been two people. He skated to a halt on the grass, turned around, and just had time to raise his gun before Della rolled over on to her back, lifted her pump-gun, and blew his stomach into rags of bloody intestine.

'That's *it*!' clipped Della. 'Now, let's get the hell out of here!'

'*Willard*!' yelled Ed. 'Willard – we're over here and we're making a run for it!'

Della's gunshot and Ed's shouting instantly attracted a whipping, whistling swarm of machine-gun fire. They lay flat against the turf as dust sprayed up all around them, and bullets penetrated the sides of the Jeep in a hurrying series of flat-sounding *clonks*. Another tyre burst, and Ed snarled at Della, 'I thought you told me that couldn't happen?'

Ed raised his Colt .45 and strained his eyes to see what was going on in the darkness. Through the bushes, he could see most of the split-rail fence where Willard and the garage-hand were hiding themselves; and he thought he could see somebody huddled by the roadside, although it was impossible to see if the man was alive and dangerous or dead and safe.

There was a long, tight silence, broken only by the occasional whistling of the grass in the wind, and by the rustling of birds, or gophers, or impatient gunmen. Ed whispered to Della, 'There's no sign from Willard. Maybe they hit him.'

Della raised a cautious hand, and said, 'Wait.'

They didn't have to wait long. A few seconds later, they heard someone running towards them. Ed lifted his head and saw two men sprinting fast and low alongside the split-rail fence. In front, holding on to his stetson hat with one hand and his shotgun in the other, was Willard Noakes; and just behind him was Ed's young garage-hand.

Ed fired twice into the air, to distract the raiders, and he was answered by a crackle of bullets. But then there was another sound – the snap of a rifle. It fired one ranging shot, then another; and then Willard collapsed in a jumble of arms and legs. The garage-hand bent over him, and Ed heard his voice on the wind like the voice of an anxious fledgling, saying, *'Willard . . .'*

Ed started to get up, but Della seized the sleeve of his T-shirt.

'Don't,' she said. 'You wouldn't stand a chance. For my sake – for your wife's sake – just stay where you are.'

Ed slid back down on to the grass. He was sure he could hear Willard moaning. And that wasn't just anybody, hit by a bullet and hurt. That was Willard Noakes, one of his father's closest buddies – the man who had taught Ed just about everything he knew – the man who had listened to his problems and given him friendly advice, and never once betrayed himself or South Burlington Farm or the good straightforward state of Kansas.

You could never have said that Willard Noakes was a great man, or even a half-successful man. He was lonesome, as a rule, and unlettered, and when he wasn't working or sleeping, he was watching television. But it took an effort of will that was almost muscular for Ed not to risk the bullets that were flying around that night and run across to tell Willard that he had always been loved, and respected, and that he wasn't going to die alone.

There were three more rifle shots. *Snap – snap – snap*. The garage-hand half-rose, batting his hands at the air as if he were trying to catch moths. Then he fell into the darkness, and Ed couldn't see him any more.

Della said, 'We've got to get out of here, Ed. I mean it, darling, otherwise we're going to be pigfeed.'

'Okay,' said Ed. 'The two back tyres on the Jeep are flat, but I guess I can still drive her back to the farmhouse. I just hope they haven't shot up the engine.'

Della looked up. 'They're trying to surround us. I can hear one of them over there, in back of the fence. Can you hear that? Like, rustling. If we're going to make a run for it, I think we'd better do it now.'

They waited for nearly ten seconds; their hearts galloping, their breath shallow. Then Ed touched Della's shoulder in the darkness, and said, '*Let's go!*'

Della scrambled up first, and threw herself into the open door of the Jeep. Ed was up next, and he had started up the motor even before he was sitting in his seat. With the driver's door swinging wildly, the Wagoneer jounced off the rough grass verge, and bucked its way on to the road. The rear hubs grated and bumped on the hard-packed soil, and when Ed thrust his foot down on the gas, the tyres slithered out from under the rims like agonised black snakes; but they were away, and heading back towards the farm as fast as the crippled Jeep could travel.

Now, for the first time they saw the raiders they were fighting. Out of the shadows, on either side of the road, men came running out of the grassland, carrying rifles and machine-guns. They wore quilted jerkins and jeans, and most of them had scarves tied around their faces.

'Can't you get this damned thing to go any *faster?*' fretted Della, as the Jeep ground laboriously along the track.

'With two flat tyres? You want miracles?'

'For God's sake! We'd be quicker on foot.'

A hail of machine-gun bullets smashed the back windows of the Wagoneer, and showered them with broken glass. Ed pressed the gas pedal flat to the floor, but although the engine screamed, and the back wheel rims screeched on the road, he couldn't get enough traction to take them clear of the running raiders. If the Jeep hadn't been four-wheel-drive, they probably couldn't have got it to go at all.

Two well-aimed rifle bullets penetrated the driver's door, with a sound like warping tin, and one of them buried itself in the upholstery of Ed's seat. He said, 'That's it. We've had it That's the end.'

But Della whooped, 'We're losing them! Ed, look we're losing them!'

Ed turned. They were travelling at almost twenty-five mph now, and the raiders were gradually falling behind. One or two of them had stopped already, and were raising their rifles and their machine-guns to their shoulders to give the Jeep a final scattering of fire.

'It's too far now,' said Della, with relief, settling back in her seat. 'They'll never get the range. Not with those peashooters.'

It was then that the Jeep's tortured transmission gave out a hideous clashing noise, and locked solid. The vehicle jolted to a stop, and wouldn't budge, even for Ed's frantic jugglings with the T-bar shift.

'*Out!*' Ed shouted at Della. 'We've got a good start on them – we can still make it!'

They were out of the Jeep and running before any of the raiders realised what had happened. But as they pounded along the dirt track towards the dark huddle of the farmhouse buildings, they heard the sporadic crackling of M3A1s behind them and the denser, sharper report of rifles. Ed – even though he was running – could feel the night air herringboned by bullets. For the first time that night, he thought, '*God – they've got me now. I don't stand a chance. I'm going to die right here, right now, as suddenly as Michael died in his car.*'

He could hear Della running along beside him – her bare feet slapping on the track. He could hear his own painful gasps for breath. He closed his eyes and pelted along faster, totally intent on survival, totally intent on living and on seeing Season and Sally again.

Then – there was another fusilade of gunfire. But this wasn't behind them, This was ahead, from the farmhouse, and from the stables. This was the bellow of shotguns and the light twig-snapping sound of handguns. His own farmhands, shooting back. The firing from the raiders broke off abruptly as they scrambled for cover, and Ed and Della found themselves running through the night in unnatural silence, as if they were trying to escape through the muffled darkness of a nightmare.

They reached the asphalt yard, and then they were stumbling up the steps of the farmhouse verandah, accompanied by an ear-splitting salvo of covering shotgun fire.

Dyson was standing by the door, and he opened it up for them as they came running along the front of the house. Then he quickly slammed it behind them, and locked it.

Ed said simply, 'Shit. Thanks, Dyson.'

Inside the farmhouse, the atmosphere was alarmed, and everybody was tight faced with tension. Even Shearson Jones had come down from his bed, and was sitting in Ed's armchair, wrapped in a white towelling bathrobe that scarcely met over the white moon-like curve of his belly. Peter Kaiser was perched on the arm of the sofa next to Karen, with his arm around her – an affectionate gesture to which she responded by sitting up as rigidly as possible.

Dyson, following Ed and Della into the living-room, said, 'We heard the shooting. Then we heard you go out to the front gate in the Jeep. I was trying to get the boys together – armed and ready – when we saw you coming back.'

Ed's chest was still heaving from their last desperate run. He said, 'Dyson, I'm glad you did. That blast of scatter-gun fire – well, that just about saved our lives.'

Dyson was carrying the light hunting rifle which he usually used for popping off shots at rabbits and rats. He went across to the window, parted the drapes, and peered studiously out into the night. The Jeep was already alight, and rolling tongues of orange flame were pouring out of its blackened carcass like a grotesque demonstration of fire-eating.

'There's a whole lot of them out there, Ed,' Dyson said,

quietly. 'Twenty or thirty maybe. I counted the muzzle flashes when you were running in. There's no way we can hold them off for very long.'

Ed said, 'I'm not going to try to hold them off.'

'You're not even going to *try* to save yourself?' asked Shearson Jones, in his fat, unmistakable voice. 'What are you going to do? Let them scavenge the few supplies we have left? Lie low while they rob us?'

Ed turned around. 'Listen,' he said, 'those raiders out there undoubtedly outnumber us. They sure as hell outgun us. If we tried to hold them off, they'd either starve us out, burn us out, or simply shoot their way in. Well – you can take your pick, senator, when it comes to the kind of death that *you* want. But right now, I personally don't feel like dying at all, and I don't suppose that a whole lot of the folks who work on my farm feel like it either.'

He turned to Dyson, and said, 'They got Willard, and they got Jack, and they got that garage-hand you sent out there. I don't even remember his name.'

Dyson said unhappily, 'When they didn't come back with you, I kind of assumed that was the way it was. Damn it, Ed, that really makes me feel like hell.'

'Me, too, Dyson,' said Ed, laying his hand on his shoulder.

Dyson said, 'That young boy's name was Gerrity – David Gerrity. He was the best we had when it came to stripping a tractor. Well, so Willard told me. I'm only the pilot.'

Ed looked back at Shearson. 'We're going to have to make a break for it,' he said. 'You can either come along with us, or you can stay behind. That decision is entirely up to you. But we're going to load our wagons with all the remaining foodstuffs on this farm and head for the west coast.'

'The west coast?' asked Della. 'Surely it makes more sense to head for Washington. They'll have government there – some kind of law and order. And besides, I want to turn Senator Jones in to Charles Kurnik in person There's no point in going to the west coast.'

Ed said, 'My wife and child are out on the west coast. I

want to find them. Once I've done that, I want to try to get out of the United States, either through Mexico or by sea. Believe me, Della, you only have to listen to the news bulletins. You only have to see what happened tonight to two of my closest friends and workmates – Willard and Jack. There's no point in pretending that things are any better in Washington. They can't be. They're probably worse. And what the hell is the point of holding on to a fraud suspect in a nation where they don't even have enough police to stop people murdering each other?'

There was a burst of gunfire outside, and somewhere across the yard a window broke.

Karen said, 'I believe we ought to stick together. I think we'll have more of a chance that way.'

Peter Kaiser rolled up his eyes. 'No wonder history has no eminent lady philosophers,' he said. 'With the possible exception of Xaviera Hollander.'

Karen looked up at him. 'Do you want to stay behind?' she asked. 'If all the rest of us go to the west coast, do you want to try to make it to Washington on your own?'

Peter looked back at her, and then shrugged. 'It depends,' he said sulkily.

Ed said, 'Dyson – how many wagons do we have? And how many cars?'

'We've got the Chevy wagon you brought back from Fall River. Then there's the Big Dooley that Carson's left here when they were shifting tree stumps. And four – maybe five family pick-ups and sedans. One El Camino for sure, and a Mercury Marquis.'

'Okay,' said Ed, 'this is what we're going to do. We're going to load the pick-ups and the trunks of the family cars with as much food as we can. We mustn't forget water and fruit juices, too. Then we're going to get everybody into their cars and ready to go, and pull out of here in a convoy, shooting all the time. With any luck, we should be able to clear the farm without any casualties.'

'With any luck,' echoed Peter Kaiser, sarcastically, pulling a morbid face.

Shearson said, 'Listen, Mr Hardesty, I may be technically the prisoner of your fancy-woman here, formerly *my* fancy-woman, but that doesn't mean I have to take instructions from you. It's essential that Mr Kaiser and I return to Washington; and if you're not prepared to come with us, then I'm afraid we shall simply have to go without you.'

'You wouldn't get ten miles,' said Ed. 'Don't you watch the television? Haven't you seen what it's like out there?'

'Your concern for my well-being is touching,' replied Shearson. 'However, I've been looking after myself for a considerable number of years, often through situations that have been a good deal stickier than this one, and I think I can manage without you, thanks.'

Della said, 'Really, Ed, we ought to try to make it to Washington. I know your wife and daughter are in Los Angeles, but I have to take Senator Jones in to the Bureau. There won't be any hope of arraigning him if I drag him out to California. He's probably thought up twenty ways of killing our indictments anyway – unusual and stressful arrest, that kind of thing. We really ought to try.'

Ed looked at Dyson, who shrugged, and then at Karen. 'Going back to Washington doesn't make any kind of sense,' he insisted. 'The whole city is practically under siege, the way they're telling it on the news. Right now, we need to get ourselves somewhere with a good climate, fertile soil, in case we have to resettle and start growing our food again from scratch; and somewhere that's close to the ocean and the border. Sure, I want to go to Los Angeles for personal reasons. But it's going to be safer, too, to stay in the West. I'd stay right here in Kansas if I could – but it's dry, and the winters can be hard, and from what's going on outside, I'd guess that we can expect raiding and looting parties for a long time to come.'

'Do you seriously think that California's going to be any better?' asked Shearson. 'Los Angeles is burning, San Francisco has turned into a latter-day Sodom, with plenty of Gomorrah thrown in; San Diego's become a looters' paradise.'

From outside, there was a crackle of heavy, sustained shooting. They heard upstairs windows break, and the sound of running feet. Dyson Kane went to the window again just as one of Ed's farmhands came into the room, carrying a shotgun that was still smoking, his face bright with sweat and excitement.

'Mr Hardesty, sir,' he said, breathlessly. 'It don't look like we can keep 'em back much longer. Jerry's been hit in the arm, sir, and the rest of the boys ain't really up to gun-fighting.'

'All right,' said Ed. 'We've wasted enough time as it is. Dyson – can you get those vehicles loaded up, and parked in a line, ready to roll? Mr Kaiser – Karen – you want to get out there and help?'

'I'm not doing anything until we've settled which direction we're heading,' said Peter, folding his arms.

Ed turned to Shearson. The senator gave him a fat, condescending smile 'The same goes for me, Mr Hardesty; and you know darn well that if *I* stay, and Mr Kaiser stays, then it's your fancy-woman's bounden duty to stay too.'

There was more shooting outside, and a child screamed. Ed snapped at Dyson, 'Get moving. I want those wagons loaded up before it's too late.' Then, without hesitation, he tugged his Colt automatic out of his belt and held it up in front of everybody in the room as if he were demonstrating it to a group of benighted natives.

'I'm going to make one thing straight,' he said. 'On this farm, I'm in charge of everything and everybody. I'm in charge, and I'm also responsible. That's the way it is, even when we *don't* have a crisis on our hands. But right now, we have, and that increases my authority even more. This country isn't safe for people to wander around on their own, particularly women, and particularly obese senior senators with a price on their heads. Our society's broken down into tribes, and the way I see it, each tribe has to hold together to survive. This is our tribe, and unless anybody wants to argue about it, I'm the chief. Now, we're all getting out of here, we're all helping to load up the wagons, and then we're all heading west.'

Shearson, gripping the arms of his chair to support himself, slowly rose to his feet. He stood there for a moment, swaddled in his bathrobe, breathing loudly and hoarsely with the exertion of getting up.

'Mr Hardesty,' he said, 'my late father once told me never to argue with fools, ignoramuses, or people with loaded guns. Since you fall into all three categories, I don't think I have any alternative but to comply with your wishes. Mrs McIntosh – shall we light out for Los Angeles?'

Della, furious, stalked out of the living-room ahead of any of them. 'Well, now,' Shearson said to Ed, pulling down his eyelid with his finger in a gesture of shared confidence, 'I seem to have made the right decision. Anything that infuriates an agent of the FBI can't be all bad.'

At the same time that Ed Hardesty's farmworkers were trying to hold off the raiders who threatened South Burlington, a small and simple tragedy was taking place in a dilapidated frame house on the outskirts of Fort Wayne, Indiana. The house had once been neat and proud, part of a row that had all belonged to International Harvester workers, foremen and supervisors and chief engineers. Now it was overshadowed by unkempt sycamores, and a rusty rundown Nash was parked in the driveway. This was where the welfare cases lived; the tired single-parent wives with their second-hand strollers and their dime-store dresses; the paraplegic husbands who could do nothing more than nod and shuffle, and whose sick pay had long since run out.

Number 8 was the home of John Frederick Walters, his wife Elizabeth, and their three daughters, Alice, Wendy and Jenna. Alice was the oldest, at six; Wendy was three and Jenna was six months.

John Frederick Walters, who always gave his name as 'John Frederick Walters', was thirty one, and a skilled electrician. At least, he used to be a skilled electrician, until 1972, when he was rewiring a house in the better part of Fort Wayne, and the owner came back half-drunk from a business reception, pulled the main switch, and electrocuted him. He was lucky to be alive. But there was a twisted burn all the way down the right side of his chest, and even after months of hospitalisation his left hand still felt a little numb, and he still dragged his left leg in an odd, teetering walk that made people in supermarkets give him a wide berth, in case he collided with their carts. Until the famine crisis on Sunday, he had worked in a Thriftee Superstore on Paulding Road, but it had been burned to the ground in the early hours of Monday. Now he was holed up with his family at Number 8, with no electricity, no telephone, no mail, and only a transistor radio with weak batteries to keep him in touch with the horror that was sweeping the outside world.

He was still sitting in his yellow-papered living-room at midnight on Thursday, listening to an extended news bulletin about the day's disasters. Thirty-six people had died when their overloaded airplane had snagged power lines over Columbus, Ohio – turning their attempted getaway from the United States into a mass cremation. Anything up to 100 people were feared dead after fire had swept a condominium in Miami from a looted supermarket next door. Washington was almost unapproachable – the US Marines had sealed off every highway from the outside world, and were threatening to shoot interlopers on sight. The President was out of his oxygen tent, but his doctors had told him he had to rest for two or three more days at the least. It was 'expertly estimated' that between seven and eight hundred Americans had died during the day from violence directly related to the food shortages.

From the outside world – from Europe, from the Far East, from the Third World – there was awkwardness and hesitation. They stood by while America slowly collapsed from within, like unwilling witnesses to a coronary. The Queen had sent a message expressing 'the grave concern of the British people', but the reluctance of America's erstwhile allies to assist her was becoming increasingly and embarrassingly obvious. Already, trade envoys from Italy, Sweden, and West Germany had made special visits to the Soviet Union, and the dollar was no longer being quoted on the world money markets. The Secretary of State, in a rare fit of temper, talked of alliances that had taken 'fifty years and one hundred fifty billion dollars to build; and only fifty minutes to tear down.'

John Frederick Walters listened to all this carefully, leaning close to his indistinct radio set. It was a hot, airless night in Fort Wayne, and most of the rioting and looting that had ravaged the town during the earlier part of the week had died down. There were no more supermarkets to break into; no more police cars to burn; and the fear and panic were collapsing of heat exhaustion. Still, John Frederick Walters could hear police sirens howling eerily out over on Tillman Road, and he knew that if he went to the top of the house, to Alice's room, and opened the window, he would be able to see the Lutheran Hospital burning over on Fairfield Avenue. He had heard it from Old Oliver, his next-door neighbour, that seventy people had died in that fire, suffocated in their beds like fumigated bugs.

He heard the stairs creak. He switched off the radio set and sat up straight, his thin hands laced together in his lap. He was a very thin man altogether – although he had weighed almost 185 pounds before his electrocution. His face was pale as water-chestnuts, and he had odd straw-coloured hair that stuck up at the back, as if it were charged with static. He *looked* an electrocuted man – as if his brain were still in that black hiatus between switch *on* and switch *off* – as if his bodily fluids were in stasis – as if his nerve-endings were recoiling and recoiling from that first fry of voltage.

His wife Elizabeth was standing in the living-room door. Her face was angular and white; her eyes as shifty and haunted as Edith Piaf, or a painting by Munch. She wore a cheap new quilted robe with orange flowers on it, Woolco's ritziest. The last time he had taken her out was in February of 1972, for her birthday, when they had gone to see *2001: A Space Odyssey*, and eaten Chinese.

She said, 'Jenna's hungry.'

John Frederick Walters looked at her. He wondered why she had come all the way downstairs at midnight to tell him that. He knew Jenna was hungry. They had scraped out the last can of formula that morning, diluting it as much as they could, and now there was nothing. There were no emergency food centres in Fort Wayne. If you wanted anything at all, you had to drive to Indianapolis, and the Rambler's battery had been flat for weeks. Besides, what chance did a cripple have of fighting his way through to the food supplies?

'Have you tried breast-feeding her?' asked John Frederick Walters.

'I tried. But there's hardly anything there. I haven't eaten in two days myself, John Frederick. I can't give milk out of nothing at all.'

John Frederick Walters reached for the red Lark packet by the radio. There were two cigarettes left in it and he shook them, wondering if he ought to have one now, or if he ought to save both of them for later. In the end, he slid one out, tucked it between his lips, and lit it one-handed with a folded matchbook. He puffed smoke.

'There's nothing left, Elizabeth. That can of franks we gave the kids today, that was it, and from what the news has been saying, we shouldn't even have risked that. They could go down with disease, die.'

Elizabeth stayed where she was in the doorway, nibbling at her lower lip. She peeled the skin off it in strips until it bled. 'I don't understand it,' she said. 'Doesn't anybody care? You'd think they'd come around with food parcels. I mean – we've got three children here. What are we going to do?'

'The whole town's a wreck,' said John Frederick Walters. 'No police, no ambulance service, nothing. How the hell can anybody expect them to bring around food parcels?'

'But we'll *starve*,' Elizabeth protested. 'The three girls will *starve*.'

John Frederick Walters stared at the burning cigarette in his hand. He felt giddy from nicotine and lack of food. 'Yes,' he said. 'I guess we will, unless something happens.'

'But what do people do in India, places like that? Cambodia? They starve, sure, but they sometimes scratch some kind of a living.'

'They know how, that's why,' said John Frederick Walters. 'They know how to live on a small bowl of rice, how to make it last. They've never seen a T-bone steak in their lives, and they'd probably puke up at the sight of it if they did. They know how to grow the damned rice, too. Do you know how to grow rice? I mean, if you do, get out back and get planting. We're all gonna need it.'

Elizabeth stared at him as if she hadn't heard or understood a word he was saying. She probably didn't. She said, slowly, 'There's some Alpo I bought for Florence's dog. There's a can of that left.'

'*Alpo?* Are you kidding? You can't eat dog-food.'

'But how can I produce milk if I don't eat? Can't you hear her screaming up there? What am I supposed to do? Stand by and watch my children wasting away? I don't know how you can sit there and smoke and listen to that stupid wore-out radio and let it *happen!*'

John Frederick Walters stared at her coldly. 'No,' he said. 'I guess you don't know, do you? You don't know that this whole world's fallen in on us, and because we're at the bottom to begin with, the entire weight of everything falls on us cripples and incompetents first.'

She looked back at him, her mouth patchy with blood. Then she turned without a word and went through to the kitchen.

He switched the radio back on, and, listened to a short bulletin about a shooting outside of Los Angeles. Fifty police had ambushed a band of vigilante looters, and slain all of them, including eight women and a child of twelve. Most state highway patrols had now formed themselves into anti-looting squads, hunting down looters and killing them on sight. What the bulletin didn't mention was that almost all of the recaptured loot was divided up amongst the arresting officers, and the district attorney's office, and anybody else the highway patrols considered to be 'close and special friends.'

It was still possible to buy certain foods on the black market. An NBC reporter had paid seven hundred and fifty dollars for a can of Chicken of the Sea at a warehouse in Brooklyn, and he had been offered whole canned hams from Denmark and the United Kingdom for well over one thousand five hundred dollars each. Pots of Marmite, the

British yeast extract, were selling at sixty dollars and upwards.

John Frederick Walters switched off the radio again, puffed twice at his cigarette, and then stood up. He limped unevenly out of the living-room, along the narrow corridor with its scenic print of Great Egg Harbor, New Jersey, still splattered with dried-up tomato sauce from the evening two years ago when he had thrown his pasta at Elizabeth in a fit of frustrated temper. He opened the kitchen door, and there Elizabeth was, sitting at the table beside the cheap cream-painted dresser, her fork raised, her eyes staring back at him in defiance and fright.

In front of her was a plate – one of the nice white octagonal plates that Elizabeth's mother had given them for a wedding gift. There were only three left, out of eight. The plate was heaped with brown glistening lumps of meat. On the draining-board was a red-labelled can, with an open lid.

John Frederick Walters walked into the kitchen, and around the table. Elizabeth kept her eyes on him warily, her fork still poised.

'Is that Alpo?' John Frederick Walters asked harshly.

Elizabeth nodded.

John Frederick Walters went to the draining-board and picked up the empty can. 'Well,' he said at last, 'you could do worse. It says here that it's a complete and balanced diet. So why don't you go ahead – eat it.'

Elizabeth hesitated for a while, biting at her lips. Then, in jerky slow-motion, she dug her fork into the dog food and lifted up two gravyish chunks. John Frederick Walters stared at her unblinking and said nothing.

Closing her eyes, Elizabeth put the dog food into her mouth. She slowly began to chew it, moving it from one side to the other, her eyes still closed, her empty fork held up beside her.

'You're lucky,' said her husband, in a shaky voice. 'Do you know how lucky you are? That's an expensive brand. Some brands are nothing but fat, and tubes, and minced up gristle. Mind you, I should think that even Alpo has its fair share of offals.'

312

Elizabeth chewed and chewed, tried to swallow, and gagged. Saliva and half-chewed dog meat trailed from her lips.

'God,' breathed John Frederick Walters, 'what are you doing? What about Jenna? How's Jenna going to survive if her mother doesn't eat dog meat to turn into milk? How are any of us going to survive?'

Elizabeth was weeping. She gagged again, and held her hand over her mouth to keep the food inside.

John Frederick Walters told Fort Wayne police officers early Friday morning that 'I acted quick.' He said, 'I never thought the day would have to come when a wife of mine would have to eat dog food to nourish our baby, and I never thought the day would have to come when my girls would go without a meal. I'm not rich, I know that, and we could never afford much since my accident, but this is America, isn't it? How come suddenly there was nothing to eat, and no prospect of nothing to eat?'

As Elizabeth choked over her mouthful of dog food, John Frederick Walters pulled down the frayed cord which was suspended over the stove for drying the girls' undervests during the winter, twisted it twice around his hands, and then once around Elizabeth's neck. She fell backwards to the floor, hitting her head on the beige linoleum. Her eyes bulged at John Frederick Walters in horror, but she was unable to speak, unable to breathe, and her face turned grey and shiny, the same colour as grey leather shoes. After five minutes, with the string cutting into his bare hands John Frederick Walters decided she was dead.

He went upstairs, leaving Elizabeth lying in the kitchen. Alice and Wendy shared a bed in the small second-storey bedroom over the living-room. They were both asleep in the darkness, in their white flock cotton nightdresses, and John Frederick Walters stood at the end of the bed watching them – their upraised wrists, traced with blueish veins, their thin ankles. He reached down and held Alice's bare toes in his hand, gently and lovingly. He wanted to kill them, he knew he had to, but he didn't know how. How do you kill children you love? How can you instantly end their lives without hurting them?

He picked Wendy up, and carried her sleeping into the bathroom. Her arms lolled beside her as if she were already dead. He felt as if he were mad, or drugged, or even as if he were someone else altogether. Supposing there wasn't really a famine at all? Supposing his radio had been telling him lies? But he looked around him at the white enamel bathtub with its green-coloured stain; at the can of lavender talcum powder with the rusted rim; at the fingerprinted mirror where Elizabeth had plucked her eyebrows and he had always shaved. And even if the radio was lying, what the hell was the use of a life like this, for any of them?

He took a safety-razor blade between finger and thumb, and then sat on the toilet seat with the sleepy Wendy on his lap. She mumbled, 'Daddy . . . what are we doing?' but he shushed her soothingly as he stroked her forehead, and then gently but firmly gripped her hair and slit her throat, as deeply as he could, from one side to the other. She didn't even protest; didn't even seem to realise what was happening. But then there was a sudden explosive gargle of blood and air, and the whole bathroom was arrayed in red. He dropped Wendy off his lap, in horror and utter fear, and she lay kicking her left foot against the side of the bath, kick, kick, kick, as she died. It was like watching a run-over dog die, only a thousand times worse, and he reeled with the dreadfulness of it.

'I didn't lose my resolve, though,' he told the police. 'I knew the rest of them had to go, too.'

He went upstairs to the small attic room where Jenna slept in her pink-painted crib. He had spent hours on that crib himself, sanding it and decorating it. Just above Jenna's slumbering curls there was a transfer of a grinning burro, wearing a straw hat.

John Frederick Walters was glad that Jenna had gone to sleep again. He doubted if he would have been able to kill her if she was crying. He leaned over her crib, kissed her, and then pressed a pillow against her face for what seemed like a half-hour. It was probably only five or ten minutes, but it was enough. Jenna May Walters died of asphyxiation, aged 179 days.

Alice was the last. Alice, too, was asleep, and all she said when he softly opened the collar of her nightdress and held the razor-blade against the side of her throat was, 'What time is it?' Then the sheets were stained with ever-widening darkness.

The police stopped him on Anthony Boulevard, trudging north. His fingers were stuck together with dried blood. They held him up against the car while they searched him, and then they sat him down on the curb and subjected him to an impromptu interrogation. He admitted murdering his family, and offered to take them back to Number 8 so that they could see for themselves. They sat him on two spread-out sheets of week-old newspaper in the back of the car, and drove him south again.

Under the emergency powers granted to the Indiana police during the state of national crisis, patrolmen were permitted in what they considered to be 'extreme circumstances' to administer summary justice and execution. The two patrolmen who had picked up John Frederick Walters were in little doubt that the homicides at Number 8 were (as they later put it) 'extreme in the extreme.'

At seventeen minutes past two on Friday morning, they asked him to kneel in the middle of his back lawn, which he did. They asked him if he had any last wishes, and he told them that he had one Lark left, in the living-room, next to the radio, and that he would appreciate the chance to smoke it. They conferred, and then said no, they didn't have time to watch him smoke a cigarette. Then one of the patrolmen lifted a .357 Python revolver and blew John Frederick Walters' brains into the peonies.

Just before he went to bed at dawn on Friday morning, the Vice-President was handed a lengthy and detailed medical report on the long-term effects of severe dietary deficiency in the United States. He was reminded that a moderately active male between thirty-five and sixty-five required 2900 calories a day; and that a woman between eighteen and fifty-five requires 2200. An estimate of available food supplies showed that even with careful conservation, and even with an intensive programme of agricultural revival,

315

there would be less than one quarter of the necessary calories available to each American man, woman, and child during the coming six months.

In practice, there would be far less. There was no question at all that 'approximately 85 million people' would have to go without food supplies altogether, and live off whatever they could scavenge. 'We are going to have to face up to the fact that the world's most technologically sophisticated society; a society capable of visiting the Moon; a society which only two weeks ago measured its anxieties in terms of breast-enlargements, jogging, psychological self-acceptance, and Howard Jarvis; is now going to have to accept the degrading spectacle of nearly a third of its citizens digging like hogs for roots.'

The report warned of rickets – a softening of the bones caused by a severe lack of vitamin D and calcium. 'This can lead to a bending of the bones under the weight of the body and the application of normal muscular pressure. Hence the bow-legged appearance of children suffering from malnutrition, and the flattening of their ribs, which can contract their chest cavity, so that their liver is pushed outward, causing the distinctive "pot-belly" of the underfed.' Rickets, the report continued, was also responsible for the high, square, intellectual-looking heads of starving children, along with their small-featured faces. Their teeth generally appeared late, and rotted away early.

Scurvy, or scorbutus, was another risk. Although it was very well known that scurvy was caused by a deficiency of vitamin C, and although in normal times it could rapidly and easily be cured, there was now a danger that many Americans would have to go without fresh fruit and vegetables for anything up to six months, and that would leave them 'wide open' to infection. The symptoms included bleeding gums, stinking breath, extravasations of blood in the skin, and even bleeding from the eyes, nose and anus. Scurvy patients were liable to suffer anaemia, agonising ulcers on their arms and legs, and, if they were still untreated, exhaustion, chronic diarrhoea, and fatal failure of the lungs or kidneys.

The medical report remarked that 'the United States is

now inevitably entering a period of disease and death that can only be described as medieval.'

At 6.35 a.m., the Vice-President took two sleeping-pills and went to bed on a cot in the small room adjoining the Oval Office. He asked to be woken at 10.35 a.m. precisely.

Through the bullet-proof glass of the White House windows, with their unreal submarine tint, he was unable to hear the brief rattles of heavy machine-gun fire over by the Arlington Memorial Bridge.

Eleven

Season Hardesty opened her eyes and tried to focus. She had taken three of Vee's little green pills last night, and her vision was blurred, like five melted varieties of ice cream. Then the pink blurs resolved themselves into price tags, and the white blurs resolved themselves into empty super-market shelves, and the yellow blurs became posters, advertising six-packs of Ale-8-One.

Season lifted the blanket. Next to her, cocooned in a large blue bath-towel, Sally was still sleeping, her thumb poised a half-inch away from her open mouth. Ever since they had left Kansas, Sally had taken up sucking her thumb again, and no amount of nagging or cajoling had been able to stop her. She never said out loud that she missed her Daddy, but there was something in her eyes which Season couldn't fail to recognise.

She sat up. All around her, people were huddled in blankets and towels and even sheets of cardboard. The early sunlight was sloping through the small high windows of the supermarket so that it looked like the nave of a church; and since it was now the sanctuary of the Church of the Practical Miracle of Los Angeles, Inc., the holy atmosphere was appropriate. There were 120 people here – men, women, and children – the majority of them from Granger Hughes's congregation, although Mike Bull and his staff had managed to bring in most of their immediate families too.

Season had resisted coming to the Hughes market on Highland until the last possible moment. The pain and humiliation she had suffered at the hands of Oxnard and his Angels had enraged her, disoriented her, and frightened her more than she could have considered possible. She wondered if she would ever be able to carry on a normal relationship with a man again. She could hardly speak to Granger, and even Carl unsettled her. Every time he put his arm around her to reassure her, she thought *what does he want*?

If there had been no famine crisis, she would have immediately sought the guidance of Vee's analyst, and tried to learn to live with the shock of her experience by joining a post-rape encounter group. The irony was that she had been discussing the subject on Monday with a woman who lived across the road in Topanga Canyon. The woman's daughter had been raped at the age of fifteen by two blacks, out at Griffith Park, and it had taken her three years of intensive and argumentative therapy to make her understand that she herself hadn't been to blame. These days, though, the girl carried a .38 in her pocketbook.

It was a brushfire, high up on Woodland Hills, between Ventura Boulevard and Mulholland Drive, that at last changed Season's mind about staying in the house. It had probably been started by someone's house burning, although under normal circumstances the fire department would almost certainly have been able to catch it before it spread to the surrounding hills. Now there was no fire department, and by early evening, with a dry north-easterly wind blowing, the sky over Los Encinos Park and all the woods around was dark with smoke. Carl had gone up to Season's bedroom, where Season had been lying on her bed in a fetal position, with a half-empty bottle of Old Grandad beside her, and said, 'Can you smell that? That's smoke. The whole canyon's alight, and we're going to have to move.'

Season hadn't looked at him. 'Do we *have* to throw in our lot with Granger Hughes?' she asked. 'Is that really necessary? Can't we make a run for it on our own?'

Carl had shaken his head. 'We wouldn't stay alive for

318

twelve hours, not on our own. It's wolf-pack time, out in the open. Come on, Season, I think I understand something of what you're feeling. I understand how violated you feel. But there's nobody around you now who wishes you anything but warmth and healing.'

Season had sat up, and scratched her blonde hair with both hands. 'I guess the worse thing was that I had a revelation. I suddenly realised that all men who enter a woman's body by force, or by blackmail, or by any means apart from love and consent, are rapists. Criminal intruders. Unfortunately, the law in California says that you're only trespassing when seventy five per cent of your body is inside of someone's premises, so I guess that lets rapists out.'

'Season,' Carl had warned her.

'I know,' Season had nodded. 'This isn't going to do me any good. But what the hell is?'

She had sniffed, and smelled smoke. 'Is the canyon really burning?'

'It's burning. We're all packed up, and ready to leave.'

'Is Sally dressed?'

'She's all ready. Come on, Season, this is the only way.'

Season had stood up. 'I guess,' she agreed, clutching herself closely, as if a window had suddenly swung open, and chilled her in an unexpected breeze.

Now, here they were in the Hughes supermarket, along with 116 other people, all strangers; along with two toilets, two washbasins, 1440 cakes of shower soap, twenty-eight cases of assorted toothpaste, and more family-sized detergents than Season had seen together in one place in her life. Since Wednesday night, Mike Bull had been working out on his office calculator an optimum practical diet for his 120 charges – a diet which would give each of them as varied and healthful an intake of food as possible – and yet which would eke out the supplies in the supermarket's stockroom for the longest time. The electricity supply was out, and so they had been forced to throw away all their chilled meat, frozen vegetables, and fish. And Mike Bull had spent an arduous two days sorting through every single container of canned foods, setting

319

aside every one of them which had been packed in the last twenty-one days. Unlike Ed, however, he didn't open them up and dump them. He labelled them clearly SUSPECT and shifted them out of sight. He reckoned that a time could well come when people were going to be hungry enough to take the risk of contracting botulism, especially if they were going to die of starvation anyway.

Tony, Mike's under-manager, had been put in charge of security. In the early part of the week, there had been a temporary police encampment on the dusty triangle of asphalt just opposite, where Franklin and Highland intersected. There had been two patrol cars, a machine-gun emplacement with sandbags, and a couple of roving motorcyclists; and although they had been positioned there to intercept looters who were trying to escape north on to the Hollywood Freeway, their presence had kept scavengers and looters well away from the battered supermarket.

Now, however, the police had been pulled back to headquarters, and the post was deserted. The looters were back, in vicious little droves of a dozen at a time. Tony had barricaded the rear exit doors with piles of wooden pallets, snopping carts, and stockroom junk. Even if the looters managed to break the locked steel-and-glass doors, they would be caught in a ceiling-high tangle of metal banding and splintered wood that would catch them as effectively as barbed wire.

The front doors, already cracked and broken from Sunday night's rioting, had been locked, and then the steel railings which separated the checkout desks had been unscrewed from their original positions, and slotted through the door-handles to prevent anyone from pushing them open.

Tony had cleared an area of five or six feet in front of the doors, and this was his 'no-go' zone. Anyone who managed to break into the supermarket as far as this would find themselves in a crossfire between Tony, with a .22 target pistol, and Gina's uncle, with a scatter-gun. That was all the firepower they had, since not one of the congregation of the Church of the Practical Miracle had brought a gun, or even owned one. Carl had a .38, which he had kept to scare off burglars, but only one round of ammunition. Tony had grinned, and slapped him on the back, and told him, 'make every shot count, huh?'

That Friday morning, one by one, the people lying on the supermarket floor in their blankets were waking up. They stretched and yawned and blinked at each other, and in every face Season saw that moment of waking realisation – *Oh, I'm not at home, in my own bed. I'm here, in this besieged community of fellow refugees.* She also sensed a distinct atmosphere of growing hostility between the people here, a resentment at being cooped up in awkward and embarrassing contact. Before the famine, most of the members of the church had been enthusiastic about Practical Miracles because the notion was innovative, fun, and always proved to be a conversation-stopper. 'You actually *believe* in miracles?' their dinner hostesses would say. 'You can walk on water, that kind of thing?' And they would answer, 'Well, it's been done before. No reason why it shouldn't be done again.' They hadn't joined the church because they were passionate and like-minded believers. They'd joined it because it was fashionable, and cute, and now the shallowness of their Christianity was beginning to show. There had been fierce arguments on the morning bathroom line already, 'Christ – you've taken hours – and now the whole john *stinks*!' There had been wrangles over privacy, 'Are you staring at my wife, buddy?' And, inevitably, there had been petty jealousies over rations, 'How come that guy has two tomatoes and we only have the one?'

Granger Hughes, however, was untouched by his followers' materialistic squabbling. If anything, the siege in the supermarket had made him even more spiritual than before. That morning, as everybody awoke, he walked up and down the aisles in a white cotton kaftan, his hands extended, nodding to each of his disciples and blessing their day. As he came to the end of the one-time canned vegetable counter, where Season was sitting up against the wall, watching over Sally, he paused, and stood above her, with the sun gilding his hair like a California halo.

'Are you all right?' he asked her.

'As well as can be expected,' answered Season. 'This isn't

exactly the Beverly Hills Hotel.'

'The Beverly Hills Hotel is a smoking ruin,' said Granger. 'It was raided on Thursday night, and two famous actresses were raped and tortured to death. So just be glad that this *isn't* the Beverly Hills Hotel.'

'What's it like outside?' asked Season.

'The looters are still there, waiting for us to weaken. But we won't weaken, of course. Mike Bull calculates that we have a good five months of food in here, and I can tell you that we'll still be eating meat and fruit while those looters out there die of starvation and disease.'

Season looked up at him narrowly. 'You still think we're chosen, don't you? You still think we deserve to live while those people out there all deserve to die.'

Granger smiled. 'It is not for me to question the ways of God. God has decided many times before to test the spiritual and moral strength of his creation – with fires, and floods, and plagues. Now we have famine. Don't you think, after all, that a famine is a fitting test for a nation that for decades has surfeited itself on steak, and candies, and sheer fat? This country has been so gluttonous that police chiefs have been forced to cut the pay of their officers if they don't lose weight; and did you hear that they had to campaign against obesity amongst students at the Oral Roberts University? America has been a nation of pigs for too long, out of sheer greed, and God has seen fit to punish us for it. Only those who have faith in the practicality of his Word will be saved.'

'I don't believe in the practicality of his Word. Why should I be saved?'

'Because you are one of my loved ones; and, in time, I know that you will come to understand that what I say is true.'

'It's not what you say that concerns me,' said Season. 'It's what you do.'

Granger raised a hand, and said, 'O Lord, thou hast brought up my soul from the grave: thou hast kept me alive, that I should not go down to the pit. Sing unto the Lord: for his anger endureth but a moment: weeping may endure for a night, but joy cometh in the morning.'

'What's that?' asked Season. 'A prayer for everlasting sexual licence? Cry tonight, but get your rocks off tomorrow?'

Granger slowly shook his head from side to side. 'You're so resentful, aren't you? So angry. But there isn't any need to be. You should feel happiness, that the Lord has protected you in this country's terrible time of trouble. You should feel content. You should forget the past and consider the happiness of tomorrow.'

'I don't think I'll ever forget those Hell's Angels,' whispered Season. 'And I don't think I'll ever forget you.' There was venom in her voice, undiluted, and crackling with hostility. Granger flinched, as if she had spat at him.

'I think I have other people to talk to,' he said, rubbing his cheek slowly with the back of his hand. 'You'll forgive me?'

It was an unfortunate choice of words. But Season didn't retaliate any more. She simply turned away, and left Granger standing there, uncertain and irritated. After a while, he resumed his beatific smile, and continued on down the bottled fruit shelves, blessing his uncomfortable flock, and wishing them a safe and prosperous day.

By noon on Friday, they had reached the outskirts of Liberal, Kansas, only a few miles from the Oklahoma line. Ed pulled the Chevy wagon in to the side of the dusty highway, and wiped the sweat from his face. Behind the Chevy, the small untidy convoy of cars and wagons pulled up at the side of the road, too, and out climbed farmworkers and their wives and children, stretching themselves and lighting cigarettes and rubbing their faces with towels and handkerchiefs.

Della, sitting next to Ed, laid her hand on his arm and said, 'How are you feeling? Are you okay?'

Ed nodded. 'I think so. Just tired, that's all.'

'Do you want me to drive?' asked Peter Kaiser, from the back.

'Later, yes,' said Ed. 'We hit sixty-six at Tucumcari, New Mexico; and I want to keep us driving through New Mexico at night. You can take over then.'

Shearson, wedged in a corner, bejewelled with beads of sweat like a Chinese Buddah, said, 'Is there any danger of getting anything to eat at this juncture? It is lunchtime, you know.'

Ed glanced at the clock on the dash. 'We'll stop to eat once we're out of Kansas. You can have a swig of water if you like.'

'Dear God for an ice-cold martini and a basket of cold pheasant,' murmured Shearson.

Without turning around, Ed said, 'Senator – if you're going to talk food all the way to Los Angeles – you'd better get out now. The situation's bad enough without you adding your frustrated gourmet fantasies to it.'

'I shall remember you, Hardesty, when all of this is over,' Shearson growled. 'I shall remember you as the only man alive who ever managed to force me to diet. Not even my doctor could make me give up oysters Rockefeller; but you did. I shall have your entrails one of these days.'

'On toast?' asked Della. 'Or *à la mode?*'

Lennie Merritt, one of the stockhands, came walking up to Ed's wagon, brushing the flies away from his face.

'Mr Hardesty?' he asked.

'What is it, Lennie?'

'My little boy Peter's real sick back there. Brought up his breakfast, and won't take nothing but sips of water. I've talked to my wife, sir, and the Billingtons, who are riding in there with us, and I'm afraid we've decided to pull out of the convoy and stay here for a while. My wife has an aunt in Dodge City, and we reckoned on travelling back up there.'

Ed looked down at the man's pinched, sweaty face, his eyes squinting against the glare of the sun. He looked like one of those labourers in those A. B. Frost paintings that Season was always going on about.

'You know how risky it's going to be, out on your own?' he asked Merritt. He didn't really have to put that question; he asked it more for the sake of his own conscience than to dissuade Merritt from going.

Merritt, of course, nodded. Nobody could have failed to miss the carcasses of burned-out trucks and cars that were strewn along the highway; or driven through abandoned communities like Greensburg and Minneola, where boarded-up houses and looted stores were now visited only by family dogs, fiercely hungry and scavenging for food, without realising how dangerous the countryside had become.

'All right,' said Ed. 'Give my love to your wife, and take a whole lot of care. You understand?'

'Yes, sir,' said Merritt. 'And Mr Hardesty, sir?'

'Yes?'

Lennie Merritt dropped his gaze. 'I just want to say that I'm sure sorry we never got the time to work the farm out the way we should have done. I think you would have made a real good boss.'

'Thanks, Lennie,' said Ed, and sat silent for a long time as the man trudged slowly back to his dusty green car.

'Are we going to move on?' asked Shearson Jones. 'Or are we going to sit here in this heat until we melt into pools of human grease?'

'You speak for yourself, Senator,' said Karen, from the tail compartment, where she was sitting amongst hurriedly-stacked cans of corned beef and carrots and peas, and two large polythene containers of water, which sloshed loudly as they drove along.

'It's okay,' said Ed. 'We're leaving.'

He blew the horn three times, waved his arm out of the window, and the farmworkers hurried back to their cars and started up their motors.

'You should have been on *Wagon Train*,' said Shearson, sarcastically.

'You should have been on *The Gang Show*,' retorted Karen.

'You're fired,' said Shearson.

'No way,' Karen told him. 'I quit your employ the night I found out about the Blight Crisis Appeal.'

Shearson tugged his shirt out of his waistband, and used it to wipe the sweat away from his neck. 'I don't know which irritates me more,' he remarked. 'Perspiration, or *naïveté*.'

Ed listened to this bickering without comment. He was still thinking about last night, and their hectic escape from the South Burlington Farm. In his mind's eye, as he drove along the uneven blacktop to Liberal, he could see the roof of the old farmhouse flaring up, and the bedroom drapes flapping and flying from the windows like fiery wings.

After their first attack the raiders had eased off their gunfire for an hour or two; and at one time Ed was convinced that they must have retreated. Maybe one or two of them had been hit by shotgun blasts. Maybe they had decided that besieging the farm wasn't worth the hassle, just for a few supplies. But shortly before dawn, the garages and stables across the yard had suddenly burst into flames, and Ed had realised that the raiders had been doing nothing more than regrouping and planning a final assault.

Fortunately, Ed had been almost ready to pull out by then. The two hours of ceasefire had enabled him to assign twelve men to loading the cars and the wagons, and the convoy was only short of a couple of cases of canned fruit when the raiders attacked in force. All the farmworkers and their families has scrambled into their vehicles, and they had driven out of the farmyard without lights, letting off shotgun blasts in all directions in a racketing parade, like Chinese New Year.

It had all been over in a few seconds. There had been a light, inaccurate spray of sub-machine gun fire in retaliation, which had broken the side window of the last car in the convoy, but that had been all. It was only a mile to the front entrance of South Burlington Farm, and even a heavily-laden wagon driving at forty mph can cover a mile in one and a half minutes.

What had hurt Ed more than anything else, though, had been the sight in his rear-view mirror of the farmhouse, blazing from verandah to roof like a galleon burning at sea. He had been brought up in that house; and apart from the family treasures stored in the attic, the old Hardesty photograph albums dating back to Edwardian days, there were a thousand memories in that house for Ed, from the strange patterns that were cast on the wall by the tiny stained-glass window on the upstairs landing, to the last rail on the back verandah, which he had worn smooth as a boy from riding as his pretend horse. It was like watching his whole childhood burn, the whole reason for his coming back from New York and setting up as a farmer. And as he turned out of the farm entrance, and drove into the darkness, he knew just why ordinary mortals should stay well out of politics and power, and never try to cross men like Senator Shearson Jones.

Liberal, Kansas, was deserted as they drove through. A gas station on the outskirts was still smouldering, and there were dead bodies lying on the forecourt, clouded in flies. They drove on, and crossed the state line into Oklahoma at 12.55 p.m.

Occasionally, they picked up random CB messages. But it was clear that most CB channels had been taken over by marauding groups of looters, and when Ed tried appealing to 'Blue Lightning' for advice on highway conditions through New Mexico, there was a suspicious silence, followed by the enquiry, 'Where are you? Where you headed? You got any food with you?'

Ed had shut off the CB and glanced across at Della. Della had shrugged, and said, 'We're on our own. I guess we just have to realise that.'

It took the convoy three hours to cross the Oklahoma panhandle, stopping to open cans of corned beef just beyond Optima. Ed appointed two of his farmworkers as lookouts, but there was nothing to be seen but dust and sun. At a few minutes before four o'clock, they crossed into Texas at Texhoma, and started the 120-mile diagonal trek across the north-west tip of the panhandle.

A few miles into New Mexico, the Mercury Marquis started blowing steam and ground to a halt. The convoy stopped under a sky the colour of violet cachous while one of South Burlington's mechanics took a look under the hood. Ed stood by, smoking a cigarette, his dark hair ruffled by the warm evening wind. One of the children, a boy of five in a grubby yellow T-shirt, was sitting a few feet away, his face still dirty with tears, watching Ed solemnly.

Della came up, holding the pump-gun in the crook of her arm. She stood silently beside him for a while, and then she

327

said, 'It wasn't your fault you know, all of this. Whatever you'd said on television, it wouldn't have made any difference. You understand that, don't you?'

'I don't know,' said Ed. 'Right now, I'm too tired to think about it.'

'You're worried about your wife?'

He nodded. 'I keep worrying about everybody else's wives and families, too.'

'It wasn't your fault. Don't you see that? This famine was going to happen whether you announced it on prime-time television or not.'

'I guess you're right. The sick thing is that somebody started it deliberately. The blight, and the radiation, and the food poisoning. And, brother, didn't they make sure they got to every source of food you could think of. Crops, grain, canned foods, frozen foods, you name it. I mean, we're checking every damned can for pinholes, but supposing we miss one?'

Della said, 'Maybe we deserved it. The famine, I mean.'

Ed looked at her. 'I hope you're kidding,' he said. 'Because whatever the politicians get up to, no kid deserves to be sitting on that rock like that kid over there, with no food and no secure future, when he should be home having his supper and getting ready for bed.'

'You think the Russians did this?' asked Della.

'I don't know who the hell did it. I'm not sure that I care. All I know is that the whole thing is totally squalid, totally underhand, and if I could lay my hands on just one of the people responsible, I'd screw their head off.'

Della shielded her eyes, and looked up at the dark purple sky, and the birds which circled above them with tireless patience.

'It's like the end of the world,' she said, quietly.

Ed's mechanics managed to get the Mercury to limp at fifteen mph as far as Tucumcari. There, its cooling system gave out completely, and the seven people who had been riding in it stood around like relatives at a funeral while Dyson Kane poked inside the steamy hood again, and pronounced it dead.

'We just don't have the spares,' he said. 'And it looks like

328

the whole engine's been damaged beyond repair. I'm afraid it's RIP.'

Ed and Dyson left everybody beside the highway while they drove around Tucumcari, looking for abandoned cars or wagons. They found three, but all three of them were wrecked, or had wheels missing. There was only one reasonable-looking vehicle in the whole place, a shiny 1968 Cadillac parked outside an odd asbestos and corrugated-iron house in a sloping street with a view of Tucumcari Peak. It was almost dark now, and they were getting desperate.

Dyson jumped down from the Chevy and quickly crossed the street to where the Cadillac was parked.

'It's locked,' he called, trying the handle. 'Maybe I can open it up with a length of wire.'

Ed looked around the untidy interior of the wagon. There was a wire coat-hanger in back, and he leaned over the seat to reach for it. He heard a snap, like someone slamming a book shut, and at first he thought it was his seat mounting, clicking into place. But then he looked up and saw Dyson huddled up on the road beside the Cadillac, with a dark river of blood already sliding across the dusty blacktop from a wound in his head.

Ed immediately ducked low in his seat, and reached for his automatic. He couldn't find it. Either it had slid backwards into the garbage on the floor, or someone had taken it. Peter Kaiser, maybe, when he wasn't looking? There was another snap, and a high-powered bullet pinged off the hub of the offside front wheel.

Inch by inch, Ed raised his head, until his eyes appeared over the sill of the Chevy's window. It was impossible to see where the shooting was coming from, although he guessed the sniper was concealed in the old asbestos house. He could hardly see Dyson now, in the gloom of the evening, but there wasn't any question at all that he was dead. Half of his head was lying on the road.

Ed started up the Chevy's engine, released the parking-brake, and slowly rolled away down the street, keeping his head down behind the door. Only when he was well around the corner did he sit up straight, and drive with howling tyres back to the highway, where the rest of the convoy were waiting.

'Where's Dyson?' asked Della, as Ed stepped down. 'Did he get us a car?'

'He's dead,' said Ed. 'There's a sniper in one of the houses back there – hit him when he was trying to open a car door.'

'A sniper?' asked one of the farmhands, a tough little Nebraskan in faded overalls. 'Then what are we waiting for? Let's go smoke him out!'

Ed shook his head. 'There's no point. He'd probably pick off two or three of us before we could get anyplace near him. I don't want anybody else dead, and that's it. It's serious enough, losing Dyson.'

'What are we going to do about a car?' asked a pale-faced woman, holding a sleeping two-year-old in her arms.

'Well, we have a choice,' said Ed. 'Either you seven find somewhere to bed down for the night, and we'll go on ahead and see if we can't find another car for you, and send someone back with it; or else you can squeeze into the vehicles we have left.'

The woman said, 'Mr Hardesty, I'd rather stay. We've been travelling all day, we're exhausted. And, besides, if we leave now, we're going to have to abandon all of our food, and I don't think we ought to do that.'

'She's right,' said her husband. 'Who knows when we're going to find anything else to eat? We can't afford to abandon fifty or sixty cans of meat. It could keep us alive for weeks.'

Ed looked around at the other workers who had been travelling in the broken-down Mercury. Old Mrs Tilsley, who had given him fresh-baked cookies from her cottage window-sill when he was young, leaning on the arm of her grandson, Keith Perks; Henry and Susan Carlsson, who had come to work at South Burlington after their own farm in Dighton had gone bankrupt.

God, he thought, it had been easy enough to accept responsibility for these people when he had been threatening Senator Jones with his automatic. But now they were looking to him to guide them through the worst disaster of their whole lives; and he wasn't at all sure he was strong enough or even willing enough. He had left his own mother behind someplace. There hadn't been time to go look for her. And apart from his mother, there were Season and Sally, in Los Angeles, who might even be dead for all he knew; and Jack Marowitz, and Willard Noakes, and Dyson Kane, who had all been butchered; and the Muldoon brothers, who had been doing nothing at all but their job. And everybody else across the breadth of the United States who had died in the riots and the looting that had followed his sanctimonious revelation of Shearson's little bit of business on the side.

If I'd just been adult enough to keep my mouth shut, he thought, then maybe the President would have had time to cope with the situation as it broke. If I'd thought the whole thing through before I started shooting my mouth off. If only Shearson hadn't asked me to be his 'representative farmer.'

He said, quietly, 'You're sure you're prepared to stay? We'll send a car back just as soon as we find one.'

'We'll stay,' said Henry Carlsson, in a firm voice. 'I don't expect there'll be a whole lot of danger around here. It looks like everything's been pretty thoroughly looted in any case.'

'All right, then,' said Ed. 'The rest of us will move on. Do you need extra shotgun cartridges, anything like that?'

'We'll manage,' Henry Carlsson assured him.

So, twenty minutes later, the depleted convoy drove off into the darkness, leaving seven people behind them. Ed glanced in his rearview mirror and saw them signal a quick goodbye with a flashlight.

In the back of the wagon, Shearson Jones said, 'I could happily get myself outside of a *filet de boeuf en croute* with Perigourdine sauce. Do you know that's a speciality of the Maisonette restaurant, on East Sixth Street, in Cincinnati, of all places? They also do an excellent trout, stuffed with crab.'

Ed said, 'I warned you, senator. One more word about food, and you're going to be hitch-hiking your way to California.'

As they headed through the hills towards Albuquerque, Peter Kaiser asked, 'Do you want me to take over the wheel now? I'd be happy to.'

Ed rubbed his eyes. 'I'm not sure if I can trust you yet, Mr Kaiser.'

'Well, maybe you can't,' said Peter, 'but you can't stay awake all night. You're going to have to sleep sometime.'

Della said, 'He's right, Ed. I can keep an eye on him.'

'Okay,' Ed agreed. 'But there's just one thing.'

'Oh, yes?'

He reached his hand backwards from the driving-seat, and said, 'You can give me my gun back, okay?'

'Your gun?' queried Peter Kaiser. 'I don't have your gun.'

'You're trying to tell me you didn't sneak it out from under my seat when we were driving along?'

'Of course I didn't. What are you talking about? Do you want to search me?'

Ed turned around in his seat. 'What about you, Senator? Do you have it?'

Shearson gave a small, contemptuous shake of his head which clearly implied that he didn't have time for weapons. His weapon was his political influence.

'All right,' said Ed, flicking on his turn signal and drawing into the side of the road. 'You can drive for a while. Three hours, straight down sixty-six; and don't stop for anybody or anything, unless you see an abandoned car in good shape that we can send back to the Carlssons.'

Peter Kaiser heaved himself up into the driver's seat, while Ed squeezed himself into the back seat next to Shearson Jones.

'I'd appreciate it if you'd resist the temptation to rest your head on my stomach while you sleep,' said Shearson.

'I think I can manage that,' Ed replied, and bundled up a towel to make himself a pillow.

As Peter Kaiser drove the wagon through the night, Ed lay awake, exhausted but unable to sleep. The shock of Dyson Kane's death on the streets of Tucumcari began to make him tremble, as if someone was shaking him to make

332

him understand something – shaking him and shaking him and refusing to let up.

He dozed for minutes at a time, and dreams danced in front of his eyes like some kind of grotesque carnival. The house at South Burlington, flaring up; Willard Noakes, collapsing into the darkness; and Dyson Kane lying on the roadway, his blood sprayed everywhere, only it wasn't blood at all, but a pattern cut out of coloured paper, and when Ed walked towards him, Dyson turned his face around towards him and grinned a disturbing, idiot grin . . .

As dawn began to rise through the Zuni Mountains behind them, they came across an abandoned white Pontiac, one of its doors still open, and its keys still in the ignition. There was no sign of the driver. Young Dave Morton, Olaf Morton's son, volunteered to drive it back to Tucumcari and pick up the seven people they had left behind.

Ed, pale-faced, unshaved, frowzy with sleep, said, 'You take care now, do you understand? If anything goes wrong, you come speeding back to join us. We'll take it slow from here, and wait for you two hours at Lake Havasu. Then we're going on, whether you've caught up with us or not.'

'Yes, sir,' said Dave, his eyes hidden behind mirror sunglasses. Then he U-turned the Pontiac around, and sped off east.

'Okay,' said Ed. 'Let's press on.'

Shearson put in, 'There's no chance of breakfast, I suppose. The merest *soupçon* of canned pork roll?'

'I see your tastes are beginning to adapt,' Ed told him, climbing back into the wagon. 'We'll have you dreaming of M&Ms before the day's out.'

Twelve

Saturday was the first day of the final collapse of American society. Millions of people, most of them used to two or three substantial meals a day, now hadn't eaten properly for three days. They were still strong enough to resist opening cans suspected of containing botulism, but few were so fussy about foods that might have been irradiated by cobalt-60. They were so convinced that 'something would turn up', and that they wouldn't have to survive on contaminated rations for more than a few days that they decided to risk it.

Something might have turned up, if the looting and the burning hadn't inflicted such grievous damage on the cities and the towns and the countryside, and if the National Guard and the Army had been able to devote their energies to distributing food and organising new crop programmes. But hunger and fear had broken down everything that had held the United States together. Brotherhood, *E Pluribus Unum*, had been a luxury that only affluence had been able to sustain. Now, each racial and ethnic and class community turned in on itself for protection, and within days the nation was tribalised.

On Saturday afternoon, declaring New York State a War Zone – the ninth state in two days – the Vice-President said that 'twenty years of Civil Rights struggle had vanished in twenty minutes, as if it had never been.' He added that 'those people who are dying today are showing us that John Kennedy and Martin Luther King died in vain.'

Although interstate communications were now severely disrupted, and it was impossible to make an accurate count, it was estimated by the besieged Department of Health that somewhere between two and three thousand Americans died of botulism during Friday night.

Worse – hunger was beginning to affect the morale of the armed forces. Men of the 101st Airborne division, based at

Fort Campbell, Kentucky, refused to go to the assistance of beleagured National Guardsmen in Lexington until they were issued with rations. Deserters walked off camps and air bases in their hundreds, many taking their weapons with them. Five men of the 3rd Armoured Cavalry Regiment were shot at Fort Bliss, Texas, for attempting to hijack a tank.

Flying across Illinois in a private plane, with special permission from the Air Force, Dan Rather broadcast one of the most moving reports of the whole famine. He talked about, 'Acre upon acre of blackened fields . . . with grey smoke rising everywhere, like the fires of a primitive, prehistoric age . . .' He was in tears as he finished his report with a prayer for the future.

The President, weak but improving, was released on Saturday evening from hospital. After he was briefed by his advisers on the national famine situation, and on the prospects of expediting aid from other countries, he asked about the freight train of supplies that was supposed to have come into Washington to help support the administration.

He was told gravely that it had been attacked by vigilantes, and burned. Bill Brinsky of *The New York Times* had appeared on television Wednesday night, and revealed 'exclusively' that the White House had arranged to feed top officials from secret stores of food, just as Ed Hardesty had claimed. As a result, angry mobs of black looters had raided each of the warehouses where government food was stored, and destroyed it or carried it off. 'Perhaps our only consolation is that we didn't have time to check the food for botulism or radiation,' said the Vice-President.

'You call that a consolation?' asked the President, with tired but offended dignity. 'The very least of our countrymen doesn't deserve to die like a rat.'

The President's economic adviser said later, 'The President always finds it easier to be expansive when the worst has already come to the worst. By God, if he'd heard Bill Brinsky's broadcast for himself, he probably would have had a heart seizure.'

During that first briefing, one report from the Pentagon

went unnoticed. It lay on the President's desk amongst a whole sheaf of papers on disease and medical treatment. It said, simply, 'We are seriously concerned at this time about the preparedness of the United States to defend itself against pre-emptive military strikes from hostiles.'

The President was too tired, too confused, too hopeless, to read it and realise what it really meant.

Thirteen

By first light on Sunday morning, the mob around the Hughes Supermarket had swelled to five or six hundred people. Season, unable to sleep, had been watching them gather. They were Hollywood suburbanites mostly — ordinary men and women who lived in the quiet small houses on Yucca Avenue and Orange Grove Avenue and Oporto Drive. They hadn't shouted or screamed or made much of a noise as they assembled around the fires of broken boxes and pieces of timber that had kept them warm during the night. But their very quietness had been menacing. They were people whose ordinary comfortable lifestyles had been abruptly taken away from them in the space of a few frightening days and now they wanted a share of what was left. They had already torn down the wooden cross that Granger Hughes had erected by the newspaper machines on the sidewalk and burned it. Now, in the grey haze of dawn, they surrounded the building in their chequered golf pants and their Bermuda shorts and their canary-yellow suntops, plain people who believed they had a right to survive.

Granger Hughes, in his white kaftan, came up to join Season at the window.

'Pretty frightening, isn't it?' asked Season.

Granger shielded his eyes against the reflections in the glass. 'No,' he said at last, 'I don't think it's frightening. They're all part of God's flock, just as we are.'

'If you think that, why are all of your friends sitting on all of this food, and why are we keeping them out?'

'Someone has to carry on the Word,' replied Granger. 'Someone has to stay alive to keep the Lord's teachings alive in the new world that must follow.'

Season looked at him for a while. Then she said hesitantly, 'Granger? Are you sure you're okay?'

'Okay? Why shouldn't I be?'

'I don't know. I didn't mean any offence. It's just that you've been acting kind of – I don't know, spaced out.'

He stared at her, perplexed, but then he smiled. 'Well,' he said, in a voice that sounded more like the man she had first met, the man who had come around to Topanga Canyon to make love to her, 'it isn't often that an Old Testament situation actually happens for real, is it? I mean, this is a real Biblical workout for anybody's faith. What next? Locusts? Seven fat kine, seven lean kine? Plague?'

Season turned and looked out at the silent crowds of people. The sun was up now, and they had let their fires burn down. They stood like ghosts of American suburbia amidst the drifting smoke. There was movement amongst them – shuffling, and rippling, as if they were trying to summon up enough courage to make a rush for the front of the supermarket.

'I don't know about tests of faith,' Season whispered. 'All I know is that I've never been so frightened in my life.'

Mike Bull came up, rolling up his shirtsleeves. He was already growing the beginnings of a beard.

'That crowd's looking pretty threatening to me,' he said to Granger, pressing his face to the window. 'I shouldn't be surprised if they try breaking in.'

'Couldn't we try throwing them out a few cans of food?' asked Season. 'Wouldn't that show them we meant well?'

Mike Bull shook his head. 'If they think we've got food to spare, just to keep them at bay, that'll only get them worked up even more. Besides, we don't want to help to prolong their stamina, do we? – not even for one day. Give them two, three days, they'll be weak as kittens, Then, if we've managed to keep them out, they'll either die, or they'll try someplace else.'

Sally, rubbing sleep from her eyes, came up and put her

337

arms around Season's waist. Season stroked her hair, and then bent down and kissed her. 'I don't know,' she said. 'It just seems to me that for active church-members, everybody here is acting pretty damn uncharitable.'

Mike Bull said, 'Listen, lady – this might not seem like charity – but charity's no use at all unless it works. If we open the doors of this supermarket and let everybody in, our whole stock of food – five months of food – is going to be gone in five minutes. Tomorrow, we'll be hungry. Now, what's the point of that? Do you want to see your daughter starve? Do you want to see her ribs showing through her skin? Because if you do, that's the way to do it.'

'I'm not suggesting anything,' said Season, defensively. 'I don't want Sally to starve and I don't want to starve myself. But look at those people out there. They're just ordinary people, like all of us.'

'They didn't follow the Church of the Practical Miracle,' said Mike Bull, in a level voice. 'And *this*, to me, is the practical miracle, with the emphasis on practical. Our people surviving this famine, and coming out the other side.'

Season turned to Granger. 'I can see why your church was so popular,' she said, caustically. 'You were only interested in miracles that helped your unworthy little selves. Wholesome, capitalist, racially-selective, no-bussing, Proposition-thirteen, private-medicine-oriented miracles.'

'What are you talking about?' said Mike Bull. 'We let in Hispanics. We even let in blacks. Tony there – he's Italian – he was going to join.'

'I haven't seen any blacks or Hispanics here in the supermarket,' said Season.

Granger laid his hand on her shoulder. 'Regretfully, we couldn't contact everybody in time,' he said.

'Besides,' put in Mike Bull, 'what are you being so critical about? This church has saved your life, hasn't it? And your daughter's life? Just be thankful you're not out there with all of those hungry people!'

Season was about to say something sharp in reply, but she checked herself. Maybe she was just tired, and frayed, and depressed. Maybe she was sick of being imprisoned in this supermarket, sick of the lines for the washroom every morning, sick of the evening sing-songs and the daily arguments, sick of the whole way in which the Hughes Supermarket had become a microcosm of American small-town thinking – we're okay because we're in here with our food, buddy, and just you keep your distance.

Season was a smart, bright girl; a city girl. In the city, you learned how to be aggressive and you learned how to survive. But somehow, sitting on your own little pile of stuff wasn't what real survival was all about. Real survival was working things out with other people – taking the risk to relate. Amongst these smug, quasi-religious Californians, Season felt even more alienated than she had on South Burlington Farm.

'Granger,' she said. 'I'm sorry. I apologise. You offered to help me and I accepted your offer. I didn't have any right to slander your beliefs.'

But Granger didn't answer. Granger was looking at her with a bright, mesmerised glassiness in his eyes that made her involuntarily turn around, to see if there was someone standing behind her.

'Granger?' she repeated. Even Mike Bull frowned.

'You're right,' Granger said, in a hoarse, slow voice. 'You're absolutely right.'

'I'm right? What are you talking about?'

Granger raised his hand, two fingers extended, a gesture unnervingly reminiscent of Jesus.

'Those people out there – *they* deserve the benefits of our faith – *they* deserve the miracles – just as much as we do – '

'Granger,' said Mike, taking his arm. 'Why don't you come and have a cup of hot coffee, and maybe some cookies? I know Nan Marneweck just brewed up.'

'No, you misunderstand me,' breathed Granger. 'I'm being tested here. This is my test. This is how my faith is being put through its ultimate workout. Don't you see it? How God has spoken to me, through Season here? How God has arranged this whole situation, this entire interface, so that I can discover at last what practical miracles really are?'

'Granger, I don't know what the hell you're talking

about,' said Mike. 'I mean, really.'

'You don't remember John, chapter six, verse five, when the five thousand followed Jesus to the mountain, and Jesus said to Philip, *Whence shall we buy bread, that these may eat?*'

Mike Bull glanced outside at the restless crowds. 'Well, yes,' he said awkwardly, 'but the plain fact is that we just don't have enough.'

'That's it!' cried Granger, 'that's absolutely it! The gospel is repeating itself! I have said to you – how are we going to feed all those people out there – and you, like Philip, have said the modern equivalent of what Philip said, which was, *Two hundred pennyworth of bread is not sufficient for them, that every one of them may take a little.* But Jesus had asked Philip this question to test him, right? Because it's written in the Bible that Jesus *knew what he would do.*'

Mike Bull stared at Granger, face to face, for a long time. Granger was trembling, and there was white spittle at the corners of his mouth. 'Okay – sure,' said Mike, uncertainly. 'But what are *you* going to do?'

'A miracle,' said Granger. 'A contemporary, practical miracle. Maybe not the feeding of the five thousand, but certainly the feeding of the five hundred.'

'It can't work,' Mike Bull told him, with hushed earnestness. 'Granger, it just *can't work.*'

'Do you think Philip believed the miracle that Jesus performed would work? Of course he didn't. The only way that anybody can ever believe in a miracle is to see it happen in front of his eyes. Now, go to the stockroom and bring me five packs of that crispbread and two cans of tuna.'

'Granger – '

Granger seized the front of Mike Bull's shirt, not angrily, but with intense religious passion. 'It's what we *believe* in, Mike. It's what we actually *believe* in. And now's our chance to show that it can happen for real. We can work a miracle, Mike, just the way Jesus did. Others have done it. Others did it in Jesus's time, and Jesus didn't mind. He approved of it. We can work this miracle, and at the same time we can purge ourselves of all of our selfishness and our greed. Don't you understand me? This one act is going to be our salvation.'

Season said, 'Granger, if you go out there, they could very well kill you.'

Granger shook his head. 'No, no chance of that. I know whose voice comes out of your mouth, Season. You've tested me before. Tested me hard, when I thought that *I* was testing *you*. They won't hurt me, those people out there. Especially when they see what I'm bringing them. Especially when they clear up after they've eaten, and realise how much they've left over.'

He was exultant now, feverishly excited and unstoppable. 'Go, Mike,' he said. 'Go get the bread and the fish. And tell young Tony to make ready to open one of the doors, so that I can go out.'

Mike hesitated, but Granger repeated, '*Go*,' in such a quiet and beatific way that Mike found it impossible to resist him. He walked down the aisle to the stockroom, and came back a minute or two later with five packs of Kellogg's crispbread and two cans of Chicken of the Sea. Seven or eight of Granger's closest disciples had gathered around him now, wanting to know what was going on, and they watched in awe as Granger arranged the food in a supermarket basket and prepared to step outside.

'That mob sure looks unhappy,' remarked one of the men, a bald, sun-bronzed insurance salesman from the San Fernando Valley. 'I'm glad it's not me that's going out there.'

Granger laid a hand on his shoulder. 'You are about to witness a miracle, Doubting Thomas. When you see what happens, you'll wish more than anything else that you were me, and that God's generosity and kindness was flowing through you.'

The man made a *moue*, and said, 'Good luck, all the same.'

Tony was ready at the door, holding his .22 target pistol. As Granger came forward with his shopping basket under his arm, he said, 'You sure you want to go? If they try to attack you, I may not be able to let you back in.'

'Attack me?' smiled Granger. He touched Tony's head

341

with the sign of the cross. 'They will adore me – and I will bring them in here afterwards friendly and laughing. I doubted my faith until now – just as you doubt it now – but this is the test – this is the time.'

Season said to Mike Bull, 'Do you really think we ought to let him go? I don't know what's come over him. One minute he was trying to persuade me that God had chosen nobody else but us to survive . . . now he's risking his life to feed a whole mob of starving people with five packs of crispbread and two cans of tuna fish.'

'I don't see what we can do to stop him,' said Mike.

'But why does he even want to go?'

'I don't know. He's always been kind of changeable. You know, up one minute, down the next. But I think he's been worrying for days about letting other people go hungry while we're all holed up in here. He tried to justify it, tried to think his way round it, but I know that it made him feel guilty as all hell. I don't think you helped much, needling his faith all the time. I guess he thinks he's found a way to solve it now. He feeds everybody outside with a miracle, and that means we can keep the rest of the food in the stockroom with a clear conscience.'

Season watched Tony sliding back one of the metal bars from the door. 'Granger's so messed up,' she said. 'I thought he was so together. But he's so messed up.'

'He's been in analysis for ten years.'

Granger stood with one hand clasping his huge crucifix as Tony reached down and turned the key in the supermarket door. In his white kaftan, he looked thin, spiritual, and vulnerable, quite unlike the first time that Season had met him, and very unlike the day he had come around to see her alone at the house on Topanga Canyon. Outside, on Highland Avenue, she could see the crowds shifting and swaying in curiosity. She looked at their faces, and in a strange way their hunger and their fear had given them the same concentrated intensity that Granger was showing on his face. It was an extraordinary confrontation of utter need with utter faith.

Tony pulled open the door, and pushed Granger unceremoniously out on to the sidewalk. Then Tony locked

342

the door again, and barred it. He glanced across at Mike Bull with an expression that meant – I didn't want to, but what else could I do? Mike shrugged, and turned away. Mike wasn't yet ready to have his support for the Church of the Practical Miracle and what the church believed in tested to the limit. He wasn't yet ready to admit that he might have joined it because Mrs Linda Javits, divorcee, regular customer, and possible replacement for his dead wife Anne, was also a member. As it turned out, Mrs Javits hadn't answered when Mike had tried to call her and tell her that the congregation was assembling in the supermarket, and for all he knew, she could be just as dead as Anne. He hadn't told anybody, not even Tony, although Tony had noticed that he went into his office more often than usual, for a quick stiff shot of whisky.

Granger Hughes stood on the sidewalk outside the supermarket with the early-morning sunlight rising behind him. The cool breeze flapped his kaftan around his ankles. The crowd on the opposite side of the road stood silently and watched him.

Granger raised a hand. 'I have brought you food,' he said, in a clear voice, 'I have brought you sustenance enough for all.'

There was a restless murmuring in the crowd. One or two of them stepped forward, until they were only a few paces away from where Granger was standing.

'You should all be seated, as the five thousand were seated on the mountain,' called Granger. 'Then I will walk amongst you and distribute what I have brought.'

One of the men, with a pinched face and an orange floral shirt, said, 'What's that you got in the basket? Samples?'

'This is all I shall need,' said Granger, with great calm.

'Are you kidding?' asked another man.

Granger shook his head. 'You may not be able to believe it now, but if you seat yourselves on the ground, I shall pass amongst you and you will see for yourselves how much is here.'

'For chrissake,' said the man in the orange shirt.

'Yes!' said Granger. 'For Christ's sake!'

He walked towards them with his wire basket on his arm.

343

Season, watching him through the supermarket window, was holding her breath so tight that her heart was beating in long, slow bumps. She could hear Mike Bull behind her breathe, 'Oh, my God.'

Granger reached into his basket and took out one of the packets of Kellogg's crispbread, offering it to the man in the orange shirt. The gesture was so affectionate, and had such generous innocence, that Season had to close her eyes. However messed up Granger might have been – however eccentric and Californian his church – he was now offering food to the hungry in the sincere belief that God would help him to satisfy them.

The man in the orange shirt, unbelievably, actually took the crispbread and stared down at it as if he couldn't quite understand what it was. But then he hurled it away from him, and turned on Granger with a screech of frustrated rage that Season could hear clearly, even inside the barricaded market. The man grabbed hold of Granger's kaftan and ripped the back of it, exposing Granger's naked back, and his blue shorts.

The crowd surged across the road as if they were runners in a marathon. The noise they made was hair-raising – a peculiar kind of ululating warble, as primitive and frightening as Zulus, or Apaches. They gathered around Granger in a furious, tearing mob, and for a moment he disappeared completely.

Tony, grey-faced, said, 'They're killing him. Right in front of our eyes. *They're killing him, Mike!*'

Season couldn't say anything. None of them had really expected Granger to go out there and pacify five hundred starving people, but for a few heady minutes they had all wondered, just wondered, if miracles could happen for real. Season held Sally close, and when Sally asked her, 'What's happening, Mommy? Where's Mr Hughes gone?' Season tried to soothe her and stroke her, and say, 'No place, honey. Maybe to heaven.'

But Granger wasn't in heaven yet. Granger was still in hell. There was a sudden struggling in the crowd, a sudden desperate fighting and wrenching and screaming. And it was then that *something* came pushing and tearing its way through the howling crowds of people, and collided with the windows of the supermarket with such force that they rattled and reverberated. *Something* that smeared red all over the glass with the feverish abandon of an action painter, trying to finish a masterpiece against the clock.

Season looked. Just once. And then she couldn't open her eyes again, not for whole eons of agonised time.

They had already torn off Granger's scalp, and most of his beard. One of his arms had been twisted around and around, right out of its socket, and there was nothing but blood and gristle where his left shoulder should have been. His scrotum had been wrenched from between his legs, and his thighs were plastered in gore. And as he shrieked and flapped his one broken arm against the supermarket window, his horrified followers saw seven or eight hands pull back his head and claw at his eyes, digging them out of their sockets in a welter of optic fluid and blood.

Then, mercifully, they dragged him out of sight. But none of the people in the supermarket knew how long they took to kill him, or what he suffered in those last minutes of his life.

Mike Bull came across to Season and touched her arm. She jumped, and opened her eyes.

Mike Bull said, 'It's – ah – '

He didn't know what to say to her. He was dizzy with shock. For some reason, he was reminded of Anne, and he suddenly started to cry. The tears streamed down his face, and his mouth was puckered with suppressed sobs. Season gently led Sally away, back to the corner by the canned fruit shelves which they were beginning to know as their home.

Tony said, 'We shouldn't never have let him out.'

Mike wiped his eyes with the back of his hand. 'You can't stop martyrs from martyring themselves, Tony. He must have known as well as we did.'

'But they tore him to shreds, Mike I mean, *shreds*.'

'They wouldn't have done if his miracle had worked, would they? Or maybe they would, I don't know. Jesus worked all of those miracles, didn't he, and they still crucified Him.'

Season, in her small corner by the fruit shelves, sat with

her knees clasped in her arms, trying to understand what was real. Sally hadn't been able to see Granger Hughes' grisly last moments from where she was standing, although she understood now that something terrifying had taken place, that Granger had somehow been hurt.

'Mommy,' she said, quietly.

Season attempted a smile.

'Mommy – is Daddy going to come save us?'

Season looked at her daughter – at *their* daughter – with a gentleness that misted her eyes. I mustn't start crying, she thought. Not now, when I'm supposed to be strong. Not now, when Sally's expecting me to reassure her. And yet Sally had put into words the flittering, irrational hope which Season had been holding out for all of these days of fright and uncertainty. Maybe Ed's coming to save us. He *must* be coming to save us. He knows what things are like in Los Angeles. No matter what happened between us, he must be thinking of us now. He can't still be in Kansas, looking after the farm. He's not that kind of a guy. He's boring, sometimes; and pretty often he doesn't recognise what a woman needs out of her life. But he knows when she needs protection, and care. He knows when she really needs help.

And now, God damn it, God damn it all to hell, she started crying. She couldn't stop the hot tears from springing into her eyes, from blurring her picture of the little girl that she and Ed had conceived between them, pretty and serious and patient. And as she wept, she touched Sally's hair, and told her, 'Of course Daddy's coming to save us. He's coming right now. Of course he's coming to save us.'

They had waited under a dense blue sky for three hours, their convoy drawn to the side of Route 66 by Topock, where the highway crosses Havasu Lake. In the western distance, five small clouds had stayed suspended close to the horizon for the whole three hours, not moving, unstirred by any wind.

The landscape was as hot and limpid as a painting by Dali, with the Sacramento Mountains up ahead, and the

346

Hualapai Mountains behind. Arizona, on a Saturday in August. A country of heat-ripples and mirages and strange illusions.

Eventually, Ed walked back to the Chevy wagon, opened the door, and climbed into the driver's seat. His passengers said nothing, but all of them looked at him with sweat-glistened faces, and expressions that pleaded: *Please – move on.*

'All right,' he said, with a dry mouth. 'We're pulling out.'

'Thank the Lord,' intoned Shearson. 'Half an hour more, and I'd have been melted to butter.'

Ed started up the wagon's engine, and the first warm blast surged out of the air-conditioning vents. He blew his horn three times, and the convoy coughed and whinnied and slowly pulled away from the roadside. They crossed the Colorado River, and then wound their way slowly north-west through the Sacramento Mountains, with the peaks of the Dead Mountains over on their left. The sky remained the same relentless blue.

'Last lap,' said Ed, as he drove. 'We're in California now.'

'Three cheers,' said Shearson. 'Do you want to try that radio again now, see if we can't pick up some news?'

Ed switched on the radio, rolling the dial between finger and thumb. There were one or two faint broadcasts, voices that were swallowed by topography and distance; but most of the time there was nothing but a heavy, colourless crackling. After ten minutes of trying, however, Ed picked up a tiny, remote voice which told him it was an emergency station, from Las Vegas, Nevada.

'We hear that the President has recovered from his illness ... and has returned to the White House to take charge of the crisis personally. We hear that several thousand people died during the past twenty-four hours from botulism ... people who apparently considered the risk worth taking ... And we also hear that Britain has flown two thousand tons of emergency supplies in to New York, against the express wishes of her fellow EEC members ...'

They were driving now through South Pass, towards the Piute Mountains and the Mojave Desert. The heat was killing. Ed had turned the Chevey's air conditioning to Max, but it was coughing and choking like a tuberculosis patient, and giving out nothing but a stream of uncomfortable tepid air. Shearson was fanning himself continuously with the wagon's instruction booklet, which he had discovered on the floor, and Peter Kaiser was sitting staring out of the window like Rodin's *Thinker* on a bad afternoon. Karen, amongst the corned beef cans and the sloshing water, slept.

As they passed the Old Dad Mountains on their way to Ludlow, Ed saw a plume of dust coming up fast from behind. It grew nearer and nearer, and as it overtook the convoy, he recognised it as Dave Morton, in his borrowed Pontiac. He pulled over to the side of the road, and Dave Morton pulled up alongside.

'You didn't get back to Tucumcari?' he shouted.

Dave waved his hands. 'I got back there okay,' he yelled.

'Then what's the matter? Why didn't you pick them up?'

'They were dead, all of them. Looked like they'd been sick or something. There was nothing I could do.'

Ed sat back in his seat. The vinyl was wet and sticky with cooled-off sweat. 'Botulism,' he said to himself. 'One of those cans of food they were carrying must have been infected.'

Della held his wrist. 'There was nothing you could have done about it,' she told him, gently. 'It's a risk that everybody's taking, right now. They took the risk, those people, and they lost. There's nothing you can do.'

Ed stared at her, the muscles in his cheeks working with anguish. '*Those people*, as you call them, were the folks who made South Burlington what it was. Henry Carlsson. Mrs Tilsley. Keith Perks. Do you know that it was Mrs Tilsley who was the first person to tell me about the tooth fairy? And now what's happened? She'd dead, in Tucumcari, New Mexico, of botulism. She wasn't even allowed to die at home.'

'Ed, these are terrible times. We're all taking risks. They took theirs.'

'You really believe that?' Ed asked her. 'All those people wanted to do was live their lives out in peace and order.

That's all. They didn't want drama, or pain, or death in a strange city. They simply wanted to see the sun rise and set over Kansas for a few more years. That's what I hate about this famine. It's killing us all, but it won't let us die in the America we're used to. It wouldn't even let me die on South Burlington Farm.'

'You don't want to die, not on South Burlington Farm, nor anywhere. Think of Season and Sally. Think of me.'

Ed looked at her, in her open plaid shirt, and her grubby white jeans. The pump-gun was still tucked down beside the passenger seat and the door. Her red hair was drawn back from her face with a green ribbon.

'You?' he asked her.

She nodded. 'Even if you've got nothing else at all, you've still got me.'

As the sun went down on Sunday evening, the President was lying propped up in bed, papers strewn all over his gold-coloured quilt, looking bloodless and tired, Sitting astride one of the bedroom chairs beside him was his National Security Adviser Louis Krupner, a sharp-faced man with an equally sharp manner. By the window, diffident and quiet, soberly dressed in a dark suit, stood Charles Kurnik, Director of the FBI.

'What I need is conclusive evidence,' the President was saying, while his thin hand picked at the braiding on his quilt. 'Until I have conclusive, irrefutable evidence, I can't possibly order any kind of retaliation.'

Charles Kurnik said, 'I don't see who else could have done it. No other country has the motive, the organisational capabilities, or the finance. Think what the whole operation must have cost. Infiltrating canning plants, sabotaging grain elevators, spreading Vorar-D over every major farm between here and California.'

'Still a whole lot cheaper than the cheapest armed conflict,' said Louis Krupner, without taking his eyes off the President.

The President rubbed his eyes. 'Charles,' he said, 'would you mind pulling that drape across the window? This sunlight's getting in my eyes.'

Charles Kurnik did as he was told. Then he stood with his hands together, like a small boy about to give a recitation.

'Mr President,' he intoned, 'unless we strike now, and unless we strike quickly, we're going to be nothing more than a sitting target. As it is, I don't think we can sustain hundred per cent national security for more than a few hours longer.'

The President picked up some papers and then tiredly laid them down again. 'You're the Director of the FBI, Charles, and a very good director. But you can't use the same street-fighting methods when it comes to international diplomacy. Just for the sake of satisfying your hunches, you're thinking of bringing the whole world down on our heads.'

'*Hunches?*' demanded Kurnik. 'We already hold a list of two hundred cannery workers from Washington State to Florida – every *one* of whom has gone missing – and every *one* of whom has forged or questionable papers! We've already found out that most of the crop virus was spread by two phony aerial photography businesses – Your Spread From The Sky, Inc., and Hi-Lens, Ltd! We already know for a proven fact that the Soviet armed forces have between 70,000 and 100,000 chemical warfare specialists, and that every line regiment has a chemical defence company assigned to it!'

Kurnik reached into his breast pocket and produced a folded news-magazine cutting. 'It's public knowledge, for heaven's sake! Look at this – from *Time*, March 10, 1980. "Using bombs, artillery shells, mortars, multiple rocket-launchers, air-delivered sprays or even land mines, the Soviets can attack with phosgene, mustard gas, hydrogen cyanide, nerve agents, botulin, and a variety of lethal viruses." What more proof do you want, Mr President, when every half-informed adult in the country already knows it for a fact?'

The President closed his eyes. He spoke without opening them. 'Charles,' he said, 'when you bring me just one of those two hundred missing cannery workers, and you establish to me beyond any reasonable doubt that your one

350

cannery worker is a Soviet agent – when you bring me just one pilot from either of those aerial photography corporations, and prove to me that your one pilot works for Moscow – then I shall act. Immediately, decisively, totally.'

Charles Kurnik waited for the President to say something else, but he didn't. He remained white-faced against his pillow, his eyes still closed.

'And not until then?' asked Kurnik, hoarsely. 'Is that what you're saying? Under no circumstances at all?'

'Charles, you're asking me to drop nuclear bombs on Moscow. You're asking me to devastate a nation.'

Charles Kurnik wiped his mouth with his hand, as if he had tasted something objectionably bitter. 'Well, why not?' he asked. 'They've already devastated ours.'

He stood silent, his eyes fixed on the floor. Outside, there was the intermittent popping and crackling of gunfire. The President said to Louis Krupner, 'Hand me those tablets on the side-table, would you? Thanks.' Then he turned to Charles Kurnik and asked, in a formal, curiously unreal voice, 'Are you staying here for dinner, Charles, or must you get back to the office?'

'*Dinner?*' asked Charles Kurnik, with an expression of disgust.

Fourteen

They drove into Los Angeles at dusk on Monday night. They had been held up for more than half a day in the Mojave Desert by burst coolant hoses, clogged exhausts, and flats. Then there had been the treacherous business of driving in convoy through the small towns east of the Los Angeles conurbation – towns where small raiding parties still roamed the streets, shooting at any thing that looked like food.

Pasadena had been a ghost town, a white mirage that shimmered under the sandy peaks of the San Gabriel

Mountains. They had stopped on the freeway overlooking the town for a twenty-minute rest, and a scrappy meal of processed meat, canned raspberries, and tepid water. They had seen nobody in the streets anywhere, and heard nothing but the persistent whistling of the warm wind. It was as if the whole population of America had eerily vanished.

As the sun glowered at them from up ahead, as crimson and sorcerous as a witch's fire, they drove slowly westwards along the Ventura Freeway, weaving their way in between wrecked and abandoned cars, until they reached the intersection with the Hollywood Freeway. Ed had ordered that every car in the convoy should have at least one gun at the ready, but the freeways were deserted, and they saw nobody.

'The first thing I want to do is check with the FBI office,' said Della.

'Where's that?' asked Ed.

'On Hollywood Boulevard, between Ivar and Vine.'

The sun had gone by the time they reached Hollywood Boulevard turnoff. As they came up the ramp to street level, they saw the heavy palls of smoke hanging over Los Angeles, and they could smell burning and death on the wind. A police car sped past them along Hollywood Boulevard, heading east, with its lights flashing and its siren warbling.

'Just about the first sign of life since Victorville,' remarked Della.

The convoy drove at ten mph along Hollywood boulevard, between the stores and the movie theatres and the parking lots, until Ed pulled the Chevy wagon in at the curb by Hollywood and Vine.

'It's here?' he asked Della.

In the back seat, Shearson Jones was asleep, and snoring heavily, with his nose in the air like a Walt Disney beaver.

'A little further, I guess,' said Della. 'There – where that office entrance is. Let me take a look at the shingles.'

Ed nudged the wagon forward, and leaned over to see the signs outside of the office building. It wasn't much of an office building – a three-story, beige-tiled walk-up in that particular architectural style which you could only define as 'Hollywood Boulevard east of Cahuenga.' A little bit Spanish, a little bit 1930s, a little bit H. G. Wells.

The signs outside read: Super AA1 Detective Agency, Inc.; Walston Retreat Tyres; BK Investments Ltd.; and YSS (Photographic) Inc.

'That's it,' said Della.

'What's what?' asked Ed. 'I don't see any sign saying "FBI".'

'You think we advertise ourselves? This is supposed to be a safe house – somewhere where agents can conceal themselves.'

She opened the door of the wagon and stepped down. 'I won't be more than a couple of minutes,' she said, 'I'm just going to check if there's anybody still there.'

Although it was still quite light, Ed found it difficult to make out her face in the shadows. Maybe it was the way her hair was falling. Maybe it was simply the fact that there were no streetlights, no fluorescent display tubes in the derelict storefronts; not even a blazing vehicle to see by. Yet the names on the wall were clear enough.

Ed said, 'I'm coming with you.'

'You don't have to,' Della told him. 'And it's really better if you don't. They're going to be pretty jumpy, and they might decide to shoot first and talk about the weather afterwards if they don't know who you are.'

'In that case, you go in first, and tell them that I'm bona fide. But I'd like to stay with you, all right?'

'Who's going to take care of Shearson?'

'Shearson can take care of himself. What do you think he's going to do – drive all the way back to Washington?'

Della hesitated, and then she said, 'All right. I'll call you when it's clear.'

Taking the pump-gun with her, she disappeared into the entrance of the office building. Ed waited on the sidewalk for what seemed like a half-hour, watched by a tired and pale-faced Karen, and by an indifferent Peter Kaiser. Shearson was still sleeping, and his rumbles sounded like minor eruptions of Mount St Helens.

In the distance, towards Beverly Hills, Ed could hear

353

firetrucks howling, and a quick rattling sound that was repeated again and again. It could have been machine-gun fire.

At last, an upstairs window opened, and Della leaned out. 'There's nobody here,' she said. 'You can come on up if you like.'

Ed walked back to the next car in the patient line of vehicles which were drawn up to the curb behind the Chevy. It was a tan Malibu wagon, driven by Jim Rutgers, Ed's farm accountant.

Jim asked, 'Are we going to be stopped here long, Ed? I think everybody's anxious about where they're going to spend the night.'

'Give us fifteen minutes,' said Ed. 'Mrs McIntosh has to try to make contact with the FBI, just to tell them that we've reached Los Angeles, and that we're holding Shearson Jones. After that, it's their problem. But they won't be able to say that we didn't do our duty as publicly-spirited citizens.'

Jim turned around to his wife, and the four children sleeping in the back seat. 'I just wish the public were as publicly-spirited as we are,' he said. 'I think about these kids, and what their future's going to be, and I can tell you something, Ed, it makes me frightened.'

'Me too, Jim,' said Ed, as comfortingly as he could. 'Just give me five minutes, and then we'll find a place to stay for the night.'

He walked back to the office building and climbed the stairs. It was so dark inside that he had to feel his way up by the handrail. There was a smell of burned paper and urine. He reached the second-storey landing, and he was just about to climb up to the third when Della appeared from a doorway beside him.

'They're in here,' she said. 'Or, at least, they *were* in here.'

Ed stepped into a small reception area, divided off with reeded glass. On the wall was a calendar supplied by Mitsubishi Aircraft, with a picture of the Diamond I executive jet flying over San Francisco Bay. There was a grey filing-cabinet, with all its drawers open and empty, and an IBM typewriter with its keys jammed together, and a blank piece of note-paper still protruding from the carriage.

'They didn't even leave a telephone,' said Della. 'But I'm going to write a message and pin it to the wall. Maybe one of their agents will come by and contact us.'

'And meanwhile we have to keep Shearson Jones captive?'

'What else do you suggest we do with him?'

Ed looked around the deserted, shadowy office. 'I suggest we let him go. Both him and Peter Kaiser. There's no chance at all that we can bring either of them to trial. Not now. And, really, what does it matter any more?'

'You were the one who thought it was so important to expose Shearson on coast-to-coast television,' said Della. 'Now you want to let him go?'

Ed sat down at the receptionist's desk, and tugged the piece of notepaper out of the typewriter. He read the letterhead carefully, and then laid the paper on the desk beside him. When he spoke, his voice was quite changed – distant and unfriendly.

'Yes,' he said. 'I want to let him go because none of this famine crisis has turned out to be what it seemed to be.'

'You're not making sense.'

'I know. But neither is anything else. If this is a safe house for the Federal Bureau of Investigation, as you claim it is, then why were they using notepaper for Your Spread From The Sky, Inc.?'

Della frowned. 'That was their cover. An aerial photography outfit. That's all. You don't expect them to put "J. Edgar Hoover" on their paper do you?'

Ed said, 'Your Spread From The Sky, Inc., was responsible for spraying my crops with Vorar-D. As well as most of the other wheat farms in Kansas. And you want me to believe that it was a cover name for the FBI? And that you're a legitimate FBI agent?'

He stood up. 'Did you really call the FBI office when you were outside of Wichita? Or were you just making it all up? Come on, Della, I think it's time you came clean with me, don't you? Why are you really holding on to Shearson Jones? You don't have any serious hopes of arraigning him.

Maybe you never intended to. So why have you brought him all this way, and guarded him so well? What's *your* connection with Your Spread From The Sky, Inc.? What the hell's going on?'

Della smiled at him, and put her head on one side, in a winning Shirley Temple kind of a gesture. 'Ed,' she said, 'you don't seriously doubt what I've told you?'

'I don't know,' Ed snapped angrily. He found that he was quivering, from exhaustion and shock, and from a sudden vertiginous sensation that the floor had disappeared from under him. 'I just want you to tell me what all this is all about.'

'How much do you actually know about Your Spread From The Sky?' asked Della.

'I know what Jack Marowitz found out. That they were flying over almost every farm in Kansas, just before the Vorar-D virus broke out. And that's too much of a goddamned coincidence to be true.'

Della carefully laid the pump-gun down across the desk. Ed didn't miss the significance of the gesture, but he didn't take his eyes off Della's face, and he didn't change his intense, unhappy expression.

'Well,' said Della, softly, 'you're right. They *did* overfly those farms. But the reason they did it wasn't to spray any poison virus on them. The reason was that they had a tipoff about the blight, and they were reconnoitring the farms in the least sensational way they knew how, to see if they could detect who was doing it, and how.'

There was a long, taut silence. Then Ed said, 'You expect me to believe that? You're trying to tell me the FBI knew about the blight in *advance*, and they didn't warn anybody? Not the Department of Agriculture? Not the President? Not even Shearson Jones?'

'Until the blight actually broke out, Ed, they weren't sure it was going to happen at all.'

Ed stood up, and walked across to the office window. He parted the lopsided venetian blinds and looked down into Hollywood Boulevard. He couldn't see the convoy of cars and wagons, but he could see Sam Gasiewicz on the other side of the street keeping guard, his rifle over his shoulder.

He turned to Della. 'Are you really FBI?' he asked her. 'Or are you something else ? Somebody else altogether?'

'What do you think?' asked Della. 'Would I have taken the trouble to blackbag a whole lot of Shearson's papers – would I have taken the trouble to keep Shearson and Peter Kaiser prisoner – would I have done *any* of the things I've done since you've met me, if I wasn't?'

'How the hell should I know?' Ed asked her.

'Listen,' Della told him, touching his arm. 'I'm only interested in keeping Shearson and Peter Kaiser in custody until I can turn them over to the Bureau. I'm only interested in helping us all to find a safe place to hide out until this rioting and raiding is all over. That's all. You can trust me, Ed. I mean it. You can genuinely trust me.'

Ed didn't answer. But after a long while, he let the venetian blind fall back into place, and he wiped the dust from his hands on the sides of his jeans.

'All right,' he said. 'If you say I can trust you, then I will. But if you do one single thing to jeopardise any of the people in this convoy of ours – if you make one single wrong move – then I'm going to have to ask you to leave the group and go out on your own. You understand that? What I'm saying?'

Della leaned forward a little and kissed his cheek. The soft heaviness of her breast pressed against his arm. He could smell the particular fragrance that wasn't perfume or soap, but just woman.

'Thank you,' she whispered. 'I know what you're saying, but I won't let you down.'

'Now,' said Ed, 'I want to go look for Season and Sally.'

The winding road up through Topanga Canyon took them on a journey of funereal fantasy – as if their convoy of wagons was wending its way through the black recesses of a mortician's nightmare.

All the grass and all the trees had been burned to ashes, so that on either side of them they could see nothing but twisted stumps that had been reduced to charcoal, and vegetation like crumbling grey hair. The north-east wind had blown the debris across the road, so that their tyres ground and scratched on the asphalt, and threw up clouds of ash and grit.

The smell was overpowering. A strong, sour stench that blew in through their air-conditioning vents and seemed to cling to their clothes. Now and then, they drove through a thick drift of smoke, and that started them coughing, and irritated their eyes, and by the time they reached Mulholland Drive, Shearson Jones was caught in an uncontrollable fit of wheezing and gasping.

'We're going to have to turn back,' insisted Peter Kaiser. 'Ten more minutes of this and the senator's going to asphyxiate.'

'We're almost there,' said Ed, in a flat voice. 'The Snowmans' house is up on the left.'

'You seriously believe it's still standing?' asked Peter.

Ed didn't answer. Ever since they had turned their convoy off the Pacific Coast Highway on to Topanga Canyon Boulevard, and seen the charred and devastated hills, his stomach had been rigid as a football with fear. The bushfire must have swept all the way down the canyon unchecked, with no firefighters and no water-dumping aircraft to hold it back; and the chances of anybody having survived it were almost absurd. Please God, thought Ed, as he reached the turn in the road where the Snowmans' driveway came down – please God don't let me find them burned.

The mailbox was still there, its post charred, its paint burned off; but Ed could distinctly make out the name *C. Snowman*. He turned the Chevy up the drive until he came to the parking area in front of the house.

From the outside, in the darkness, the house didn't look too bad. But when Ed climbed down from the wagon and crunched his way closer across the drifts of ashes, he could see that the interior was completely burned out.

Della came up behind him. 'I'm sorry,' she said.

Ed clambered his way over fallen beams and blackened skeletal furniture until he reached the place which had once been the living-room. Incongruously, one part of the living-room wall still stood, and attached to it was a white telephone, drooping and distorted by heat. Ed almost expected it to ring, and to hear voices from the past. Next to the phone, still half-legible, were the words: '*Ed Hardesty called from South Burlington Farm. Says he's on his way to LA.*'

'The cop who wrote that said the place was empty,' Ed remarked. 'With any luck, they didn't try to come back. But the question is – where are they now?'

'I can tell you that,' said a keen, sharp voice.

Ed turned around, squinting against the glare of the convoy's headlights to see who was talking.

'Who's that?' he asked. Della stepped to one side, and raised her pump-gun.

'No need to be afraid,' said the voice. 'I'm not carrying a gun or nothing.'

'Step into the light where I can see you,' said Della.

There was a hesitant, shuffling sound, and then a small, soot-smudged man emerged into the headlight beam. He looked like a grubby, tattered, erratic second cousin of Donald Pleasence. His jacket was singed at the back, and he wore burnt brown mittens.

'Pearson's the name,' he said, brushing ash from his sleeves. 'Longtime resident of Topanga Canyon and environs. You looking for the folks who used to live here?'

'That's right. Carl and Vee Snowman, and the people who were staying with them. A woman and a little girl.'

Pearson coughed, and wiped black-speckled sputum from his lips with the back of his mitten. 'You carrying any food?' he asked.

'Maybe. Do you know where the Snowmans are?'

'Sure I know. But it wouldn't be right to tell you for nothing. You got any canned meat? The safe variety, mind. I'm not giving out information just to get a dose of that botulism.'

'How do I know you're going to ell me the truth?' asked Ed.

Pearson coughed, and cackled. 'A can of meat in this town, mister, is worth its weight in any kind of currency you care to mention. You can get yourself a woman for a can of meat. Or a whole heap of narcotics. Down on Santa Monica Boulevard, you can fix yourself up with a bag of good quality heroin for just one can of Campbell's condensed oxtail, provided it's carrying the right date of manufacture, and no pinholes. I even hear tell they've set up places for changing the dates on suspect cans, just to re-sell 'em.'

Pearson came closer. He carried a smell with him, of sweat and ash and poverty. 'With a can of meat being worth as much as that, mister, I wouldn't care to double-cross nobody for it. Folks are getting killed for cans of meat. Don't you think I don't know you wouldn't come hunting me out, if'n I gave you wrong information, and don't you think I don't know you wouldn't kill me?'

'You're right,' said Ed, with exaggerated ferocity. 'I would kill you. Della – will you go get me a can of that Moms Kitchen Corned Beef?'

Della hesitated, and then walked back to the wagon. She came back a few moments later carrying the red-and-yellow can with the smiling woman's face on the label.

'Okay, where are they?' asked Ed. 'And you make sure you tell me straight!'

Pearson stared at the corned beef as if it were the Holy Grail. His stomach rumbled in audible peristalsis, and saliva ran from the corners of his mouth.

'I haven't eaten nothing since Wednesday,' he said. 'Only a pack of taco chips I found in one of the burned-out houses.'

'Where are they?' insisted Ed.

'I'll tell you where they are. They're holed up at the Hughes Supermarket on Franklin and Highland. Them and maybe a hundred more from one of those nutty churches. You can't get in there if you try. They've got the whole place barricaded. The rumour is that they've got themselves a whole stockroom of food, enough to last them for nearly a year; and that's why the place is surrounded.'

Ed looked at Pearson acutely.

'That's the God's-honest truth, mister. I swear it on my liver,' the old man promised.

'All right,' said Ed, and tossed him the can of corned beef. 'Don't try eating all that at one sitting. You'll be sick as a dog.'

Pearson may have been starving for five days, but he caught the can of corned beef as neatly as a professional ballplayer. Then he was off, hopping and skipping over the ashes with his prize held against his chest. Ed called, 'Pearson!' but it was too late. The old man was gone.

Ed walked slowly back to the Chevy. Shearson had managed to control his coughing now, but he was breathing in deep, shuddering wheezes which sounded as if every tube in his bronchial system was clogged with mucus.

'Are you *ever* going to let us rest, you infernal farmer?' he wanted to know. 'Or are you going to trail us around the west for the rest of our days?'

'The senator's sick,' said Peter Kaiser. 'Unless we get him someplace where he can rest, he's going to get a whole lot worse.'

Ed said, 'My wife and child are apparently barricaded in a supermarket on Highland Avenue, along with a whole bunch of other people. From what that old hobo said, they have plenty of supplies, maybe enough for a year. It makes sense to me personally to try to go join them. I mean, my family's there. But I also think it makes sense for all of us to try to get in there. Even if we don't stay for more than a day or two, at least it'll give us a breathing-space to get ourselves orientated, and decided what we're going to do next.'

Shearson wiped his face with his handkerchief, and coughed. 'For goodness' sake, Hardesty, stop giving us lectures in logic and feasibility and take us somewhere where we can get something to eat. And drink, too, if that's not too much to ask.'

'Senator?' said Karen, and passed Shearson a Dixie cup of lukewarm water.

'I shall have nightmares about tepid, plastic-tasting water for the rest of my life,' said Shearson, swallowing it noisily. 'Do you know something? I'm so much thinner than I was last week that if I stood up, my pants would drop to my ankles.'

'You could have fooled me,' said Ed, glancing at Shearson's huge belly.

Della said, 'I don't think we have much of a choice. I vote

361

we try to get into the supermarket.'

'I suppose that means I go too,' put in Shearson. Della gave him a grin like caustic soda.

'Okay,' said Ed. 'I'll go have a word with everybody else in the convoy and tell them what we've decided. They'll all be able to stay with us, or go to their own way, whatever they want.'

'What about me?' asked Peter Kaiser.

'You stay with me,' Shearson reminded him, hoarsely. 'I still pay your salary, remember, or at least I will do when I can get my hands on those bank accounts on Grand Cayman.'

'The world's collapsed around his ears, and he still thinks about his swindled money,' marvelled Della.

'My dear,' Shearson reminded her, 'everything that ever happens in this whole world has something to do with money. Even in the middle of a famine, you can't lose sight of that.'

Two of the convoy decided to drop out and make their way to Mexico straight away – Jim Rutgers and his family, and everybody who was travelling with Sam Gasiewicz. There was a short but emotional goodbye on the Pacific Coast Highway at Topanga Beach, while the shadowy ocean seethed and foamed, and distant fires burned far away to the south. Moira Gasiewicz wept on Ed's shoulder, and then her husband tugged her gently back to their car, nodded to Ed, and climed into the car himself.

Ed stood watching the red tail-lights curving away towards Santa Monica, and then he said to Della, 'All right. Let's go see what's happening at the supermarket.'

It was the third attack that night. Soon after dark, the first hails of bricks, bottles and chunks of broken curbstones had racketed and splintered against the supermarket doors, and blazing gasoline had been splashed on the sidewalk outside. Then, like demons from purgatory, the crowd had come rushing through the flames with home-made cudgels and axes and fenceposts wrapped in barbed-wire, and they had hammered on the doors, so furiously and so hard that

362

many of them had smashed their fingers and knuckles. Inside, the congregation of the Church of the Practical Miracle had stood silent and frozen, waxworks, unable to do anything but watch.

A second attack had come at nine o'clock, when one of the crowd had climbed on to the supermarket roof and tried to throw a Molotov cocktail in through the skylight. Tony, crouched behind the liquor counter, had shot at the intruder five times with his .22 target pistol as the man tried to light his home-made bomb, and had hit him twice in the arms, flesh wounds. The bomb had flared up, and splashed fiery gasoline all over the intruder's clothes. Screaming, his hair on fire, his arms flapping in great circles of flame, he had run across the roof and toppled head-first off the edge. His body had blazed on the sidewalk for almost twenty minutes.

Now, they were attacking again, and this time the thunder of rocks and bottles against the doors was relentless and deafening.

Carl was sitting next to Season in her corner by the fruit shelves. They had been sharing the last of their dinner – a can of soya hamburger helper and a can of Green Giant spinach – while Vee had been singing Sally to sleep. Carl looked at Season with wide eyes, and he didn't have to say anything at all. They both knew that it was only going to be a matter of time before the mob broke in, and when they did, there wouldn't be any mercy for any of them. It was no good pretending that what had happened to Granger Hughes wouldn't happen again.

'Do you think it's possible to – make things easier?' asked Season, in a high, dry voice she scarcely recognised as her own.

'In what way?' asked Carl.

'Well, for Sally. To make it painless.'

Carl pulled at the skin of his cheeks as if it were tired pink elastic. 'I guess Mike Bull has a whole lot of pharmaceuticals we could use. Aspirin, something like that. But that would take time.'

There was a crash of reinforced glass as the mob outside began to hurl themselves at the supermarket doors with

363

hammers and tyre-irons.

'You don't want to do it too soon,' said Carl. 'And on the other hand, you certainly don't want to do it too late.'

'She's so pretty,' said Season, looking across at Sally's fine blonde hair, her eyes filled with tears. 'I couldn't bear it if they hurt her.'

Vee could hear what they were saying, but she continued to rock Sally in her arms, smoothing her forehead to calm her down, and singing to her.

'Roon, roon, rosie,
Cuppie, cuppie, shell,
The dog's away to Hamilton,
To buy a new bell;
If you don't take it,
I'll take it to myself.
Roon, roon, rosie,
Cuppie, cuppie, shell.'

Her voice was drowned by a tumult of shrieking and banging. Carl laid aside his uneaten food, and said, 'Mike's going to need some help. For God's sake, look, there must be a thousand of them out there.'

The hammering grew louder and even more determined. One of the chromed steel bars that Tony had slid through the door-handles to keep the mobs from breaking in was actually *bending* now, and the door was half-torn off its hinges. The reinforced glass had held together, even though it had been crushed into a wired-together slush; but now the sheer weight of hysterical people outside of the supermarket was beginning to tell. One blood-smeared hand appeared through the opaque glass like the hand that had reached out of the lake for Excalibur, disembodied, groping blindly, unable to pull itself back because of all the furious people behind.

Sally sat up. She was pale, alarmed, with dark circles under her eyes. Vee stopped singing now, and looked across at Season with an expression that conveyed all the fright that a sister and a woman could feel. The noise of screeching people and shaking doors was so loud that when Vee said something, Season could only see her lips move, and indistinctly hear the word '. . . *please*.'

Mike Bull came across, walking with unusual speed and economy. He leaned over Season and said as quietly as he could, 'I thought we could starve them away. But it doesn't look like we've succeeded. We can't hold them off for a whole lot longer.'

Season gave a wobbly smile. 'You've done your best,' she told him.

Vee said, 'What are we going to do now? You saw what they did to Granger.'

Mike cleared his throat, looking from Vee to Season and then to Carl. 'You've got that .38 of yours, don't you, Carl? With one shell?'

Carl nodded, His face was lined, and as white as typing paper.

'Well, then,' said Mike, 'I suggest you use it on . . .' and he inclined his head towards Sally. 'Back of the head, she won't even know.'

Season felt as if it were totally impossible to breathe. The noise outside the supermarket was hideous, and yet inside her head was nothing but silence and coldness and disbelief. *Back of the head, she won't even know*. Where that fine blonde hair is parted into plaits, where I've caressed her so often as she dreamed herself to sleep. And she won't even see her father again.

Mike could sense what Season was thinking. But he muttered, 'It's the kindest way, you know. That mob's out of their skulls. It's going to be rape, torture, you name it.'

Carl cleared his throat, strangely formal. 'Well,' he said, 'thanks for the hamburger helper, if nothing else.'

Mike tried to smile, but he couldn't. All he could say was, 'Good luck, people. I mean it,' before he went off to warn the others.

Sally said, with as much childish dignity as she could, 'Mommy? Mommy, I'm frightened.'

Season reached out and touched her cheek. 'Yes, baby,' she said. 'We all are.'

They had seen the fires and the crowds from ten blocks away. Ed had ordered the convoy to draw up on the wide triangular piece of rough ground by La Brea Avenue, and now they were sitting in their wagons while gunfire popped and echoed through the night, and people rushed and ran and stumbled past them on their way to Highland. The word must have gotten around that the Hughes supermarket was on the brink of collapse, and that there was going to be plenty of food to be looted.

'Do you think we're too late?' asked Karen, from the back. 'My God, just *look* at them. They're like crazy people.'

'They're hungry, that's why,' said Peter. 'Hunger always makes people crazy. Whether it's for food, or sex, or money.'

'My wife and daughter are in there,' said Ed, flatly.

'We know,' replied Shearson. 'And don't think for a moment that we're going to leave them to the distinctly untender mercies of this mob. We're going to think of something. *Do* something. Your wife and daughter must be saved.'

'As well as a year's supply of food,' put in Della, sharply.

'What's wrong with wanting to rescue the food?' Shearson protested, angrily. 'Don't you understand, you stupid woman? Didn't you hear what that hobo character said? A year's supply of canned food could buy you anything you could conceivably dream of. That's edible gold in there. In fact, it's *better* than gold. It's even better than heroin. Only a limited number of addicts crave for heroin. But everybody craves for food. Give them what they want, and in a few hours, they're begging you for more. Don't you understand what *power* that food in that supermarket could give us?'

'Christ, you make me heave,' said Ed. 'Della – there's little enough law and order in this country as it is – why don't you elect yourself judge and executioner and blow the senator's fat head off?'

A running looter collided blindly with their wagon, but carried on his way, waving a long kitchen knife.

'I couldn't execute the senator,' smiled Della. 'The senator is running absolutely true to character, and as far as I'm concerned, that's fine.'

'*Fine?* What do you mean, *fine*? Didn't you hear him?'

'I heard him. And that's why I've been protecting him so carefully all the way from Kansas, both from you and everything else. Senator Jones has even shared half of my food ration, haven't you, senator?'

Ed stared at her. 'You gave him half your food? But what the hell for?'

'Because, my darling, it's my mission to keep Senator Shearson Jones in one piece. Alive, well, and avaricious. That's why I agreed to come west with you, instead of taking him to Washington, because you were quite right about the dangers of travelling east. Too many looters, too many marauding mobs. And my superiors would have been very irritated if I'd lost him. Or his clever young assistant.'

'Will you explain this to me, in words that I can understand?' asked Ed. He knew now that it was urgent for him to find out what was going on; although he couldn't help himself from glancing anxiously down Franklin Avenue towards the lurid gasoline fires that now lit up the outline of the Hughes Supermarket.

'It's very simple,' said Della. She raised the muzzle of her rifle slightly. Not more than a half-inch, but enough for Ed to notice.

'If it's simple, then we should be able to follow it,' put in Shearson. 'I'd love to know why you consider my overweight carcass to be so extraordinarily valuable.'

'Years ago,' said Della slowly, as if she were speaking from a remembered script, 'years ago – when this famine was being planned – it was decided by my superiors that as soon as the President had surrendered, a new President would immediately have to be installed in his place. But, he couldn't be a Russian. To have a Russian President, all of a sudden, would be too much of a shock for the American people, and they would react violently. You are a violent people, as the frequent riots in your cities have shown us. Apart from that, a Russian President would find the nation too difficult to handle with any degree of success. Yours is a complex, unstable, hedonistic society. Very hard for a Russian to understand.'

She paused. Shearson had cupped his hand to his ear as if

he were hard of hearing. Peter Kaiser's face was stiff as a meringue.

'We went to considerable trouble to pick as our future *Gauleiter* of America an established politician who would be able to carry off the burden of Presidential duties without feeling overwhelmed by them; a man whose face was already familiar to the American public; a reassuring, fatherly figure. And yet a man whose personal morals were so flawed that he would easily be encouraged by the gift of instant Presidency and great financial wealth to assist us in taking over the administration of your country as painlessly and as quickly as possible.'

Shearson Jones' lips were opening and closing wordlessly.

Della turned to him, and smiled, and said, 'Of course, Senator Jones, our first choice for *Gauleiter* was you. And that is why I consider your overweight carcass so valuable, and that is why I have been cossetting you and protecting you all the way from Kansas to the Pacific ocean.'

'So,' breathed Ed, 'we were right about Your Spread From The Sky. And I was right about you. You're not FBI. You're a Soviet agent.'

'In a manner of speaking,' Della nodded.

'In a manner of speaking,' puffed Shearson, scathingly. 'You're a Red, my dear. An economy-size Mata Hari. There's no "manner of speaking" about it.'

'But what about the Blight Crisis Appeal?' asked Ed. 'If you wanted Shearson for a puppet President, why did you bother to steal all those incriminating papers?'

'Because they're incriminating,' smiled Della. 'We like to keep our friends in line; and if Shearson ever misbehaved himself, we could quite easily oust him from power and imprison him on the evidence of his past swindles. How could the rest of the world complain about that? The man's an obvious, proven criminal. Apart from that, we needed to confiscate his personal millions, so that he would no longer have the means to escape us, nor to bribe anybody to help him.'

'And why are you telling us this confidential and privileged information?' asked Peter Kaiser. 'Shouldn't you have waited until Russian troops were actually wetting their boots on Malibu Beach?'

'I'm telling you because there's no other way I could have explained that there's been a change of plan. We're *not* going to attempt to rescue Ed's wife and daughter; and we're *not* going to attempt to lay our hands on that stock of food. Look at it – there's a full-scale riot going on down there. All the people in that supermarket will be dead in an hour, and all the food will be looted. It's not worth the risk.'

'Risk?' asked Peter Kaiser. 'What risk?'

'The risk of losing the next President of the latest addition to the Union of Soviet Socialist Republics. That's what risk.'

Ed gripped the steering-wheel with sweaty hands. He could try to wrench the pump-gun out of Della's hands, but he knew that it was hopeless. She would have blown his face off before he had even turned around. He stared at the leaping flames at the intersection of Highland and Franklin, and his eyes watered with hopelessness, with tiredness, and with glare.

Shearson said, 'I'm a man of some influence, you know, my dear Della. A figure of respect. I'm quite sure I could go some way towards quelling that mob of lunatics.'

'They'd rip you apart,' said Della. 'They're no better than wild animals.'

'Well, if you say so,' shrugged Shearson, drawing Ed's Colt .45 out of his voluminous coat and pointing it at the back of Della's head.

Ed stared at Della in total horror. She caught the look on his face, frowned, and said, 'Ed, what's the – '

Shearson fired, and Della's face seemed to expand in front of Ed's eyes like an over-inflated carnival balloon. Then there was blood and glass everywhere, and Della jerked forward in her seat. Ed's ears rang with the noise of the shot.

'Well,' said Shearson, handing the .45 to Ed. 'Severe times merit severe measures. I may be morally flawed, but I'm still a patriot. You're next to her, Mr Hardesty. Do you mind kicking her out of the door?'

Ed opened the driver's door, climbed down, and walked

around the hood. He opened the passenger door, and lifted Della carefully down to the sidewalk.

Shearson said, 'It's more than she deserved,' as Ed climbed up behind the steering-wheel again.

Ed said, 'I made love to her once, that's all. Now, what are we going to do?'

'Well, we're going to have to be quick, and we're going to have to be bold,' said Shearson, leaning forward in his seat. 'We're pretty reasonably armed, compared with most of that mob. Shotguns against clubs. So my suggestion is that we form up these wagons of ours into some kind of a flying wedge – drive straight through to the supermarket doors – and keep the looters at bay while we let the people inside get out, and while we organise any able-bodied men to load up whatever food they can.'

Peter Kaiser ran his hand through his hair. 'If you don't mind my saying so, senator, that seems incredibly risky. There have to be seven or eight hundred people there. Maybe more.'

'I *know* it's risky,' said Shearson, with exaggerated patience. 'But consider the alternatives. Either we spend the next six months scrabbling for food like the rest of these poor wretches, or we load ourselves up with enough sustenance to keep ourselves independent and self-sufficient. And *solvent*, apart from anything else. Remember you can buy yourself a woman with a can of meat.'

Ed said, 'I'll have to go ask the rest of them. And the women and children will have to stay behind here someplace.'

Shearson twisted himself around in his seat. 'There's a hotel back there. That looks likely. Less chance of disturbing any irate and gun-happy householders. Now, I'd get moving if I were you. The way that supermarket's burning, it doesn't look like we've got ourselves a whole lot of time.'

It took Ed five minutes to persuade two out of the remaining three farmworkers in his convoy to join in a rescue attempt. One of them – Roy Gurning – had always had a soft spot for Season, and so he was pleased to volunteer. Nat Petersen was a little more reluctant, but he was single, and physically strong, and a good shot with a scatter-gun, and eventually Ed managed to talk him around. Jerry Stone wouldn't go for anything. He had his wife and children with him, and in any case he thought Ed was crazy.

'I'd rather throw myself into a volcano,' he remarked. Ed shook his hand, said okay, and left him to look after the remaining two farm women, his wife, and his four children.

Ed went back to the Chevy, started her up, slammed the door, and said, 'Ready? Peter – you cover the right side with the pump-gun. Senator – since you're so handy with a .45 – you cover the left. Karen – keep your head down.'

He pulled the wagon out on to Franklin Avenue. Behind him, Roy Gurning drove on his left three-quarter flank in his Pinto wagon, and Nat Petersen drove on his right three-quarter flank in a Cutlass. Between them, the three cars formed a spearhead which took up the width of the whole road.

'I just hope we know what the hell we're doing,' said Ed. He was sweating all over, and he couldn't stop.

'All right,' growled Shearson, 'Let's go.'

Ed waved to Roy and Nat, and then slammed his foot down on the gas. With a throaty bellow, the Chevy surged forward, right into the running crowds, with the Pinto and the Cutlass hugging close behind.

Ed felt the wagon's bumper hit two – three – four people. Their bodies made firm thumping noises, like huge insects hitting the windshield in summer. Someone screamed, and two men tried to run along beside him and claw the driver's door open, but he was driving too fast, and Roy was coming up so close behind them that they had to dodge out of the way.

Then, it was hell. They reached the intersection of Highland and Franklin and they were in the thick of it. Sticks and stones drummed against the sides of the wagon, and there were screeches of agony and fright as he forced the hood of the four-wheel-drive vehicle right into the surging mob of people around the supermarket.

He heard Peter Kaiser shoot the pump-gun four or five

times. He heard windows at the back of the wagon breaking. There was a chaotic howling ocean of distorted people around him, and yet he was still driving the wagon forward – slower now, because of the dense press of bodies – but still relentlessly forward over crushed arms and legs and bursting skulls. The banging of clubs and sticks against the vehicle's bodywork was utterly deafening, and he knew that his face was pulled into a ridiculous expression of fear and concentration, but there was nothing he could do about it.

The last few feet were the worst. As the wagon pushed its bumpers right up to the supermarket's doors, ten or twelve looters were caught in front of it, and shoved bodily through the wire-reinforced glass, like ribbons of raw meat through a grater. Then, with a last burst of low-gear power, Ed brought down the whole row of doors, and collided with the liquor counter.

They had miscalculated, badly. The mob was wild and unstoppable and far more numerous than they had realised. Peter fired three more shots and his pump-gun was empty, Roy Gurning's Pinto had been swallowed up by the crowd, and Ed glimpsed its offside wheels as it was turned over, with Roy still inside it. Nat Petersen's car had disappeared altogether, Shearson screamed, '*It won't work! It won't work! Just back up and get the hell out of here!*'

But Ed, looking around the wrecked supermarket, had momentarily caught sight of Sally in the far corner, and nothing was going to get him out of that store without them. He forced open the Chevy's door, pushing over two struggling looters, and elbowed and shoved his way between the shelves to where he thought he had seen them. Behind him the mob had begun to surge through the broken-open doors, and scrambled towards the stock-room. It was going to be looting first, revenge second.

For three insane minutes, Ed remembered everything his college football coach had taught him, and he pushed and shoved and bulldozed his way through the screaming scrum of people towards the shelves at the far back of the supermarket. Then, in an instant that was too fearful to be anything but blurred, unmemorable, and confused, he had scooped Sally up in his arms, and pushed Season ahead of him, and they were fighting their way back to the wagon.

'*Vee!*' screamed Season. '*I can't see Vee!*'

'*Get out of here!*' bellowed Ed. '*Just get to the wagon, and let's get out of here!*'

He was thrown back against a shelf, with an agonising jar against his back; but he managed to thrust his way on to his feet again, with Sally still awkwardly clutched in his arms, and struggled on. Somehow, bruised and sweating and grazed, his adrenalin at bursting point, he reached the wagon and threw Sally in through the door on to Shearson's lap. Then he pulled Season up behing him, shoved her across beside Peter Kaiser, and started up the engine.

Slowly, grindingly, the Chevy backed up into the mob. Now that the supermarket stockroom had been broken into, few of the looters took any notice of the wagon at all, but pushed their way around it. It was food they were after, and the maelstrom of fighting and bodies in the supermarket was too confusing for most of them to understand what was happening.

They were almost out on to the roadway again when their rear bumper caught up with Roy Gurning's overturned Pinto. Ed rocked the wagon backwards and forwards, but it still refused to budge. He pressed his foot harder on the gas and prayed to God for the Pinto to move.

Slowly, it did, with a grating screech of metal on concrete. But now the wagon had begun to attract the attention of some of the late-coming looters – the ones who knew they were going to be lucky to pick up a few battered cans of corn. Twenty or thirty of them started tearing at the doors and banging their fists on the windows, and Ed looked out in fright at a world that seemed to be nothing but grotesque, staring faces.

Abruptly, Shearson Jones's passenger-door was tugged open. Shearson shrieked like a girl, and Peter Kaiser tried to reach across and grab him, but five or six pairs of hands pulled Shearson's coat and pants, and heaved him bodily out of the wagon.

'*I'm a United States senator!*' screamed Shearson. '*I'm a*

United States senator!

Then he was swallowed up by the mob; and it took all of Peter's strength to slam the door closed again, and hold it shut against the scratching hands of frantic looters.

Ed, sobbing with fear and exhaustion, jammed his foot down on the gas pedal once more. Slowly, slowly, the wrecked Pinto began to slide out of the way. Then, it toppled, and the Chevy was clear. They surged backwards into the crowds, and drove backwards with their transmission whining in protest all the way to La Brea Avenue, almost a quarter-mile.

Ed stopped the wagon when they reached La Brea, and turned forwards in his seat to look at the supermarket. It was blazing from sidewalk to roof now, with huge tongues of fire licking at the night with a lasciviousness that could only remind him of greed, and pain, and hatred.

He stared at Season. She was wide-eyed, shocked, scarcely able to speak. Sally, in the back seat, was whimpering and shivering.

Then Ed held his hand over his mouth to try and stop the tears. But he couldn't; they ran freely down his cheeks; and they sparkled in the flickering glare of the burning supermarket as if his eyes were on fire, too.

The next morning, when the burned-out shell of the supermarket was abandoned, they went back. Season walked amongst the bodies which lay between the empty shelves while Ed stood silently by the smashed and blood-smeared doors.

'Vee's not here,' she said at last. 'Nor Carl. I can't see Mike Bull, either. They must have escaped. I knew this girl, though. Clara, her name was.'

From outside, Ed heard Peter calling, 'Ed – come here. In the parking lot. And come on your own. Don't bring Sally.'

Ed walked around the side of the building to the parking-lot. It was strewn with twisted shopping-carts and burned-out automobiles. But Peter was standing in the far corner, where it seemed as if another, smaller, fire had been burning; and where there was an elaborate arrangement of

shopping-carts which seemed to have been linked together
to form a kind of barbecue.

When he was fifteen feet away, Ed realised what it was,
and what had happened. Beside it, in a congealing heap, lay
the naked remains of Senator Shearson Jones. Inside it, still
half-cooked, were strips of flesh that had been cut from his
thighs, his arms, and his belly.

Ed stayed where he was, and didn't approach any closer.
Peter Kaiser looked at him, unblinking, unmoving, as if he
was a statue of a time that neither of them could remember.

They drove northwards, through Santa Barbara, on a day
that was hot and clear. They spoke very little, and Sally, in
the back seat, slept.

Peter and Karen had found Nat Petersen's car, un-
damaged, but with no sign of Nat Petersen. After a half-
hour talk together, they had elected to head together for
Mexico, along with Jerry Stone and his wife. Ed had taken
the Chevy, and his new-found family, and decided to try to
find a new life for them in Washington or Oregon, out in the
backwoods maybe, or in some secluded valley.

Season said, as they passed through El Encanto Heights,
'I guess I should never have left you, really. I guess it was
foolish of me.'

Ed smiled at her, not forgivingly, because she didn't need
forgiving, not for anything; but with that kind of love that
sometimes feels like sorrow, because it's so close, and yet
it's never quite close enough.

They pulled off the road a little further on, at Gaviota,
overlooking the ocean; and they opened up a can of
Mexicorn. The wind blew warm and fresh, and for the first
time in days Ed began to relax. He felt impossibly tired.

They were almost ready to move on when they heard a
low, vibrant, thrumming noise. It grew deeper, and louder,
and closer, and within a few minutes they saw a formation
of four-engined airplanes, turbo-prop bombers, approaching from the sea.

Thunderously, the bombers passed low overhead, and
they shielded their eyes against the sun to watch them. Ed
tried to count them, but there must have been more than

fifty or sixty. All of them were camouflaged in khaki and blue; all of them left behind them long white vapour trails which scored the western sky long after they had headed eastwards over the Sierra Madre. All of them bore the red star of the Soviet Air force.

Ed looked down at the glittering ocean, at the spray on the California shore. Then he turned to Season and said quietly, 'Well, we'd better get moving. We've got a life to lead.'